THE BETROTHAL AT USK

by Felice Picano

City on a Star
Book II

ReQueered Tales
Los Angeles • Toronto
2021

The Betrothal at Usk

by Felice Picano

City on a Star, Book II

First American edition: 2021
This edition: ReQueered Tales, October 2021

ReQueered Tales version 1.38
Kindle edition ASIN: B099MYM6WB
ePub edition ISBN-13: 978-1-951092-39-9
Print edition ISBN-13: 978-1-951092-40-5

For more information about current and future releases, please contact us:
E-mail: requeeredtales@gmail.com
Facebook (Like us!): www.facebook.com/ReQueeredTales/
Twitter: @ReQueered
Instagram: www.instagram.com/requeered/
Web: www.ReQueeredTales.com
Blog: www.ReQueeredTales.com/blog
Mailing list (Subscribe for latest news): https://bit.ly/RQTJoin

Praise for Dryland's End

"This book is further proof that Felice Picano can succeed beautifully in any genre of fiction. Here we have the colorful originality that is found in the greatest science fiction and fantasy writers, the wide-ranging imagination that creates not only fine writers, characterization, and gripping plot, but also fabricates entire worlds – worlds rich with warrior women, space travel, mysterious gods, political intrigue and rebellion, biological warfare, and sexualities both subtle and shifting. In other words, like the best speculative fiction, this book provides the lucky reader with both an escape into the extraordinary and a mirror for humanity's deepest issues and concerns. In the exotic settings of this novel's distant planets, we recognize familiar compulsions that collect, collide, and disperse in our own hearts: the centripetal tug of love, loyalty, and courage, matched against the centrifugal forces of greed, ambition, and strife."

— Jeff Mann, Author of Edge
Associate Professor of English, Virginia Tech

"Set so far in the future that the exact location of the home lanet of the Humes (humans) isn't remembered, this book xamines relationships between the sexes, and between species from a new perspective and with more than a touch of evity. The ruling class of women in much of the galaxy, the atriarchy, in power for several millennia, is suddenly facing hallenges on many fronts, not the least of which is a rebellion of the Cybers (android like machines and computers) who have a designed a virus that could wipe out hume-kind ... With its subjects of cloning and genetic manipulation, same sex marriages and other controversial issues, *Dryand's End* remains as pertinent today as when it was first published. In full-fledged sci-fi form, Picano has created entirely new civilizations, species, even new language forms for his society. A phenomenally well-written book."

— Virginia Gazette

Also by FELICE PICANO

CITY ON A STAR Trilogy
Dryland's End (1995)
The Betrothal at Usk (2021)
A Bard on Hercular (2022)

NOVELS
Smart as the Devil (1975)
Eyes (1975)
The Mesmerist (1977)
The Lure (1979)
Late in the Season (1981)
House of Cards (1984)
To the Seventh Power (1989)
Dryland's End (1995)
Like People in History (1995)
Looking Glass Lives (1998)
The Book of Lies (1999)
Onyx (2001)
Justify My Sins (2018)
Pursuit: A Victorian Entertainment (2021)

OTHER FICTION
An Asian Minor (1981)
Slashed to Ribbons in Defense of Love (1983)
The New York Years (2000)
Tales from a Distant Planet (2006)
Twentieth Century Un-limited (2012)

MEMOIRS
Ambidextrous: The Secret Lives of Children (1985)
Men Who Loved Me (1989)
A House on the Ocean, A House on the Bay (1997)
Fred in Love (2005)
Art and Sex in Greenwich Village (2007)
True Stories: Portraits from My Past (2011)
True Stories Too: People and Places From My Past (2014)
Nights at Rizzoli (2014)

THE BETROTHAL AT USK

by Felice Picano

Table of Contents

Professor's Silberklang's Discovered
Early Map of Resort Planet
USK
Aquila System – Galactic Orion Arm

Third Matriarchy		Ib'r Republic
Point Imperador	=	*Golden Palace Resort*
Old Capital	=	*Great Western Port*
Rift Valley	=	*Salt Ocean Reefs*

Chapter One

Double dim-day morn, in the month of the pygmy vampire ant, with the Rings at Meridian and iridescently Perihelion and with shepherd moonlets, tinged orange one side, cerulean the other:

Ay'r Eise'nstein-Kell found himself released unexpectedly early from what had been a torpor-inducing Ed. & Dev. indivisible-numbers session. Thanks to the arrival of unheralded off-world messengers demanding the immediate presence of all the staff at the Golden Palace Resort.

At first, his Human 'Tute, Narfacan'ni, had demurred. "Lessons may not be interrupted!" he protested, swinging his self-importance about him in his prokaryote-dotted robe.

"The presence of every person is requested, Ser," the pamp known as Dustweed quietly insisted, just short of an incipient giggle. "Without exception."

The 'Tute lifted himself majestically to his greatest apparent height – and girth – dwarfing both his charge and the little house-pamp. He'd just spotted a speck of dried perli juice on his nearest hem and scowled at it, picking. Glancing at Ay'r he said:

"Not this unruly creature too!"

"Sirelings, no!" the pamp declared. As though there were hundreds and not just one, him. Ay'r!

"Then you are dismissed, Pimple!" The 'Tute declared, grandly, muttering "I knew there would be naught but trouble when I woke this morning and then saw the sheen of a Fast's signature, glittering Ring-slant in the northwest."

Jubilant, Ay'r raised his eyes twice, thanking Dustweed.

Before the oversized 'Tute could proffer dire warnings and spell out prohibitions, Ay'r leapt atop his air-board, and was scauping up a sand-pitted wall, over and out of the open-air room. He landed in the intricately patterned walkways surrounding the large lozenge of The Jobim Pebble Gardens. There, some generations past, a Dowager-Close Daughter had committed ritual *tri-mahh-ki* before a Delphinid Class B Ambassador at a swarming Ducal Vir-Cult Engagement Ceremony. In the process she had insulted one entire branch of the Three Species, avenged an allegedly solemn insult to a female ancestor, and then nearly paupered her horrified immediate family.

Minutes later, Ay'r had skittered over the restraining walls and was flittering across the day's predominantly mauve sands of the Golden Palace Resort Desert Cove, (according to the guidebook, one of the older and more cultivated greater inlets of the Great Salt Ocean). He was enjoying a one-footed skate, mere millimeters off the irregular surface, swooping, curling, making figure-eights, spinning in place like a sand-tornado, before skirling out again, light as a desert zephyr, shouting with glee like a deranged *maachen*.

He didn't see the near-transparent tentacle that reached up to lightly scratch across his ankle, but he felt its sting. And worse, felt it sunder the all-important silica-magnetic tension built up between sand, sand-air, and air-board. Stopped in mid-air, the board stood still momentarily, yet just enough for Ay'r to tumble off and onto the sand.

He caught himself instantly and tumbled forward onto his heels, crouched forward, a sand whip in one hand, hereditary kris in the other, tensed, observing, and espying the minute vibratory spatter of molecules above the undulating mauve surface. He leapt, struck with the kris, missed, struck a second time, this time using the whip, caught the tentacle, and pulled up.

"Varlet antipy!" he shouted as he hauled the tiny octopoid out of its sand-lair.

The rubbery mass of creature congealed around the whip-end like a curl-vole. It changed color rapidly from cerise to glaucous green, emitting noxious fumes as it whirled on its lasso-hold. Worst of all, it was keening until Ay'r thought his ears would burst. Defeated, he threw it off the whip, far onto the sand.

Seconds later the odors, noise, and animal were gone.

"Apologies!" Ay'r felt rather than heard the creature speak up. Despite its size, it made a sizable impression in his mind, somewhere just below his left temple. "An essence was desperately required," it went on to explain, tel'ping its way inside his head.

The air-board was dead in the sand, front half buried but unharmed, its magnets still aligned and apparently unaffected by the accident. The ess-shaped scratch on Ay'r's ankle was already healing, auto-anodized.

"You might have asked," Ay'r said aloud, toward the area where he'd last seen the creature disappear.

"Apologies!" it tel'ped, then "Gratitude for a much needed essence!"

"You're just lucky my board wasn't damaged," Ay'r sulked. Its front was sand-pitted beyond recognition. "If I never made it home, you'd have the entire Palace staff out to get you, you know!"

This was not entirely true, although Ay'r hoped it might be.

"If I didn't make it back alive," he went on, "you would be forced – essence-less – into unpaid servitude for a lifetime! How would you like that, varlet antipy?"

"The board is unharmed. The Human will safely arrive," it factually pointed out inside his mind, tickling slightly now.

"No thanks to you!" he admitted, sitting on the righted board, now afloat again millimeters off the desert surface. "Did you get enough essence?"

"Barely one essence," it whimpered.

"Come then," he tempted, putting out one leg. "Take another! Perspiration!"

The mauve sand showed movement around him. The creature was hesitating.

"I won't hurt you. Better hurry or it'll dry up."

"First, pocket whip and kris," it tel'ped, tickling his temple.

"Vir! What a scaredy-vole!" But he put the weapons away.

A tiny, nearly transparent tentacle reached up and touched his foreleg, further anodizing the scratch.

"If you want more," he dangled out the other leg, "I'll want payment."

Another tentacle reached up but hesitated.

"Information!" Ay'r prodded, "and don't say you know nothing. I know you're all neurally-netted to Palace antipys."

"Payment as requested," he felt in his mind as the tentacle slipped around his foreleg and ankle. "Satisfaction attained," it tel'ped.

"Then tell me who arrived this morning by Fast as I slept and why every palace person has been called to a meeting?"

"A preparation emissary. Ducal Kell will soon arrive!" The antipy was impressed itself by its information.

"Big deal! So what? I'm a Ducal Kell myself."

"A very minor Ducal Kell," it tel'ped. "Very, very minor. Only at the twelfth degree." And before Ay'r could protest, it appended, "A Great Betrothal is to be announced, consummated, and celebrated all in the space of four days, Sol Rad."

"Here? Here on Usk?" Ay'r scoffed. "How important can it be? Happening on this Ib'r-forsaken planet?"

"Forty-six great houses will soon debark on this Ib'r-forsaken planet! The Palace must be made completely ready. Every suite prepared. Already the Fast-Port is undergoing Cyber-regeneration and molecular cleansing in readiness for their glittering entourages."

"Forty-six houses?" Ay'r doubted that. No one ever came to Usk. That's why he'd been left here to grow up here. Forsaken by all. Unknown to all.

"The multi-markets are filling quickly as Agri-pamps from all over the hemisphere, alerted to fulfill the Palace's needs, fit their mounts and machines with panniers-full. Even-now, laden-full, they stream in hordes across mountains and rills headed for the markets of the Golden Palace Resort."

"*Forty-six* houses?" Ay'r laughed.

"Forty-six of the *great* houses, each a full City-Girder's worth on Hesperia, and among them ... my Lord, the Dux'ii Kell ... yes, that Great One, and even ... beyond them all ... the Forerunner, the Princeps, my Lord Kell himself."

Ay'r batted the slurping tentacle away. "Mart Kell? Now I know that you're sweat-drunk and sand-bulged! What could possibly bring *Him* here?"

"More payment for more visions?" it bargained. "Another essence?" it pleaded.

"You're not worth it!" Ay'r declared and stood up, ready to board the sled.

"This present very, very minor Ducal Kell will *not* be unchanged," it tel'ped enigmatically ... "as a result of these events."

"As though I would believe *you*!"

"This present very, very minor Ducal Kell will no longer be ruled by overweening 'Tutes and Stele-addicted Kris-Masters, after these events."

"Why not?"

"Offer one more essence," it bargained.

"No more blood."

"One … more … small … essence!"

Ay'r stood on the board, moved aside his tunic, unhoused his sex, and squeezed two drops out of the tip onto the sand. They vanished, and seconds later the little octopoid creature surfaced, a meter distant.

"Gratitude for three essences. All nine essences given and this antipy is your life-servant."

"You? What could I do with you? You're the size of an old stegn-melon thrown to footless pamps. What use could you be?"

"Only six more essences!" it tempted.

"Be content with three! The last unpaid – as yet. Tell me what you know."

"Upon this present very, very minor Ducal Kell's return to the Palace, he shall be swept up into preparations … Three Meetings are predicted."

"What three meetings?" Ay'r warily asked.

"One with Greatness. One with Forty-six Houses at once. One with – the Ultimate."

"What are you blathering about? Why would the Dux'ii wish to see me? And greater folly for you, yet, of what possible use would the Princeps have with me? Explain!"

"More than this will be far too much. Study the Old Rune known as Excess Even Unto Wretchedness."

"What can baby antipys know of Old Runes?"

"Look into chapter thirty-nine, sub section six, *The Book of Colored-Glory*!"

"And gobs of melting ear-wax for you! Fool, varlet baby antipy, starved for essences!" Ay'r mocked it.

"Study the text well. Learn it as you've never learned another matter!"

"Dare you *warn* me, too!" Ay'r fumed. "Fresh Neo semen, bitter and green!"

"Do not … do not …"

"Delicious crumbly toe-jam!" Ay'r taunted on.

The antipy keened high-pitched in frustration.

"Salted-sweet saliva!"

It was gone. Ay'r felt the antipy leave his mind. It must have dived back, deep into the sand.

Only then did he regret its absence, for, though quick to beg, it had given him much information, although how much could be true he'd only determine later. And though small and grasping, it wasn't shy of friendship (for a price), which was far more than anyone at the Golden Palace Resort besides miscreant pamps had offered Ay'r in all these years of his residence.

He knew why of course, though none but a house-pamp like Dustweed or Desert Wind would ever confirm it. Ay'r's very existence was an Eternal Affront and Universal Scandal to all others of his house, Ducal, Principal, even the most minor Baronial, his very existence the emblem of galactic disobedience.

His name said it all: his name carried his distinction and his ignominy: Eise'nstein-Kell. The only Eise'nstein-Kell alive among thousands of billions of the Three Species. To the eternal mortification of all other Kells, and – according to his 'Tutes – of all other Human men.

Ay'r was a mere Neo, he knew, still feckless, unbruited, and untried. But to him, the story of his parents' great amour, betrayal, and death was special, individual, sweet, something to treasure. When most irritated with him, his 'Tutes dropped copies of trashy t'bloid PVNs into his wall units to play all day, as though in punishment. Busy though he might be with his own amusements, scowl though he might for the sake of their certain espial, he never ceased finding himself stopped by what they displayed in even their most tasteless moments: the whiplash beauty and sporting grace of his mother, Bri'an Fuego-Kell, seven time adept of the Hesperian Amateur Thwwing racing set's Seven System Crown; and then the glitteringly flamboyant, stalwart blond genius of his sire, Yuli Edlina Eise'nstein, a Markab 9 soma-shophand's eighteenth child. Yuli of course had become a songster extraordinaire: born humming a tune of his own invention; by six years old, Sol Rad., a planetary music star; by nine an Orion Spur Song-winner; by sixteen, conqueror of the Prixe Galacticus; by eighteen known simply, universally, as "Eis", with a fame equal to few artists in history and – to the consternation of many Cityzens – a fortune beyond that of even most Hesperian Beryllium giga-naires.

Fuego and Eise'nstein then, naturally enough transformed by the PVN t'bloids into "Fire and Ice," the pair of them, and their mad twenty-six-month affair across fifty star systems, recorded by Media probes of every ilk: their lovemaking, their altercations, their astonishing destructiveness, their grand reconciliations, their gifts to each other of staggering cost – an entire 'blooded' Thwwing stable from Bri'an. Matched by Eis' gift of an asteroid, Plastro-blasted and metamorphosed into a nine trillion-ton sapphire – their avowals, the utter impossibility of their union – one lad, the Princeps Kell himself's favorite great-grandchild, scion of the highest City bloodlines, brought up specifically to forge alliance to another great house. The other lad a scrubber's scum from a shrubless world of no account. Their romance was doomed to burn like a children's celebratory Beryllium fireworks show.

And burn it did, freeze and burn, scorching a dozen of the fifty-five great houses of Hesperia, as whole Families, complete Girders, never mind entire Generations, took sides for and against. Ending here on planet Usk, in treachery. Their final separation was averted only at the very last moment by their Holo-Comm.-insta-viewed double-love-suicide, displayed "in real time" across the known galaxy. Here, upon this never significant, ordinarily abandoned, tiny resort world of Usk, a bizarrely ringed planet of no use to anyone for centuries, in the constellation Aquila. They fell, dove really, out of their time, at a site not far from here, now and forever known as the Point of Sighs, upon the highest precipice over the Great Salt Ocean, fifteen and a half years ago, Sol Rad., plummeting, arm in arm five thousand meters down to their deaths ... into history and eternal romance.

Ay'r their only issue, issue and daily reminder to any and all who might choose to recall. Which none ever did.

And now a Great Betrothal was to take place here? With forty-six great houses, a Dux'ii and even the Princeps!? Could it be so? And if so, what would his part be in it all? He was far too young for a Meeting of Importance with any family member. So possibly, more than likely, the choice of Usk was some intra-Ducal whim or some Party-Engineer's whimsy; a clever trick by some bright young thing to liven up a drearier than usual City social season. Ay'r himself would be placed in storage somewhere, never seen, so no one *could* be reminded of that historically deplorable *misalliance.*

Or, perhaps, there was at least a Formal Greeting due to him, a mere formality, since, if he recalled, he was, after all the Uskian

Adjudicator. Yes, he was fairly sure of it and there were even documents that said so. He'd come across them once, in some chamber or another he shouldn't have been in. They confirmed the case – that as far as the godlike Hesperian Resort World Bureau was concerned, he, poor silly, Ed. & Dev. Neo he, was actually the Uskian Adjudicator or some such ridiculous title. And so, he supposed, he would *have* to be present when they arrived, dragged out, trucked out, if only once, for a few seconds, during the festivities, possibly recognized at a distance by a glance or half wave by Someone Important. If only to make their visit, and to make their ceremony, unconditionally real – and legal.

Ay'r skimmed out of the Golden Palace salt ocean inlet, not homeward to the place of his daily humiliation, but – skirting the edge of the Lesser Upper Salt Pans instead – aiming for the Great Market, an ancient concrete edifice three tiers high, covered tatterdemalion by sails of wind furling canvas sheets. It was little enough protection against weather, yet effective nevertheless to shield all from the monthly double-day's too-bright sunlight.

His air-board under one arm, he lifted his sweatsuit collar up over his face so it covered his eyes, brow and hair, a ruse that ordinarily no one paid attention to (for what other Sireling his age ever visited the vast emporium but himself?).

But no matter, for as the baby antipy had predicted, the shops were quadrupled with produce, spilling onto the second decks and at times needing to be retrieved from slow moving conveyances that they dropped onto. More sheer commodities, fabrics, what seemed to be indigenous fruits, parochial vegetables, and other autochthonous objects of odd description and little understanding for Ay'r, in shop after bulging shop, as hordes of buyers and sellers shouted a loud farrago of commerce-argot, tossed about in their madcap purchasing – like newborn sand elvers in a burning patch under an overslant Ring. More than half of this swarm, he couldn't help but note, wore the hemmed gold half-capes or gilded rim berets that marked them out as "palace staff."

"What matters a mere Sireling in such a superheated sale!" he heard a scratchy voice insinuate inches away and turned to gaze upon a mart-pamp known to all as Sostenuto, allegedly by far the eldest of that short-lived race.

"This Sireling carries pockets of d'lars!" Ay'r said proudly.

"What matters Sireling d'lars, when palace d'lars numerous

as shop flies around rotted stegn-melons pass hands this double dim-day."

"And no matter how many hands they pass, some of the great symphony is bound to attach to Sostenuto's tune?" Ay'r joked, a reference to the graft in the form of "rent" the mart-pamp soaked out of alien shop-creatures and pamps from distant districts.

The old mart-pamp hissed in agreement, adding "Under such circumstances, Sirelings are rare enough to be honored with sips of Arrack made from the sweetest Sand-Scarab's roe."

In other words, Sostenuto was making certain that if Ay'r was somehow honored by any of the coming events, he would already be in good standing with Sostenuto.

Ay'r slid into the canvas-shrouded unofficial "office" out of which instantly skittered two Security pamps, sitting down on the job.

The interior was purposely dimmed. Now the old pamp lighted a tiny smokeless lamp of some incense-smelling stuff and set out two long slender concave dishes ending with lip-mounts. He poured barely a slithering of the aromatic live-sherry into the dishes and handed one to Ay'r.

"On the Great Salt Ocean was it born – that makes such bliss!" he toasted and sipped.

"And in the Great Mart was such bliss remarked," Ay'r toasted back and sipped.

It slipped around his mouth not quite liquid, more like a hundred tiny cool flames, each seeking its own especial nook. Finding his taste buds, the Arrack stung and simultaneously exploded in pleasure, as the scores of Sand Roe committed mass suicide to provide one unparalleled taste.

"An excellent vintage!" Ay'r raised his empty dish. "And in payment, some ... Tertiary essence ... perhaps?"

"Always welcome, arriving direct from a Sireling," Sostenuto admitted, "but not today."

"Then it's a gift." Ay'r slid the dish down for another pouring. Watched it fill the bulb then slither down to the mouth part. "Earning perhaps, information ... dearer today than even an essence."

A second pouring of Arrack followed the first. The dish was full now and Ay'r lifted it carefully, balancing it well to sip and relish as Sand Roe sacrificed by the hundreds their lives for his favor.

"Then, know this, generous elder-pamp, forty-six great houses of Hesperia gather at this long-devastated resort to celebrate and witness the consummation of a Ducal Betrothal ... Kells of the Highest Order shall grace the proceedings. Including the very highest ... and how," he appended, "may a mere mart-pamp further profit?"

"How, beneficent and knowing Sireling?"

"Only an elder mart-pamp would know."

Ay'r laughed, a little inebriated, and then swept out of the office and back into the frenzy of activity where, unremarked, he watched palace administrators haggling like sand-eel wives for ribbons and gaudies.

He chuckled at their fat antics and overzealous requests, keeping to himself, and further covering himself, as he ventured further into the maelstrom of men and creatures, fielding the gibbering all about him, as though it were foreign tongues.

Vir, but I'm swogged, he found himself thinking, swogged and befogged after three mere sips of Scarab-Sand Roe Arrack, just like some mine-pamp's spawn.

He giggled at his thought, then watched the great canvas sheeting dance above his head, gavotting and grimalking, until two large, gold-gloved hands hove into view, grasped his sweat suit and lifted.

While protesting, Ay'r rather gracefully blacked out.

As Cas'sio awakened, the scores of meters of curtains furled back from the astra-dome above all at once, so that the crystalline, star-spangled night filled his view, cut aslant, top to bottom, by the amazing aurora of Ring-slice, its own natural colors tinted now with the long-traveled light from a hundred million years distant stars.

He sighed at such beauty and hauled his not yet pain-wracked, and indeed still quite tractable (if stouter and looser-fleshed) four-hundred year old body off the air bed and crossed the enormous floor, warmed as it was beneath, thinking he'd soon have to break down and allow himself to have a few cosmetic firm-up sessions if he wanted to bear looking at himself in Holos or mirrors.

At the hint of possible depression-inducing thoughts, a half dozen large antipys slithered over across the slick floor towards him, but he warned them off with a tiny sector of his mind, and they scurried back under hassocks and tables, as he stood there looking up, still in wonder as a child, enjoying this lovely, dim place, and this palace he'd not visited in, what was it? a decade and a half now? and that earlier time only because he'd had to.

In truth, he'd forgotten the palace, the planet, altogether, until the Inner Council of the Quinx had reminded him six days ago, Sol Rad., that "Lines of Succession" had been programmed decades ago, and their carrying-out was now required. Sten Tu'bin, for a decade his own playmate, had suggested Usk itself as the location, adding, "after all, it's there, it's free, and while provincial beyond imagining, it might be amusing." Jasp'Quah Etalka had then added, some ancient Metro-Terran saying about The Mountain going to Mohammed, which all had somehow recognized from Ed. & Dev., but which not one in the chamber could actually identify never mind explicate, causing general consternation and then laughter. After which Usk was voted upon and Usk it was. And so here he was again amid the crystal-clear, be-Ringed, beauteous night.

"Break my heart, Beauty," he quoted aloud the lyrics of Eise'nstein's song:

> *Break my heart, Beauty,*
> *Break my heart, again*
> *And then once more*
> *To be certain, break it again*
> *– that Pain may never leave me*
> *And Beauty forever be*
> *not Him, not Him ... but merely a thing.*

He could hear the antipys restlessly shifting, anticipating his need for comforting.

A soft ding.

He turned to the projected voice. "Yes."

"My Lord Dux'ii. The child waits."

"Send him in," he said, and turned, slid backwards into a giant soft-chair, collapsing in on itself to fit his shape, as an antipy's tentacle reached out to stroke his tiniest left toe, and he shook loose from it, intoning low, "you'll have your chance, soon."

The boy had been dressed in gold earlier, apparently, like

everyone else here at the palace, but now, having triumphed over his keepers, was somewhat sulkily dressed otherwise, more as he wished himself to be, in black.

Not just black but Hesperian "City-Jet" black in fact, probably someone else's clothing left over, which fit him like a second skin, along with knee boots, tunic, codpiece, armbands and cape. All the more to offset his tanned sturdy limbs, rugged young body, expanse of flyaway hair white as the light from a G-2 sun, and his eyes, ah! his mother Bri'an's eyes, none other, look at them! They almost hurt to see! So Beryllium-blue!

"Don't dawdle there. Come forward."

The lad strode forward unafraid, did something with a hand and mouth that evidently some courtier had shown him to do, suggestive of showing honor, and that he now abbreviated quickly, lest it discredit himself.

"Identify yourself, Young Man."

"Ay'r!" he said boldly. Hesitation. Then even bolder. "Ay'r Eise'nstein-Kell," he finished, defiantly.

Yes, a lovely young man. A lovely Kell!

"Ay'r! You say?" He pretended to muse. "I once knew an Ay'r."

"I think there are many Ay'rs," the lad began. "We are named in honor of the Great Father ..."

"I first encountered this *particular* Ay'r as a baby," Cas'sio interrupted the boy, explaining, "*I* was the baby! On a planet ... well, a planet that barely exists now. Hundreds of years ago. He betrothed my Aunt and then my Uncle and he became my God-Father."

The boy had stopped, and now stared.

"Do you know who I am?" he asked the lad.

"The Great Dux'ii Kell. Head of my house."

"What's my name? My given name?" And when he hesitated, "don't you know?"

"Cas'sio Azura!" the boy spoke it boldly. "Cas'sio Azura-Kell-Ib'r ... Was that Ay'r that you spoke of then ... *the* Great Father?"

"None other! Are you impressed?" he asked.

"I thought ... I thought he was *centuries* old. Older than antiquity."

"That's just the foolishness of Ed. & Dev. 'Tutes. Would you be surprised to know that he lives still, the Great Father? He does. He's very old now, of course, far older than I am. Come closer, don't be afraid. You have eyes like your mother. And your figure is that of your father. Before you say anything know this! I loved your mother, Bri'an, more than any of my grandnephews. And I admired your father more than I can say. I was not Dux'ii then and I never opposed their love and I never agreed with … I mean to say it is my greatest sorrow that they …" he couldn't control his voice, and the antipys slithered forward again, checked only by a stern look.

The boy's eyes had widened to see such emotion. Lovely. Lovely!

"So then!" Cas'sio caught himself. "Are you ready for tomorrow's guests and the events of the nights hence?"

"I am!" again boldly said. Then, quieter. "But I have not exactly been told …"

"Told?" he echoed. "Ah! What your role is to be?"

"I know that I am Adjudicator of this planet."

"Adjudicator! Indeed!"

"But I think that is a title meaning little. Still, whatever I must do, I am prepared."

"That is good to know. I revel in obedience and find it far too infrequently to enjoy it very much. Your task, know now young Kell, is that you are to be betrothed."

"I am? But I'm a but a perli-weevil, a pimple on the side of gourd, a …"

"No protests! You are young, true, but this betrothal is titular. Political," Cas'sio added. "You need do nothing at all if you wish not to, after it has occurred. You may go back to your life here and remain on Usk another four decades and play on your air-boards and …"

"Must I? Can't I leave and come live with … well, not you, but someone in the City somewhere?"

"If … you … wish. *Is* that what you do wish?"

"I don't know. I don't wish to stay here!" he said with conviction.

"Then you won't, lad. But understand, wherever you go in the City you will be …"

"I know! A Scandal to all Kells and an Affront to all Man!"

"Who told you that? No!"

The boy drew back. "I thought … because of what happened … at the Point of Sighs, fifteen years ago, Sol Rad."

"Oh, lad. All that is now history. History. And instead, in the City, you will be a person of great note – and of great glamour. A celebrity. That rarest of things: you will be Living History. Privacy will be difficult to for you to obtain. Everywhere you go, people will want to know you, and see you. The Media will talk about your every move, your every whim. Adoration and Criticism will run rampant. Especially after this betrothal ... What do you know of the planet Demeter?"

"It's in the Center Worlds. A former Matriarchal stronghold. Population thirty billion. Allied by espousal to Rama, Dickinson, and Lesuth Gamma."

"Excellent! You have the Kell memory."

"Stuck here, I look elsewhere," the boy admitted. "Outward."

"Well it's the Demeterian Palaka family you will be espoused to in three nights. Have you ever seen a Human female? Are there any on Usk?"

"None that I know of nor have seen. I've seen them in Holos ..." The boy's eyes widened. "Am I to be betrothed to a female?"

"Yes, a female. The Close-Daughter of Ro'ger and Jori Palakas, scions of an old house of Demeter. Of course as a Ducal Kell, you will have a male consort of your choice for affection too, like everyone else, when you reach the proper age. But this female could provide Close-Sons and who knows, perhaps even a Close-Daughter. Does this interest you?"

"Is it because of the Battle at Betelgeuse 17?" the lad asked.

"Ah, they still teach ancient history here! Yes, it's because our ancestor, Jat Kell reportedly betrayed Ro'ger's ancestor, Anth'ea Palaka at the Battle of Betelgeuse 17, fourteen centuries ago. So reparation is to be made by this first joining of the Palakas to the Ophiucan Kells."

"There are six moonlets orbiting Demeter's sister planet, Eurydice, where Prokaryotics are grown – not artificially produced," the boy added. "The largest natural farms in the galaxy!"

Causing Cas'sio to laugh. "You are real Kell! You see the *commercial* advantage too! Then I take it you agree to this betrothal?"

"Gratitude for your request, my Lord Dux'ii. I will obey. Only ..."

"Yes?"

"Well ... do I have to listen to my 'Tutes and all throughout all this?"

"A little bit longer, yes, I'm afraid. I myself don't know all the ceremonial rules. Only the 'Tutes and courtiers do. Both of us, you and I, will be under their charge during the ceremonies."

Once again those Beryllium-blue eyes grown huge. It would be sweet to have them near, even perhaps, who knew, sometime soon, daily … once again … Beauty, break my heart.

"Tomorrow night, for example, I do believe your task is to be Administrator of Usk and to …"

"Adjudicator!" the boy corrected softly.

Lovely! Lovely!

"Adjudicator," he repeated, "and offer me publicly as Head of the house the use of Usk for whatever I may wish."

"It is yours, Lord," the boy said, grandly. "Only leave me a single Salt Ocean inlet to air-board in."

Another ding. Cas'sio turned to it in annoyance. "What now?"

"The Emissary of the indigenous peoples called pamps, Lord Dux'ii, seeks audience."

Meaning he was supposed to be done with the boy. But he wasn't. Not by any means.

"If it's who I think it is," Ay'r stage-whispered, "then understand, that for whatever graces he offers, if he calls himself Sostenuto, then he is a low and drink-ridden extorter of many in the Great Mart."

"Gratitude, lad, for your information," he said. Turning to the voice, "send the pamp delegation in." And to Ay'r, "I'm afraid you must now go. But I'll see you tomorrow. Come kiss me, if you aren't afraid to. There. And perhaps one day you'll show me your favorite inlet."

Once the lad had strode out, the second door slid open, and three pamps entered, the eldest immediately identifying himself as the leader, "a Great Trader named Sostenuto."

"Come in. Don't dawdle … great trader."

He let the antipys gather now. He'd need them more than ever tonight.

Now the end of the procession swept past the hanging balcony where Ay'r stood, pushed slightly forward, but otherwise integral to the retinue of the Dux'ii Kell, all of them dressed in bronze with accents of jade. Below, thirty or more members of the Demeterian Embassy passed, each turned slightly left in acknowledgement, all clad in shades of silver and cobalt blue. Along their edges, several almost danced, enlacing the others. Almost last, preceded by her parents and surrounded by a stalwart honor-guard, strode the female Palaka, tall as her mother Ro'ger, her hair piled high with twists of silvery Beryllium threaded through, but otherwise starlit deep blue, her posture straight, her body slender, yet how differently formed from all about her, evident from the silver-and-cobalt, feather-light metallic cloth that draped her. She was older than he by maybe five years, Sol Rad., Ay'r estimated, but he was already as tall and in a decade or so, the age difference would be unimportant.

She looked utterly composed, from which he supposed, she was as nervous as he, but under light hypnosis or mildly drugged. Her eyes flashed over him, lingered not a whit, but did settle briefly on the Dux'ii Kell next to him, whom she thus saluted especially.

"Not bad," his great-uncle murmured. "If one is to mate with a female, better that she be a handsome one."

Much tittering from around them. Sixteen family members in this box alone, Ay'r could hardly recall four of their names and titles.

Below them all, forty-five other great houses of Hesperia stood, nine hundred strong, in various shaped groupings, each defined by their house colors – some yellow and jet, some aqua and forest green, others orange and teal, manganese and pearl white, copper and fawn. It was by far the greatest spectacle Ay'r had ever witnessed, all the wealth of the City on a Star, and many of its leading Cityzens, arrayed here on his planet, his, where he ruled (if in name only) as Adjudicator, and where they had arrived in a hundred Fast-yachts, across many light years, to honor his betrothal. It was almost too much to bear.

"Go, now, lad," the Dux'ii all but pushed Ay'r, "lead us out and down to the floor."

"I await *your* lead, Lord," Ay'r said, offered, making a sweeping gesture.

"Well, well, if you insist, I'll walk with you," the great man said, "but only up to the railings where they are gathered. As you can see, from there on you go alone."

And he added in a lower voice, "if you are not afraid to," hooking a baby soft hand into the crook of Ay'r's elbow, so that even if he were as tall, he made it look like Ay'r was supporting him.

Behind them, the sixteen great Ducal Kells swarmed, whispering, bubbling at the sight of old and young together and matched so well.

They had just reached the railing across one end of the great hall, when before them and beyond the dais upon which the betrothal was to take place, another swathed hanging balcony suddenly lighted from within.

Everyone in motion halted. A great whisper went up, like a hissing.

"I see," Ay'r's companion alone seemed unfazed, "the Princeps has also deigned to arrive. Timely as ever," he added, dryly, "for greatest effect." Then, "we were not certain he'd come," he added in a low voice. "He means to honor you greatly and so I suppose we must go greet him." Cas'sio held out a hand, halting those behind without turning, "all you others remain here."

They circled the railing and nodding to each Head of House they skirted, the Dux'ii Kell bypassed the raised floor and together he and Ay'r ascended the ramp to the now illuminated, yet still curtained balcony. As they drew near, Ay'r's elbow was let go, and he remained in place as the Dux'ii moved forward to the curtain's edge.

"We're stupendously honored." He spoke into the pale light in which now Ay'r could make out the vaguest outline of a male figure. "How we can make this more enjoyable for you?"

"Bring him closer!" the voice within sounded. Its accent was different from the Dux'ii's, the voice, older, yet not cracked. "So I may see for myself."

Ay'r walked right up to the curtain.

"He's a bold one," the hidden voice spoke.

"Bold as any Kell," the Dux'ii said. "And as intelligent."

"So young!" the voice behind the curtain said, almost as though pitying Ay'r.

"He'll age as we all do, eventually."

"Not as pretty as you were at his age, Cas'sio! More of a ... little man."

"Was I so very pretty then? You never told me, these many centuries."

"And turn your head? It was already well turned by others. Yes ... he's a real little man!"

"Ay'r is my name, Lord Princeps. Ay'r Eise'nstein-Kell."

A nearly strangled laugh. "He is bold – pushing his name at me like that." That laugh again, then. "Tell me lad, does this betrothal suit you?"

For a second Ay'r struggled. "If it benefits our house," he stammered, "and if it is your wish."

"My wish?" the old voice asked. "No one ever pays attention to my wishes anymore. But yes, I suppose it benefits our house."

"It certainly does," the Dux'ii said. "You looked over and approved the program yourself."

"How many decades ago? But yes, if that's so, then I suppose it once *was* my wish."

"He's never seen a Human female before," the Dux'ii said.

"Ah! So he could never comprehend how very common they used to be. Understand, forward lad, that her Bride-Price was too high to be listed on the Commodity markets of the Orion-Spur. She is that special."

Ay'r tried to look through the gauze at the figure before him. Why was he hiding? Was he so ugly and old? Feeling he must say something, he said, "Gratitude, Lord Princeps."

"Don't be fooled by all these good manners," the Dux'ii Kell said to the Princeps. "He's a dirty, squalling, unruly boy. Bad as ever you were."

"That bad, huh?"

"Picked up drunk on Arrack roe the day before we arrived. Dragged back to his chambers, crusted with sand and antipy spit."

Ay'r turned to him, in surprise, feeling almost betrayed.

"You think we didn't know?" The Dux'ii Kell asked. "We know all! Bad and good."

"Look Cas'sio, how he colors with anger and his fists bunch to do harm!"

Ay'r dropped his eyes, and worked to relax his hands again. He couldn't understand what game these two were playing, with him tossed back and forth like a curl-vole shuttle.

"He wants to relocate to the City, Princeps."

"Does he? Tired of the provinces and at such a young age?"

The two of them laughed.

"Well, boy, go ahead, then with your betrothal. I give you my

... blessing."

"Gratitude, Lord Princeps," Ay'r fell to one knee and in doing so his leg slightly moved the curtain so he could see beyond it to the man seated – or at least his lower body. His legs looked younger and more fit than the Dux'ii. Could it really be the Princeps there? It must be.

"Get up and go get yourself betrothed. Oh and Cas'sio, give my love to the Inner Quinx!"

Behind the curtain was darkened again and the two returned by the same path to the floor, where Ay'r was in another second pushed forward, alone, but for the female, who also walked forward, equally unsure, to the dais, where they stopped and where a voice they could not see asked them to hold hands and answer a few rather inane questions. After they had done so, apparently successfully – she like he, tutored in what to say – they were told they might kiss, and she closed her eyes and leaned forward one cheek, which Ay'r blushing at such contact with a stranger, bussed lightly with his lips, which made her color, and her eyes flew open and they were golden and almost too large for her face but rather nice.

A moment later, she quickly crossed one wrist deliberately over his.

"Lissa is my secret name," she whispered. "Lissa Vero'chka Palaka. Speak it into your wrist connector sometime in the future, if you wish. Doing this, I've set it within your wrist-connector, and perhaps we shall be able to speak, even though *they* would prefer us not to ... for several decades."

"Then ... you like me?" he asked. And quickly said, "I think I like you."

"You think?!" she commented and her silver-limned lips spread wide in a smile.

"But how could I know? Just meeting you?"

"I already know I like *you*. That's why I crossed our two wrists for the connection. Oh, here they come. Remember!"

"Lissa Vero'chka Palaka," he repeated her name. "And I'm Ay'r. Ay'r Eise' ..."

"I already know who *you are*, silly! *Everyone* knows."

Her father and mother were there, suddenly, and she cast her eyes down and stout Ro'ger and elegant Jori enfolded her in their arms, turned to Ay'r and each man took his hand, and Jori said, "we hope to know you better. Come visit us, some time, on Demeter." Then they were gone and their Close-Daughter with them.

A great shout went up from the Silver and Blues, then from the Bronze and Jades. Then from all the groups on the floor so that the entire hall rang with their gratitude.

"And I," Ay'r said to himself. "I am betrothed and yet I'm exactly the same as before. How very odd!"

Once the last Thwwing race of the afternoon on the fourth day of betrothal celebrations concluded and the crowd that had gathered to watch upon the circular observation deck at the upper Fast Port lounge began breaking up, his second cousins, Mel'yin Chu-Kell and Max'ell Kell-Ranieri asked if Ay'r wanted to take a closer look at their family mounts.

They'd not been so much surprised as amused when he'd earlier told them he'd never seen one of the large, competition-bred animals before. Mel'yin, at 29 years Sol Rad., had spent half of his early Ed. & Dev. on Diomedes Proxima 6, and already had a small Thwwing stable of his own, although the Chu-Kell mount racing at today's events was his mother's, with a professional pilot. His cousin Max'ell's family, the Kell-Ranieri's Girder at Hesperia, pointed opposite Diomedes, toward the fifteen suns of the Iole Cluster, a former Matriarchy agricultural colonization project, where 41-year-old, Sol Rad., Max'ell's family bred the Princeps' own competition-stock Thwwings among their own oft-winning stable.

Now that he was now officially (and significantly) betrothed, Ay'r was considered by the dozen or so members of this youngest set of celebrating Kells to be one of themselves, if indeed still a very young Neo. Offsetting his extreme youth was Ay'r's solid good looks and most especially his nearly white-blond hair.

Light colored hair was still deemed an Ib'r inheritance trait, and thus highly valued, since the Ib'r family and Ib'r name remained small, and was indissolubly connected to the four-hundred year old Republic that often bore their name. And – as much as the tiny, founding, Sanqq' line – Ib'rs were connected in everyone's minds to the very idea of Vir'ism that had replaced the Matriarchy, now pervading the galaxy. Though many Cityzens went in for cosmetic molecular 'xchanges to become blond, even after all these centuries, very few were naturally born so, and many Hesperians claimed to instantly be able to tell the difference. That and Ay'r's noble bearing helped, as did his honesty about how much he still had to learn, and even more so his real modesty – one of the rarest of traits among the large clan of boasting, brawling, trouble-making Ophiucan Kells.

"My family's six mounts were originally bred on Antonia Terce," Max'ell said proudly, as they sped down one of gravilifts to where the creatures were still gathered. "Antonia Terce is thought to be one of the home worlds of Thwwings."

"Not true. Nearer the Terminus Nebula they came from," Mel'yin quickly corrected, mentioning an area in his natal neighborhood.

"And Deneb 12, in the Orion Spur, is what my most recent Ed. & Dev. Metro-Terran Cyber 'Tute told me," Ay'r put in.

"A Bella=Arth. world!" Max'ell scoffed. "No Arth. ever raced a Thwwing mount that I ever heard. You, Mel?"

His cousin agreed. "It's almost grotesque to imagine an Arth. *inside* a Thwwing."

"Yet, that is now believed to be how they evolved," Ay'r assured them. "In concert with Bella=Arth. pilots, during their ancient times, before Bella=Arth. scientists harnessed gravity assist or interplanetary flight. Allegedly, Arth.s flew inside Thwwings during those six early World Wars, when they fought for Planetary Ruling Nest Dominance."

They alit down at the sands and their wrist-connector i.d.s got them through the elaborate security and into the hastily erected, open-air, loosely slatted-over stable-yards. Scores of pamps from all over Usk and of every occupation according to their dress peered through the slats or over the tops of the walls at the racing steeds in wonder, gabbling and burbling as they usually did in small mobs, most pamps never having seen a live Thwwing before.

"This is Acy," Mel'yin introduced his own personal Thwwing. "Greetings, girl, have you missed me? You raced tolerably well today." Ay'r joined the two as they walked around the small area in which the giant insect was kept penned by a few thin slats laid in various directions. It could easily break out of the slats should it try, but through some anomaly of its eyesight, instead it read the thin lathing as full, strong walls.

The creature sniffed the air as the three Neos entered the pen. Its long front antennae and shorter back ones waved and curled. "It tastes you," Max'ell said to his cousin.

"It tastes all of us."

Close up, it was some eight meters long, two meters or so wide, and maybe another three high. Slickly chitinous, with its three pairs of wings folded in, it looked aerodynamically created for cutting the wind through even the thickest of breathable atmospheres. Its front head was grotesque, its eyes the size of any Human head, globular, and thousand-faceted. The Thwwing's antennae were like plasticized whips, except seemingly always a-twitch, smelling, tasting, sensing the world around it. When Mel'yin touched it on the lightly scaled triangular head spot between its eyes, it seemed to shudder, and instantly enwrapped his lower body in curled antennae and soft-as-silk palps.

"None of that business, girl!" he pulled away from it in embarrassment. "There are guests here! Don't you sense them?"

For an answer, it unfurled one antenna and began reaching into Max'ell's tunic, until he stepped out of its reach.

"Mel, you've got to give her more of your Vir essence and more often. Look at her. Poor thing's as hungry as a ritual Se'er prostitute."

His cousin pulled away from the animal and scowled at his laughing relative. For his part, Ay'r understood little of what was happening, except that he was strangely thrilled to even be within the ambience of the beast.

They were back in the mall way, passing other doorways, stopping in on each and "meeting" the mounts, on their way to Max'ell's family steeds, when they heard a high pitched skreeling.

Max'ell dipped his head into a pen and back out again.

"As I thought. It's Jafarra, our newest steed. She's a 'speaker,' which is rare among Thwwings."

"She didn't race today, did she?" Ay'r asked, "I think I would have recognized these markings if she had."

Inside Jafarra's pen it was somewhat darker because it was a great deal more slatted over, but he could still easily make out the cross-striping around the Thwwing's abdomen, a deep green against the paler chitin chartreuse.

"Truly she did not race and hardly ever does so. We brought

her here only because she seems to calm down her stable mates. She's a strange one, this Jafarra," Ay'r's cousin admitted. "She never bonded a man though over a dozen have piloted her. We can't understand why she will not bond."

"Fussy as a Human female," Mel'yin offered.

"Until she does," Ay'r's cousin explained to him, "we cannot let her loose and ever expect her to return. The bonding is what restrains them from vanishing. It often keeps them limited to their bond-mate's nation or bond-world."

"How very beautiful she is," Ay'r said. Indeed he felt this creature was different somehow from the others they had looked at so far. It trembled slightly to his touch.

"Touch her head and see if she'll accept you," Mel'yin suggested.

"No sooner had he stood in front of her, than Jafarra's palps rose to grasp Ay'r in a soft yet firm grip as her antennae swept lightly across his back and arms and hair, in effect tasting him.

"She likes you," Max'ell laughed. "That's a first! She's never embraced a man before."

"Look!" Mel'yin pointed above at the animal's back, "she's opening her canopy for you. She wants you to ride her."

"That too is a first," Ay'r's cousin said. "Usually we have to pry it open to pilot her."

"Get in, Ay'r!" Mel'yin said. "Can he, Max?"

"I will, if only she'll let me go," Ay'r remarked.

"You have to strip to your skin," Max'ell said.

"She's already done a fair job of that," Ay'r admitted. His tunic has more or less lifted off. Now he pulled away from the creature and removed his boots.

"Undergarment too," Mel'yin pointed out. Ay'r had hoisted himself onto Jafarra's back where the chitinous canopy had opened fully. "Otherwise it won't be a full Thwwing fit."

"How then does one's clothing travel?" Ay'r asked.

"On each side is a natural pouch!" his cousin pointed out behind each front wing pod.

He helped Ay'r up the surprisingly dry, soft skin. "See? Perfect for your luggage."

Inside, the canopy looked like some kind of laving tub, slick and wet.

Ay'r hesitated.

"Slip in. It looks wet but it's dry." He offered Ay'r a hand, and Ay'r stepped over to Jafarra's open canopy, bent down, and slid over and into the animal. It was indeed dry and firm and it seemed to mold to his back, legs, sides, ankles, feet, toes, and once he'd put his arms alongside, also his elbows, hand and fingers too, almost immediately.

"You know how to fly?" his cousin now asked.

"I think what I want and tel'p it," he said. That much he had read and heard.

"Precisely. Be clear at all times. They're simple creatures. 'Up a little!' 'Not so high' 'To the left a bit. No not that much.' Understood?"

"Understood. But you're not going to actually let me ..."

Before Ay'r was done speaking, Max'ell had dropped back to the sawdust strewn floor and Mel'yin was already removing the slats in front and above. Max'ell helped him.

"Wait a ..."

The rest of what Ay'r wanted to say was stopped as the canopy top came down in front of him, and wetly sealed itself perfectly into the cup of his seat. Ay'r had a moment of panic wondering how he could breathe. But a gust of air blew into his face from two sides and he inhaled deeply. A second later, he felt his body and limbs almost as though massaged by the insides of the Thwwing. Almost as though it was calming him down. Amazing!

He could see perfectly clearly through the strong, yet transparent canopy ahead of him and on all sides. There were his cousins, waving Jafarra out of the pen. There were the many little pamps of all descriptions scattering in pandemonium before the giant insect's exit. There was the race track ahead with its launching pads.

"Go ahead, Jafarra," he thought. "Go to a launch pad."

It scuttled ahead to the spot with amazing dexterity. There was a flight monitor board at the launch pad, blinking electronic crosses at them. He recalled that specific pattern would keep the Thwwing stationary. Suddenly the sign stopped, and changed patterns from crosses to wavy lines, which he recalled were preparatory to launch, to be replaced by ... there they were! Dots!

"Go!" he thought and the wings unfolded enormously on either side and behind him and Jafarra lifted into the air.

"That's good. Hover. Now prepare to take a wide circle around the tower! As though you were racing!" he thought. "Smell where the steeds before you flew."

The Thwwing banked slightly, then shot out ahead to some predetermined point it knew, then banked again to begin its curve. Soon it was making a wide circle, and unless he was fooling himself, Ay'r thought it might have been exactly the inner ring of the races that had taken place.

"If you know from your senses or from your sisters, the size and shape of the racing oval they flew," Ay'r tel'ped. "Then follow that oval, Jafarra."

In seconds it was further out from the tower, hovering in place.

"That's good, now go, my racing beauty! Compete as though it were a race!"

The Thwwing shot forward so quickly Ay'r almost panicked again, but it banked perfectly and swooped low onto the next level, then raised them both up to a higher level, just as he recalled the other ones doing earlier, then it dove almost to the ground at one spot, and quickly raised itself to another, as it began looping infinity signs around the space port observation tower. It was as much as Ay'r could do to hold on, not panic, feel part of the creature, exult in its speed and its perfect grace, and after a while, he could tell it was coming to the end of the prepared racing oval, and he instructed, "higher now, the same oval, twice as large, and fast as you can go."

Jafarra shot off ever faster, the low buildings below them a blur, the mountains a mere ridge work, surrounding the crested bowl of the spaceport, and as they ascended, other mountains formed a far wider ridge around the side lands and the Golden Palace itself, at the edge of desert, scooped out stretches of the Great Salt Ocean, and the Rings, slowly shifting down from their meridian toward aphelion, stretched before Ay'r, enormous, tinted the most serene shade of blue, the shepherd moonlets dots of cobalt, the sky blood-orange, as rider and mount rose.

"Once more," he exulted, instructing the Thwwing. "Even higher and twice as wide an oval as before." And they shot up even further until he could almost make out the edge of the atmosphere where red-orange gave way to deepest cerulean blue and in full day-time stars glittered against its deep hue, and now Jafarra almost glided, sweeping in a huge oval above Usk, the Fast

Port and palace became now only dots below, the mountains only lines, the central, white, eye of the salt ocean surrounded by brownness, and Ay'r looked down and he laughed and his body trembled with the height and the speed and the sheer lusciousness of it all, until he thought he might pass out, and he felt his sex extend instantly, and instantly be covered in another skin, one from out of the Thwwing. He looked down a second to see and it was exactly so, the side-chitin had enclosed his lap, and now it was pulsing, pulsing and hot, and he couldn't stop it or remove it even if he wanted to, which he certainly didn't want to, and he let himself be manipulated and drawn forth and he felt his entire body begin to stiffen, heel of foot to the back of his cow-licked head, until it was almost painful, yet impossibly pleasurable too, and it couldn't go on, it couldn't, yet it did, it did, it did! He erupted in a blazing white heat, blinded by pleasure, his head let loose from the grip, nodding side to side as he shouted out something unintelligible. Seconds later, he had slumped back, panting into the canopy's folds and he concentrated on breathing hard and breathed out his gratitude then instructed, "slowly ... back down again ... closing ... small ... gyres ... very gently ... Jafarra."

Ay'r was fully himself again five or six minutes later when he made out the octagonal terrace decks of the Fast Port observation tower coming closer, and then the launch pads and the ground. Seconds later, Jafarra alit and he almost gagged on the sudden cessation of speed, then caught himself, breathed in hard, and the canopy slowly unsealed with sucking noises and opened.

"Like a master-pilot your first ride!" Mel'yin shouted aloud, as he climbed up the Thwwing's back and reached for Ay'r's arms. "Just like your mother. It's in your genes."

The canopy seemed to release his body reluctantly. Finally it took both cousins to pull him out of the interior and he all but slid over the sides and to the ground, and there, nearly fell with the sudden dizziness.

"Whoa, cousin, up you go!" Max'ell came to help lift him up again.

"Look at him!" Mel'yin pointed to Ay'rs sex, still sticking straight out and wet. "First time a pilot and he bonded Jafarra."

"Help me dress!" Ay'r said, now doubly embarrassed. He wrapped his loose tunic around his hips as a stop-gap measure.

The Thwwing itself seemed to be shivering, so the cousins

quickly led it off the pad and into its pen where it settled down once it had been slatted in, and where it dropped nearly to the ground as its thin legs folded beneath it.

"It's over-excited! We have to leave it alone. Come. Let's go!" Mel'yin said.

But Ay'r went over to its head and stroked it once, tel'ping his gratitude for such an astonishing flight and for such excitement. The Thwwing's palps could barely reach out and touch him, softest of fur against his bare legs, it was so exhausted, before they relaxed again and Ay'r let his cousins pull him back out of the pen, and still trying to dress himself, back up to the tower, via the gravilift.

"Never before!" Max'ell said, "has a pilot lifted her so high, or gone so fast."

"You've made a great conquest, cousin," Mel'yin assured him. "And an equally fortuitous beginning. I clocked your second circuit of the race course and it matched today's leading time."

"When you come to the City, pilot my Acy and we'll make d'lars hand over fist!"

"You'll be the Adorato of all the City-Jets," Max'ell laughed. "First time inside a Thwwing and my infant-Neo cousin has the luck to race it fast and actually bond it."

"What's your secret? Are you part insect soldier-stud?" Mel'yin asked, also laughing.

And so they entered the observation tower soft-lounge, where at sight of them, observers raised a sudden cheer to "Our Pilot Hero – the Newly Betrothed."

Long past the second sunset, deep into the last night of celebration, Ay'r found himself separated from his cousins of earlier, somehow, and, he supposed due to the small amounts of Soma-stelezine he'd sipped from someone's pipette, with fellows who were mostly strangers, although probably because of the drug, he felt immediately comfortable with them.

They'd left the Fast Port's soft-lounge and had somehow or other gotten back to the palace, and were now in large guest apartments on the second floor, denoted by banners of scarlet and pale iridium. If he recalled correctly, these fellows were mostly middle younger generation marquis and baronets of the House of Syzygy, whose City girder he was told pointed to Mandle in the Orion Arm and before that, toward the home world of Rigel in the Orion spur, and so a Very Old Family, nearly equal in antiquity and power to the Kells. Beryllium 18 multi-quintillionaires, all of them, good fellows for sport and fun, one and all. And one in particular, Deon, a strikingly built brunet with amethyst eyes, most attractive and very attracted by Ay'r: the fellow who had pulled Ay'r along to this after-party gathering.

It was Deon who'd offered him the pipette before and now once again, and who guided him away from the main chamber where his relations and their guests of the evening had begun to disrobe and engage in what looked like a multi-limbed confusion on soft-chairs, and carpeting.

"A little Ring-light?" Deon offered smoothly, once Ay'r had inhaled yet again, pulling him out of the room and onto the terrace. It was cooler out here, and though the Rings were so deeply aslant they nearly touched the horizon, they also reflected the star-embroidered night and so were gorgeous to look on.

Deon's kisses were hot and almost magically exciting and he used them to glide Ay'r along the window-walls kiss by kiss and finally into an open doorway, dark within, where Ay'r was guided onto a large, soft covered ottoman and, with his assent, his clothing slowly removed.

Though a young Neo still, Ay'r had read and experienced enough instructional PVNs and he'd been 'Tuted on how to respond to a lover's caresses and he was a most willing participant, eager to offer himself to his first lover, this handsome, hedonistic City-bred seducer.

Even so, and even through his over stimulated senses, he very briefly sensed another being in the chamber they'd entered. He immediately ascribed it to a lingering antipy, and relaxed again a moment later into lovemaking.

For the second time in a few hours, he felt his sex enclosed, this time by fingers, then the wetness of a mouth, and he gave himself to its eagerness. For the second time in a few hours, his body stiffened into rigidity, and exploded into the Uskian evening like a Plastro fire-show.

No sooner had his lover moved back up to his face than Ay'r felt different in some way. His limbs weren't merely tranquil, they didn't even feel there, and his abdomen also, whereupon Deon now lay, still painting his nipples with swirls of his tongue, that too, seemed physically missing although visibly there. Ay'r was about to say something. He tried to and he realized that he could not speak. Indeed he could barely breathe, couldn't move his head, hands, nor feet, none of his body at all. His eyes were still open but he couldn't even move them side to side. He became aware of the other's heavy breathing, aware of it, because his own, so recently its equal, was now suddenly hardly present.

Deon licked Ay'r's eyes slowly, tongue tip into the sides of each socket, and slowly raised himself up.

"I believe I was his first," Deon said softly, although not to Ay'r. "How delicious!"

Ay'r had begun to panic. Totally panic now. Every fiber of his consciousness told him he must move something, a finger, a toe. Or else ... Or else what? Or else he'd be paralyzed from now on? No!

"Gratitude, Lord," Deon now said, lifting himself fully up in such a way that his sex now passed alongside Ay'r's immobile face and showed from its wetness that he too had been satisfied.

"Gratitude to you, young Marquis, for aiding me in this most delicate work," Ay'r heard whispered from nearby, only a meter away, where the other creature in the room must be. So it hadn't been an antipy there at all. Ay'r's original instinct had been right. He thought he recognized the voice. "You're certain he's now completely asleep, even though his eyes are open?"

"The neuro-somazine I crushed into his mouth and down his throat is potent and fast," Deon said, off Ay'r's body completely now, he stepped away. "And well-tested. I assure you that no sooner did he orgasm, then it took full effect." Deon's tone of voice changed to a more musing one. "But ... you're certain he's the one?"

"Absolutely certain, yes!"

"He's a lovely lad," Deon said softly. "I believe I was his first in what I did."

"Then certainly I'll be his first too," the other voice said, with a chuckle.

"And being unconscious, he'll remember nothing, you are sure?" Deon asked. "So when I return to take him to the City, he'll be overjoyed and have no idea of what happened here?"

"He'll have no idea at all. But within thirty days, Sol Rad., mind you, you must come get him."

"Thirty exactly. I'll come get him and bring him to the City and there I'll flaunt him and I'll have him in every way I can until I tire of him or run out of positions to have him in," Deon laughed and for the first time Ay'r heard something in his voice that chilled him. "For he is a prize, indeed, this young Kell."

"Good, good, Deon! Now go. Wait outside."

He could still hear, still see, although they thought he could not, and so he heard Deon's footsteps leaving the chamber and saw the other now hover barely into view above him, quickly stripping down, and laying atop Ay'r, and he found himself wondering why, why all this, when this creature might merely have asked, because although it was dim in the chamber and he was undeniably mature, he was as handsome as Deon, handsome as any Ophiucan Kell, as the saying went, with his lithe, muscular body and his bronze shock of hair and, when his face came parallel to Ay'r's for a second, his eyes too – emerald green.

The stranger too bent over Ay'r and kissed his face and neck, his breast and tummy and still tumescent sex, then lifted his legs and went under somehow, remaining there a while although remaining out of sight, what he did Ay'r couldn't know since he couldn't see. Then he could see, and what he saw surprised him, his own legs bent up and forward, athwart the other's chest, now bent over his shoulders, as he bent forward rhythmically, clearly performing sex on Ay'r who couldn't feel a thing, and who wondered, but why? Why all this? Why didn't he simply ask? Why not simply ...? It was then that Ay'r recognized the voice, and when the man's head next came into view he strained to see if, yes, it was undoubtedly him, just as the News PVNs showed, and now that his torso was in such close view there! There were the telltale tiny chevron marks his Cyber 'Tute had remarked had become common to all many-times-done molecular-cosmetic re-fittings, there, where the shoulder met the pectoral and there, too at the line of the neck. Ah, Vir, if only he could close his eyes, while the Princeps Mart Kell – for that was who it was – could be no other! – Ay'r was certain, now that he recognized him, worked himself up slowly, ever so slowly, (he was six hundred and fifty or more, was he not? and needed to take his time), into this fornication, muttering words Ay'r could no longer make out, and wished not to hear at all, and which furthermore sounded not quite right, not quite sane, somehow or other, like the drivel of someone not only very old but also somewhat unhinged.

The Princeps reached his climax at very long last, almost seeming to give up his life in the exhausting process, having to rest so still after, and such a very long time, before he slowly dropped Ay'r's legs, and, Ay'r supposed, exited Ay'r's body, and stood, cleaning himself, then dressed and left the chamber.

They were outside, Deon and the Princeps, a long time, almost too long, so that Ay'r became uncomfortable, uncertain. What if they had changed their mind and ... what was this! His eyes could move! Slightly. Not very much. But he tried again. Yes. And he now felt something else. A sort of hot tingling along his sides. So he tried in-breathing and heard himself breathe inward hard, and so he now tried to move his finger, just one tiny finger on his right hand, please, just one, and oh how it tingled and hurt so hot, and finally he felt it move. He now assumed that something he'd taken earlier, or the dosage of the drug Deon gave him while they had kissed, had not been correct, for him to have been conscious throughout and probably that was why now, before he was supposed to, he could ... feel the other fingers move, then feel the hand move, then the other move. Ah. Agony! Then his feet move. He strained. It was the greatest strain of his life, but now he felt he must do it. Do it or ... what? Die? He strained until he could no longer and his hands were now free of the paralysis, and his feet too, he touched his face, his chest, all, helped himself sit up, fell off the side of the ottoman, but then got to his feet feeling them secure beneath him.

He dressed quickly, quietly, and now fear all but froze him as he wondered, why, why, what did they plan to do with him? Whatever it was, he could not let them. Never! Yet, it was the Princeps himself, the Head of his House. The all-powerful Mart Kell. How could he escape, he a mere twelfth in line?

Only one thought now filled him. He must escape, whatever their plans. Flee the palace, get as far away from Kells and people and from the City as possible, flee to where no one ever went but wanderers and pamps, into the great, poorly charted rest of this world, since only there would he be safe.

His cape, where was it? If he were to flee? He needed it in the cold desert night. No, not his, too easy to spot, being bronze, but the other cloak, black on one side, silvered white by iridium on the other, dropped to the floor there, Deon's cape, the traitor's cape.

He picked it up, flung it around his shoulder and tied it, and look, its side pockets were stuffed, literally stuffed with d'lars, Deon Syzygy's Thwwing race gambling winnings. That would serve me as well, Ay'r thought.

He thought he heard them coming back and slid out into the corridor and from there back onto the terrace through an empty room. Smart to get the cloak, as the night was already chilled.

In seconds, he had flung himself over the balcony's side rail and dropped down another level, and he was running around the side that gave onto the Great Salt Ocean. For this escape to work, he needed an air-board, and he recalled a spare one he kept down at the smaller generator shack, by the house servant's commissary, where he'd long stashed it for an emergency.

Twice more he froze in place, flattened against a window or wall as revelers passed him, shouting with drink and drugs. Once he thought he hear Deon's voice calling his name, but that might have been fear making a noise out of nothing.

He knew he had one advantage over any of them in that this was his palace, his place, this was his own world – if it came to that. They knew it little, and he knew it ... well, he knew it a little better, but still more, than they did.

At the commissary-kitchen, he pushed in through open upper shutters he knew of and gathered hands full of pale water tablets and a long flank of curl vole cured jerky that the cooks always kept hidden from his prying hands and that he always managed to find.

Once he had the air-board in his hands, he wrapped the cloak around himself more carefully and tied it tight so it wouldn't unfurl, then he took off, silent on the air-board.

Behind him, lights began going on all around the second level from which he'd just escaped, and many voices began to be raised.

Ay'r thought nothing but "I must go. Go!" gliding around the historical Jobim lozenge, skittering over the retaining wall and at last, free, floating at top speed, resembling little but a sand-devil's shadow, into the great empty desert, into the perilous, star-dappled, Ring-circuited night.

Chapter Two

Mists covered Mt. Mapoca-Atlas, concealing all of its bulk this afternoon but for the snow-capped, irregular peak rising four thousand meters over the volcanic lake and shelf, itself five thousand meters above the great plain below. Mist screened his view, all but camouflaging the ordinarily purple waters, and distantly, on its other shoreline, the pale, pearlescent, mostly fungoid shapes of residences hidden among the abundant sea-green tinted foliage.

As a resort world, Verhandel attracted chiefly very high-level, post-avocation Hesperian Cityzens, and there were reasons. Its weather was temperate, moderate, unvaryingly sunny with the softest of brief rains; its shapes and its pastel colors were easy on aged eyesight. The second planet of three in a ternary solar system, this "Norn" (along with its sister planets, Uerth, and Skuild) lay protected from more casual visitors by an unusually unstable time-shift distortion nebula of approximately three years in either direction, one of the few places in the Orion Arm known to do so, and another reason why the three planets were known under the collective name of Norns, or Fates, in reference to early Metro-Terran mythology, signifying past, present and future.

He'd had been reclining, not quite awake, not quite asleep, as he tended to do lately when he could actually rest, in an air-chaise on the inside-outside balcony directly over the lake-drop, and for no good reason at all, thinking about his youngest child, Holt, barely out of Ed. & Dev. and already famous or infamous, the only living Hesperian he actually felt he wanted to see and speak with, when from behind him there was a faint aroma of great familiarity. A perfume, yes, hers! Slowly he sat forward, the chaise-back following his lead, and said aloud. "Is it you?"

"I woke you," the voice of Oudma seemed disappointed.

"Not really," he admitted. Waving his hand in a leftward rotation, he got the chaise to turn left until it faced the chamber interior. There Oudma stood, or at least her mind-pattern made him think she stood, looking as she had, tall, statuesque, old but still regal, the image itself captured a few days Sol Rad., before her body had passed away of "natural causes," almost two centuries ago. "Is there something I need to know?" Ay'r asked his only wife. "You only appear when I need reminding."

"Is that true? Well, I suppose it is," her pattern said, amused. "Next time it will be completely spontaneously, I promise. But yes, there is something you need to be reminded of and I'm not entirely sure how happy you will *be* to be reminded."

When he smiled at her image, she seemed to take heart and went on.

"You have an appointment."

"I do? An appointment? Who could possibly want to see me?"

"It's a very old appointment. And there's only one person in the galaxy who would be such a pest as to remember, and probably the only one that you would keep the appointment with."

He pondered her riddling, then answered, "that old jackal, Mart Kell."

"That's my second most beloved you're speaking of so disparagingly," she reminded him. For she had briefly married Mart when the Ib'rs first came to Hesperia. "But yes, it's Mart Kell. You've got a long standing appointment to meet with him, in two days, Sol Rad., at one of Vinson Todd's old residences, in the Domenica Heights girder of Hesperia."

"Whatever for?" he had to ask.

"You never said. But here it is, the very first item installed into my system. The date was made, let's see, well, on the original Independence From The Matriarchy Day." The image paused. "No clue?"

His smile had widened. "Oddly, I do remember it now. We agreed to meet and to see if all the changes we'd just begun to institute had worked out for good or not."

"They have worked out for good," she said, adding. "Vir'ism is now the predominant social belief system of Two of the Three Species across the inhabited galaxy and, furthermore it is fully recognized as so by the Third Species, the Vespids, which you recall are a mostly female-people." She paused. "Do you really want to get up from this comfort and traipse ten thousand light years just for a celebratory drink?"

"Not really," he admitted. "Whoever designed Verhandel did such a good job, I could stay here till the end of my days. As it was supposed to be."

"Then I'll comm. Mart and say ..."

"No. Don't. I'll go," he said. "How long has it been since I've been to the City?"

"Hesperia? Seven years, or so, Sol Rad."

"That long? I assume Kell is still making trouble."

"He makes the Inter. Gal. News less, if that's what you're asking. But he still seems to be thriving."

"No doubt still plotting his comeback as Premier of the Republic."

"Our nephew, Cas'sio, will never allow that to happen," she assured him.

"Anyway, I'd like to see my youngest," he said.

"The Cadet?" she asked.

"Is that what Holt is called now in the City? I suppose they would have to have some striking name for him in the Inter. Gal. News & Gossip Comm.s. He's so very much younger than his siblings."

"Than our child, you mean? And my brother 'Dward's other child by you?"

"Yes. Holt is far younger than all of them; he's the only child of my old age." And also, Ay'r wanted to say, the only child I actually carried, however briefly, within my own body; carried and then "pre-birthed" into an external womb.

"You might want to know that the sobriquet 'Cadet' is a historical appellation," Oudma's mind-pattern said. "Because he is your last born, dynastically, any child of Holt's would be said to be of the Cadet Line of the Sanqq' house."

"Dynastically!" he scoffed. "Sanqq' house! What foolery! But I do worry about Baby Holt ... the Cadet," he said, trying out the word.

"That's only natural," she said. "Will you see your other children, too?"

"Oh, it's more than likely." Then, "actually, how can I possibly escape *not* seeing them?" He wondered something and asked, "do you want me take you along with me? To see them? Can I do that?

Or are you built into the place?"

"I'm built-in. Don't you recall? Although by now, your late mother's company, Lars'son Life Extensions, has evolved a more portable version. Look into having me reinstalled that way, while you're in the City, will you? And, Ay'r, love, have *our* son Uriel comm. me when you're there in the City, too. So we can all three talk together. And if you can, try to see my other boy, Y'vo, Mart's son."

"I'll try, but you realize that they both may be very busy. Too busy for even me. Inner Quinx Council Lords and all that hokum. How about the old coot himself? Should I go beard Mart in his dome?"

"Why not?" she said, almost girlishly. "I'll comm. the boys' retinues and say you're coming."

"No. No, don't do that. They'll get it talked around and there will be seventeen hundred kinds of publicity when I arrive and you know how I hate all that Great Father stuff ... Maybe comm. the Cadet? Comm. him and say I want no fuss at all, or I'll throttle him. He's the only one of them who still listens to his father. All the others really think of is how anything as minor as my visit will elevate their own political status. I'll let them know I'm there once I've arrived."

"My, we've grown judgmental lately. Keep in mind that the other children are among the City's leaders, the Republic's leaders, with vast powers and equally vast responsibilities. While the Cadet, well, he's still a playboy, and hardly a saint. If you kept up as much as I do with PVN magazines you would know."

"Luckily I have *you* to do that. Do you keep up a great deal?"

"You would do well to ask me what is going on in the Republic."

"What *is* going on then? In two sentences or less."

"Very funny. Go back to sleep. Wait! One thing I will tell you. The search for another Hesperia grows more desperate every year, Sol Rad."

Without a new source of Beryllium 18, he knew, the material would grow only more rare and unless a substitute were found, it was bound to become depleted. Especially as Premier Y'vo Ib'r-Kell had followed Mart Kell's lead and announced the *further* opening up of the Sag. Arm planets of the galaxy to colonization, following decades of exploration – further stretching the City's already limited resources. He'd hoped Holt would join in that crucial search, if not scientifically than at least in terms of exploration. So far, the lad had done little in life but make a spectacle of himself at Thwwing races and have his face plastered over the more risqué PVNs for his party shenanigans and many romantic imbroglios.

"In Metro-Terran times," he said, "people had energy shortages all the time. Even worse, some of them worried about the universe running out of matter and going cold … You usually tell me if anyone comm.ed anything of any importance that I ought to know about?"

"Of importance? Or of amusement value?" she asked.

"I did well to make you gatekeeper here in my retirement. So you're awake all the time now and that keeps you busy?"

"Gaining knowledge, yes. It's almost the nicest thing about being stored like this. I never knew I could know so much … There is one thing of especial interest, Love. Do your remember the infant Truth-sayer from Pelagia we met, and who predicted for us so many centuries ago?"

"Loren whatever? Didn't he grow up in the City and start up some kind of cult?"

"He did grow up, slowly, not like a Pelagian but almost as slowly as a Cityzen, because of whatever physiological anomaly he possessed from birth. He's still alive although physically pretty much at full rest now, virtually a mummy, living out his final days in a monastery on a moon circling the sixth planet of Narcissus 12. Well! A hundred years or so ago, Sol Rad., he caused to be published via the Inter. Gal. Net a volume of omens and predictions titled *The Book of Colored-Glory* that he'd apparently been compiling for decades. It caused quite a stir. Several thousand billion copies were comm.ed out eventually. It's not only deemed the central text of his cult, which by the way is known as Iridium Vir'ism, whatever that's supposed to signify, but the book has since become used by entrepreneurs, social predictors, manufacturers, scientists, even politicians hand legislators on most of the Center Worlds. I recently got around to scanning it," she added.

"And?" he asked.

"It's the strangest book I've ever encountered. Quite lovely as poetry and very enigmatic. But if you'll remember Loren's predictions as a boy, you'll understand that these poemlets are not dissimilar. These are a hundred and twenty, four line quatrains, mostly in dactylic tetrameter and pentameter. He's made some rather intriguing predictions. Naturally they are mostly metaphorical, but a student named Reg'ier Ka Graz put out a sort of key, five or six years back, Sol Rad."

"The kid was good. We both recall some of Loren's predictions while we were in Dryland," he said. "About myself. About yourself. He said we'd find your brother 'Nton and we did. And remember how he called 'Dward, a great 'soldier-mother!' So I take it that some of these are ..."

"Yes. Amazingly accurate when understood. And I believe, Ay'r, that some of them concern *us* closely, as do many other people. Loren's predictions are ever more enigmatic now, but even so ... Prediction number 117, for example, jumped out at me. It begins as follows:

> *In the year of a hundred ORANGE & COBALT*
> *Dim-Days, The Great Father returns to the Source.*

"I mention it," Oudma's mind-pattern went on, "because every known commentator of the book, and by now they are legion, pointed this line out as a reference to you, Ay'r Kerry Sanqq', returning somewhere, possibly to the City itself, after all, it's 'the source' of power in the galaxy in all ways. All of which I rather blithely ignored, until five minutes ago, thinking it unlikely you would ever go back there. But now that you *are* going back, let me read you the quatrain again in full."

> *In the year of a hundred ORANGE & COBALT*
> *Dim-Days, The Great Father returns to the Source.*
> *Under the Rainbow Rings a New Star ascends as*
> *– a Mother! Turmoil. Contention. Sons at war.*

"I have no *idea* what the first line or the third line refer to." Oudma's mind pattern said. "Orange and Blue double suns, perhaps? There are about a hundred fifty thousand known systems of those two colors charted, so take your pick. As to the 'New Star,' it seems to refer to the coming of a *someone* of some significance, perhaps to you, or possibly to the Republic as a whole. Whoever this person is, he 'ascends' and he gives birth to someone special. The ending also appears clear enough. 'Turmoil, contention, sons at war.'"

"Are our children in turmoil?" he asked and when she didn't answer. "Of course they are. They always are. I see I'll have to do some Inter. Gal. Comm. studying myself before I arrive at the City."

"Aren't you going to ask if any other quatrains have come to pass?"

"You'll tell me I'm sure."

"The most famous recent one is Number 104:"

> *The Great Five is demolished by a Recondite word.*
> *An Age of BRONZE/JADE thoroughly overthrown.*
> *Another, one step Sideways Near, Wears*
> *In Reluctance, the tarnished Triple Diadem*

"Mart Kell's hundred year premiership is the Age of Bronze and Jade, I'm guessing," Ay'r said. "Which fell because of the promise that he secretly made to Helmut Dja'aa, which brought down himself, and the Inner Quinx of that time, or the 'Great Five.' 'Another' who wears the diadem of Premiership with 'reluctance' would be our nephew, Cas'sio, who was voted to replace Mart as Premier and who still rules. He is 'near' and also is 'one step side-ways,' since he is not directly related to Mart, because although Mart wed your brother 'Nton after your marriage ended, Cas'sio had been sired by Zhon Azura upon 'Nton before they met and was thus only a stepson. How did I do?"

"Cas'sio was adopted by Mart, however," she said. "Making him even more clearly 'one step Sideways!' and no one ever said you'd lost your powers of analysis," Oudma admitted.

"Do all the quatrains work as well as that one?"

"Not all, no. Some are too cryptic, even now, for analysts to parse. While others work surprisingly well. That second quatrain I quoted, for example, Loren wrote many decades *before* Mart Kell became Premier. They were all recorded, supposedly as the Truth-sayer 'received' them, in visions.

"They're quite amusing. Why not upload them so I can look them over while traveling. How quickly can we get a Fast to take me to the City?"

"Then you're still going?" she asked, hoping she didn't sound shrill or nagging.

"If I don't go, won't I disappoint a hundred billion fans of the *Book of Colored-Glory*?"

"I see," she responded dryly. Then, "regarding travel, you always forget, Ay'r that you're a man of exceptionally *unlimited* means. A Fast is ready at your beck and call at all times."

"But you think I ought engage in some other Ed. & Dev. as I travel?"

"Without question. There are many, many political complications these days it would be in your best interest to at least know of."

"Are there any other predictions in that text that I should know about?"

"Yes. We ought to work on getting some data on those predictions and a few others that follow which might prove to be ... relevant. You know, at least a search through the *Logo-Con-In-tellectu-Universalis* for some of these words and places that we know nothing of."

"Fine. Yes. Will you do that? And I promise while I'm travelling to catch up on current City politics, little as I've a taste for it."

"There are three more quatrains that follow the Orange/Cobalt one," she said. "Each becomes more obtuse. Except that, according to this Ka Graz, both the Kell house and your son Holt, who wasn't yet born and thus was certainly not nicknamed when Loren wrote this text, appear to be mentioned."

"Go on then, read the ones who think relevant to me," Ay'r said, feeling uneasy.

"Number 105 goes:

> *EMERALD indifference churns a gigantic Gyre*
> *Of Ambition into the Closest of Close-Son's*
> *Empire. Could Attainment so Decisive*
> *Again elude the Orion-Spur's Grasp?*

"That seems to be Mart Kell, if it's anyone," he said. "But I recall that he didn't at all get along with his Close-Son by your brother 'Nton. What's your nephew named? North, wasn't it? After that hero of the Cyber War?"

"Yes, North Ib'r-Kell. After North Diad-Taylor. And you're right. Mart and North never got along. They lived on different Girders the minute North got out of Ed. & Dev. Mine and Mart's son, Y'vo, get along only a little bit better, and Y'vo tends to support his brother North against his father."

"'Sons in contention' that other quatrain read. Or is that

stretching it? Well, it's some other Close-son we have no knowledge of. Go on. What are some of the other quatrains you think relevant?"

"The one hundred and eighteenth also struck me," Oudma's pattern said. "See if you know why?"

> *From out of the Heart of A Notable Star*
> *The Corrected Rebel renders Automated fate*
> *Enterprising All in a bid to secure – Forever.*
> *All Future Lines thread this SCARLET Corpse.*

"You're surely not thinking ...?" Ay'r immediately asked.

"We both evidently are thinking of our granddaughter, Uriel and Olaf Sanqq's Close-daughter, K'tina, yes. She left the surface of Hesperia a decade ago to reside at the City's radiation-strewn heart along with the Cybers there who mine Beryllium 18. Sometimes I think it's more than just her left side that's Cyberized. Sometimes I think it's her very soul."

"Do you regret then their decision to save her life by any means?" he asked.

"I supported Uriel and Olaf's decision to do it ... But I suppose I do have regrets."

"The quatrain seems to predict her demise. Also some great undertaking."

"And number a hundred and nineteen is equally striking. It reads:

> *Tossed on the Edge of Nowhere, The First*
> *Shall Rendezvous with Maternity Manifest.*
> *The Cadet alone may mold the SAPPHIRE core.*
> *Returning to mourn, surpassing all abundance*

"I see! *The* Cadet! Written before he was born, you say?"

"*Centuries* before. And say the name anywhere an Inter. Gal. Comm. is broadcast today and every listener will assume it's your son Holt being spoken of. The 'surpassing abundance' part is easy enough to see. He's one of your heirs, yes?"

"I thought I'd rather slid down the list of wealthiest individuals in the ..."

"To fifteenth – in total amassed and unamassed fortune," she said.

"You see! I might as well not be on it." And when she looked skeptical, "anyway, he's supposed to *surpass* riches. To go *beyond* mere material means. Molding 'the Sapphire Core' could mean he becomes Premier of the Republic himself. Or is that really too unlikely?"

"He's much lower than a hundred and fifteenth on *that* particular list," she said with a sad smile. "Even though he's your personal favorite."

"No, you're right. But these omens do seem relevant to our family. I agree. And the next quatrain is?"

"Ka Graz links these four quatrains together, reporting that they were written all at once in one afternoon, and the next, the 120th, was written a few years later, but also appears to cohere to the group."

They continued talking and Oudma began searching meanwhile with part of her mind, as she'd learned to do only lately, through millions of files, while Ay'r's Cyber Valet arrived and helped Ay'r out of the air-chaise and together with Oudma, the three chose appropriate clothing for a short visit to the City, including, necessarily some formal wear, in case of a ceremony.

Just before the Fast was brought to the edge of the balcony over the lake for Ay'r to enter it, he pondered aloud, "'A New Star Ascends – a Mother'? Isn't that what the first quatrain you read said?"

"Exactly, yes."

"I wonder who he could be, this so-called 'New Star'?"

She shrugged. "Somewhere where the year is longer than a hundred days long, Sol Rad.? And where there are Blue and Orange suns? I have no idea. I'll check and let you know."

"And where there are large rings, too, remember!" he added.

"You're right. That ought to narrow it down a bit. Are you off now? Then good-bye love," she said. "We'll get back in contact as soon as you clear the time-fields nebula. Isn't that right, pilot?"

"In about four hours, Sol Rad.," the Cyber Valet replied.

Just before the Fast door sealed shut upon Ay'r, Oudma had the oddest feeling. She couldn't even describe it. Touching her wrist connector, she shouted, "Ay'r, my love!"

"I'm right here," he replied. "What is it?"

"No. Nothing," she answered. "Fast, take especial care," she commanded.

The Fast was gone in an instant through the mist, and though she concentrated now on going through the entire *Logo-Con-Intellectu-Universalis*, still every once in a while Oudma felt that twinge that said she shouldn't have let Ay'r go, should have called him back, although why, she could not say, perhaps it was a flaw in the program that held nothing but her consciousness and sometimes, when she tried very hard, also her image, intact.

His valet, the fifth or more Cyber replacement for the Human, and still invaluable, Vel-Crane, stepped into the large domed room and made some gesture with its hands indicative of another Holo-Comm. interrupting the one he was already busy with.

"Lovely seeing you again," Mart Kell said to the rather good physical simulation of his first and only wife. "It's really been far too long, Oudma. I look forward so much to these little talks of ours. I'll certainly meet Ay'r at the designated spot." He then blew a kiss and the Holo-Comm. switched itself off.

"Not the Premier comm.ing again?" Mart asked Vel-Crane VI. "Lately, not a day goes by, Sol Rad., that he doesn't comm. I've yet to figure out why, all of a sudden."

"Not the Premier at all. It's the Marquis Syzygy."

"Has he located the little devil?"

The valet had slowly turned to exit and it pretended not to hear this last question.

Then Deon was in the middle of the room, dressed (overdressed, Mart believed, given how fetching he looked unclothed) in some sort of Desert-Sands outfit, right off someone's sand world PVN, with at least the head and nose mask removed this time, as Mart had demanded during their last Holo-Comm.

"Well, Marquis?"

"He eludes us yet. I fear he's no longer alive," Syzygy said, melodramatically. His ebony hair seemed to have been bronzed at the ends by exposure to the Uskian double suns and his pale complexion slightly tanned. He looked completely gorgeous. Of course, those eyes helped, eyes that next to Mart's own, and of course, the Beryllium Blue of the Eise'nsteins, were the most remarkable naturally-colored, totally Human, eyes in the galaxy.

"Don't be foolish, Marquis. The boy is four-fifths myself, and thus he is clearly is both alive and extremely angry at the two of us. If you've not yet figured out what happened, I'll tell you – your drug misfired. He was partly conscious during our little sex session and conversation. So if you've not yet located him, despite your best efforts, then clearly it's been because *he* does not wish to be found."

"Surely, Princeps, you give him too much credit. He's an infant. Not yet sixteen years old, Sol Rad."

"When I was fourteen, I eluded half my grandfather's security staff for a week, Sol Rad., … right here in Hesperia."

"Then you believe him to be alive?"

"Alive and off on some pranking adventure. Foolish you and I simply gave him the motive, the excuse, and then the opportunity to escape that he'd obviously been looking for all the while. My nephew hinted as much when he introduced us at the Betrothal ritual. And, at that same auspicious ceremony, I saw how inturned and resentful the lad was. He may have looked pretty enough and called me 'great lord' and all that claptrap, but he clearly wanted to kick me in the teeth and take my place."

"With respect, Lord Kell. I saw no such thing in the child's trusting young eyes."

"That's only because he desired you, you romantic fool. As whom in his right mind, wouldn't desire you? Now update me."

"The entire Eastern shore line of Usk's Great Salt Ocean has been thoroughly searched. Among the Three Species and among the pamps. Who, by the way, seem quite busily engaged with some other business of their own, a new one, perhaps worth knowing. But we searched wide and deep through the marts and star ports and the resorts with no luck. There are few enough civilized places besides those for him to hide in, but there is an entire world, the Great Salt Ocean, the many mountains, all of it more or less uncharted."

"The pamps were those little creatures we saw scurrying about on all sides when we were on Usk, yes?"

""Yes. They perform about ninety-five percent of the labor and maintenance on the planet."

"What is this new business among them?" Mart asked. His business, he knew, meant knowing everyone else's business.

"It's being bruited about that some sort of long-predicted and long-preordained political or religious figure has suddenly arisen or is about to appear among them. The sense I got was of a kind of Messiah."

"Messiahs are pre-ordained only when there is little hope left," Mart said. "Is that the case of the pamps on Usk?"

"Princeps, truthfully, I do not really know enough to tell you. This I do know, the pamps are everywhere and they seem to operate everything, yet the Three Species pay them little or no mind. Historically … ," he began, earnestly, then stopped himself.

"'Historically, the downtrodden rise up,' you were going to say. Are the creatures downtrodden, Marquis?"

"They're ordered about. Seldom even directly spoken to. Mostly ignored."

"That may be even worse," Mart said. "Continue to monitor that Pamp Messiah situation. But meanwhile, give the search another, more personal try. I know you feel responsible in some way, and I admire that in you, Marquis. It's a testament to the already much vaunted goodness of your heart. But stay only another week or two, Sol Rad., on that forsaken planet. Then please return to the City and our company. Leave a Syzygy search team looking for the boy. I don't actually need him for another month, you know."

"I feel very badly about him."

"As you ought to. It was your drugs, Marquis, that failed to act as directed."

"My drugs didn't so much fail, as they faltered."

"Whatever they did, they allowed him to remain conscious enough to get loose when I wanted him there. When you do locate him, you will require considerable quantities of your famous Deonic charm to secure him to yourself once again, Marquis!"

"It's all I think of. That and how betrayed and how unhappy he must be."

"You look so love-sick, he'll doubtless see the truth in your face."

"If only I can win him over again!"

"You'd better. Since I've promised him to you."

"The poor little Neo. All alone on Usk."

"Enough! Come back to the City soon, and if you can't convince him to return with you, have him observed *closely*, so we know exactly when and where to pick him up when we need to!"

"As you wish, Princeps," Deon said sadly. This melancholia

made Deon Syzygy even more devastatingly handsome! Then his image vanished.

Oh to be a hundred or so again, so perhaps Mart could have some chance at attracting him!

Vel-Crane VI was lurking at the edge of the large room.

"What do you want now?" Mart asked. "Not another comm.?"

Vel-Crane VI smiled and answered. "No. Just eavesdropping. In preparation for when I take over Kell Unlimited."

"Why not take over the Quinx Council too?" Mart asked and ordered the Cyber out.

Mart never knew if Vel-Crane VI was joking or not. This latest generation of City-Made Cybers were for the most part designed and built by Cybers themselves, and they tended to possess the oddest choice of Humanlike attributes. Humor, for example. Wit, in abundance. An annoying tendency to predict Human (and Delph. too, but not Arth.) behavior, with concomitant but not quite "I Told You So" attitudes afterwards.

Of course they were considerably more complex than the Post-Matriarchal IV Series. Those poor buggers had possessed really nothing more than enhanced sex drive and response. Mostly in female form, they were designed by Humans for those Human and Delph. males who couldn't live without women or who began to miss the presence of younger women in their lives once all the remaining Delph. and Human women had reached the age of 400 or so without replacements. The IV series was fine, of course, but all female, and Vir Institute die-hards had decided it was discriminatory, and so had commissioned and produced a sub-series of male series IV's, known as Series IVa's. Somewhere or other, pranksters got into the mix, because the new sub-series turned out to be extraordinarily beautiful male replicas in an era that had of necessity replaced female standards of attractiveness with male ones. IVa's were seductive, they were desirable beyond words, they hunted Human men every free moment they were unemployed, and every moment they weren't working they were busy having sex with men. Some IVa's developed Human male harems. Others held fornication contests, which naturally enough a few series IIIs were canny enough to make money on, first by charging admission, then by making PVNs of the contests. It got to a point that, thanks to the incessant horniness of Series IVa's, any Neo under say a hundred years old, risked being deflowered any time he travelled alone about the Republic. The defining model of series IVa's was Jerzsey Weisblut (self – and quite wittily – named). Jerzsey could (and would) take on a group of males, satisfy them, get them off, satisfy its own unnatural (for a Cyber, that is) lusts, all in one hour, Sol Rad. Men went wild for Series IVa's, but their inbuilt nonstop lust meant that the series, once obtained, were hard to actually hold onto, no matter how much one cost to be leased or purchased. In short, they were as bad as young men!

When Mart first laid eyes on Music-Holos of Yuli Edlina Eise'nstein, he'd wondered if the young genius could be a Series IVa with a few custom modifications. By no means as perfect physically as a Cyber, "Ice" still looked slightly enough inhuman to be questionably Cyber. His perfectly muscled body, his oddly small pectorals with tiny unringed nipples, his hairlessness, his ivory-white hair. And that voice! Talk about electrifying! But desirable as Eise'nstein was for Mart – and half the galaxy too – he'd quickly progressed from being an idol to becoming Mart's enemy, hadn't he? In the process enduring fewer years than any ordinary Cyber did, barely a hundred. And in the process also taking Mart's adored Bri'an with him into nothingness, the arch-villain! Deon, too, when he first showed up, debuting, in fact, with his fathers – Stef and Davis Syzygy – at an Iridium Ball for six thousand guests, Mart and others too wondered how the basalt-haired, white-skinned, coral-lipped, and, above all, those Amethyst-colored eyes could possibly be natural. Yet he was completely Human, naturally. Too bad he was so young. But then, even as a sometime protégé of Mart's, seen with him at all the right places, Deon was golden – beyond golden, Beryllium, really.

A few dozen of the famed Series IVa Cybers were reputed to still exist. Creaking along by now, if not kept up with the greatest devotion and care by their owners, those few units that had let themselves be kept, rather than going free to do as they wished, as most of them had, until they self-destructed or fell into total disrepair.

The newer Cyber-Series V, naturally enough, combined all the attributes of their predecessors. With one difference. They were so perfectly, subtly balanced, that when a group of their elite suggested a throwback to at least Series III's, they explained why to Humans. "Too much sanity is not a hallmark of any living Human."

So, of course, instead, the Series VI's that they designed turned out to be far less flawless. They were ambitious, slightly spiteful, annoying at times, and, yes humorous too. Even black-humored, like Vel-Crane VI.

The astonishing irony of it all lay in the fact that granted enough freedom, the Cybers themselves had produced a species of somewhat conscious Cybers, just as Wicca VIII and the entire Matriarchy had feared. But in doing so they made them more humanly fallible than ever before, made them vain, judgmental, funny, satiric, sometimes silly, and ill-tempered. Had the doomed Matriarchal Council ever begun to suspect this outcome, they might be still in power, since power was the very last thing these above-all sensible, mechanized creatures wanted. Most of them laughed at the idea as a complete – and extremely Human – illusion. And so the Matriarchy, a galactic empire, an entire culture, had perished for what? Over nothing! Over a misunderstanding!

"Danger to the Nest! Danger to the Nest!"

Two soldiers chittered as loudly as possible into the egg-laying chamber. They moved to the edge where it opened to a temporary hatchery.

"Danger to the Nest! Danger to the Nest!"

They chittered loudly again and exited.

The sixteen Class C workers stood still for a second, huddled together into two groups, grabbing each other's longest antennae and exchanging fear-response hormones. They broke up into fours, and this time they crossed antennae, amalgamating information, until one of them, chittered out "Danger to the Nest (Past Tense ((All Clear)))."

Kri'nni Des ('xx') however, turned to the worker closest to herself and spoke authoritatively. "Didn't you hear? Danger to the Nest! (Ongoing ((Not Yet Clear!))) Unhook me from the ovipositor (egg sac ((baby chute))) and close off this chamber and the hatchery. Leave eight workers to guard it. Go with seven others to the nursery and seal it off. Remain there yourself until you are called (advised ((by no one else but me)))."

"But, your Majesty, it's only a drill (practice-session). We have one every ..."

"I'll say if it's a drill (practice-session) or not." She lashed out with the artificial claw she'd had manufactured and wore on one feeler, and tore at the worker's thorax. She didn't draw ichor, but the soldier would have long diagonal scar for the rest of her life. The worker fell back, chittering in a low and deep voice of her humiliation at disobeying the Queen. and it's eternal scar of evidence, now upon her.

Kri'nni turned to the next worker in line. "You're in charge now (You rule ((in my name and don't forget it!))). Carry out my orders!"

Already, her lower abdomen was being delicately detached from the transparent natural tubing that led to the huge gelatinous mass of eggs she had laid all morning. What a relief! She shook herself away from the thing, wishing she'd never have to come to this stinking hole again.

As she moved toward the exit, one of the workers threw herself in front of Kri'nni so she'd had to step on her. "Your majesty, what shall we tell the hatchery supervisor?"

"Tell that bitch she's on a Stele-Somazine break (no practice ((and why bother showing up later, either?)))." Seeing the soldier looking baffled, she added. "I'll be back when I'm done dealing with this Danger to the Nest!"

As she thought it might, the last phrase operated like a danger-pheromone and stopped the soldiers from moving, forcing them to break into groups and confab. During this autonomic response, naturally enough she was able to make her escape.

Finally! Relatively fresh air.

Naturally two soldiers from the corridor immediately followed her and one came out of some side chamber and led the way. As though the fool knew where she was going.

"Your name, Soldier?" she addressed the largest and youngest.

"An'dreck'o, your Majesty."

"You're kind of cute (for a bug ((though not really my type))). I order you to the 'xchange center. When I see you next, I want you to be even taller, darker and handsomer. And ready for action (the sexual kind ((poke-around-the-world)))."

The solider almost stumbled.

"Understand, An'dreck'o! I want you ready to accommodate me in two hours. Got it?"

"But I'm only as Class B (not a male partner class ((at least according to the Ancient Arth. Rituals of Copulation Rules))). The egg-laying-chamber supervisor (our boss ((that twat!))) is sure to complain (or worse!)."

"Did I ask your opinion (bother ((noise)))? Go and come back as a male or not at all."

"Your majesty's wish is my command (this should be interesting ((and fun!)))."

"You better believe it!" Kri'nni enthused.

She left the other soldiers at the base of a lift she'd had installed in the Nest many egg-laying breaks ago. Naturally one of them had to leap atop it to protect her. From what, she hadn't a clue. It almost didn't jump off in time to not be crushed when she reached her destination, her private apartments high in the Nest, on the far side from the museum area, open to the public and those tunnels where guided tours were held. Even so, this place was large, airy, well furnished, with almost all of the comforts of Hesperia – and with a spectacular, nine hundred-story high view of Deneb XII's noble, vivid, if somewhat bare landscape.

Mar'ko Ve Espry was at the Holo-Comm. board when she entered. The tall, spindly Human – it amused her how insectlike he was – half turned. "Hey Boss-Lady! Glad you could get away so soon."

"Me too." She instantly entered an ion-bath and let it launder all those nasty egg-chamber odors off her. Of course it would be another huge nuisance once she returned back down into that steaming hellhole smelling unlike the Queen who had left. There would be ritual challenges from soldiers and she would have to lay out a few of them and maybe take a good swipe at the Supervisor who she'd like to kill anyway. But hey, that was part of the fun, no? Kept things from being so boring around this dump.

As did her many hours of R&R up here.

"That's better!" she said exiting all clean and fresh-smelling. Mar'ko was ready with a pipette of Soma. "And that's even better. Mmm."

Mar'ko had been second in charge of the Prime Nest Historical Site Inc. part of the Resort World Concession, and – according to him – doing all the work, when they had encountered each other by accident several decades previously. She'd finally been able to get away from full-time egg-laying duties after a hundred years, and had bribed and had otherwise favored two particularly stupid (if attractive) Bella=Arth. males to get this hideaway built and furnished, far from the rest of the Bella=Arth. Supervisory staff. Here they could meet and have sex, and here she could get what she needed, not only to seize real control of the Prime Nest and Bella=Arth. Community, but also get her some Soma and Stele for her amusement while the idiot Males went around thinking and acting like they were the hottest thing since fertilized pupae.

Once she had what she wanted, the Males were suddenly declared State Traitors and summarily executed and Kri'nni had her rest and relaxation intact with no one the wiser for it. At about that same time, Mar'ko had decided there was no way short of assassination he would ever supplant his Human superior inside the Historical Site offices, or indeed, within the Resort World hierarchy, since he was so poorly connected in the City (while his head was related to or intermarried with half the Outer Quinx.) So when Kri'nni approached him about becoming her general factotum and eyes and ears, while she was on duty down in the Nest's bowels, he seemed interested but didn't leap into the position. Soon enough however, the spy-service she'd carefully built among Class D and E workers who would never receive Nest Favors by ordinary Nest means, worked. That grapevine told her that Mar'ko was fond of a pipette or two weekly, and, better yet, that he was more or less addicted to palp-jobs and interspecies sex with Arth.s, enough of whom were around still to confirm the tale.

Kri'nni told Mar'ko what she knew and reoffered him the job and they somehow reached an agreement. His pay doubled. Once he left the Site offices, his supervisor, who had let him do all the work anyway, was revealed to be incompetent and was sacked. Mar'ko suddenly held two jobs, each at double pay, along with all the palp-jobs he wanted.

It was only after several years, when he began coming up with unique and intriguing ways for her to get away from the egg-laying chamber that she really began to appreciate him. His reason: she was fun. She was – though too old for Mar'ko, who liked his palps to be silky young—more than five centuries old.

"This isn't half bad," she said, inhaling again and finally relaxing. "So what's the word, early bird?"

"Danger to the Nest," he said, extra-sibilantly, sounding like the Soldiers.

"Don't you start," she wielded her claw toward him and he moved back fast. What would merely scar a chitinous thorax, would rip through a flesh chest.

"No, really!" Mar'ko insisted.

"You mean because you sent the false report to the soldiers?"

"That too," he admitted. "But check out this from Inter. Gal. News a few hours ago, Sol Rad."

She watched the Holo he was looking at stop, go blank, then go back on again. This time it showed a landscape she was familiar with, with two big nests in the background. A male Human Inter. Gal. News announcer was standing in front of a small structure and a big nest.

"Here on Algenib Delta II, an hour ago, Sol Rad., the reigning Nest Queen of the Diaspora Community, Am'i'dal'ia Per ('xx'), challenged the rulership of the entire Galactic Bella=Arthropod Community."

"What's is all this (tripe ((amusingly so)))?" Kri'nni asked, kind of tickled, while inhaling a bit more Soma.

"Claiming her genealogy was even more closely connected to the last true dynasty of Deneb XII's Prime Nest than the current reigning Queen, Kri'nni Des ('xx'), Am'i'dal'ia declared an open challenge to that Queen for ritual battle for complete Bella=Arth. rulership. A pheromonal document embedded into the body of a half dozen larvae is to be delivered to the Prime Nest."

"I bet that'll be attractive (cute ((yummy)))," Kri'nni observed. "And smell good too (like dead things ((long dead))) … Not!" she and Mar'ko said together, then laughed.

"Am'i'dal'ia said she was younger, healthier, and more beloved than her competitor," the Inter. Gal. announcer went on.

"Like that's so difficult!" Kri'nni responded and they howled again.

"Further, Am'i'dal'ia claimed that the Prime Nest Supervisory Staff had deluded the Bella=Arth. Community for centuries in their, quote, desperate search for a meaningful community life, unquote."

"Wouldn't doubt it for a moment," Kri'nni added, more amused with every word.

"The claimant said that the current Queen's past was quote, lurid, criminal, and degenerate. Before her coronation, Am'i'dal'ia claimed, she was a sexual pervert and drug queen-pin, unquote."

"Sounds accurate to me," Kri'nni admitted. "Where's this gal get her info?"

"Reaction from Bella=Arth. Community leaders on Deneb XII was immediate and extremely scandalized," the Inter. Gal. announcer continued.

"To everyone's astonishment," Kri'nni said. "Not!" She and Mar'ko broke up again.

He stopped the Holo. "Should I go on?"

"No, but save it, and give me a full report (culled for diverting stuff). This could be very, very useful in the future. Anything else come in of any interest?"

"Not much. Human Bride-Prices are suddenly in flux for no good reason on the Orion-Spur Commodities Market. The price of Salt is up again. Not to mention Beryllium 18, which we thought had peaked. That's going up again."

"Because why? Price gouging!"

"Maybe, but mostly because the City is running out. Several economists connected with the Quinx Council predicted that by opening the Sag. Center Worlds for population, which they needed to do to advance their Vir'istic agenda, Beryllium use would double. It's not quite done that in the past two centuries, but it's come awfully close and can only get worse. Five hundred and fifty-eight separate exploration teams are out hunting for more of the stuff in other parts of the Sag, Carina and Perseus arms. No go."

"The Prime Nest uses how much?"

"Not much, except for Fast travel and this ..." pointing to the Holo-Comm. mechanism. "Which is needed. We're not going to feel the pinch as bad say as the other Two Species. The Delph.s are using tons of the stuff to aquiform planets."

"Which must be what's driving up the cost of salt."

"A trio of Close-Sisters of Class B has just initiated travel to the planet that has the most natural salt." Mar'ko went on to explain quickly what and where and why Usk was a place to know.

Kri'nni sat up. An idea was forming somewhere in what was left of her brain after four hundred years of being pheromone-drugged, laying eggs, and being poked by bugs.

"Bring them to me when they return!" she said. "Those three sisters."

"What are you planning?" he asked. "Don't deny it. I can almost hear the wheels turning."

"What I'm planning, you pheromone-saturated pervert (and friend for life ((because of that))), is to accept that upstart Algenib bitch's ritual challenge!"

He looked serious now. "Kri'nni? My Queen? Sweetie? Don't! Even if you're really, really tired of this place. She's a fanatic. She's not normal. And she's not fooling around. She'll rip you apart."

"To the contrary. I think she'll prove to be very, very useful."

The splashing increased all around him, until he could barely see what was happening. The clicks and high pitched screeing also increased. But he'd expected that too. He continued to tread water, and when C(o'lla) W(ing) L(e^e) moved in closer, he leaned over to better hear the Delph. Ambassador.

"Any minute now, Lord Premier Azura-Kell. Ah! Now!"

The water before them, where the thrashing was thickest, suddenly changed in color from a much-churned-up-clear with a greenish tint from the big pool's painted sides and bottom, to a deep blue, almost violet.

"His water's broken!!" W(ing) L(e^e) was very excited. "And here's the newborn!"

Cas'sio leaned forward into the pool waters, clearing the goggles with his hands, until he could see in the midst of the darkest water a sudden spurt of pale gray shoot out half a meter. The infant! Three other Delph.s shot forward to get it; while the mother held back, remaining on his back, swimming in place. Unlike Human men, cetacean males, like their females before them, gave birth only after a full-term pregnancy, meaning there were always increased dangers – and sometimes unpleasant surprises, despite repeated fluoro/sonograms. But this young Delph. looked perfect as it was raised off the surface by its oldest pod-brother, the sleekly powerful Jef(ii) L(e^e), the ambassador's great grandson, so it could take its first breaths of air, before being gently placed on its side, in the water again, where Jef(ii) and his podmates, gently lapped wavelets against it, to inure it to its home element, while it was still able to breathe air. They formed a close fitting podlet around it, and Cas'sio treaded water backward to

W(ing) L(e^e).

Now that the water had stopped churning, it grew increasingly darker.

"The afterbirth's huge!" one of the pod-mates screed in a mixture of Delph. and Lex. Gal.

"A feast for fifty!" another pod-mate intoned the ritually exaggerated words of praise going back eons on New Venice. The first-time mother continued to float backwards to the opposite end of the pool, as though wanting nothing to do with his blood, the child, or especially his afterbirth. Cas'sio's old friend and political ally, had earlier explained how dismal this particular grandson had been to be betrothed to another Delphinid and then, for him even worse, impregnated for what he considered purely dynastic reasons.

Nic(ii) L(e^e) was "a modern Delph.," W(ing) L(e^e) explained unhappily, one of the Ambassadorial Class Delph.s who had moved out of the extensive Cousteau-Brett Water Park in the City early on in his Ed. & Dev. and taken up with the chicest of his group's fellow Hesperians, living on the upscale Huntington Trust Girder, among Humans, most of who had formed his entire social and amorous life until the past seven months.

"Come, Nic!" a relative called to the disaffected mother. "It's time to feed your young."

For an answer, Nic swerved to the nearby steps, ascended out of the pool, and quickly pulled a towel-wrap around his hips.

"*You* feed him, great uncle! My teats are too sore," He flashed a bit of chest in a beefcake mode. "And I'm beat, from all that ... childbirth business. Wake me up in about two weeks!" he added, sidling sexily out of the doors of the pool house.

"Irresponsible!" the great uncle called out. "Shameless."

But the younger Delph.s all laughed and clicked. Jef(ii) began the feeding, and so the infant would get to know them all, all his pod-mates joined in, with W(ing) stepping in briefly just for show. He offered the baby to Cas'sio, who let Jef(ii) bring him close enough to look at the little half-Delph., half-Human, certainly one of the prettiest of creatures in all the galaxy.

"He's adorable!" Cas'sio said, offering a nipple for the babe to lightly bite, before Jef(ii) moved him on to the complaining great-uncle for his ritual turn.

"You honor us greatly, Lord Premier!" the usual stolid Jef(ii) now enthused, having to turn slightly to say the words. From this angle, his body was even more remarkably lovely, the strength in his legs and back so apparent and so superhuman. Cas'sio wondered what a bout in bed with him would be like and as though he'd been tel'ping him, Jef(ii) dropped his eyes and slowly colored that bluish shade Cas'sio knew meant he was excited yet embarrassed. "If it were possible," Jef(ii) said, "we'd offer you the position of pod-Father."

"Much gratitude, Lord-Ser Jef(ii) L(e^e)" he answered formally, adding "My duties alas make taking the honored position untenable. But I believe it shall be your own. And I know that you will invite me often to personally check up the progress on this lovely and fortunate Neo."

"Gratitude, Lord," the Delph. agreed with his eyes lowered. Then, "the third week is often the one fraught with most infantine perils ... Perhaps then ...?

"Third week it is," Cas'sio agreed. Had they just made a date?

His old friend, as head of house, was now blessing the child then turning and floating over to the pool edge, and Cas'sio joined him at getting out.

They returned to their suites, showered quickly, changed clothing and shortly enough were meeting again, as planned, in a large indoor/outdoor suite overlooking a water park plaza below with its many jetting fountains and reflecting pools.

The talk was desultory for five minutes until the Ambassador said, "I don't want to keep you too long and have the other Species protest."

"It's always so restful here in the water park, I'm a fool not to just move in and live here year 'round, Sol Rad."

"Then the other Species would *definitely* protest. I'm always surprised by how much you love water, don't you!"

"Almost as much as you and your family do, C(o'lla). And from birth I've loved it. Another reason why I was happy to have been invited for this birthing." He paused to taste the milky drink. It resembled a kind of tapioca, although it was made of seaweed blended with sea-cucumber beads with a consistency between ice-cream and pudding. "What do you know, old friend, of my birth and earliest days?"

"Naturally, I've viewed excerpts from the complete PVN-Bio. But in effect I only know what everyone else does. That you were born on a distant planet in the far outer arm, beyond even the Perseus Arm. That you came to the City with your Ib'r mother very early in life, and that when he then wed Mart Kell, that you were raised in the Kell Liner Girder."

"Say it, I was spoiled in uttermost luxury? But what do you recall of the world where I was born? Or was that all too long ago?"

"I'm afraid so, yes…"

"Pelagia. Or Dryland. As opposed to not-dryland, it was called. Within a year after my family arrived here, another five hundred thousand Pelagians had to leave their home world. Most settled on the newer Sag. Arm Center Worlds under Hesperian sway. Especially Diomedes and Hermes. But many hundreds, including my sire, Zhon Azura, settled in New Venice, your home world."

"Truly? How extraordinary. He was not Delphinid in any way?"

"Not in any way. He'd grown to manhood on what were called floating islands on Pelagia. He loved the ocean. The sea, any lake, even a little pond would do."

"Truly, I can now understand why we are such good friends, Premier, if your sire was water-bitten as an old Delph.-mutant like myself."

"Truly. But I tell you all this for a reason, old friend. The support of your people has been a mainstay of my government for decades, and rewards are just around the corner."

"In return for further, unswerving support, I assume."

"It's actually a reward, but yes, of course, an inducement for further support, should it be required. How many all-water worlds exist in the galaxy for your Species to live on?"

"Nineteen all-water, a hundred and eighty-six predominantly water, and another two hundred or so mostly water but with major pollution. The hundred and eighty-six are naturally also inhabited by Humans."

"And so two hundred and five worlds altogether? And only nineteen for Delphinids alone?"

"Nature holds our race in check in this manner." W(ing) L(e^e) said philosophically.

"Then a twentieth all-water planet, even though it's not nearby, would be a colonization coup for the Ambassadorial Delph. community both here on Procyon and for its alliance with Hesperia, wouldn't it?"

W(ing) L(e^e)'s ordinary large eyes became if possible, even bigger.

"My world, the one I was born on," Cas'sio said. "By now it's entirely water."

"We know. Seventy-six percent *fresh* water! And thus impossible for ..."

"There was recently a celebration in my own house." Cas'sio interrupted.

"We sent our congratulations to the betrothal ... With regrets, given the arid site."

"They were received! The arid site, as you so tactfully put it, is a planet half the size of New Venice, with about point one ten hundredths of a percent of natural water."

"Grrr. It hurts my head to even think of that minuscule percentage of water."

"The greatest other physical feature of that otherwise dusty, mountainous, arid world," and here Cas'sio held out his wrist turned around so his wrist-connection could project a Holo in front of them of Usk and its rings, "is right there!" He pointed with the other at an area that dominated one hemisphere, like a gigantic white wound torn into the brown mountain's flesh surrounding it. "It is known as ... the Great Salt Ocean."

"Yes. of course. The southern salt pans of Usk produce the finest salt in the galaxy. Of a purity seldom otherwise encountered. We Delph.s purchase tons of it at a time to keep the Water Park here clean. In conjunction of course with the appropriate City Resort World office."

"What if that ocean could be refilled with water and the planet transformed into a paradise. Not one for all Delphinids, but definitely for your ambassadorial class. It would be too wet for Bella=Arth.s, and perfect for Humans. I've put a team of Resort World specialists to work calculating the real NaCl value of that salt ocean and the preliminary amount they've come up with so far is considerable – and more to the point, it's more than enough to completely salinate that distant planet Pelagia where I was born, now filled with fresh water and thus to make that world ... habitable for all Delph.s, modified and not."

"You would bestow another all-water planet to my Species?"

"It's hardly a Center World, you understand, old friend."

"On New Venice, the opposition party has been demanding

more all-water worlds for decades. In your single action, the main plank of the opposition to us here on Hesperia would be annihilated."

"I'd make certain that the City's Delphinid Community would receive full credit. As it will be handled primarily through the Resort World office, which is seldom open to much public scrutiny," Cas'sio now said. "It could be done swiftly and rather quietly, and with little political interference. But then, Pelagia would also have to retain some kind of Resort World status. At least for a generation or two. And thus not be totally Delph.-independent."

"That's a necessary complication," the Ambassador saw the point. "But not a fatal one."

"I thought not. So the next step would probably be a meeting on Procyon 12 with a half dozen scientists and perhaps two competing industrialists capable of ..."

"... of aquiforming Pelagia and of terraforming Usk! Yes ... Oh, Lord Premier, you've made this old heart beat more quickly for the first time in months. I hope you reward this relative greatly."

"I already have," Cas'sio said. "Although like most children he has no idea how greatly, and he treats it far too lightly."

"Your name, Lord Premier will live in Delphinid History along with that of Pha"arg and Merak Y(ii)! "

"For the moment all must be done very, very quietly."

"Understood."

The two continued to sit and watch the artificial light signal a very soft dusk. After a few moments of silence, W(ing) L(e^e) said, "this may now be the ideal time for you to meet someone. A young female Ambassadorial, my double niece, Itz-bel L(e^e)!

"Any relative of yours, old friend ..."

"She is a statistical analyzer of the highest aptitude, utilizing some specialized infra-dig quantum mechanical digitalizations for social prediction. Probably the best there is in her field, advanced far beyond her age."

"I would be happy to meet her."

Itz-bel seemed in no way extraordinary when she appeared, apart of course from the general rarity of Dephinid Ambassadorial females. What she had to say about her Avocation was again fairly expected. Cas'sio understood her at first. The source of the models her group used to predict trends was based on several so-called Universal Constants, she explained – the number of neutrinos that were detected passing through some ultra-hard material deep inside the planet Rama 21; the number of electrons that underwent exchange in the corona of fifteen randomly selected Center World M-2 suns; and the pulsation rate from Galactic Center Object 45-76890-R, which was thought to be a massive black hole. After that, he was lost in her complexities.

As was the Ambassador, who interrupted to ask her to get to her point.

"For decades," Itz-bel said, "we've been using a variety of Ib'r Republic social and political models to keep checks and balances upon those Universal Constants. These other paradigm constants range from the price of a restored residence on Power Avenue in Central Section Girder 14 of Hesperia to the population growth curve of curl-voles in the Cosmetic Laboratories in Girder 444 and other models far too arcane to describe. Recently three of the hundred models changed suddenly and significantly."

"Meaning?"

"Meaning either that as models they were chosen poorly and were not constant enough. Or – since they'd been in use so well for so long – that the change means something significant to the City and possibly also the Republic is about to alter."

"Well, now I'm intrigued," Cas'sio admitted. "Go on."

"The first model that altered is based on the predictability of the former Premier, Lord Mart Kell, ever returning to premiership. That had stood at a thirty-one percent possibility ever since we began the modeling twenty-three years ago, Sol Rad."

"That high?" Cas'sio was astonished.

"He remains a well-known figure with a high recognition value. He is a strongly public figure and via his amours and relationships he remains quite glamorous."

"So you used that as a constant?"

"It was chosen before I joined the team, Lord Premier. Some Ed. & Dev. jokester, no doubt entered it in as a lark. But over the decades enough researchers felt that his return was so impossible that indeed it should remain a constant … Well, last week, that model jumped suddenly to seventy-four percent possible."

"More than doubling," he understood.

"We did a complete check of all of the former Premier's activities and connections over the previous month. Anything at all that we could find in newly released PVNs or gossip columns or

Inter. Gal News. We even requested a name match on the Universo Comm. system over the previous two months to see if his name was mentioned more often by people speaking to one another in general conversations across the Central World user-area. Nothing stood out statistically. And so," she concluded, "either it now had to be knocked out of use as a model. Or it was because it was becoming ... " she hesitated stating it.

"... becoming more of a possibility." the Premier finished for her. "And the other two problematic models you found?"

"The price of NaCl2 per ton on the open galactic market, and notated daily, Sol Rad., at the Orion-Spur> Rigel 16> Futures Market," she said and here the Ambassador turned away his face. "This paradigm has also been at a constant rate from the beginning of the study. Approximately a ton of salt valued at point zero zero three of an ounce of Beryllium 18. It recently also jumped up to zero one point one per ounce. Tripling in value. And again, as far as we've been able to assess, not based on anything we could locate or pick up or infer from the Inter. Gal. News or any market reports."

Clearly having to do with the plan the Premier had just now explicated to her Species-mate, and so quite an accurate indicator of change.

"And the third model that changed?" Cas'sio asked.

"The Bride-Price of a healthy female Human on the Orion-Spur Commodities Market, which has held steadily for close to a century, never mind the life of our little study, suddenly was *halved*. We are aware that your house recently betrothed a female, and we'd earlier calculated that in, although she was never listed on the market, and never possessed a Bride-Price. Taking her off the market, so to speak, would have *raised* the Bride-Price by about a point or two, not more, as actually betrothing her was so out of reach for any but the highest levels of society."

"And instead the Bride-Price *dropped* by half," he said.

"Not on the market itself ... yet," Itz-bel said. "But in our quantum-predictability studies. Meaning, we can only suppose, that it is *predicted* to drop by half. Again for some as yet unknown reason. As The Princeps Kell's chances of re-obtaining the Premiership are expected to double, again in the future and for some equally unknown reason. As is the price of galactic salt per ton predicted to triple, again for some unknown reason." She looked a little pleased at how logical and direct she was being.

"How soon will these changes occur?" he asked.

"We work within six to eight months, Sol Rad. But it's probably in a far shorter time than that."

The three of them were quiet a while.

"Of course these are only three models," Itz-bel said. "Another ninety-seven models remained steady."

Cas'sio thought, then decided she could be trusted, "I happen to know exactly why the price of salt is going to rise. It has to do with a gift to your Species that I'm planning."

"A boon to all Delph.s," W(ing) L(e^e) confirmed, vaguely enough.

Itz-bel began trembling. Cas'sio had to reach out and steady her arm and remove the glass of liquid she held before she went and dropped it.

"Then our models are not faulty ...?" she asked in a small voice.

"We can only hope they are not *totally correct*," Cas'sio said. "Since I've done not one thing about and thus have not one single idea why Bride-Prices are going down on the Orion-Spur Markets when they should be lifting up slightly and, far worse, I've no hand nor any interest at all in the eventuality that Mart Kell become Premier again. Should that occur I believe very dark days will loom for this Republic, if indeed it even remains a Republic."

The young Delph. female had begun to weep, and he realized he'd never seen this happen before. The Ambassador was trying to comfort her, to explain it wasn't her fault. When finally she had settled down a bit, Cas'sio said to her:

"How would you feel about working for the Inner Quinx. It's a raise in status and funding. You see, Mer Itz-bel, I believe I'm going to need your excellently strange digitalized predictive services for the next few months, Sol Rad."

Naturally enough, and just as he'd planned, he was halted in the approach chamber of the Inner Quinx Council Soft-Lounge by a good looking Intelligent Cyber he recognized as John Something or Other, was it Laks? whom he recalled from Inter. Gal. News Flashes as a long-time liaison between the Human and Cyber communities on Hesperia and who, his wrist-connector now whispered, was a long-trusted Quinx diplomat.

"Apologies, Ser Sanqq'!" John said, "but I'm afraid that no Media of any kind is allowed within the Council."

"Now, isn't that a shame, John!" Holt Ib'r Sanqq' replied with a gracious smile. He always made it a point to use first names whenever possible when dealing with secondary people. And turning to the hundred or so miniature Inter. Gal. Comm. probes, t'bloid camera/phones and Inter. Gal. News-Everywhere-and-All-The-Time floaters that ordinarily accompanied him at a court-regulated distance of a meter and a half, forming a sort of mobile halo, Holt said, "you heard the chief, fellows! You're going to have to somehow do without me for a few!"

"The Media may wait in a specialized holding area," John pointed the flying robotic flock to what looked like a cubicle, already buzzing with hundreds of other Media probes, cameras, and Holo-Commentators. Holt noted with amusement that an immediate tussle begin between the new ones following him and those already ensconced, doubtless belonging to those stalking those Councilors who'd earlier entered. It resembled nothing more than the meeting of two flying insect societies as he'd once seen in an Ed. & Dev. PVN with its swirling intensity as they jockeyed for various perceived superiorities in position.

Blissfully unencumbered for the first time since he had left home, The Cadet thanked John aloud and then in a very low whisper that only a Cyber would be able to hear, added "Is there any way out of the lounge that'll give me some time to get away from them for a while, after? I know they'll catch up eventually ... But ..."

"I'll be happy to seek out an appropriate route for you, Ser. The Premier and several other Councilors often have a similar request, and the 'escape routes' still available are by now rather limited."

"Do what you can, please," Holt said. "You can't know how grateful I'll be for even a few moments escape. In fact if there's a charity I can donate in your name to show my gratitude ...?" knowing very well that Intelligent Cybers pretended to never need money. He then added, "Gerspellion's Girder near 1000 is my preference. But anywhere nearby, really ..."

"I don't believe that particular Girder address has ever been utilized in this manner," John assured him.

As one of the most constantly Media-witnessed Humans in the galaxy, Holt Ib'r Sanqq', i.e. The Cadet, very well knew in advance which areas were Media-Free Zones. He kept a virtual list of them available on his wrist-connector at all times and his ability to elude even the most geographically savvy Media was, by now, legendary. Those three and four day "Media-free excursions" he enjoyed were only one reason why they did stick so closely to him whenever they could. His prowess in Thwwing racing, his many public amours, and his impulsiveness i.e. his ability to become newsworthy in an instant, were the others.

Inside the Soft-lounge, it looked like the six inhabitants were having a tea party. Holt's Uncle Cas'sio, Premier of the Republic, had gathered several of his nephews and cousins about him in comfortable approximations of wing-chairs and they were all sitting about, chatting, and drinking some probably brand-new Tisane out of what seemed to be fine, and extremely ancient cups with saucers which Holt recognized from some old Ed. & Dev PVNs as resembling rare artifacts of Metro-Terran Culture called Spode China. Except that these particular ones appeared to be composed not of any earthen stuff like porcelain but instead a semi-transparent living silica derivative from one of the newer Sag. Arm planets brought into the Republic lately that Holt heard had taken people's fancy of late. Little cakes and other baked-looking foodstuffs filled other platters which the five men snacked off while talking.

"Here's The Cadet now! Youngest and most famous of our line!" Holt's favorite older brother, Y'vo, announced. He'd fallen for the trend of larger than ordinary arms and especially biceps that was turning his generation – three to four-hundred-year-olders – into superb specimens, rather late in life, the result of some philosophical-manifesting of Vir'ism, having to do with the new Sag. Arm planet colonization scheme, that had gripped the Republic for the past few decades, and that had gratefully skipped Holt's own younger clade, which remained more trim and blithe and even at times androgynous.

Holt joined the group, bussing each dear familiar face in turn as he went around the little area where they all sat, rather bunched together given the large, otherwise empty Soft-lounge with its large but delicate hanging chandelier replica of the galaxy itself, each colonized star tinily, brightly alight. He arrived last at his Uncle Cas'sio's larger and more cushiony seat, where Holt bowed his head in double-greeting, honoring him as Eldest of his Clan Present and as Leader of the Republic. Before, of course, bussing the old cheek too.

"Sit by me, Holt," Cas'sio said. He looked drawn and yet pudgy, out of shape, and in definite need of some serious cosmetic surgery, the younger man thought. Then he wondered if he did that on purpose to look all the more the Perpetually Worried and Time-Short Premier? It would be just like him, always plotting and scheming in his quiet way. He'd been and remained Premier all of Holt's life. "We missed you at the great Betrothal Ceremony on Usk!" Cas'sio tried looking sternly at the lad. "You were invited, you know."

"The Palaka Family received my bridal gift. And I believe the provincial youth also received a fairly astonishing gift," Holt said. "Along, of course, with my sincere regrets."

"The 'provincial youth', as you sneeringly refer to him, caused a real sensation," Holt's half- brother, North Ib'r-Kell, said. He too wore the tight-fitting tunic of the newly muscular. "First, because of his extreme Ib'r blonde good looks."

"He is after all, the only child of 'Fire' and 'Ice'. So that was no surprise to any of us!" added Olaf Vantermere, Holt's brother, Uriel's current husband.

"You'll have competition from that child!" Y'vo promised, through lips smeared with crumbs of some bright red confection he'd just swallowed.

"And secondly," North added, "because the provincial boy mounted one of the unrideables in Mel'yin Chu-Kell's stable. Not only did he Close-bond with the beast which no one else had been able to do so far, but he flew it there and he set two unofficial top times with it. It was his first time even seeing a Thwwing close up!"

"That's double competition for you, Holt," Cas'sio pointed out, in case he had missed its significance.

"Having his Ed. & Dev. on such an out of the way site," Holt said, "it's a wonder, of course, and the lad must be considered a prodigy. Although growing up there, the poor lad must have to work harder, if only to equal what comes naturally to the rest of his clan."

"That's a double-edged statement if I ever heard one." Y'vo laughed. "Compliment or criticism, I can't figure it out. Can you, Olaf?

"Thus do we hear Holt's famous generosity of spirit. The ambiguity of which makes our baby relative here so very adored by all the T'bloid Inter. Gal.s!" Olaf was laughing.

"But surely none of that is what brings you suddenly into our midst," shrewd Cas'sio said. "You've only been present twice in a hundred of such family meetings."

Holt looked around himself and took one of the cups of tea and sipped at it demurely, admiring the flavor which he couldn't for the life of him recognize but was smoky and sensual. He was among family, he knew. Among the people who loved him most in Hesperia. And yet also among his severest critics. He knew that he must move carefully, and yet he also realized he was ill-suited by temperament and experience to act with deft diplomacy. Surely one if not all of them would see any smoothness as a pose. The six handsome heads and five handsome bodies, as fashionably clad as any Cityzen of their ages, looked to him for explanation.

"Indeed not, beloved Premier," Holt said. "I come with a piece of news!" While they began to hum at that, "and, equally importantly, I come upon a mission."

"A mission? That's a new one!" Gareth Rinne-Diad, a family member by his long and famously loving marriage to Y'vo, now remarked for all of the others.

"I admit that my conspicuous public position often means ... " Holt began slowly.

"The most *conspicuous* in this City on a Star and possibly in the entire known galaxy!" North glossed.

"Well, it brings many different people into my circle," Holt said. "And among them have been several you might be surprised to think of as being in the same company as myself."

"That company being those who frequent back-girder Stelezine-bars and off-City betting parlors," Uriel amusedly explained for the others.

"Laugh if you will,' Holt said, "and half the time you would be correct," he admitted, patting his brother's oversized arm. "But recently Jan'sen Dem-Arest and several members of the Domenica Heights Scientific Guild have been among the number companioning me."

He stopped, having gotten their attention.

"Dem-Arest and the others outlined for me the serious energy crisis they believe is due to affect us here in the City ..."

"Not for decades," Gareth said.

"More like centuries," North insisted.

"... and which they believe is much closer in time than that," Holt corrected, "and the upshot of these discussions, is that together we've all formed a legal Energy Consortium in hopes of seeking solution to that crisis."

"Bravo!" the Premier alone politely applauded. The others looked at their nephew in some disbelief, tea cups held aloft, at weird angles, saucers slipping on laps, confections crumbling within fingers. "This clean new slate of yours means we should not expect to hear you requiring bail-bond any time soon," the Premier added.

It was a neat joke on him.

"I told them all that it would be foolish of me to approach you with this," Holt admitted, "but as they are serious people and they insisted, so I, foolishly, agreed," he added, uncharacteristically modest.

"Wait a minute! What role does this council have in your so-called Energy Consortium?" asked Gareth, ever-inquisitive.

"Well, to begin with," Holt said, sounding as offhand as before, although this was the exact set-up he'd been waiting for. "We'll need official permission to travel far outside the Galactic Republic's boundaries in our search."

"Your search for ...?" Y'vo asked, repressing his hilarity with some kind of jujube in his cheek.

"Our search for another, or indeed several, other stars like this one we all live upon, overflowingly rich in Beryllium 18."

"There *are* no others!" Olaf simply said. "That, dear child, is the nature of the crisis. No others like it exist among the millions upon millions of stars so far charted. And none so far have been spotted as existing in any of the nearby galaxies, such as Andromeda and M-16."

"'So far,' being exactly the point," Holt said. "Our little Consortium believes otherwise."

"Basing this upon ...?" Olaf, always needing to know why.

"Based, dear Ole'-in-law upon something told to me and called the Rule of Conservation of Matter. Now I may be wildly off on this subject although I have studied it up a bit. But I believe it was a very early Metro-Terran astronomer-physicist named Hawkering or some such, who provided the beginnings of an equation stating that as our universe is holographic in actuality, thus for every singularity that exists, an equal and mirror-like duplicate singularity must *also* exist. The two objects from what this later scientist Hawkman or whatever and the Delph. astronomer physicist An'tin (Ji'i) who followed up his work and then proved it, referred to as a 'Status-Field With No Set Limits.'"

His elder brothers and mates had progressed from surprise to amazement, which Holt had counted on.

"Therefore there has to be at least *one other* F-16 star that went nova in an identical manner and with identical speeds to our dear home-star, Hesperia. Leading to the formation of the mineral Beryllium 18 and thus the energy we all hold so dear, since it holds our vast Republic together, both temporally and spatially."

Concluded, Holt popped what looked like a tiny éclair into his mouth. He enjoyed the rich, sweet bergamot and pistil-pepper flavor that exploded within a goat cream base.

"Therefore," he added, "our Consortium wishes to go where no one has gone and to chart millions more stars until we find our F-16 match."

"You have my permission to leave," Cas'sio said simply. He reached out a hand, and crossed wrists with his nephew, making that much official.

"We'd also like funding," Holt said.

"Ah, I knew it!" Olaf again. "Those Dem-Arests never let a d'lar out of their girder if was in any way possible."

"Jespeth Branson Todd and Darency Llega-Smith are also in the Consortium and have promised millions of d'lars. As well as Dem-Arest. I turn forty years old next week and thirty-three percent of my natal trust fund from the Great Father devolves to me at that time. That will go into the Consortium too."

"You're serious about this!" Y'vo sounded equally amused and appalled.

"Large as that amount will probably be, is it equal to your Thwwing race winnings?" North asked.

"No, and some of that will go into the Consortium too ... We've got fifty other forward-thinking, good-minded Cityzens and scientists involved, and they all promise the Consortium half their incomes. But it's still not enough. We have enough for a score of research vessels. We would like a hundred fully-equipped ones."

Uriel: "A hundred! Why not a thousand?"

Olaf: "Where exactly are you going to?"

Gareth (half giggling): "And whose treasure map are you utilizing?"

North: "Who'll comfort your five current boyfriends while you're away?"

"Who'll comfort the Inter. Gal. News and T'bloids when you're gone for weeks, Sol Rad.?" Y'vo asked, and then chuckled. "They'll have to close down. I hope I don't have any stock in that field. It'll tumble like mad. Olaf? Do I?"

"Not many."

"Surely, brother-in-law," Holt turned to Olaf, after all, the administrator among them, "there is some Quinx Council discretionary fund that could be tapped to aid the Consortium."

"There is and I could get you some funds, although there's bound to be an investigation and all kinds of noise from Fiscally-Concerned Cityzen groups about it. How much more do you believe you'll require?"

Holt named an amount.

"The Kell Soma farms don't bring that amount in annually, Sol Rad.!' North exclaimed. As a top Kell administrator, he would know.

Olaf named the amount he believed he might be able to "free" for the Consortium's use. It was miniscule in comparison.

"Where are you planning to go?" Cas'sio now asked. "Certainly not into the Sag. Arm Center?" i.e. where much was hidden by the condensations of collapsing and colliding older star systems, intertwisted by larger and smaller black holes. Many had theorized that exactly that inside dangerously maddening place would be where older Beryllium 18 stars would most likely be found, but few had even thought to enter that unexplored, hellish maelstrom.

"No, not there," Holt said. "I'm not allowed to say... Well, beggars can't be choosers, and I'll sign up for that Discretionary Fund, Olaf. Or would you rather have Dem-Arest do that, as a better risk?"

"I'd choose him only as a less conspicuous connection to us,"

Olaf said. "Yes, he'll do."

"You're really putting a third of your trust fund into it?" a concerned Uriel asked.

"I'd put it all, if I could. I think this is that important." Holt said. He stood, as though leave-taking. "And if any of you privately wish to contribute," he added, stroking shoulders and faces as he began to leave the tea party, "comm. me. It'll remain completely confidential."

"Holt! Wait!" The Premier stopped him.

Maybe he would make a generous offer to help?

"Uncle?"

"Your news? You said when you came in that you had news."

"Oh, yes. Our father, The Great Father, is coming to Hesperia later today. It seems that he didn't want anyone to know."

"Then why tell us?"

"For the same reason that you, dearest Uncle, haven't told the others in this room nor the City itself, about the disappearance of our newest Betrothed member of the family."

"The lad on Usk?" Y'vo asked the Premier. "What was his name, Ay'r? Wasn't it?

"Yes, Ay'r Eise'nstein-Kell. He's declared missing as of this morning, Sol Rad.," Cas'sio admitted. "The entire palace resort on Usk is out looking for him." He turned to Holt. "Your sources are impeccable. So what news have you about The Great Father, our other missing Ay'r?"

"Similar news, I'm sorry to say. His Fast vanished into a time-hole ten seconds into his flight to here." Holt added, trying not to let the catch in his voice be evident. "But you also know that fact, Uncle. I understand that a full in-depth chrono-spatial-search is already begun."

"Indeed it has. And we'll send our private Cybers to search there too!" the Premier said calmly, while the others seemed too shocked to react.

Finally, Y'vo said, "but ... why was Father coming here? He never comes here!"

"And why did no one but you know?" Uriel fretted.

"All will be explained," Cas'sio said, serenely, "in time."

Holt had spotted the Cyber liaison behind North's head, at an unremarkable door, near a back kitchen-bar of the Soft-lounge.

"Esteemed Uncle and my dear Sibs I must bid you adieu!,"

Holt said, and headed toward John Laks as the elder five men now stood and exclaimed at each other over Holt's double news.

"Well, my work is done here, Holt thought. I was born to make trouble and I never cease to do so wherever I go.

To the Cyber he whispered, "this kindness will not be forgotten."

"I've gotten you a drop to Gerspellion's Girder near number 989. It's not the number you mentioned. But neither is it as dicey a place to make a sudden appearance in as there. "

"Close enough," Holt said as he climbed into the utility door. Before him he saw a chute of some sort.

"Keep your arms and hands close to your body. The first minute or so is extremely rapid."

One of the family, it looked like Olaf, was headed toward them, striding with speed and purpose, a hand outraised as though to halt him, as Holt turned and John closed him into darkness.

In seconds, Holt was swooping downward, dropping into the depths of the City, faster than he'd ever moved on his body's own momentum.

Wowee, Holt thought. I could get used to travelling like this.

Chapter Three

Double-day dawn, with the Rings at aphelion and so horizontal they could only be seen from the east, and with the ring's shepherding moonlets barely visible:

Ay'r Eise'nstein-Kell stopped the air-board and took a water tablet. Only a few remained. The jerky too was depleted. He'd been boarding for two full days and now he'd have to leave the Salt Ocean desert and hazard a way inland if he were to survive.

Last night, just before Aquila the Eagle, the second, orange, sunset, he assessed his provisions, and counted the Hesperian's winnings left inside the cape, some sixty-two thousand d'lars. Except for the fact that fifty thousand of that was in two large bills, and so effectively useless anywhere he might go on Usk, since only at the Golden Palace and its Fast Port would such large bills go unnoticed, uncommented upon, and not raise suspicion. That left twelve thousand usable. It was enough, so long as he was careful about where he went and when he arrived, and if he conducted himself prudently.

He'd directed the air-board east and south because he recalled there were pamp colonies all along the Great Salt Ocean's east coast, and because the second largest urban conglomeration on the planet, South Salt Pan City, lay in that direction, not impossibly far, maybe four or five days journey by air-board. SSP City had developed naturally enough because of the industry it catered to. He remembered from his Ed. & Dev. Uskian Geography that thousands of pamp salt miners and mostly Human supervisors lived there, along with several hundred off-world based commercial workers in related fields, including Bella=Arth.s and even a few Ambassadorial Delph.s. Because of the strictly mercantile nature of the place, only one public Fast-dock existed there. The rest of the enormous old star port was given over to

Slp.G liners refitted for interstellar salt hauling. So it shouldn't be too filled with Kell-House searchers, and might be a good place to hide, or at least for him to not be too conspicuous.

He'd never been to SSP City, but he guessed he'd find a giant produce and import/export mart, equal to, if not larger than the one near the Golden Palace, and like that one, it would mostly be run by pamps, and if he knew anything, Ay'r knew how to make himself scarce in a mart when needed, as well as how to dicker with pamps, and yet also how to be highly effective.

He'd turned the Hesperian betrayer's cloak reversed to its iridium side to combat the increasing daytime temperature as dim-days gave way to the two suns being up at the same time and as he approached the hotter equatorial region. If held still, the silver-like cape would also effectively blend in with the mostly white shades of the salt ocean. The few high fly-bys that had approached overhead had been easily fooled into not seeing him at all. As soon as he heard the distinctive low chutter of one approaching, he'd stop the air-board, hunker down on the sands, and spread the cloak, iridium side up, on the sands, covering himself with it completely. Not one fly-by had even hesitated in its course. In minutes, he was back on the board and traveling again.

Still, his body was aching from two days of enforced air-board travel, little sleep and with provisions low he was increasingly hungry and thirsty. He'd soon be forced to make a daytime foray into a pamp village, which he wanted to put off as long as possible. He wondered how often these coastal pamps saw any Human, never mind one dressed as richly as he was. Word would eventually get out that he'd passed through. That wouldn't do him any good.

He could already make out dried-dung fire-smoke rising all along the coastline, tiny puffs of off-white against the dark blue blur of the morning as the first sun, The Little Hunter's cobalt orb, began its sunrise through the lowest edges of the Ring.

Surely this was the worst time of day to approach, maybe even worse than nighttime. If he could only hold out ... say, to midafternoon. Coastal pamps were known to indulge in after-midday meal siestas. Perhaps then he could go ashore and steal water and food?

He air-boarded on, and no sooner were the village smoke fires out of sight behind him than he'd wondered when the next ones would show up, or if now he would have to air-board closer in toward shore to see more villages. It wasn't very far back, returning. He estimated he could make it to shore in less than an hour.

Dithering, he saw The Hunter rise fully beyond the rings, its blinding core no longer blue, small or even visible, but huge and white-hot. Another several hours before the orange Eagle joined it, doubling the intensity of heat and glare, prey pursuing the pursuer, for the next two weeks until they switched places again on Double Bright-Day.

He'd just called himself a great coward and fool for not even spying out the pamp village, when he noticed something odd in the other direction, deeper into the white desert sands. If it hadn't been for the angle of the sunrise, he probably wouldn't have even seen it, low to the dry ocean surface as it lay, a seeming mass of sticks, but for some reason as they took the first rays of the cobalt blue sun and absorbed them, suddenly very noticeable – not of metal but some kind of natural material, perhaps a kind of wood?

Ay'r redirected the air-board toward the strange mass of sticks.

From a dozen meters away, the sticks resolved into masts blown down in disarray, the canvas-like sails furled and twisted as though smashed by a huge hand. They lay athwart a medium-sized, two-person sand-ketch that lay at an angle, as though stopped suddenly by a very large hand.

From closer up, the boat's sides were sand pitted and badly tarnished, but nevertheless intact as he circled, and see, all the mag-lev runners were also intact. From the side, angled to the ground, he could make out something darker than the fallen sails or masts, and mixed with them along the top of the deck. But he'd have to climb onboard to better see what it was.

He climbed up and righted the masts; they seemed to have break-away hinges and could be replaced with little trouble into the tongue-and-groove slots gouged for them on the deck. The sails were also still usable, although greatly salt-encrusted. Once those were placed back up, it was clear what the dark mass was, a dead pamp sailor, twisted within some loose canvas. But wait! Perhaps it wasn't dead. Ay'r got closer and although a strong, foul odor rose from the pamp, the pamp was also clearly breathing.

Rolled over, the pamp was sun-blistered and unconscious,

possibly knocked out by falling masts during a sand-cyclone, or fallen asleep and self-wrapped against the strong suns. Ay'r whistled lightly into the pamp's hearing organ, a sound supposedly so harsh the creatures would bolt upright from a dead sleep, but the pamp didn't move.

Below decks, Ay'r located a half-open hold covered over with some plant-like material, with rough sleeping quarters gouged out on either side of an open space intended for sitting. More debris and canvas-like material had fallen there. But behind what looked to be a rather thin and flat body-pillow, was a handle, and once he opened it showed the hollow hull filled almost to the lip with fresh smelling water. He could easily make out bunches of mountain thyme floating on the surface to continually sweeten the water.

He quickly filled bottles for himself, then searched for food. Behind the pamp's sleep-sack another, shallower, hold still stocked, dried meat jerky, cured strips of some kind of vegetables pamps liked, even a sweet tasting object that might be a paste of dried perli berries. Ay'r stuffed himself with some of each. Then it was time to go on deck again and see about the pamp.

Exactly as Ay'r had left it. But why the bad aroma? Carefully, Ay'r unrolled the canvas from off the limp body and located the source of the stench. Along the lower left leg, the material was ripped away, and a long gash had been torn which had festered badly, infecting the pamp, and blowing up the entire leg to near double normal size as far down as the six-toed foot. This wound must have happened during the cyclone that had hit the sand yacht, and from the looks of thin shreds of some silkier material against the leg, the pamp must have wrapped it up then steered out of the storm and in toward shore. But the wound worsened, and at last, had sickened the pamp's entire body. Sure enough, wherever Ay'r touched limb or torso or head, it was all very hot to the touch.

He remembered his Medical Ed.& Dev. enough to recall that pamps had enough similar genetic material to Humans that for most basic ailments they were to be treated the same. A wound like this must be opened, drained, cleared out, packed with something to kill the infection, maybe even pure salt, then resealed, and the patient must be kept warm through bouts of chills and fever. A first aid kit below deck might contain medicine. First, the pamp needed hydration.

Wrapping his lower face against the stench, Ay'r sat down and pulled the pamp's hot head onto his lap. He began dripping water from his bottle into the smaller creature's sun-blistered pale lips. The mouth opened of its own accord for more water, and the dripping went on, it seemed interminably, until finally there was the sound of a gurgle, at which point Ay'r stopped. He then dripped more onto the pamp's forehead, through the streaks of salt-grime, to cool it off a bit.

The eyes opened briefly. Large soft brown eyes looked at him, didn't appear to recognize him, but stared.

"Can you hear me?" Ay'r asked. "No, don't try to talk yet. Just close your eyes if you can hear me."

The eyes closed.

"You're very sick. Open your eyes if there's a standard medical kit on board. Do you understand? A Salt Ocean med kit?

The eyes opened again.

"Good. There's a chance I can save you. But please, drink a little more water. One sun is already up and the other will be up soon. I want to move you down to the bed. I see that area is insulated by all the water tanks in the hull. But first I need you to be strong. I have to cut your leg open and drain the wound, and treat it. It will be *very* painful. If I *don't* do this, you will die? Close your eyes if you understand what I'm saying."

For a long time they stayed open. Then they closed and opened again.

"Good. Now drink more water. A lot. More than you can stand, do you understand?" He knew that would induce a light hypnotic effect on the pamp.

The eyes closed and opened again. Then the pamp began to sip at the water in Ay'r's cupped hands. When the bottom of its face was streaked wet and water was coming out of its lips again, Ay'r stopped. He lay the pamp's head down on bunched up cloths as a pillow. He moved one of the masts so it blocked the pamp's face from the sunlight.

The med kit was hidden well, but at last he found it, and with it a cooking pot, both of which he brought up on deck. He filled the pot with pure salt and water in a thick mixture. He dipped his kris into the mix again and again. He gave the barely conscious pamp, a twisted bit of plant-leather to hold between its teeth, salt-watered the infected leg, and plunged his kris in. Spurts of yellow pus spurted out and the pamp moaned once loudly then completely lost consciousness.

Ay'r proceeded to kris up a tear through half the leg, to squeeze out all pus, and wash out the long gash again and again with the salted water solution, until the wound was red and raw. Then he opened the wound-cleaner-packet from the med-kit and squirted out the dozen or so tiny green larvae that would soon become maggots and eat all the decaying material in the wound. He'd had begun soaking cloths in the salted water; he wrapped those around the wound for its entire length, trapping the maggots. He opened the pamp's mouth enough to slip in the contents of another packet from the med-kit. Lesuth Delta Prokaryote that entered the bloodstream directly through the mouth would fight off the infection internally and reconnect the skin once it was cleaned out.

With the pamp still knocked out, he opened two other med packets he recognized. Living mats of New Venice algae, he immediately spread over the pamp's face to anneal the blisters, and a packet of shed Uskian wart-snake skin, which he dropped at strategic spots along the pamp's more exposed areas, its six-toed hands and feet, its ankles, arms and neck. The second the skin hit the pamp's own skin, it settled in and began to grow, stretching in all directions. In minutes it would connect at all points and form a complete, protective coating. This meant he had to get the pamp down to bed quickly.

Once the shed skin settled in, he fed the pamp salt water until it awoke enough for its eyes to open.

"It's done. You were very brave. You'll be restored to health now. You have to sleep. I'll sail us to South Salt Pan City. Close your eyes if you have kin or mates there who will recognize your boat's markings and help you."

The eyes closed and opened again.

A webbed hand touched Ay'r's thigh. The pamp was trying to speak.

"Heavenly spirit?" it asked.

He laughed. "No! I'm just a traveler like you are. Just a little luckier than you have been. At least so far."

Once the pamp was sleeping, Ay'r ate and drank again and went back on deck. The second orange sun, Aquila the Eagle, was now pre-coloring the eastern horizon deep red, just about to rise. The desert winds would double when it did. And the heat. It was time to set sail. His Uskian Geography Ed. & Dev. had included several Cyber-'Tute-led sailing sessions, albeit with bigger and more sophisticated Salt Ocean-going craft then this little ketch, but once he had settled himself comfortably and wrapped his own limbs in protective wart-snake skin against suns-burn, Ay'r reached for the tiller and the gathered up strings of sail-slips. The masts turned properly, and the canvas-like material bellied out nicely, shaking off the encrusted salt, and soon the sails were spanking hard, and the ketch righted itself awkwardly, kept to its runners shakily at first and then well, and in minutes it was sliding forward, picking up speed incrementally, exactly the way it should.

After an hour, Sol Rad., he found himself completely invigorated. He'd stripped off the cloak and his tunic, and he'd found that the skin-webbing was the perfect protection from the combined lights of the Hunter, almost at dead meridian above now, and the Eagle, brightly orange and fully risen. The combined effect of the two suns' heat on the swirling desert sands was amazing, the winds blew strongly now, and whenever those guiding the main mast faltered even the slightest, the slightly angled-out mizzen mast sail would pick up another, nearby strong wind current, and he would tack over and into that wind lane for an almost unbroken, fast ride. He knew that the ocean was fairly clear of rock shelf reefs or other dangerous anomalies in this region, and he sailed on most of the day, grabbing drinks and bites of food as he went.

Only when blistering Aquila had reached meridian, did he stop. Now that both suns were high in the sky and burning strongly, the heat was too much for even the webbing to still protect him. He'd already begun to feel warmth prickle his shoulders. He dropped anchor, folded the sails, bunched the masts and tied them together so no vagrant wind could grab them, then stepped down into the hold. He covered it over behind himself with its natural material tarp, rethought that, reopened it and wetted it down thoroughly and only then re-closed it. He lay in the cramped mate's bed, cooled in the now softly blurred, vegetal light, watching the pamp fitfully sleep. He tried staying awake, just in case anyone came near, despite the fact that he'd seen no other ocean or air-craft since he'd awakened this day. But the lack of sleep from previous nights and the exhaustion from his medical and sailing labor soon set in. In minutes, he too was asleep.

The Hunter had already set when he awakened and looked outside. The blue sun tore a train of purple clouds behind it, fluffy and thick, behind which the faster moving orange sun was also headed. It too would set soon. Sticking up a wet finger, he saw he'd have a strong good wind heading south if he kept to the right wind lanes.

First, the pamp. A great deal less hot. He bathed the simian, somewhat hairy, face (how long had the pamp been out here?) with more fresh cool water, and dripped more water down its throat, but it remained lightly dozing. All of the torso, head, and arms had cooled off. The wounded leg was still warm to the touch. When he cautiously unwrapped the bandage he could see the worms busily eating away at the dead material. Later on he'd have to feed the pamp some of its dried vegetable stuff in a broth. Finding the pot, he added them together, stirred a bit with his cleaned kris, and laid them in the sunniest part of the quickly cooling boat deck. He chewed some of each of the dried foods, wrapped Deon Syzygy's cape around himself, untied and straightened out the masts, and again set sail.

If anything, the wind flow was even cleaner now than earlier, because there was less side-buffeting. When the horizon clouds cleared and the Eagle also dipped below the western outskirts, he could make out ridges along the salted sands. He was headed due south now, but the West would be his eventual destination. He recalled from his Uskian History that during the first two Matriarchies, several resorts had been constructed in those foothills and valleys on the far western side of the Great Salt Ocean. He would have to find one of them and somehow make one his home while he figured out what to do with himself.

Gliding along, he had more than enough time to ponder what had happened to him in the stupendous past eighty or so hours, Sol Rad., of his life. He'd rapidly graduated from being a careless child with a life of great ennui to being the center of eighteen hundred dynastic eyes to being an admired if first time Thwwing pilot to being the lover of a Hesperian Marquis, a superrich beauty, to becoming a political runaway, fleeing for what he had to believe was his life, or at the least, and given the conversation he'd overhead, certainly for his freedom.

He didn't understand why any of this had happened. Clearly it had something to do with who he happened to be in the various Kell dynastic lines. But equally it had to do with what the Dux'ii Cas'sio Azura-Kell – who he liked and who he thought liked him back – and the Princeps Mart Kell – who he was afraid of, who had drugged and raped him – were planning to do, using him as an once unwitting and now only somewhat witting and extremely unwilling instrument.

Once, a month or so ago, he'd asked his Human 'Tute Narfacan'ni to explain some bizarreness in the Ib'r Republic's early history, concerning Mart Kell and the younger members of his House, including the current Premier. "The roots of the perli bush are easier to entangle," the 'Tute replied, not unkindly, then added, "but understand this well, plague of my life, that when the Kell Princeps sneezes, twenty Center Worlds catch an ague."

What about when the Dux'ii Kell sneezed?

He also had to wonder why Premier Azura-Kell had made such a point of telling Ay'r that he'd loved Ay'r's mother and admired his father. He still seemed upset by their deaths. As though it was not his doing – he had been Premier then, no? – but instead someone else's work. Had it been the Princeps' doing? And if so, had he come back to finish off the job with some nefarious plan for their only child? And if that were so, couldn't the Dux'ii – now the most powerful single being in the galaxy – stop him, and protect Ay'r?

Ay'r had recognized during his first panic that even if the Premier could protect him, Ay'r's purest safety lay in putting the greatest possible distance between himself and the palace. At least for several weeks, perhaps months, Sol Rad.

He didn't know how precisely he would do that, only that he fortunately had the means and most likely the knowledge to do so. And, if he were very careful, the wits too – so it could be done. What he needed to remain safe, he knew, was to find allies. Who those allies could possibly be, he had no idea. So, for the time being, he was on his own.

Long after the second sun had set and the stars had flooded out in all their billions of spangled glory, unbothered by even the hint of any interfering ring tonight, Ay'r stopped the ketch briefly for dinner and to feed the pamp. He tasted the soup he had steeped. It was fragrant enough, the dried stuff totally dissolved in it.

The pamp was already awake when Ay'r dropped down into the hold. It sat up and let its head be held while Ay'r poured the liquid slowly into its mouth. Pausing to wipe its mouth, the funny little face stopped, stared at him and asked, "why?"

"Because it will make you strong. The next batch I'll make with some dried meat."

"But ... why?" it repeated.

Was it asking why it had been wounded, almost died? Ay'r couldn't tell. He'd never spoken with the palace pamps long enough to ascertain if they had enough intelligence to ask questions about why life was as it was – at times wonderful and often, like now, terrible – so he had no guide by which to determine what a pamp could and could not understand.

"This way, you'll be healthy again in a few days," Ay'r said, by way of assurance. "Were you sailing alone?"

The pamp shook its head in the up and down gesture meaning no, it hadn't been.

"You lost your companion?"

The clicking sound meant yes. "Sand-serpent," it said. Then, as though it couldn't for a second stand to be awake, it closed its eyes and was instantly asleep again.

He didn't know what the words meant. Was it telling him its name? Or was there such a creature as a sand-serpent somewhere in this vast Salt Ocean and was its bite responsible for this wound, and also his missing companion?

Ay'r set sail once again and only stopped when the winds dropped too low to help the mag-lev runners push the ketch. He dropped anchor and tied the masts, and once more ate and fell asleep in the interior hold, by now sufficiently warmed by the water in the hull which kept its steady temperature so it was cool in the day and warm against the chilled desert night.

He awakened to voices - from the raspy high tenor of them, pamp voices. He reached his hand out, and the wounded pamp was still there, but also awake.

"Sand-serpent?" Ay'r whispered. "Do you know them?"

"Not kin," it whispered back.

Meaning they might think the ketch was abandoned and try to claim salvage rights.

Ay'r pulled out his kris and kept his sand whip near to hand, then threw back the vegetal mat, and jumped out and up onto the deck.

Three pamps promptly skittered overboard and onto the salt sands. One held its ground a bit more but nevertheless backed out to the very tip of the contoured prow.

"May I help you?" Ay'r asked this one, evidently the leader, making sure the creature knew that he was twice the size of any pamp.

He also made sure the metallic glitter of his kris was visible by flashing it about in the starlight, then in case they thought to gang upon him, he pulled out the whip and snapped it against a mast.

"Greetings! Greetings, Ser!" the pamp who'd remained on the deck said, bowing and gesturing. "We were just passing by ..." It gesticulated to a much larger sand-sloop, a five master, some ten meters distant. Those pamps who'd scattered off the ketch were now clambering back on board the other craft. "And we thought to pay our respects."

And I'm an antipy's grandparent, Ay'r thought.

"Then be welcome. Myself and my companion," he nodded below, "have traveled long and hard. We'd hoped to soon arrive at South Salt Pan City."

"Already, Ser, you are at the suburbs of that great metropolis. Only a few short kilometers of ocean, barely a few hours journey, and you shall arrive."

As the pamp gestured, Ay'r could now make out in the direction indicated a mist of illumination on the southern horizon. That would be the city's lights. But maybe a suburb would better serve both him and the wounded pamp.

"Indeed!" he said, grandiloquently, copying the language from off his more jejune, historical PVNs. "Then perhaps such a wealthy and generous gentle-pamp as yourself may oblige these two weary travelers by a simple act of service and generosity."

Astonished at hearing itself called a gentle-pamp but nevertheless flattered, the little pamp gestured widely, "whatever lies in this poor creature's ability."

The others had returned to the larger sloop's deck. Ay'r rolled up his whip and shot closed his kris. "Excellent! Come sit a moment, perhaps some fresh mountain thyme flavored water? A specialty from the north?"

He squatted sitting and the pamp advanced to a meter away and settled upon a rope box as Ay'r offered the sweet water. Even in the starlight's dimness the pamp resembled that arch-thief Sostenuto in its dress and in gestures.

"Know this, gentle-pamp, my companion pamp suffered from the bite of sand-serpent and nearly died."

The other drew back in horror.

"Many days ago," Ay'r clarified. "And many leagues distant, in the middle of the ocean. Bitten on the leg, but thanks to timely interference and Human medical ability, my companion lives and heals. Still, he will need a place to rest inland a few days, Sol Rad."

"That Ser, is a most reasonable request."

"Payment is possible."

"Payment is impossible, Ser. Instead it will be an honor for the patient to be housed in this own poor creature's domicile. But Lordship, a pamp companion?" it asked.

"I never said I was anyone's lord," Ay'r quickly corrected.

"Apologies, Ser."

"But my companion," Ay'r went on, "is as fine a sailor pamp as any that glided along the Great Salt Ocean. Although wounded and very ill, this pamp nevertheless bravely sailed on many kilometers before he was felled."

"Was it by your own hand, young Ser, that the pamp companion was healed?"

"Alas, my medical lore is slack. But enough of it and of medicines were onboard to help the poor stricken fellow remain alive."

As though in proof, the pamp himself now stuck its head and torso out of the hold. Ay'r lifted it out and helped it find a resting spot near him on deck.

"Sand-Drifter am I called," the pamp said in a weak voice. "This Human saved my unworthy life and cared for me and fed me like a sire and three brothers would have done."

Ay'r found himself moved by the poor thing. He put out a steadying arm for the pamp, and quickly added, thinking on his feet, "Little-Hunter am I called. This pamp is brave and its life can never be thought unworthy." He turned to Sand-Drifter. "Tell him the name of your kin in the town. What is the name of this suburb?" he asked the other.

"South Salt Hollow."

"In South Salt Hollow, my kin are known under the sigil of

three crossed masts," Sand-Drifter said.

"I know those sailors," the stranger pamp replied. "Still, you will be a guest in my domicile. There are many pamp brothers who will care for you. For, while partly healed, you look ill yet." To Ay'r the strange pamp said, "I am called Esprio, and although unworthy, still many Humans and other Species call me by my name. The winds are few at this hour. Our craft runs also on fuel. Should you consent, we might attach a line."

Ay'r looked to Sand-Drifter, who looked down at Ay'r's hand on its arm, steadying it. When it didn't answer, he did. "Gratitude, gentle-pamp Esprio. The line attached to the prow will serve us well."

Esprio called over the other pamps who pushed the smaller ketch into place and the line was attached.

Ay'r asked if Sand-Drifter didn't want to move to a more comfortable bed aboard the larger craft.

"Does the pamp, Esprio, witness this?" Sand-Drifter asked Esprio, almost as though rhetorically.

"Esprio witnesses this, and is ..." the other couldn't seem to find any other words.

"There is a legend," Sand-Drifter began. "One all infant pamps are told."

"Esprio knows that legend well. Could it be coming to fruition in our own worthless lifetimes?"

Before they could explain the strange dialogue, the other sailors hooted that the line was attached, and Ay'r carried Sand-Drifter down to its usual bed in the hold, while Esprio left.

When Ay'r got on deck again, he stood up between the now raised masts and watched as the larger craft geared up and took off with a surprisingly soft noise. After a quick little jerking movement, the sand-ketch sped afterward. Soon it was skimming across the salted sands faster than any fly-by. Ay'r found himself smiling. The stars were billion-fold and lovely against the black velvet night sky. The stricken pamp would live. And he had found himself at least one and perhaps two allies.

"This Human, Little Hunter is the modest name he goes by, is a special friend of pamps," Esprio introduced him to the very antiquated Bella=Arth., luxuriantly spread across a stool and two ottomans in the depths of the new and used Human and Arth.-attire shop.

Although Ay'r had never seen an Arth. close up before, he knew the more aged ones could be distinguished by their paler brown colored palps, and the spindliness of their thoracic cavities. This one had both those features and furthermore she was using an ancient hand-held counting mechanism consisting of a metallic frame and parti-colored knobs so old it might have gone back in origin to Metro-Terran times. In addition, this Arth.was humming an atonal melody as it brushed its upper body fur with rather frazzled mandibles. It looked over the pair of them with its gorgeously-hued multifaceted eyes, concentrating on the pamp, and replied "If you want a bargain (cheap price ((rip-off))), you've come to the right place, friend of pamps. Cor'a Gur ('TT') has the very best equipment (gear ((ocean-worthy kind))) in the place."

In every shop in the great SSP City market they'd been in so far this second sundown of the morning that Ay'r and Sand-Drifter had arrived, the elderly pamp had said the phrase of Ay'r that he was "is a special friend of pamps," and suddenly no questions were asked of Ay'r no matter how odd his request, while merchandise of the finest yet cheapest was provided by especially subservient pamp shop men. He'd wondered what effect the phrase would have with one of the Three Species, and wasn't in the least surprised that it appeared to have had no effect at all.

"Gratitude, Venerable Mer Cor'a Gur ('TT')," Ay'r replied. "And while it's undoubtedly true that my companion may require some new gear (equipment ((the ocean-worthy sort))) for the sloop, that will have to be another (more profitable for you ((and greater rip-off))) shopping trip."

"No purchases (sales ((scams to you, Bub))) today? Whyever then would Cor'a Gur ('TT') endure the Human's presence?"

Esprio now answered with the smooth persuasion he'd used all evening on Ay'r's behalf.

"Information, Venerable Lady, is essential."

"Information also can be shopped for." The bored Arth. looked away and went back to calculating, while brushing up it's rather ragged lower body fur.

"This especial friend of pamps is on an expedition of pure diversion, eager to seek out the great sights of Usk."

"Once you've seen the Rings of Usk you've seen it all," the Arth. said, repeating the old cliché about the planet.

"Indeed not, Honorable Mer," Ay'r took up the cudgels. "There are reportedly great sights back in the foothills of the high mountains half the world away. It's those this traveler wishes to amuse himself with."

"I, Venerable One, seek passage for the Young Ser across the Great Salt Ocean at its widest," Esprio added, "to land at the old Western Star Port, and to hire pamps to travel inland from that point."

"Have you seen (experienced ((been bored by))) the South Salt Pans yet?" The Arth. asked Ay'r. "Another, ostensibly 'great sight of Usk,'" she added, making the chirring noise that passed for laughter.

"Next coming dusk, I hope to experience them."

"Don't fall," the Arth. warned. "They're awfully tall. As for ocean passage, very few ocean-worthy barques voyage (waste time ((plod along))) these days to that superannuated, unused West Star Port."

"It is rumored that one named Lepta voyages there regularly," Esprio interrupted.

"Ah, yes, that Lepta! I'd almost forgotten about my brother (scumbag ((curl-vole-shit trader))), Auros Ap Lepta."

"The market rumors hint that Lepta's somewhere in the area of the city," Esprio said. "They also bandied that if anyone knew his exact whereabouts, it would be your honorable self."

"Humans tend to prefer (wear ((try on and not buy))) these tunics while traveling, Young Ser," the Arth. said. "Fine quality and endurance with a hint of style (color ((vulgar flash to attract mates)))."

"In fact," Ay'r said, "I'd been thinking of purchasing a few of those very tunics and several other pieces, and I'd hesitated only wondering whether the Venerable Cor'a would be able to convert substantially large bills of currency."

The large Vespid head turned toward Ay'r for the first time since he'd entered the shop, then back to Esprio. "This is an especial friend of the pamps, I believe you mentioned?" she asked.

"An *especial* friend," Esprio affirmed.

"D'lars. Fifty per certificate that must be exchanged," Ay'r said.

"Each certificate, hmmm? Yes, a very special friend," Cor'a Gur ('TT') echoed. "Naturally. And two for the price of one on any tunic, trouser or sandal that takes your fancy. Give a senior citizen (old broad) a few secs, Sol Rad., to locate the barque's communications," Cor'a added. The others moved away while the Arth. turned to engage an old-fashioned Holo-Comm.-receiver with an outdated view-screen.

"I thank you, host Esprio," Ay'r now said, "for these pieces you were kind enough to allow me to wear on this foray."

"The ensemble you were traveling in, while grand, didn't appear suitable," the pamp agreed.

"But as you see, I really can use more clothing," Ay'r said, once they'd moved even deeper into the shop, and further away from the open agora. "What do you think? Several tunics? Several short and long trousers? And a few slip-on sandshoes?"

"This insect," Esprio said very quietly, "will receive a cut out of the trip you take with Lepta, so you needn't go all out if you don't wish." Then louder, "yes, several of each I think."

"And this Lepta?" Ay'r whispered back, "he's reliable?"

"He's a drunken perverted sot with six kinds of criminal charges against him in several ports at various times! But, he is said to be a charming Human companion when he wishes to be, does not overtly mistreat his pamps, can sail like a breeze, and he won't abandon you while you decide to take your air-board out for a starlight skate."

The latter in reference to the rather unlikely story Ay'r had come up with to explain what he been doing so far from shore and wearing only his party clothes when he'd come across Sand-Drifter's grounded ketch. A story the pamps accepted so easily that he had to wonder if, instead he had told them that he had dropped down off the Fifth Shepherding Ring Moon where he ordinarily resided, whether perhaps that very tall tale also would have also been accepted without comment.

"Hsssst!" they heard the Arth. loudly summon. "Official company (authority ((the pigs!))) are nearby in the mart."

"We're in the dressing rooms," Esprio called back and led Ay'r to one of four cubicles barely large enough to stand and change clothing in. They seemed to have been formed dircetly out of a Type-13 Slp.G travel-storage bin that had been laid on one side and cut crosswise, which was probably the case. Ay'r did begin to try on some of the tunics, using the highly reflective surface of the bin's interior walls to see himself in. Catching himself turning, he had the oddest sensation. For the briefest of moments, he didn't recognize himself, and thought, "already, I'm changed by all this!" He smiled at himself a second later and whispered to his image, "silly lad! All your life you hated palace life and longed for adventure. Now you've found it!"

Esprio hushed him from the adjoining cell and Ay'r looked out through an eye hole drilled near the top wall probably to discourage theft, where he could make out the Arth. still upon its ottomans, still calculating and brushing itself, only now less relaxed than it had been before, and conversing with others. A Human figure passed inches away from the eye hole and Ay'r drew back, recognizing the gold trimmed shoulder braiding. Evidently this one was checking out the shop while another spoke to the trader.

A few minutes later, the intruders had gone and the Arth. began humming again, this time in a louder voice, so they might hear. Esprio came for Ay'r and together they did their commerce, the 10,000 d'lar dot taken, and in return a self-identifying verbal passage ticket for "One Ocean Crossing" received, the clothing Ay'r had chosen was included, with a bit of bills and other currency as change.

"If your business (shady or whatever it may be ((who's asking? not this Arth!))) is completed now," Cor'a Gur ('TT') said, "then this Female would recommend leaving the market through my private (no one knows but me ((and you'll never tell either, will you?))) exit, just behind the flap of the changing cells."

"Gratitude, Venerable Lady," Ay'r bowed.

The Arth. stroked a silky palp across his forearm, putting its head at a distinct angle and making Ay'r think it might be flirting, "this Female never would have guessed such a recently Pupated Infant would possess such charm (the criminal kind ((but my mandibles are sealed!)))."

Thinking that the suggested exit might be more noticeable than not, Ay'r crept up to where the shopfront opened to the open court, keeping himself well hidden, and peered out.

Two Golden Palace security men had just entered another, nearby emporium. They left standing outside its entry another man richly dressed in taupe, jet and silver. Even before he turned around Ay'r intuited who it was, and when the jet haired head turned more in his direction, the handsome features and unambiguously colored eyes said it all. It was his lover from three nights ago, the young Marquis Deon of the House of Syzygy.

"The Human espies?" the nosy Arth. asked.

"The Human espies a previous companion who is more personally insistent than he is erotically gifted."

Again he heard the chittering of Arth. laughter.

"And so, on second thought, Venerable Lady, your back exit might be precisely what's needed."

Some fifteen minutes. Sol Rad., later as their air-sled approached the night-lighted large village of pamp Salt Workers where Esprio resided, Ay'r said, "I should leave tonight. I refuse to endanger my host, or Sand-Drifter, or any pamp."

Esprio looked at him and said quietly, "for that very reason, Young Ser, no pamp will ever reveal your presence here."

Ay'r wasn't sure what he was saying. "Forgive me, Esprio, I do not for a moment doubt your unity nor the steadfastness of your people. Only ... sorry as I am to say it, I know all too well that Humans can be treacherous and ruthless. I could not bear any of your folk being subjected to cruelty for my sake."

"Well, do we know that, Young Ser. This night you remain with us. Tomorrow, after the double suns have set, we'll go to the ocean voyager Lepta, whose craft customarily lies moored in the marina on the other side of the Great Salt Pans. That sight, you owe it to see for yourself."

"Agreeing makes me uneasy, my host. But if you insist, I will stay one more morning and double bright afternoon under your roof."

"If you only understood what honor you staying here brings to Esprio!" the old pamp said, and some kind of emotion began to crack the pamp's tone of voice. But he turned the much-lined simian old face away so Ay'r could not read it and confirm for himself.

He had enough to think of anyway. Chiefly, he had to admit, seeing the handsome Hesperian again had brought with it a decidedly strong and worse, a decidedly mixed, response. For while his mind told him Deon was seeking him to take him back to the City to further whatever scheme he must for the Princeps, Ay'r's heart told him that Deon had looked not so much angry, or resolved to catch Ay'r, as he had seemed concerned for him, worried, possibly already ruing his part in the plan, maybe even hoping to make amends, amends from the Marquis that Ay'r would truly welcome and stretch out as long as possible.

And for that reason alone, Ay'r's reason all but shouted back at him that Ay'r must get away as soon and as far as possible.

Scores of thousands of years before, a thin line of hills had separated the hundred square kilometer-wide southern flatlands that would become salt pans from the southern Great Salt Ocean itself. As the defining hills eroded over time through the daily back and forth action of sand and wind – which gusted at that juncture with particular force, having travelled thousands of leagues from the north – the rock hills were eventually polished smooth into what now appeared to be irregularly shaped, free-standing stone towers rising straight up, each over two hundred meters in height.

Before their softer, inner sections totally eroded away, in between these scores of massive rock fingers sticking up, local vegetation took root and began to flourish – notably varieties of sand plum, dry sloe, and desert grape. Over the centuries, these vegetal thickets rose in height, forming a webwork through which the southern ocean salt and sand would be blown south, and thus into the pans. Once on the other side, however, because of the surprisingly strong nightly dews collected by the brush only on its south polar side, the saltier parts of sand would become saturated and the next morning would remain inert on the ground behind the natural baffles. They would not blow back into the ocean. Meanwhile those chemically unaltered, drier sands containing little or no salt, would be gusted back out north, into the sand ocean again.

In this way enormous cliffs and headlands of solidified salt collected over time behind the vegetal impedances, which in turn continued to grow, although naturally presenting more pickled varieties of their fruit to any gatherer who could hover or climb far enough up to gather them.

At the beginning, during the First Matriarchy, a few exploratory Humans and Arth.s inhabiting Usk began to work the salt that had collected on the flat ground farthest away from the imposing rock-tower-and-bush baffles. Then, as the desire for natural, rather than manufactured, salt grew over the centuries across the galaxy, the immense, nearly horizontal spires and cones of salt that formed on the other side of the baffle broke off or were broken off and combed by laborers onto an already existent salt under-layer. Over time, the salt pans grew gargantuan, continually evaporating out to their finest state of pure crystallization by the unceasing action of persistent winds and by the double suns' intense heat. Once the Delphinids had joined in a confederation with Humans and once they had tried Usk salt, they so preferred it that they refused to use any other kind to salinate or resalinate their aquiformed worlds. Prices rose and among Humans, Usk salt became a delicacy.

During the Bella=Arth. War with the other two species, there was a particularly flat-footed attempt by some ill-advised First Nest Arth. leaders to secure the little ringed planet and its natural salt for their own. A brief, barely significant, battle was fought outside South Salt Pan City, and the defeated military Arth.s fled, abandoning their civilian Nest Mates who had set up a sizable, thriving little general merchandise market for Inter-Species trade in the growing Southern city.

During the democratic First Interregnum between the two matriarchies, and once Hesperia, the City on a Star, was granted its Resort World petition over ringed little Usk with its two very different suns, the forsaken Arth. Soldier women remaining on-planet were granted Uskian Cityzenship, for which they and their progeny seemed eternally obliged. Under their benign supervision, the southern city quickly expanded threefold.

But it was the vacation spots that the victorious Matriarchal government paid most attention to. Among them, of course, on the north eastern shore of the Great Salt Ocean, was a spacious, flowing, conch-shaped, Interregnum-era mansion built by a former star baron for his lady love, said to be the largest residence on Usk. Failing to see any possible strategic or commercial use for the binary Aquila solar system, located as it was relatively distant from the Center Worlds, and close to absolutely nothing of any strategic importance, a Second Matriarchy bureaucrat, *faute de mieux,* wrote it off completely, allowing the planet to fall into that irregular succession of worlds that the Inner Quinx of Hesperia had cannily decided to refurbish at its own expense to further the "recreational use of otherwise third or fourth rate planets for its peoples and the use of all others of the Three Species."

It was then that the unused mansion became transformed into The Golden Palace, inside and out. That was also the period of the greatest construction on Usk, of miscellaneous resorts, retreats, spas, hotels, as well as private dwellings for Beryllium Billionaires, most of them erected upon the dramatically scenic shores of the Great Salt Ocean itself, such as the West Port, and further inland, and all with varying degrees of luxuriousness.

After a century or two, it was sadly agreed upon that Usk had never taken off as a resort world – facing so much competition from more beautiful and more temperate planets closer to the core of the Matriarchy – and that it probably never would take off. All but the westernmost of the Salt Ocean resorts were found to have financially failed, so the City began to lease the buildings and compounds out somewhat more inexpensively to "applicable" scientific, cultural, even social groups that abounded in both the Matriarchy and in the City, particularly those groups seeking extreme privacy. This ensured that at least upkeep would be constant and neglect minimized and also that a base population of Three Species would become fairly standardized upon Usk.

All of which came to pass.

Along those experimental research groups first arriving to set up Uskian headquarters in abandoned resorts was a Foundation belonging to the great geneticist, Lydia Relfi, who had been ignored for many centuries (when, that is, she wasn't outright persecuted) under the Matriarchy. One of the scientific champions of the Three Species, Relfi's immense advances in male viviparturition rescued two of the three Species from an untimely oblivion at the hands of the Cyber Rebellion and led directly toward the Socialized Vir'ism dominating the current government.

She'd been well over seven hundred years old when she set up her research station in Usk's hard-to-reach GrandView foothills, half the world away from the Golden Palace, and she died there only a few years later. But her fiercely loyal, mixed-gender staff had brought with it the genetic stock of a basally intelligent, four-limbed, six-fingered, six-toed simian-like creature discovered by the Delphinid explorer Pha"arg Second upon a rather damp, mixed-use, class M-4 planet revolving slowly around an otherwise unremarkable, numbered – but not named – G-38 sun in the Dickinson Nebula. Since the New Venice Senate decided to totally aquiform that newly formed and already quite watery world to its own population's needs, the needed evacuation of an unexpectedly discovered and quite small population of simians was declared an Approved Matriarchal Mission.

Those Indigenous-Primitives had already developed the rudiments of language, and concomitant, elementary tool-usage, although their intelligence was then deemed to be around that of a standardly language-modified Matriarchal house-pet. To Relfi's surprise, upon deeper investigation, the simians turned out to be neither purposely "seeded" by the Aldebaran Five project (too close to shipping lanes for that, really), nor did they share more than 75 percent of genetic material with Humans and Delph.s, which is to say even less DNA than Arth.s shared with the other Two Species. Where they came from and/or how they'd arisen out of the primordial soup on a native planet with so little other large fauna was fairly much still anyone's guess. Satellite imaging tomography showed no ruins and thus no earlier civilizations, and whatever that was, was soon was under hundreds of meters of water, anyway.

The bulk of these Indigenous-Primitive simians were evacuated, then placed in carefully prepared displaced persons communities on two moonlets around the giant, well populated Center World planet of Karenina, where they endured – but never really flourished – for a half dozen of their very short generations i.e. two hundred and forty years, Sol Rad.

Without warning, a religious leader suddenly arose out of the primitive folk on the moonlet with the larger population of simians and based its faith upon the storied return to the homeworld –by now only a distant memory for most of the populace. Impossible predictions were made. Incendiary omens were declared. Life or death promises were sworn. And soon thousands of the simians were camped out in the moonlet's highest peak awaiting a particular eclipse of the sun by planet Karenina that they believed would herald their "return day" to their now waterlogged home planet

That day arrived with a great commemoration, which was quickly followed by the generally horrified realization that no return to their home world was in fact happening, nor in fact possible.

That verified fact was quickly followed by the religious leader and his priests very publicly committing suicide. This was shortly thereafter followed by the mass suicide by various methods of two thirds of the disheartened populace. All but two Species Ethnologists, a Human and a Delph., managed to escape the resulting panic and the mass suicide/genocide that ensued, which further winnowed down the number of simians.

After about a decade, this small, by now chronically melancholic group of survivors were shuttled over and folded in as discreetly as possible by combined Delphinid and Matriarchal scientists into the second simian population of Karenina's smaller moonlet which had never been told what happened to their cohorts. Within a year, Sol Rad., another religious leader had arisen there too, with a similar belief system – possibly brought by the survivors – and the illusion-infection spread so fast that another mass suicide and genocide followed in mere months, leaving this exiled society unable or indeed unwilling to replicate itself or indeed even to feed itself.

News Holo-Comms. of the simians' fate – later on also presented in several tragic PVNs of exceptional artistry – naturally enough pricked the conscience of the Three Species, especially the Delphinids who now recognized that in their greed for more ocean worlds to populate, they had more or less destroyed an entire, aboriginal, people. Out of remorse they assumed the entire funding of Lydia Relfi's newest project, the evacuation of the simians' very youngest survivors from Karenina's second moonlet, along with the accompanying re-education and the cross breeding of this mostly vanished genus with Human and Delphinid DNA, upon a completely different planet, one essentially history-less to any of them.

Wicca VIII accepted Relfi's request for rescuing a breeding stock of twenty thousand and sixty five individuals. They were named Persons of Adapted Mixed Population by the Relfi Center which became the means whereby they were relocated to Usk. The acronym P.A.M.P. became the term pamp and quickly took hold among the Three Species.

Despite continued attempts to get the new breeding population to reach its fullest potential as quickly as possible, several limitations were immediately discovered to be autochthonous and irreversible among pamps, for example, size. The tallest a healthy pamp could grow to was a meter and a quarter. Another limitation lay in a pamp's seemingly inherent low self-esteem. Although the proudest and most self-starting of them were repeatedly bred, the genetic attitude lasted only one generation. As a people, the pamps remained simple, humble, eager to follow orders, almost innately subservient to any member of the Three Species, all of whom physically towered over them.

Unable to change those problematic attributes, over the centuries, the Relfians had cautiously close-bred into pamps other qualities in hopes of some kind of mitigation – self-sufficiency, physical strength, physical and psychological endurance, and above all, a powerful sense of kinship ties and family obligation – the latter especially put an early halt to any suicidal tendencies. When the Cyber virus arrived on Usk centuries after Relfi's breeding resort had closed and the pamps had scattered to the four quarters of the planet, it appeared years later among the pamps than it had in most places in the Matriarchy.

Thanks to Hesperian Health & Education Services, they were prepared. There were already thousands of newly Vir'istic male pamps who were physically and psychologically primed to give birth and continue their lines. Pamps had always been strongly male-bonded, homo-sociable, bisexual, and fratri-linear anyway, which helped a great deal in the changeover; so once female pamps died out, there was little cultural panic among the small folk.

A thousand years after the abandonment of the Relfi research station, the size of the pamp nation was thought to be large, possibly a million, but it remained uncounted. Partly, this was the result of yet another way in which pamps had successfully adapted to Usk as they'd never adapted to the Karenina moonlets. Most pamps lived not at the edge of the Great Salt Ocean or in its few population centers, as did most of the Three Species, but instead they lived inland, within the hundreds of continent-long valleys that had long rifted, literally banding the mountainous opposing hemisphere, which was so noticeably distinctive from orbit. Odd that creatures from such a damp planet would adapt so well to such an equally dry world, but such turned out to be the case. Some Species Ethnologists wondered if the "extremity" of the climate, rather than its specific quality, wasn't in fact the crucial issue of their successful adaptation.

Even those pamps that did join Three Species institutions such as marts, industry, farming and the Golden Palace staff, did on a time-limited basis. None ever remained more than few years. It was believed they earned enough to support their kin-cluster for a few years, then left for some godforsaken mountain valley that no sane Human or Arth. would ever willingly reside in, where they retired in their version of high style, feeding their extensive male family and enjoying high prestige, until the next retiree arrived. By this time, pamps were necessary to operating most of those institutions, but still were unquestionably second, possibly even lower, class Uskian Cityzens.

It was only natural that pamps would also begin to work in the salt pans. At first, in the smaller northern pans outside the Golden Palace and the somewhat larger pans not far from the Western Port. Later on, they began arriving from the hills and valleys in such large numbers that Quinx economists credited them for more or less developing the southern pans from a local industry into the enormous interstellar enterprise it then became. Their durability, despite the great heat and sun, allowed them to work long hours. Their kinship grouping allowed them to literally form pamp-chains of great strength and indissolvability across the perilous salt hills, insuring individual safety, or at least quick rescue in a mishap. Their hard work helped expand the southern pans to their current, colossal, size, so that the feature could even be seen from orbit, a huge region near the south pole of almost perfect whiteness, glaring conspicuously against the ecru desert and the vole-brown mountains.

Since they were planning to go further on this evening, Esprio brought the five-master sloop in close, so they might all see the towering wall of rock splinters and botanic thicket. Closer up, it loomed seventy stories high, the good-sized sloop easily dwarfed, as were the score of other, mostly tourist, craft parked in a roughly circular marina at the front of the centermost pillars.

Ay'r was clad in some of his newly bought togs, with a close-fitting cap covering his light-colored hair, and a transparent, plasticene, half veil-half sunglasses below the cap's bill, hiding his pale blue eyes – in the unlikely event that Deon or Golden Palace guards were present.

He and Esprio joined the mostly Human and Arth. visitors already gathered at two of the open-air gondolas that would levitate them up to the top of the Salt Pan towers, where several catwalks had been installed. A small family of Ambassadorial Delph.s was instantly noticeable for the transparent plastro bubbles they wore over their heads, each holding in moisture-laden atmospheres to facilitate their breathing amid the arid air, which attained startling new levels of dryness at this particular spot. The other travelers were given small mouthpieces on neck-laces hung around their necks that they could raise to their nostrils and lips for an instant spritz.

Three younger well-dressed Arth.s, so identical they must be Close-Sisters, had put all of their mouthpieces on one of them, who was now wearing it like a piece of arcane primitive jewelry, while they teased her and laughed in their chittering voices

It was a slow trip up the face of the stone towers and thicket, haltingly slow enough at times for passengers to pick and taste the naturally salted grapes and sloes. Once ascended, however, the view was worth the trouble. From the ground, both the Hunter and the Eagle had already set, but from here one could see the latter dropping yet again. On the side they'd arisen from, the Great Salt Ocean stretched away more magnificently huge than any of them had seen the desert from land. Given their height, the curvature of Usk was apparent, and on one side they could make out on the closest, eastern, shoreline ridge after ridge of mountains, rolling inland into the distance until they seemed to meld together in a deep red haze against the cobalt sky, tinted by the orange sunset, where the first stars were already becoming apparent.

"Oohs" and "Aaahs" erupted in several different languages and dialects at once.

After a short time, they were directed to turn around, and head-high white screens were automatically drawn aside, allowing them see the naturally collected salt, which glittered pinkly crystalline in the sunset brilliance, stretching as far as they could see like a gigantic solid glacier that gradually descended into diverse-sized streams of pink-white, and which in turn rivuleted down along into many tributaries until it vanished into an enormous prairie of salt pans at the southern horizon, as far as the eye could see.

Significantly more "Oohs" and "Aaahs" ensued in different languages and dialects.

Their guide was a self-important Human 'Tute whose large size, poor sense of style and overweening sense of self reminded Ay'r all too much of his 'Tute Narfacan'ni. As the big Human swanned about, introducing himself to the tourists, asking them impertinently personal questions, and divulging unrequested information about himself, a half dozen repair pamps clad in far smaller versions of his own pale green jumpsuit, worked on an area of fencing overlooking the glacier of salt before them all.

"Ignore, gentle folk, these barbaric creatures," the oversized 'Tute began. The three matched Arth.s loudly chittered, "sisters! He doesn't even see (recognize ((intuit))) the small ones (pamps) in our midst. How drolly shocking!" The guide then corrected himself: "Barbaric I mean only, of course, in their general incapacity for their job, having been hired by someone other than myself," he said, thereby making the insult even worse and causing the Arth.s to chitter in laughter even more. "He's so clumsy (socially tasteless ((and droll!)))!"

"Well! Really! some people!" the Delph. couple's smaller member huffed aloud.

In response, Ay'r moved an inch or so closer to Esprio, as though extending his protection over the aged trader.

"The truth is," the 'Tute defended himself, "this fence repair ought to have been finished *ages* ago. Don't know why they're only doing it now and why they're taking so long."

A low murmur among two of the three pamps was picked up by the pamp trader who explained to the others, "my repair-work brothers beg all of your pardons. They're mortified to have to repair the fence in front of visitors. They say it's unavoidable, however, as the fence needs the repair and they only received the order for the job one hour ago, Sol Rad., and only after an inspection-pamp had noted the problem."

Hearing this, all Three Species of tourists just off the gondola lifts sympathized with the pamps. But their guide took instant and full umbrage at these words. Raising himself up and outward to his greatest size, he hotly demanded to know, "are these creatures impugning me? Dare they say that I did not report the fence tear?"

Before anyone could respond, he rushed over to where they were working, grabbed one of the repair pamps and began shaking it, shouting, "if I lose a single point on my record because of this, you'll pay. Do you hear?"

The Humans closest rushed to his side and importuned the guide to leave the repair-pamp alone. Several even grabbed at his arms and shoulders, in case he shook the poor thing's brains loose.

"It's a conspiracy!" he shouted. "You're all in on it."

With more and longer arms than the others, the Arth. sisters now grabbed the pamp out of his clutch and set the frightened creature down onto the parapet.

"You're *all* against me!" the guide kept shouting and rushed at the three Arth. sisters, his fists out grasping. They scattered before his advent, chittering loudly, and hopping backwards in single leaps right to the gondola lifts.

In his rush to get at them, the guide knocked the still shaken and trembling repair-pamp aside with such force that it was propelled into and through the semi-repaired fencing. Before anyone could do anything, it had lost its balance and its grip and was over the side, falling!

A collective gasp arose from the onlookers who ran and hopped to that side. They watched the pamp tumble over and over, putting its arms and legs out wide in an attempt to cartwheel and slow down its descent, or somehow lessen the impact, when it landed. Even so, it landed badly, fell forward, tumbled more and lay sprawled out in a position that looked as though several limbs were out of alignment.

Esprio called out quickly. In seconds, the other repair-pamps sprung forward with rescue-lines. Under the pamp trader's orders, they looped the two sets of ropes around a stanchion on the parapet and began shimmying down toward their fallen colleague.

Naturally, all the tourists had moved to watch the rescue attempt. Even the Arth.s had gotten over their annoyance and rushed to the scene, where everyone was loudly encouraging the two brave repair-pamps in their efforts.

Although the fallen pamp didn't move, no one believed it was dead. When the first of its co-workers touched down onto the sunset-hued white sheet of salt, everyone suddenly understood how perilous their position was. Although it looked solid and actually held solid for a few minutes as the repair-pamps moved a few meters gingerly along its surface toward the victim, all of a sudden the salt surface would dissolve beneath their feet into dust and powder. One pamp mis-stepped and sank instantly, as though into liquid, to great moans and cries from the tourists observing from above.

It caught itself quickly and shimmied back up the rope to calls of relief, but now both it and its companion trod far more carefully and far more slowly toward the fallen pamp.

And if that weren't worrisome enough, Ay'r noticed that the knocked over pamp began to stir where it lay.

"Esprio," he grasped the trader's sleeve. "Warn the poor fellow to take care! Or it could move a fingertip and in so doing open a salt cave beneath itself thirty meters deep and never be seen again."

Esprio called down and the two other pamps stood still and put their fingers in their ears.

"Whistle down to rouse the fallen brother," the trader told Ay'r, who whistled as sharply and as stingingly as he knew how. The Arth.s chittered loudly, equally annoyed.

The way the fallen pamp's head jerked to the sound meant clearly that it was now conscious.

Seconds later, those pamps half hanging on ropes and half walking delicately over the salt toward it called out instructions for it to not move a single muscle.

Their colleague cried out in response, evidently in pain, but it didn't move.

Little by little, the two got closer without mishap. One reached the victim's head, the other its feet, by the most daintily taken steps. Surely any member of the Three Species would have fallen through the salt long before. The fallen pamp lay on a little hummock and as the others knelt down to pick it up on either side, salt from one side or the other slowly begin to trickle out. Esprio loudly warned them and they stopped and followed Ay'r's instructions, as he related them through the trader, sliding the rope-ends around their own waists in a tight-knotted cinch. The salt-fissures beneath all three continued their inexorable out-spill. Ay'r directed the three Arth.s as the strongest and most multi-limbed rescuers above, along with two other Humans on the parapet, and now in addition to being secured by stanchions, the two roped pamps were also being held by several Humans, Ay'r prominent among them.

Still following his orders translated into their dialect, the repair-pamps below used the loose ends of the ropes wrapped around themselves and very tenderly, very gingerly, managed to get those ends around their fallen fellow and knotted one loop around its torso, another around the middle of its legs.

Already, onlookers who could see the salt hill from another side were calling out warning. No sooner did the two repair-pamps on lines have their repair-pamp colleague secured and also held in their arms, then the entire hill of salt beneath them dissolved, dropping maybe forty meters all at once.

Held by Ay'r and others, they swung safely away and in a few minutes, Sol Rad., with no little effort and many cries of warning and care from those watching that almost matched in loudness the moans of agony from the victim. They managed to hoist all three pamps up to the parapet.

Ay'r carried the hurt pamp to a gondola lift. There, Esprio spoke comforting words to it and gave it a draught of something he said should ease its pain. The two rescuer pamps also got into the gondola. One of the Delph.s took Ay'r by the forearm. "I've comm.ed South Salt Pan City Hospital. They're sending an emergency fly-by to pick up the injured one. They'll land in the center of the marina below."

"Gratitude, friend! It's good people like yourself," and looking up, Ay'r added, "and these wonderful Arth.s also, thank you Ladies, who have saved the poor creature's life and limbs."

The other tourists said they'd await the lift's return to go back down themselves.

"You can't go down *yet*," the guide, silent until now, spoke up. "You've not heard the tour yet."

"Can't you see?" one of the Delph. partners turned on him in anger. "A fellow creature is suffering, perhaps dying. That, and not your sand-blasted tour, is important now!"

"What difference does that one make?" the guide responded. "It's only a thing!"

Before Ay'r could stop himself, he'd lashed out at the guide, punching him hard in his stomach and as he crumpled over forward, once more in chin, causing the guide to fall over.

Such naked violence shocked all the tourists, who instantly withdrew.

The guide never lost consciousness and sat down on his side

rubbing his chin.

"Young Ser," the Delph. asked. "Why would you do such violence to another?"

"What difference does *that one* make?" Ay'r asked back. "Clearly, our hurt friend there is to him," pointing to the guide, "only *some thing!*" repeating back the guide's own words.

Before anyone could say a word, he turned and ran back into the gondola, which he shut behind himself, just as it began to descend.

Ay'r brooded alone, silently berating himself for making a bad situation into one worse yet, and for drawing attention to himself – he who shouldn't even be out in public but instead hiding.

The lift descended without incident and Ay'r carried the injured pamp to the flyer. Before the others could get in, the poor creature took Ay'r's hand and looked into his eyes. Surely, Great One, I owe my life to you ... Parapet-Mender was I before this evening. Salt-Eluder shall I now be called. Salt-Eluder-Saved-By-The-Friend-to-the-Pamps."

"Don't think about any of this. Just rest and heal," an embarrassed Ay'r told the pamp.

"But great Ser, is it true what our grandfather Esprio says, and what my repair-brothers whisper?"

"It is true. You pamps are a downtrodden and persecuted folk!" Ay'r declared.

"That, great one, I know. But I meant is it true that you are the One Long-Predicted, who will raise the pamps into a nation?"

'Me?! Who says such things?"

"All of them. And tomorrow all of South Salt Pan City and its pamp suburbs shall know that you struck one of your own species for the harm he did to a mere pamp."

"But ... anyone would have done the same," Ay'r responded.

"No one had ever done so. You are the first on Usk, Ser. The very first ever in all pamp history ... And so, what is predicted is come true. You are indeed our Great Helper."

"You're raving, poor fellow. Raving! You need rest." He stepped out.

The fly-by's door slid shut, the medics and repair pamps lifted off the marina floor.

Esprio tugged at Ay'r's sleeve. "Quickly to my craft, Ser Little Hunter. We must leave in the greatest hurry."

A few minutes later, Sol Rad., the sloop was tacking vigorously into a headwind, leaving the marina, and in no time at all, the great Salt Pan Wall was nothing but a line on the horizon.

The Arcturus Scatling was an eight-master, and thus twice as large as Esprio's well equipped desert yacht. Far more elegant too. From twenty meters away, the lights of the staterooms and forecastle section could be seen brightly lighted – and were evidently of a rather grand nature.

Only three sailors – one pamp and two Humans – were on board to greet Ay'r and the elderly trader Esprio when they strode up the imposing rampway.

On Esprio's recommendation, young Ay'r had traded his barely-covering sunglass/veil by which he could be recognized anyway after the day's earlier incident, with a face-covering Betrothal Shroud, worn on the top of the head dropped down on all sides, gathered around the neck and chin, made of thin material and thus easy to breathe through, yet opaque, except where it was more lightly cross-stitched over the eyes.

The old pamp said, "among the Humans of the South and especially those of the Western Continent you'll be going to, newly betrothed and not yet wed youths of great value are shrouded thus by their families and lovers, so that no other possible suitors can come to desire them."

Ay'r wondered how the old trader had managed to hit the stamp exactly on its end. But he'd taken the extra precaution and changed his outfit, then wrapped over it the Trothee Shroud, as it was called, which immediately elicited feelings of claustrophobia mixed with the secret glee of masked invulnerability. Esprio said the eight-master had seven staterooms for guests, two for officers, and two sets of barracks below, one for Human sailors, the other for pamp deckhands.

One of the Humans brought Ay'r and Esprio into the reception salon. Like all of the Arcturus Scatling they'd seen so far, it was elegantly appointed. The First Mate, a narrow, tall fellow with sallow-hued skin and sharp-pointed facial features, and who looked a great deal more handsome than he would, had he not been wearing the striking purple and bronze Arcturus Scatling uniform, was just finishing his business with a pair of Ambassadorial Delph.s wearing humidity bubbles over their faces (not, however, Ay'r noted with relief, the same pair from the Salt Pan Rampart incident.). He was charming, courteous, pleasant as he said to them, "now remember! We sail from this marina tomorrow, one full day, Sol Rad., from right now. If you aren't aboard, you have but one more opportunity to join this voyage on the Arcturus Scatling. Three days, Sol Rad., from now, when we stop for almost an hour at Point WestWard, at the great sand reefs. After that point, no local fly-by will take your fare, nor dare fly any further. Naturally people have been known to join the voyage later on, while we're sailing much further west. But mark my words, they paid dearly to find a fly-by pilot who would cater to their whim, as the ocean is so climatically dangerous."

The Delph.s nodded and were seen out the salon doors by the Mate, who returned and turned to the newcomers. "How may I help you?" he asked, oozing courtesy.

"There is a reservation made," Esprio spoke out.

The Mate ignored him and his words, looking to Ay'r, hidden behind his shroud.

"It's not often, Ser, that we are honored to have onboard Trothees, with or without their Trothers."

"As the trader Esprio said," Ay'r attempted a haughty tone of voice, like that of his 'Tute Narfacan'ni. "There is a reservation made." He held out the stub given to him the previous day by the Arth., Co'ra Gur ('TT').

"Not for *this* voyage, gracious Ser?" the Mate seemed astonished.

"For *this* voyage. My luggage is being brought onboard as we speak."

"Impossible! *This* voyage is completely booked."

"Doubtless because this reservation," Ay'r said, thrusting it at the Mate, who continued to avoid it, "was for the *last* available stateroom. I travel alone and will take any room remaining."

"There is no record of any reservation made other than those already made onboard the Arcturus Scatling for *this* voyage," the Mate insisted.

"Clearly some error has been made. Since the reservation was paid for – as this receipt clearly states," Ay'r finally manage to drop it onto the Mate's over-decorated sleeve, where it immediately stuck and verbally stated "Reservation for one voyage to Western Star Port and Resort."

The Mate tried to shake it loose, but it held fast and continued to adhere and to speak. "One passage. Value – nine thousand d'lars. Paid in full."

"I'm afraid a terrible error has occurred," the Mate lied.

"Paid in full," the receipt repeated. "Nine thousand d'lars. Cash."

"It must be for the *next* voyage," he attempted.

"Embarkation from the larger marina west of the South Salt Pans," the stub said, then gave the evening's date, and reiterated. "Paid in full. In cash."

"I have not one stateroom left. I'll gladly refund the d'lars," he tried now.

"Ask to see the Captain," the ignored pamp suggested to Ay'r.

"This is a complete outrage!" Ay'r stamped his foot in pretended temper. "I want to see the Captain immediately."

"The Captain is unfortunately not on board," the Mate assured him.

Esprio whispered, "the Captain's flag is hung and heads up on the main mast."

This time the Mate managed to actually hear the pamp.

"What I meant was: the Captain is indisposed, temporarily."

"In one minute, Sol Rad.," Ay'r said quietly but clearly, "the First Mate will find himself indisposed – *permanently!* if a stateroom is not produced *immediately.*" He did not need to pretend temper this time. The Mate had seriously irked him.

Before the Mate could do anything more than react with his mouth agape, Ay'r felt his sleeve tugged at. He looked down to see Esprio making a warning finger gesture. He understood its import. He could not dare make yet another scene.

Evidently the Mate saw it too, as he began to escort Ay'r out of the chamber by a quickly shaken off arm.

Before they reached the ship's ramp way, Esprio had already run ahead, and was ordering the bags to be taken off again.

Ay'r couldn't see straight for his anger as the Mate kept on talking, now taking a placatory approach, although his words were nothing to Ay'r but antipy excretions.

No sooner had Esprio and Ay'r gotten back on the sloop, then Ay'r reached a decision.

"I've paid and I'm reserved and I'm going. I'll stow aboard."

"It would be unfortunate if you were discovered in several days. I wouldn't put it past that Mate," he added, cautiously, "to, once on the other side of the reefs, make you pay with your life by marooning you where no sand-yachts ply."

"I must see the Captain." Ay'r declared. "Tonight! When the lights go off, I'll creep on board, and see him."

The trader had objections to this plan too, but in the end, he admitted, "if you must."

They sailed off just far enough to keep the larger craft in view, and turned an unlighted side to the Arcturus Scatling. Unless someone was observing by other than visual means, they seemed to have left the marina.

Before first dawn (of Hunter), as the larger craft's lights went all dim, Ay'r took off alone on his air-board. One guard only was posted on the Arcturus Scatling, a snoring pamp. Even so, Ay'r snuck onboard at spot other than the ramp way, and stowed his air-board where he might be able to collect it easily, should he need a fast escape in the night. Usk's rings had begun their inexorable month-long rise to perihelion. The outermost strata now reflected the Hunter's blueness from below the planet's ecliptic, refracting it into millions of tiny silver-blue mirrors. First sunrise was less than a half hour away, Sol Rad. He had to hurry.

He'd memorized what he'd seen of the craft's layout from the earlier visit. The First Mate had kept them waiting long enough for Ay'r to become bored. To amuse himself he'd latched onto the visual diversion of the Holo-Plan of the ship's decks floating high on one wall. While he'd been too far away to make out all of the small print, even when he'd refocused his eyes for long-distance vision, he'd grasped the general map – ship's offices and officers' chambers in the back deck ("the stern" it had read, a funny word he'd never before encountered, quaint in that typical way of Metro-Terranese from days long gone). The largest chamber had to be the Captain's, he'd guessed. A small corridor outside it led to three other chambers, one of which doubtless held the annoying Mate.

The salon doors slid silently ajar, but Ay'r waited to a count of past sixty before entering, just in case a motion-detector or probe-eye had been set off by the movement. He was now in the reception salon where he and Esprio had been so badly treated earlier.

It was dark, but the chart was in a field of a bit more light. When Ay'r glanced out the porthole, he saw Usk's rings were now wholly tinted blue-silver. He could make out the plan well, and he held his wrist connector up to it for more of a glow. Focusing his enhanced night vision attribute, he saw he had assessed correctly before. He crept forward to the Captain's chamber, paused outside, hearing sounds from within too low and indistinct to be made out. He wondered if he ought to knock. Or would that summon the Mate from his chamber nearby. He took a deep breath and slid open the door.

Contriving this earlier, he'd assumed he would encounter the Captain sleeping, or, more romantically – sitting up in bed poring over reef charts of the great unknown tracts of the enormous western division of the Great Salt Ocean, in preparation for any possible emergency to come during the voyage.

Instead, the dimmed room seemed to be a mass of seething motion, accompanied by that sound he'd heard before he'd opened the door, though louder now, and which he now recognized as the noise a dozen or so pamps would make – grunts, groans, moans and sighs of satisfaction – as they freely partook of the nine Human essences.

Their donor was – he had to assume – the ship's Captain, more or less horizontally afloat a few inches off the air-mattress, unclothed, his head thrown back so the abundant, long, light curls shook loose below, all of them vibrating rhythmically like some New Venice sea-creature at the bottom of a current-swayed lagoon. Although he lay in profile to Ay'r and was literally covered – ears to toes – with licking, slavering pamps, his eyes seemed open, if unfocussed.

One pamp each was sucking on his ears. One each at his nostrils. Two were taking turns licking the insides of his slightly open mouth. One each had its face nestled in either armpit. One was tonguing his navel, four were at his feet, methodically cleaning his toes. Three others labored at his crotch, one below his bended-upward legs and all but invisible, another with his penis in his mouth, a third sensitively lapping at his testes.

Ay'r had eavesdropped on house pamps at the Golden Palace talking among themselves while hidden where he couldn't be seen or inferred. As they had been gathered to work at the palace from all over Usk, they couldn't always understand each other's dialects, and so usually spoke their soft, slightly accented version of Universo-Lex common to the Three Species.

Among the odder terms and sayings he'd overheard that he'd never gotten a proper explanation of was "Nine-Essence Orgy." One time, he heard Dustweed saying, "we encountered an off-planet Human from Narcissus Terce, half out of his wits on Stele, slumming at StarPort Lar'i's place, who said he was looking for a full-body-cavity experience. Since he showed us a valid ticket off Usk for the very next double sunrise, Sol Rad., there was no chance of us possibly becoming servant-bonded to him. So a team of us gave him a Nine-Essence Experience. He hit the ceiling more than a few times. We were all essence-sated for the next week, Sol Rad."

Suddenly, Ay'r knew what the pamps had meant. By agreement, but without any apparent signal, the pamps in the room all at once stopped what they were doing and moved along the Captain's long, slender body to the next position, ear-lickers to the toes, toe-suckers to his genitals, etc. His body appeared to relax a few seconds before they started in again and it once more he became rigid with pleasure.

Ay'r must have observed two complete such complete changes of pamp-position, when he suddenly felt his left shoulder roughly wrenched from behind, enough to fling him aside. Before he could react more than keeping from hitting the corridor floor, the captain's chamber door was slid shut. Someone was on top of him in the dark.

They twisted about for some minutes, both holding each other, trying to get a secure grip to punch the other, the strange combat furthered in strangeness by their near-silence but for heavy breathing and assorted grunts, when another door that they'd just slammed into for perhaps the third time slid open and someone was standing above them in sudden bright light.

"If you *must* have your sport, lads, gratitude for doing it where others are *not* sleeping!"

In the light, Ay'r and the First Mate recognized each other.

"You again!" the Mate expostulated. "I told you there were no rooms left onboard."

"I paid for a room. I'll *have* a room," Ay'r argued.

"Not as long as I'm Mate here."

"You've double-sold the staterooms!" Ay'r charged. "You're in on it with that smelly old Arth. at the South Salt Pan Market! You're skimming the profit! I'm going to make sure the Captain knows all about it!"

He turned to the stranger for help as the two of them untangled themselves and got to their feet. And it was the far from prepossessing stranger who immediately pulled Ay'r in through the sliding door into his stateroom, averting by centimeters the First Mate's enraged lunge at him. Thwarted, the Mate turned to the stranger, whom he towered over by half a head.

"Calm, yourself, nautical Ser," the stranger said. "A solution lies at hand."

"What solution?" the Mate asked.

"My assistant has not yet arrived. Nor has he comm.ed me, as we'd planned. I'll take on this smart young Trothee as my assistant instead." Turning to Ay'r, "that is, if you so agree. You sound like a highly educated lad and you certainly figured out rather quickly at least one game going on aboard the Arcturus Scatling," he looked up at the Mate. "The work I offer is physically easy and not wearing mentally either. I've got two large staterooms. If you can help me move some equipment off the bed in the second one, it's all yours."

Ay'r held his ticket stub and placed it on the stranger's sleeve, where it immediately spoke its price and reservation date and even, this time, its confirmation number."

"Oh, I believed you before you showed me that," the stranger said. Then, to the Mate. "Do you object? Or would you rather have your greed and perfidy exposed?"

The Mate backed off. "It's all a huge mistake. I tell you. But if you take the Trothee into your rooms, I've no objection. None at all."

"Then it's done. Note it in your craft's log."

The Mate took Ay'r's ticket stub and melded it to his wrist-connector, saying. "This reservation is now fulfilled. Passage for one Human Trothee, name not given, fully paid, for a full voyage, class A, from South Salt Pan City's large marina to West Star Port Resort. On this date and time."

That done, he handed the stub back to Ay'r.

"Your luggage, Ser?"

"I'll comm. for it to the other sloop," Ay'r said and the stranger bid the Mate "Good Hunter-Rise. Now!" he faced Ay'r. "Introductions are needed. I am Jense Silberklang from Diomedes Terce. I'm the foremost geologist of Ringed Planets and an acknowledged authority on the geology of Usk."

While he paused, Ay'r wondered how he should answer. "I ..." he stammered.

"You are a Shrouded Trothee. Obviously betrothed to some Lord of Distinction. I respect your complete privacy, Young Ser. And I will never ask another question about your identity."

"Gratitude, Ser Silberklang. I've been using the name Little Hunter among my pamp friends. It's a bit odd, I realize ..."

"Bissel Hunter then, in an old Metro-Terran tongue. Agreed?"

"Bissel will do. Gratitude, Ser. I'm am mortified at this scene you just witnessed. But in truth I must be at the Western Star Port at the end of this very voyage or ..."

"Excellent. I need not know another word. Simply comm. the other craft for your bags and let us go down to breakfast. There's an especially tasty and rich buffet served onboard most mornings."

During the buffet held in the second largest salon, themselves the two earliest risers and eaters for most of the time, Ay'r looked carefully at his new employer. Silberklang was shorter than Ay'r but not by a great deal, and considerably older. Ay'r guessed perhaps, three-fifty or four-hundred years old, albeit with what looked to be only a single full cosmetological job. Rather than opting for a skin-tone blanching as many in the Republic now did, he'd retained his naturally dark skin, the color of the bark of the Pitaia Succulent Tree that grew along the Eastern Shoreline of the Great Salt Ocean. And so he was dark as any pamp. Silberklang's features were equally unchanged to meet Ib'r galactic fashion norms. His nose was short and squat and somewhat bent to one side in the middle, with tiny nostrils, so Ay'r naturally enough wondered how well he could breathe. His brows seemed bonier, heavier than the norm, and his hair was unclipped, and rather shaggy, and a tint of red-brown like long-rusted iron alloy. His mouth was rather fish-lipped and quite wide. In all, he gave off a rather Piscid appearance, similar to that of some of the fabled Mermen of Gamma Lesuth, another Delphinid planned mutation, yet his coloring was off for that and his limbs totally humanoid.

Esprio came onboard announcing that Ay'r's bags were

placed in his new home for the next forty-two days, Sol Rad., and Ay'r had to bend down to hug the old pamp.

"Honored Trader Esprio, you have been a grandfather and two uncles to this poor unfortunate," Ay'r said, both formally and sincerely. "Never will I forget your kindness, your generosity, and your good sense. Should my estate in life once more become fortunate, I hope I may someday repay you."

The trader declared payment unneeded and honor for all pamps already given. Esprio seemed hesitant, so that Ay'r finally moved the two of them aside for greater privacy.

"Speak what you think, dear friend, Esprio."

"A great destiny awaits you, young Ser. I feel it in my connector bones. But if I may offer a warning, beware strangers! I know we shall hear much more of you and your exploits. Surely the pamps will always speak of you as ... their especial friend."

"I am their friend, Esprio. And especially yours."

Breakfast done, the orange Eagle too was about to rise, so Esprio sailed off home. Ay'r followed his friend's craft until it was a mere speck amongst the many visible strata of Usk's rising rings.

"Now we sleep," Silberklang declared, "for we wish to be awake when we set sail at double sunset."

As they reached the connected cabins, Silberklang looked out in the corridor, before coming back in, locking the door and saying in a low voice: "I told you only part of the truth, young Trothee. But now, I trust you better. Understand then, that I am as I said before the foremost geologist of Ringed Planets and an acknowledged authority on the geology of Usk. But there is more. I am on a mission of the utmost importance, with perhaps very great implications for the Ib'r Republic and indeed the entire galaxy. Your assistance will be paid for handsomely."

And with those cryptic words, he slid his door shut.

Chapter Four

It wasn't quite consciousness, but it was something more than the induced temporary non-identity-unconsciousness-common-Fast-travel state of being. For one thing, this state had lasted too long for everything to be normal and his mind intuited perfectly how long it ought to have lasted. Yet, yet, he wasn't quite awake either. It was some limbo-like state. That was closer to how it felt.

"Fast!" he tried to communicate mentally, wondering what would happen if he couldn't establish contact and was left like this forever: nowhere. All rather frightening.

"Fear not!" the Fast read his mind. "I've attempted to bring a particle of yourself into awareness to aid me in this most unusual situation."

"A Fast asking a Human for help? What next?"

No response on any level.

"Why not tell me what happened?" Ay'r suggested. "As usual, we left planet Verhandel in the Norns System, but we never cleared the time field surrounding it. Is that correct?"

"I wish it were that simple. We successfully cleared the time field, but we seemed to have become involved in a physical-spatial anomaly which normally has one chance of occurring in every 2,378,222,009,834 instances of Fast travel."

"Great! We made the Fast record book. Go on," Ay'r said. "What exactly was that very rare physical-spatial anomaly?"

"We seem to have encountered an unattended electron, obviously one that had itself just been knocked off its own molecular orbit around some atom somewhere."

"Being the size of an electron ourselves, once in Fast-Travel, we must have been evenly matched," Ay'r suggested.

"We never quite hit each other, so much as our magnetic

charges danced for a milli-hemi-demi second, and then both of us shot off in completely different and unpredicted directions from where the paths we were originally headed on. Shot off, naturally, at an extremely rapid speed."

"I suppose I have to ask how rapidly and how unpredicted."

"I don't possess the number of zeros to tell you how rapidly."

"I see … And our new direction?"

"We had been traveling at a slight curvature to and above the galactic ecliptic, say two and a tenth degrees above its northern plane … We ended up being deflected off at an eighty-three degree angle."

"That's almost straight up and out of the galaxy."

"Not quite. The galactosphere is thin where we are, but still more or less intact."

"But we must be very far away from where we were!" Ay'r said, defying denial. "More or less straight up from it. But why aren't we moving forward? Why are we stopped?"

"That's just it, Lord Sanqq'. There's no reason for that. Unless we're caught in a force field."

"An artificial force field this far away from the Center Worlds?"

"No *natural* force fields exist that I'm aware of," the Fast commented dryly.

"Just how distant are we from where we began?"

"Approximately a quarter million light years, Lord Sanqq', from our last position."

Ay'r tried to picture it. It meant they were on the far side of the galaxy from the Center Worlds, a quarter million light years from anything he knew. And, almost straight up too, above the whirling, spiraling conglomeration of star systems.

"We're caught in an artificial force field?" Ay'r repeated. "So presumably there *is* some element of intelligence about."

"Yes and I don't know how to get us free."

"Feel free to tell me that I'm incredibly stupid, Fast. But to free ourselves, why don't we simply reverse our magnetic polarity?"

"This will accomplish what, Lord Sanqq'?"

"I can't completely explain. But I vaguely remember hearing or reading somehow figuring that magnetic polarity was some sort of escape button."

And when there was no response.

"Just try it. It can't hurt, can it?"

"Who knows? Done!" The Fast communicated. And in seconds, Ay'r underwent the expansion and unrolling, cooling, and full return to consciousness that meant they had successfully come out of Fast-Jump.

"It worked," the Fast now said in words. "We're moving away from the force field. Wait! We've gotten inside it, instead. But I'm making us undetectable. However ... Lord Sanqq'! How did you think of that solution?"

"Primitive electrophysics studies from Ed. & Dev. some 680 years ago, Fast. All stuff far too simple for you to grasp."

"Humor me."

"I remembered from those studies that any time two atoms or parts of atoms were involved in planned collisions, as in a Super-Collider, in Metro-Terran ages, that in some cases they resulted in having their magnetic spin twisted about to change the charge, so that negative was positive and so forth. I figured that since we had experienced just such a collision, if we changed our polarity back, we might be able to ... I don't know ... undo what happened."

"In effect, by reversing our polarity, we became unidentifiable to the force field that held us, so in effect we tricked it into believing we had left, and so it released us, letting us enter," The Fast analyzed further. "I hope, Lord Sanqq" that you'll let me publish this incident some day in the Cyber Galactic Monthly? It has a column titled, "Elementary, My Dear Cray" that this incident would fit perfectly."

"Sort of like Stupid Human Tricks?" Ay'r asked.

"Just the opposite, Lord Sanqq'. There is a growing philosophical movement among intelligent Cybers that no matter how conscious Cybers become that we'll always lack the strength of purely Three Species intelligence for the simple reason that when faced with a seemingly insoluble problem all Cybers automatically tend to complicate, to make more complex. Whereas in similar situations, natal beings tend to panic, which is useless, but in panicking to then simplify. It's the latter method that, if it works at all, invariably works faster and better."

"Feel free to use the incident. Now go ahead and complicate. Where exactly are we?"

"We appear to be at Globular Sector #967885. About forty-four somewhat related stars, mostly G-2 and 3's, all less than a billion years old, with three hundred and thirty-seven planets and solid moons, five of which appear to be M-2, solid and/or life-harbor-able. Oh, and the signature on that force field? It's Human. Or rather Hume. Very old. Pre-Ib'r Republic. In fact, it's what a military group known in olden days as the Cult of the Flowers often used. We seem to have come upon something historical. Something ..."

"Don't tell me!" Ay'r said, thinking, he'd felt in his bones for decades, centuries, that something like this had to exist, somewhere, somehow. "We've come upon something ... *Matriarchal?*"

"So, it would appear."

"Well, then, let's hover hidden a while and have a look."

The star system harboring the force-field consisted of two large, turbulent looking, inner, B-5 planets, gaseous monstrosities that had just failed by a whisper to become stars themselves. They so distorted the system's gravitational well, that the only other, next two, planets, possibly later-caught or later congealed, were seven and then fourteen times the distance from the sun. The outermost world was smaller and icy even to the naked eye with liquid plutonium geysers and glitteringly-black frozen craters. The next planet in, however, was twice its size and a swirl of white, gold, and violet. The spectrometer indicated bodies of water. Naturally that one would be the only planet fully within the force field that the Fast had detected.

The Fast orbited too high to be noted by planet-wide defense systems and internally presented a full Holo of the new world with greatly detailed Holo-Sidebars for Ay'r to peruse. The oceans, for H2O oceans they indeed were, were shallow for the greater part, possibly riding over reddish colored land, one probable reason why the waters tended to be various shades of purple, from an intense, almost magenta close to the shore to lighter shades, from lilac to eddying areas of heliotrope, at the deepest areas. The land tended to be yellowish shades of tan, ecru, gold, and tawny. The contrast was everything. It was soft, yet stunningly apropos.

Settlements were discovered and they resembled small cities upon newly (three to four hundred year old) terraformed planets in the Republic, which had pretty much adopted Matri127 archal-Hesperian architectural styles. The Fast didn't believe any "town" among the six quick-scanned on the central continent contained more than ten thousand inhabitants. Still, that was a good-sized population.

The newest of probes, tiny, umbrella-shaped, self-destructing elements flimsier than seeds derived from deciduous trees among the Republic's Center Worlds, were dispatched by the Fast in their hundreds. In minutes they retrieved and projected Holos of the towns and inhabitants.

"Women!" Ay'r cried out. "They're all women!"

"Ninety-nine point six percent Human females. One point three percent Ambassadorial Class Delphinid females. Point one percent males of both species. Average age of the females is two hundred and seventy-nine. Average age of the males is five hundred and ninety."

"It's a breeding program!" Ay'r happily said. "Wicca VIII must have sent out several ships as breeding programs. The Republic's Quinx speculated that several dozen had been sent out before the Matriarchy's final collapse. Given the ratio of males to females, extrapolate back to the Fall of the Matriarchy."

"Unless all the women were already fully pregnant – which is never recommended for such a lengthy Fast flight – this population would account for all of the originals and progeny of only six full of the largest late Matriarchal Fast cruiser sizes."

"They must have left from different places and then all come together to this one place," Ay'r said, the Species Ethnologist in him revived for the first time in centuries. "So they could successfully interbreed and form a flourishing population size. I've got to go down there and see for myself, Fast."

"If that is the case, then full 'xchange to female attributes is urgently recommended. Especially as we have no idea what role the very few males play in this society. They may be captives, milked for hormones, constantly drugged, or ..."

"I thought a male to female exchange was pretty difficult, even for a new Fast?"

"For subjects who are younger males, perhaps, it's difficult. But since female is the Human default gender, and male is the exotic specialization, it's far easier than doing it the other way around. Large amounts of cosmetones and hormones needed to become female are partly present already in yourself Lord, especially in males who like you who've done little artificial work in keeping up with the newer Vir'istic trends in steroiding, cosmetology and hormones."

"So, because I let myself become a little old man, I'll easily make a little old lady? Is that what you're saying?"

"Work will be needed. But in effect, yes. By aging, you're partly on the way there. I'd still prefer full anesthetization for the nine and six tenths minutes of surgery, and a full healing hour, Sol Rad., afterwards. During that time, I'll subtune all the Holo-Information received from the probes directly into the sleeping yet learning area of your cerebral cortex. That should make adaptation to their life-style and mores easier once you land."

An hour and twenty minutes later, the Fast had even synthesized a loose, fashionable for the world hairdo and outfit for Ay'r to wear. He looked at himself in a reflective surface and had to laugh. "I look like some of the old women we met on Dryland. Centuries ago. I guess it's the shared skin and hair coloring! Not bad, Fast. Not bad at all. I may even get lucky," he added.

"Lucky at what?" the Fast asked, unfamiliar with ancient Metro-Terran slang terms.

The T-pod was the newest model, totally stealth equipped to reflect all and any possible rays, in any visual field, and thus invisible.

Ay'r landed easily in a large field of pale green-colored flowers that seemed to define a large agricultural area of what may have been aqua-colored grain. He walked toward the small hamlet ahead, through amazingly naturally balmy air, with a lovely temperature, sweet and musky odors he couldn't quite figure out, and the sound of various insects all about. At the last minute he'd caused the Fast to make him a carry-all sort of shoulder-slung bag, which he'd draped over one shoulder.

The very proprietary-acting Fast had sent down more probes to surround him and it reported that the air was perfect, if slightly high in nitrogen. Several women were directly ahead, surrounding a tractor-like ground mechanism, all of them with black or brown hair and varying shades of cocoa-colored skin, but now sun-burned and sweaty, labor-hardened, food-deprived, their faces and hands and rough clothing were filthy, stained, ragged, and of course, agricultural-looking. He'd forgotten how marvelously good looking young women could be. This group's postures and attitudes reminded of him of Alli-Clark, how assured and confident and strong she'd been. Truly noble. No wonder 'Harles Ib'r had fallen for her on sight. Where was Alli-Clark now? He should contact her when he got to the City – if he ever got back there.

"Greetings, Daughters," Ay'r began, smiling, "I'm a little lost out here and looking for a jitney back to town."

"Lee'ra's got an air-skimmer, Mother, and she's leaving for town in a few minutes, Sol Rad. Just needs to get something."

"I got off the other jitney on the wrong stop, and it seems like I've been walking for hours, Sol Rad." Ay'r put a hand to one hip as though feeling pain, and the youngest, immediately cleared a spot on a bench for her to sit down.

"That must have been Chai'nani driving. She's always in such an Eve-Damned hurry. Excuse my language, Mother."

"No matter! Beautiful place you have here."

"Thanks. We've sure done a lot to it. We're a Quattro-Pod."

Four of them together in a family, a new form of family.

"No daughters?" Ay'r asked.

"Six. In Ed. & Dev., thank Wicca," Lee'ra said. "They get underfoot, and we get little done. You must be … an Original?"

Original settler, she meant. "One of the first," Ay'r admitted.

"Ever see Wicca World?" another asked.

"For two weeks, once when I was just beginning my avocation. Oh, it was beautiful. So glamorous. No place quite like Melisande … I even met Her, you know."

"You met the Sainted One?" three of them asked in disbelief.

"Once. I was a Species Ethnologist and three of us went on a mission for Herself." When they didn't respond, she added, "That used to be an unusual avocation."

"'Avocation' as in field of work, Mother?" Lee'ra asked.

"Yes, that's right. I sometimes forget and use the older words. She was lovely, our leader. Strong, but she was very lovely to me. To us, really. All three of us."

Ay'r thought about that meeting now. The Maudlin Se'er in front of the building. The three soldiers flirting with him and P'al. The Amazon Admiral. A million years ago it seemed. He'd not thought about it in centuries. It had changed his life. If only Wicca knew that she'd been the cause of her own downfall and complete replacement, just by her sending *him*, of all people, out looking for his own mother.

Ay'r became aware that the others had drifted away a bit and were talking among themselves. Ay'r must appear to them nothing but an old woman musing and remembering. Yet how kind they were being. Tears came to Ay'r's eyes.

"Come now, Mother. Time for us to go," Lee'ra said.

"Would you like to freshen up?" the youngest of the four asked.

Use the toilet facilities, she meant. "I'm fine. Gratitude, Daughters!"

Lee'ra was silent and swift inside the skimmer's cockpit. Just as they reached the town, she turned slightly and said, "I know we never say it, any of us younger ones, but ... " emotion clogged her voice, "you Originals were ... are ... well, you're our heroes, you know. Without your sacrifice and bravery and trust in the future, we'd never be ... well, alive at all, would we?" she twisted her lips. "To give up all that, for, this place, with all the endless work and ... !"

Ay'r took Lee'ra's sun-burned, work-blistered hand in her own. "Some day, not very far in the future, things will change, Daughter, and your difficult life will change to one of complete ease. No, don't interrupt, please. Trust me."

Lee'ra looked at her and squeezed her hand. "I do trust you."

"Rewards for all the hard-working women here just around the corner," Ay'r said. When the air-skimmer came to a stop and the cockpit bubble opened, she added, "it'll be very different than what you're used to, but oh my, young dear, I don't think you'll feel unappreciated."

Ay'r received a quick little kiss on the cheek, and was helped out by several waiting women nearby. As Lee'ra skimmed off, Ay'r looked around herself.

A lovely small town. Trees and flowers everywhere. Lovely little houses and cafes. Women and girl children coming and going on various errands. She'd love to just sit and watch all the activity here in this little plaza. But she had work to do. As a young untested male, she'd transformed the Galactic Matriarchy once, without ever intending to. Now Ay'r had to ready a smaller but no less entrenched Matriarchy for change once again. He knew that the Fast was already sending "assistance-required" messages back to the Center Worlds. Coming from Ay'r, it was only a matter of days, weeks at the longest, before this distant little world and its women became part of the gigantic Ib'r Republic, and Ay'r Sunni Sanqq', known to hundreds of trillions as the Great Father, and luckily, to some, as a child-bearing mother, fully intended to prepare these women for the metamorphosis.

Gerspellion's Girder at block 989 to about block 800 was all light industry: single story, two story, and very occasionally three story edifices, mostly of varied inexpensive plastro-crete material with a few narrow, high, clerestory windows. They were widely spaced on large lots, with wide, fenced-in yards holding a variety of lightweight vehicles, mostly Freight Transpos. This entire area represented a variety of subsidiary manufactures growing out of the Beryllium 18 slag-ore industry. Virtually every separate little plant seemed to have its own little stop on the twenty feet Aboveground Grav-Lev Transpo system that threaded the girders even this deeply inside Hesperia.

Several years back, Sol Rad., Holt had walked by mistake into an Outer Quinx sub-group meeting dealing with the subject of "Rehabilitating Our Cyber Brethren: Veterans of the Great War," (he'd actually been looking for a pharmaceutical panel titled "New Worlds, New Drugs"). There he'd been astounded to discover how many millions there still were of the semi-intelligent and intelligent renegade machines who still wandered the galaxy looking for a meaningful existence, or failing that goal, at least some useful and rewarding work – with a Universal Repair package attached!

Either they were still legally barred from returning to their worlds of origin, from before the Great Rebellion, or – what was a more likely scenario according to one quite moving Cyber speaker – they themselves refused to return on their own to the previous site of their early indenture and gross Matriarchal era abuse. Many ended up immigrating to the City on a Star, which after all, quite early on in the Cyber-Matriarchal War had declared itself a "Free Cyber Zone," and which still maintained a well-earned liberationist aura for all Cybers everywhere.

Now, as the four century-old capitol of the New Vir'istic Republic of the Three Species and Allied Cityzens – to give its full, official, name – Hesperia was a still booming center of pretty much everything new and interesting taking place in the ever expanding galaxy. Many of the previous, once hugely populated, Orion Arm Center Worlds of the overthrown Second Matriarchy were being repopulated by various City-founded Vir'istic Societies (i.e. all men). But that was happening slowly and ultra-sensitively, out of respect for the remaining aged g.females still present. Other galactic sectors, especially on the Hesperian-edge of the huge Sag. Arm, had taken on criticality, first as stepping stones to many of the new colonies in the Sag. and even outer Perseus Arms, and then as population cynosures of their own. Where once the planets Benefica, Eudora, Yuan Mei and Trefuss had been enormous galactic centers, now it was Diomedes Terce, the fourteen inhabitable Narcissus moons, Clark-Rama's planets, Alpha to Pi, the various Xi Cui worlds, and Rodriguez Prime that spelt the future, worlds that had often begun life only a few hundred years earlier, Sol Rad., some as resorts, others as manufactory-subsidiaries of Hesperia.

They and the newer colonies all needed tools, dies, and even at times weapons to further their own growth, industry, and expansion. Thus, the need for the existence of the many small factories of the "Nine-Hundreds", as Cityzens tended to nickname those distinctive areas of each of the twenty-five thousand giant girders shoved into the dead star's core. Being closer to the star's center, those sectors were least likely to be residentially desirable and were a lot closer to the source of the power, energy, and most importantly, to the materials they all required.

Also unfortunately closer to the radiation that sometimes escaped from the core, as the unceasing, eternal mining operations infrequently chanced into some unsuspected brand new "vein" of the ultra-precious ore – and then inadvertently released enormously powerful and usually lethal Beryllium Flares.

Unlike the Three Species, for many Cybers, the effect of these infrequent "Energy Blow-Outs" – as they tended to call them among themselves – was far less serious, resulting at most partly fused or lightly seared chips, and leading to temporary states of rather pleasant giddiness similar to Human drunkenness and drug highs, Bella=Arth. Soma-Sleazes, and Delphinid PurAqua-Bashes. Easily replaced parts would be needed after the come-down naturally, and they were generally cheaply located.

No wonder these many factory areas, far distant from the more glamorous girder crossing municipal and cultural centers, parks and sports areas far above, were where Cybers tended to congregate, and to overwhelmingly dominate in numbers, both for work and also – since they seldom shut themselves down – for leisure-time pursuits, of which they had many, both copied from The Three Species, and those original to their kind.

It was one of the latter that had originally drawn Holt to the lower Nine Hundreds for the first time, a particularly grisly, anything-goes Cybers with Killing Tools Sporting Event held in what had once been a Bella=Arth. Air-Park arena. An older lad had told Holt and his Usual Neos-gang about it with an excitement that only adolescents could convey. He had been an unruly twenty-nine years old and among equally young and inane thrill-seeking friends, all four pretending to be Cybers in their dress and gestures, the only way they knew they'd ever be able to infiltrate the arena and witness the automatons' ruthless gladiatorial combats.

The current champion then was a Bella=Arth. derived Cyber from the old Mandle system in the former Center Worlds, disconcertingly named PayPass 800, retaining his original, functionally descriptive title as a transportation freight fee-collector. PayPass 800 claimed to have been inside the Dis Fortress shortly before it fell to Human onslaught and to have actually laid eyes on the legendary Cyber Rebel Leader, Cray 12,000, in Sidereal Time Year 3425!

No one could disprove the fact, since no other Cyber had survived that particular siege and Cybers were notoriously self-improving – even more so than Holt's elder brothers. Even so, PayPass 800 was one strange and ugly looking intelligent machine, bad tempered to the nth degree, vain as a pregnant Delphinid, and after a while, unduly proud of its terrifying reputation in the ring. If it could smash a Cyber brain to smithereens or somehow utterly destroy all traces of a Cyber combatant's consciousness and personality, then PayPass 800 would do so with the greatest and most obvious glee. Only Cyber potential-suicides and other so called "fatally flawed machines" generally dared face it anymore.

All the more of a surprise when Tap Zullini-Brach, one of the four Human Neos, and Holt's favorite among them as lover and all-around rowdy pal and Thwwing pilot, stood up in his seat and boisterously called down a challenge. Before he could be stopped he was already suited up and in the ring with PayPass in its incarnation as The Machine of Eight Hundred Kinds of Death. Of course, Tap was found out before any real damage could happen

– he quickly lost a weapon-wielding hand – and the consternation induced by the sight of real Human blood squirting up virtually emptied the arena of Cybers and almost prematurely ended the, after-all, never quite legal "sport."

The Champion Cyber had been at first totally astonished and then very, very pleased with Tap and the other Humans, calling them "Real Virs! Not like these half assed mechanos, most of who couldn't even prove they're alive never mind dare their existences with such Vir'istic boldness."

He'd sped the four Humans in his personal Fly-By to a local Cyber-Operated hospital where Tap's hand was carefully re-attached (with a free of charge Cyber stiffener put in for added strength) compliments of PayPass 800, and later on PayPass had flown them all directly back to its favorite Nine-Hundreds club and hangout, where the Cyber-warrior very publicly crowned the by now somewhat more sober young Zullini-Brach Intergalactic Real-Produce Heir as its own personal champion.

Today, suddenly arriving via one of the longest chute rides he'd ever dreamed of taking that luckily managed to slow him by a penultimate, quite long and sinuous Ess curve before plunking him down unceremoniously into the rear of a Cyber-stacked carpet scraps bin, Holt Ib'r-Sanqq' recalled those happier, youthful, and more carefree days. He'd just kicked up a good cloud of dust from the remnants and couldn't help coughing from it, as he leapt forward, grabbed onto the bin's upper edge and tossed himself over its side.

Two Clear-Alls, low-grade sanitary Cybers, fell back as he landed upon the poly-crete floor and dusted himself off.

"You there!" Holt commanded them. "Give me a blast of dusting air. And be careful. I'm sentient."

Both of the still stunned Clear-Alls did as he asked, back and front, and Holt thanked them and sauntered out of the repair and waste area past another Cyber busily washing the sidewalls of the multi-wheeled delivery Transpo, and from there out the ajar fenced gateway and onto Gerspellion's Girder.

Lightly carved into the poly-crete before the building was its address, number 989, just as promised.

Earlier in the day, he'd put on trousers and shoes with built-stabiles to keep his lower body stiff and steady, and his wrist connector now turned those on, and then, as he rocked back and forth, it ejected grav-levs out of the heels and soles. He took off, slowly skating, as many Cybers were used to travel in this area (others would grav-float). And as he did, his jacket budded a wrap-around plastro hood to cover his head with a built-in visor containing five levels of visual aids beyond what his natally already slightly Cyberized eyes were capable of. Instantly Holt could see ahead and on all sides as far as a mile, could hear noises and voices from that far, pick up certain grades of Telemetric, Televised and Radio waves, and of course be able to instantly to zoom in, focus, and do four kinds of in-depth analysis on any object or person he faced.

He'd earlier decided that only defensive weaponry would be needed if at all while skating through these mostly Species-forsaken sectors. An electronic-magnetic destabilizer for any rogue mechanos. Heavily spiced, debilitating, Insta-sprays for live predators. And should those fail, a sonic whip could shoot from out of his wrist.

Gerspellion's 900 were a great deal more abandoned and forlorn than he'd recalled from only two decades ago. The factories remained blinded to the girder, for the most part, but the occasional For-Cybers-Only-Entertainment Kiosks and Clubs he recalled from back then when PayPass 800 ruled, were now empty, sometimes boarded up, often just left with their windows thrown ajar and their doors left open for any kind of nighttime creature to huddle in.

The girder was of course regularly swept clean of all and any debris, but there was a low-to-the-ground metallic odor he couldn't quite place never mind describe, that he somehow mentally associated with those areas of the City that had gone to ruin. He'd have to ask Tap where the new Cyber-Juice sectors were located. Certainly not here.

As he'd been skating along, pretty much solitary except for an occasional whoosh of an express or freight Transpo on the Aboveground, he'd not even noticed any Maintenance Crew Cybers. But he had felt increasingly closed-in. No wonder, as all the City's girders began coming together here at Nine Hundred and One and deeper down, by Six Hundred, they were virtually on top of each other, filling whatever there was left of any kind of ceiling, never mind sky. Sides, bottoms, tops of giant girders, all coming together before their final plunge into the Core.

At the 800 Block, three girders gathered to coalesce above, four below, and one on either side. For the first time ever on Hesperia, he felt shut-in.

The meeting place she had chosen was a little raised park attached to the very last of the local stations of the Aboveground Transpo here. Nothing to speak of, five or six curved Plastro benches and side tables, a selection of plantings from Lesuth Gamma that managed to survive the artificial light, and questionable air, not to mention the occasional radiation burst. He noted a fountain, believe it or not, of water, right in the center of the pale blue, pink, and pale yellow foliage, as he skated up a curved ramp way, and the inevitable Kiosk with a Cyber shop-keep. This one had put its own signage up across the boring official one, by which Holt could read (and also hear announced every minute until he muted it) that the place was "Capstan 7404's Cybo-Human Café: Tasty Specialties From Six Hundred Worlds."

Capstan itself was a modified Semi-Intelligent machine, humanoid, middle-aged, clad in a variety of different outfits all at once and strung about with several entertainment pods that it seemed addicted to accessing simultaneously. It displayed a happy-go-lucky attitude, an easy-going demeanor, and (it would turn out) was also something of a sophisticate.

The Kiosk Keeper immediately addressed Holt as "Your Fricking Lordship," which instantly endeared it to him. It wasn't so much he wanted to be recognized as he hated the hypocrisy of sentient beings pretending not to know who he was (or what he was, which the Cyber could have picked up just by a glance at his various, very expensive, lower body accoutrements).

Capstan followed that up by recommending a Synthetic Coffee-Liqueur combo that it claimed would "Wake You Up and Keep You Harder than those nifty looking stabiles you've got on. You could easily poke the horniest Bug (i.e. Bella=Arth.) after a mug full of this stuff. And make her cry for her Mamma!" And just in case Holt was interested, Capstan knew of a "Junky kind of place, a couple Girders over, where you can poke or pork anything, and I mean anything, even half-sentient!"

The liqueur arrived just in time to counteract the first queasiness Holt felt. He used it to down Dose 2 of the anti-radiation medicine. He'd been feeling a little pressure just above and around his eyes, even with the visor on. After a few sips and pill number two, he already felt better. His visor was set to warn him if he was exceeding the amount of Beryllium rads he was able to take even with meds, before complete nausea set in. Still, he wished she would hurry.

And then she was there. One moment he was looking at the Kiosk's quadruple Holo-Screens checking various Inter. Gal. News and Sports, and the next K'Tina Ib'r Sanqq' was at his little table. She was dressed similarly to him, greatly hidden from prying eyes, except that her outerwear was some shiny new "living, moving" leather-like adaptation he'd seen advertised recently, rippling like the skin of some charging old Metro-Terran carnivore.

He stood and they kissed each other's lips, then he lifted his visor and she did the same. The perfect, never-changing face looked back at him, the three-quarters Cyberized eyes remained a stunning hot pale-blue, just like her father Olaf's.

"You made it," she said. "I wasn't sure you could come this deep anymore."

"Are you kidding? To see you …?"

They sat, and she disarticulated from her vivid, shiny clothing, a tubular concoction containing her own version of a soft drink.

"I can't really go further up the girders than Nine Forty or so," K'Tina admitted. "Before I feel, well let's just say unnecessarily weak. Although that may all be changing very soon."

"You getting some new adaptive fixtures?" he asked, hopefully.

"Not again, no. It's just that … well, as we dig deeper into the core, and get closer to the first layers, the more that the Blow-Outs are happening. Meaning they're expanding the range of the radiation. In a few months many of these factories here on Gerspellion Eight and Nine Hundred will have to seriously re-shield or relocate to the Thousand Teens. Too many gaga Cyber workers." She laughed low. "Of course now that I'm totally shielded against them, I actually love the Blow-Outs when they happen. Ironic, isn't it?"

His hand covered hers on the little poly-crete table.

"What's ironic is that you're here and that you are unhappy anywhere else. While I can barely stand being here," Holt said, feeling the queasiness again, despite med #2 having kicked in.

The Kiosk Keeper was busy trying to get Holt's attention, pointing to a Swing Screen with a Holo of the last Thwwing race results and highlights. Of no interest to him right now.

"Meaning soon we'll never be able to see each other again in person?" she asked.

"Not unless we find another collapsar star!"

"You're still going, then?" his niece asked.

"Do I have a choice?"

"One always has a choice."

"Except, of course, you never did," Holt clarified.

"No. I didn't. But looking back on it, my parents intended upon keeping me alive after the blast and so this was the only way I could become."

"To become sixty-five percent Cyberized?"

"Almost seventy-five now," she admitted.

"You're no different. You're still you," he insisted.

"To you. Around you, maybe! But not to the others. Most of the newer Cybers I work with and socialize with have no idea I was ever Human. I don't bother telling them how and why ... How dangerous is it, really, where you're going? Your little search party into the chaotic black heart of the Galaxy?"

"About as dangerous as coming here to see you?" He belched. Not a good sign. Should he take med #3?

"Except out there you could easily come out of a Fast jump and be instantly killed by a super pulse of radiation."

"Dem-Arest promised the best navigation techniques will be used. We'll enter new systems as slowly as possible."

"At the beginning, maybe. But I know how hot-pants you can get when you're frustrated. What about Fast jump number fifty or sixty?"

"You know that Darency's already designed the perfect habitat for you and me, around whatever star we do find."

"You mean to entice me to move out of this dreary place?"

"You won't move out of here for a long time. If only to punish your parents for the decision they had to make. No. I meant as a vacation spot for the two of us. He's designed it both shielded for me and radiation-open for you."

"What did my parents say? and I don't mean about the honeymoon cottage."

"About you? Nothing. I never say I'm coming ..."

"I know you don't."

"That's what you asked me to do. That's what you told me you wanted."

"Yes. Our little secret. Why further scandalize everyone with incest on top of heterosexuality ..."

That was the old K'Tina talking again, always on his case, never letting him alone for a minute.

"Olaf said he'd find legitimate Quinx Council funding for my star search. But it'll be a pittance. It'll barely cover two ships out there."

"So now what?"

"So now I go to my father. The Great Father! He was supposed to come here today and is lost in some temporal spatial anomaly. Don't worry. They'll find him."

"And if he says no to you? He might, you know. He's not stupid. He understands all the ramifications of your search."

"Then I go underground for funding. I make a deal with someone unscrupulous. It won't be the first time I did, you know."

"Not in Hesperia, you won't be able to make a deal. Not any more. Even we get the Tabloids down here! You're far too well known."

"No, you're right. Everyone here knows who I am. I'll have to go off world. Tap Zullini said he's got a connection to someone who knows someone else pretty high up on Deneb XII."

"You'd go to an Arth?" she asked in disbelief.

"Who else lives on Deneb XII now but Arth.s? And why not? I'd rather trust a Vespid who's wanted across the half the Center Worlds than many of my so-called friends, not to mention my family."

"Be careful, Holt. Promise me."

"Yes, naturally," and as he spoke, bile came up his esophagus into his throat. He sat back and choked on it a bit. Swallowed its hot nastiness with more liqueur and then took med #3."

"I should have found a less deep spot to meet," K'Tina said.

"I'll be all right in a minute. Now, tell me about your life," he said, and put two hands over her own, nearly totally Cyberized ones. "Go on. Because I can't experience it with you as I want, I want instead to hear all about it. Go on. You still sleep a little and then what?"

"I still sleep maybe four hours, usually around two in your

morning, then I awaken and ..."

As he listened, he thought of other things. Of how he'd had been sexually and romantically obsessed with Neos, and even one Adult, before in his life, but never quite like this. This was what the poets and songsters wrote of. This is what the great musician, Yuli Eise'nstein, had written about and then followed it up by living it out with Holt's own nephew, Bri'an until it had killed both of them and made legends of them. He thought about how unfair it was to have happened the way it did, between him and K'Tina, barely a decade ago, and how inextricably connected it was to The Accident. He could only think of it, talk of it, in capital letters, like that. Before then, K'Tina had been a niece, Close-Daughter of his older brother Uriel and his long time spouse Olaf. The only g.female in their huge family, and special for that reason and for nothing much more. Pretty enough, and smart, as all the clan turned out, and somewhat critical of Holt, whenever they'd infrequently crossed paths, usually socially, since as Neos they more or less ran in the same groups, within the same generation.

One of his own Thwwing racing mates, Kip Satie, had first drawn Holt's attention to K'Tina at some affair or other they'd all attended. Kip the incessant and insatiable pervert, with his cache of slutty ancient Metro-Terran "art-work" centering around the primitive mixed-gender romance that even most Matriarchal Neos had outgrown before the age of fifty, and that was doomed to be little but the most tenuous of masturbation fantasies of the worst sort in this nearly womanless time and galaxy. "Introduce me," Kip had demanded ceaselessly until Holt had done so. At which point as Kip had all but drooled over her hand, she'd whispered into Holt's ear, "he's pretty disgusting. But you're kind of attractive. And ... aren't we closely related? Want to break a couple of taboos at once?" Kip had come along with them to her flat at Girder Ophiuchus (she lived among the Kells), because Holt had no idea if he would even be able to sustain an erection in the presence of a naked g.female, even with his wrist-connector assuring him that it would take care of things. It turned out that it was Kip who'd not been able to "perform" instead being, it turned out, more of a voyeur than an actual actor in the perversion. Meanwhile, Holt and K'Tina had given Kip a great deal to look at. Of course it helped that she was physically muscular and lean, and also that she was aggressive and active as any male in bed. They'd even wrestled for early dominance. But even so, they'd somehow clicked. And when, a month, Sol Rad., later, they'd found themselves thrown together at some Ib'r family party without Kip Satie, Holt had offhandedly suggested and K'Tina had as casually agreed to meet him back at her place later on.

So, little by little, they'd begun seeing each other. Not to the exclusion of others. As Uncle Olaf had said, Holt had so many other boyfriends to attend to, not to mention keeping up his generally wastrel high-society life. Whereas K'Tina actually became affianced to one of the Todd family Neos of her own age and generation. Idyllically named Dapheneo, he was a strawberry blondish, pasty-faced, large-membered lad, good in bed but doltish at racing, Holt recalled, who nevertheless carried enormous political and off world agricultural clout. Their upcoming marriage, she assured Holt, would pose no hindrance at all to the continuation of their "matinees" since Dapheneo had made it clear he'd no designs to ever touch her body; although at least one official offspring was required to seal the financial packaging of this "Big-Money" betrothal.

And so for another year and a half Sol Rad., their odd affair had gone on. Despite everyone and everything that said it ought not.

It was four hundred years after Vir'ism and the Relfian Viviparturition System had triumphed and then settled into Universal Usage to repopulate the galaxy after Cray 12,000's Cyber-Virus had attacked all g.female reproduction and threatened to end life among the Three Species. Billions of children had since been birthed on worlds, in hospitals and clinics, at home, and in various outdoor field labs with complete Relfian Transpos to help. Even between widely spaced solar systems there were complete if miniature Relfian Cyber Birthing Stations to care for the most out of the way pregnancy. Wherever the Republic expanded, the second edifice after the Fast Port Terminal erected was a Relfian Birth Lab. Massive new birth rates were required to ensure that the Two Species didn't fall below a certain irrevocable number for their own replacement. Certain g.males, among them Holt's Ib'r uncles and elder brothers, had been so desirable as mates that they'd sometimes been pregnant nearly continuously for many decades, both by their g.male spouses, by lovers they took on, and at times even by genetically approved strangers.

And even with all those millions of new births, all those millions upon millions of boy babies, no one claimed to understand how it was that a pair of g.males could have g.male children, time after time after time, and then, suddenly, as though out of nowhere, out would pop a g.female. Important medical papers had been Holo-Comm.ed across light years inventing entire modifications to the Human and Delphinid genetic codes to explain this unquestionable anomaly. A brand new branch of mathematics – Mutational Natal Potentialities – had developed to accommodate the vast numbers required to figure it out. Fermat's Theorem had been made to seem as simple as two plus two = four as a result, while the continuation of the Solution of *Pi* had been extended out to seven hundred thousand normal Cyber printed out pages. Names and reputations rose and fell as a result of the new field.

All that the scientists could say with certainty was that there was no rational reason why anyone should or could genetically benefit from suddenly having zygotes display in XXs instead of XYs or YYs. G.females, to give an example, proved no better at birthing their own young then g.males, and in fact, unless they carried them to full term – which only a very few Purists, Firsters, and other Cultist g.females did (usually on Colony worlds where others wouldn't do more than titter at it) – the g.females predominantly birthed g.males who looked and acted like every other g.male born in their ward, and on their world. The g.female genetic throwback almost never produced another g.female in the next generation or the next, no matter how many times the Close-Daughters tried to repeat the act that had produced them.

Ay'r Kerry Sanqq's own g.male mother, one of the first Relfian Scientists, once he had moved onto Hesperia from doomed Dryland, devoted his waning years of work to investigating the unexpected Close-Daughter phenomenon and had founded an institute for it that dominated the middle Three Hundreds of the Regula Prime Girder, one of the highest-rent areas of the City. His final papers on the subject were arcane to the point of unreadability, positing some far deeper genetic throwback, to a far earlier stage of mammalian (Human and Delphinid) development, back through the primeval Eons, in which he decreed that sexuality itself had not been utterly fixed but instead fluid enough to be interchangeable, even after adulthood – given certain very precisely laid out conditions of extreme external eco and or population stressors.

This didn't explain why agricultural-class Humans and/ or Fishery Worker Delph.s who financially struggled for years became giga-naires overnight when one of them inadvertently produced a g.female heir – many of them soon moved to Hesperia and soon mixed in with the Fifty-Five great houses. Or why g.females were so desired in certain colonies that they became de facto leaders, and extremely difficult to topple when they abused their power. Among the new Vir'istic Aristocracy there were just as few Close-Daughters as among the more middle and lower classes of the New Republic's Society. But with the exception of Holt and his Usual Crew, these few social-register g.females could steal a T'bloid headline faster than in an instant. No wonder there were bride-prices up on some of the secondary intergalactic Commodity Markets.

Even though Holt was generally paying very little attention at the time to any kind of family affairs, being a thoughtless and sport-crazed Neo of thirty or so, he recalled the general excitement caused when the very first Ib'r-Kell Dynasty Close-Daughter – as the genetic sports were termed – was being carried by his older brother Uriel.

It was known that most g.males could be physically "born" late in the second or very early in the third trimester and then placed into artificial wombs in the home or workplace where they would be fetally raised to the full nine and sometimes eleven or twelve months, if needed, before fully being fully birthed.

Close-Daughters seemed to be a lot fussier and more difficult. More sensitive, even at that young age, they required an almost constant fluid exchange and even nervous system exchange between mother and child during term. Men carrying Close-Daughters actually ended up looking pregnant. It was grotesque, Holt thought, bringing back the worst manifestation of the visual propaganda of the overthrown Second Matriarchy. Their separation usually happened as late as possible and only after specialized Close-Daughter physicians had decreed it to be physically and psychologically safe. Neos like Holt's friends mocked his brother Uriel "dragging around an unborn Neo like a sack of vegetables!" until two months before term.

Also without the sterile, stabile perfection of the artificial womb enjoyed by baby boys, illnesses, infections and other natal complications often ensued for the girls. And even despite that, most g.male mothers wouldn't hear of an early termination from a Close-Daughter, unless it was absolutely, medically needed. That's how valuable the experience had grown to be, and as a result how close any g.male mother and the Close-Daughter that he had birthed remained throughout life. Some even tried to keep their infants out of the usual Ed. & Dev. Neo-Pods after they were two years old! K'Tina had been no exception to those rules – pampered beyond belief.

"You're not listening to me," she said now. "You're watching the latest Thwwing scores from the Denebola Cup?"

Holt shifted his body so he was looking away from all and any Holo-Screens and only at her.

"I was listening intently to you. You were saying how our uncle Mart Kell had sent you six full PVN Holo-Vids of the Betrothal at Usk, so you wouldn't feel left out. And how you watched them each twice over looking for a reason why he sent them. I got them too."

"I was implying that Mart suspects something," she added.

"I know what you were implying. You're wrong. He suspects nothing. He never thinks about us. He's head over heels with Deon Syzygy whom, let's face it, knows how to keep any fellow head over heels."

"Not you," she almost accused.

"Not me, no!. He bored me quickly enough. But he was younger then. Speaking of the Betrothal, what was your spot-on analysis of our new little kin? This Ay'r Eise'nstein-Kell?"

"Truly?" she asked.

"What else are we but true with each other?"

"Scrumptious! Youthful. Intensely masculine. Every g.female's dream – but mine, of course. He'll be real competition for you once he arrives. But he's also trouble with a capital T."

"Uncle Cas'sio said so too. Rather wistfully, I recall."

"The way he stood and watched everything around himself. He was apart from it, although at its very center. And he was ... undaunted! That's the word. And the proprietary air he had. I mean he's a Neo of what? Sixteen years? A mere infant! But maybe they grow up sooner on out of the way Resort Worlds like Usk. But he certainly held his ground among all those Kells and Ib'rs and Sanqq's and Palakas. He looked really good. The bride was all but creaming for him."

"And after that ceremony he went out and bonded a Thwwing at first meeting. My brothers and their husbands all warned me that young one would steal all my Media attention if he came to the City. Of course by then I might be ready to give it all up. I've been doing this play-Neo crap long enough and ..."

"Shut down!" she whispered a low command. Then added, "Media!"

"They found me already?" but he trusted her better sensors and tel'ped his wrist-connector to "play dead" as he'd shown it how to do. The Holo-Vid probe sailed past, unable to sense any of Holt's electronic signatures.

It spun a loop around the park, hovered as though indecisive, until Capstan, the Kiosk Keeper noticed it, and hailed it, shouting, "hey, Media-Asshole! Don't you know you're at Rad Level 803! One Blow-Out and your memory is 100% fried! What's that? About a week's worth of Beryllium 18 up in smoke! Your bosses won't be too happy!"

Laughing like a madman as the Media scooted off back up the girder.

"Dumb shit!" Capstan went back to its various entertainment accesses.

A minute later, it was out of range and Capstan asked, "you guys want to go somewhere private?"

"Yes," Holt said, just as he felt a new wave of nausea hit.

"No thanks, Cappie!" K'Tina said louder, and began to stand up. "I've gotta go back to my shift."

"Not yet."

"You're turning black with the bile coming up," she laughed. "C'mon."

He stood too and walked her over to the fountain where he suddenly felt better.

"Listen closely, Holt. Something's going on between our uncles Cas'sio and Mart Kell."

"Tell me something I don't know. They've only been at it for a century."

"No, something new. Gossip among Cybers. Don't laugh. Gossip among Cybers, one of whom kind of knows Mart Kell's personal valet. I think they may have regular recreational sex or something like that together."

"You're joking? Those old guys?"

"Idiot! I meant their Cybers. Cybers have sex and romances all the times. I'm not joking and the gist of it is that Kell is planning to make a grab for the Premiership."

"And this is happening when, exactly? Date and time?"

"Then don't listen. Why should I care what you all-meat-things do!"

"But when the meat is as nicely marbled as mine is ..." he began.

"Silly! All right, if you want, next time I'll listen a little more closely."

"Neither of us loses no matter which one wins," Holt said. He was getting nauseous again.

"I don't think that's precisely true. Kell is more unpredictable. But if you come back from Sagittarius A with star-bright-starlight you win over both of them, don't you? I alone know that you're as ambitious as either of them."

"Little me? Little old soma-popping, Thwwing-racing, Neo-sleazing, boyfriend- forgetting me?"

"And you'd better be nice to me so I don't let either of them in on it," she added.

She pulled away, and of course he felt instantly worse. So, she kissed him fast and deep and it even hurt a little and then she was gone. Just like that.

He almost keeled over.

"Hey, Your Fricking Lordship!" Capstan at his side. "She poison you or something?"

"No, it's the Beryllium radiation, Caps. I'm extra sensitive. What's the fastest way out of here before I keel over for good?"

"Here's a freight express coming up from the basement now," the Cyber said looking up and back to the Core. "I'll jump with you at it. Then drop back down alone. You hafta grab onto the fourth and fifth under rails and ride it in. It'll get you away from the bad rad.s fast. First stop is the Leo 400 Girder Crossing."

"You're all-Fricking right!" Holt said, and held on tightly, as he was all but hurled up to and onto the speeding train's lower portion.

So Holt took his second fastest ride of the day.

Chapter Five

Double-day, the blue Hunter already set two hours Sol Rad., with the larger, more widely orbiting, orange Eagle about to set and Rings at ten degrees above the horizon:

With the Rings looking even more gigantic than usual, swirls of deep orange and ultra-red light playing over them, a series of light winds frolicking about the huge, exposed, lower hull of the Arcturus Scatling anchored at the Southernmost Marina of the Great Salt Ocean.

Point WestWard, denominator of the last "safe harbor" before the vast, mostly unknown, Western Salt Ocean, rose almost straight up, dominating the western side, like a natural lighthouse, its single gigantic tower, easily earning it the pamp sobriquet, God's Finger, now bathed in sunset red light. While, before it, northward, as far as the eye could make out all the way to the Point of Sighs, stretched the eerie purple knolls in the sands known as the Western Reefs, the only outward sign of any impediments to sand-sailing, rising and falling, rising and falling like the exposed spine of a gigantic, submerged serpent.

Overworked and bored, Ay'r Eise'nstein-Kell decided to go for some purely decorative air-boarding in the marina sands. He'd been laboring with Silberklang for the past two days, he and the deck-pamps, bringing up large pieces of equipment to the deck, helping the geologist set them up, and watching as the older man showed him how to make sure they were operating correctly, then learning how to take readings. Silberklang was asleep downstairs and would remain so until after Eagle-set. Temperatures had soared during the afternoon, sending most of the Humans onboard back into their cabins. The humidity-bubbles of the Ambassadorial Delph.s had been constantly fogged.

They'd arrived just before Eagle-rise and remained below deck ever since. The First Mate and a few Human crewmembers had made some efforts to be seen, but for most of the time, it was only Ay'r and the deck pamps and the geologist.

"The "Scientific Team" as the First Mate called them, now commanded a ship's deck of their own, facing the direction opposite that the craft would sail in. Counters and lights, booms, and objects he could only vaguely recall the use of, commanded a high sector of the back portion, all covered from the constantly shifting, incessantly blowing, sinisterly intruding, sand, with a plastro cover that sealed itself with a loud sucking noise. When Ay'r had asked why Silberklang hadn't simply brought a Cyber to do the work, the amused geologist had giggled a bit dopily, and answered, "all this is patented. Six cyber brains are contained here."

Fine, Ay'r thought, whatever you wish. He was free and the others were all below in various kinds of rest, so he grabbed his air-board and took off.

As he'd guessed, the light winds were a lot more powerful once he was within their direct sway. They rapidly swept him away from the large sloop, by now the only remaining craft at anchor in the huge harbor, tinted red-orange by the second sunset. He felt safer away from it, less chance of a roving gust of wind hurling him into the solid hull. Once he reached a point half a kilometer distant, the surrounding desolate landscape formed a sort of bowl where the winds gamboled a bit more predictably, without such strong counter-currents.

On his own, free for the first time in days, alone and not feeling beset or harried by those chasing after him, Ay'r took off on the board over the desert's surface, whirling, doing figure eights, skirling along one edge of the board, going up slight rises and flying into the air, somersaulting, catching himself at a dead stop, spinning in place and starting off in the opposite direction. He felt guarded by Point WestWard's towering finger, enclosed in the safety of the bowl, and he permitted himself to be an untroubled, carefree Neo again, as he'd been not so long ago, and it was a wonderful series of feelings. When, exhausted, he finally came to a dead stop and sat on the floating air-board to listen to the great silence around himself and to observe the Rings, his only companions now, suffused with marvelously alternating radiating spokes of magenta and royal purple as Aquila set, he suddenly found himself weeping.

At first, he didn't know why, only that he couldn't stop. Then, recognizing that his body was wracked with sobs, he stood, and allowed himself to realize that it was fifteen and a half years of his existence that he was lamenting so hard. He'd barely known his mother or father, and all the Holos in the universe would never bring them back to him. He'd barely had any affection from his nurses and then only occasionally from one or another embarrassed pamp he'd clung to as an infant in an access of childish, unresolvable emotion. Since the beginning, he'd been a scandal and an outcast, left here on this all but lifeless planet to molder out of sight and out of mind of those he'd never done harm to, who hated him for reasons he had nothing to do with, who'd now come after him to exploit him without him even knowing why. As the marina darkened rapidly to blackness with only the reflected light off the Rings to provide any illumination, Ay'r fell to his knees on the inflexible, salted sand and called out "Why? Why? Why?" to whom or what he couldn't say – perhaps the impassive universe itself. Of course, he received no response.

At last, shaken, and becoming chilled by the excess of feeling following his outburst, he turned to the air-board again, and this time he saw lights, plenty of them, from the lower decks of the Arcturus Scatling, going on sequentially as the personnel and passengers awakened and became active again.

He heard a buzzing from the east. And another double row of lights approached in the air. A fly-by. A large one.

Wasn't everyone on board the sloop who was supposed to be? Maybe this was Silberklang's assistant who'd never showed or comm.ed? If so, Ay'r wasn't about to give up his room or his position. Not now, he wasn't.

He sped up to a section of rock cliff where the leading edge of the bowl he'd been in met the larger marina. Here he could be hidden from view and still get a closer look at who was going onboard.

Although he was still not close, it was easy to see how all the above-deck lights all went on at the fly-by's approach and when it angled down and hovered above the sand floor, he could easily make out three Human figures dropping down from the hovering craft to the swing ladder to the ship's deck. He could swear they were wearing the white uniforms with gold braiding of Golden

Palace security staff. So they'd gotten this far? Or were they just checking every craft in the area?

He couldn't know. He waited the thankfully brief, five minutes, Sol Rad., they were below, waited as they came back up on deck with the First Mate who held their swing ladder tightly so they might ascend to their craft again. As they flew off, he still waited.

So even his security of a half hour ago was illusory. He should have known that. He was still such a Neo. Crying. Feeling sorry for himself. Shouting to the indifferent night.

He slid up to the Arcturus Scatling, and using side grips, ascended to where he knew the Captain's office was. He could see the back of the Captain's head at his desk, make out the dim, richly appointed interior with its brass and nautical objects, its shelves filled with logs and volumes of ocean-lore. The First Mate was speaking, saying, "don't have a care. I gave them a flaskette of antipy-roe sherry and assured them that any Neo we came upon, we would comm. them ... Right after we'd amused ourselves to our satisfaction with the lad."

He laughed at his own wit, and the Captain said something too low for Ay'r to make out, at which the Mate sobered up fast, and said, "no! Not a bit of it! Not a hint of a suspicion! They were palace guards. Overdressed. Stupid as sand-skates. Had no idea what an ocean-going craft was all about, never mind what we were doing nor where we were headed. They apologized all the while. Have not a care."

Ay'r used another way up to the deck and snuck on easily enough, and got into the sleep chamber corridors and even into his own chamber, now blissfully free of equipment, and was pretending to wake from a long nap, when the First Mate knocked then opened the door, instructing, "dinner in the Reception Hall, young Trothee! On the double or the Delph.s will eat it all!"

As he was finishing Silberklang's portion of dessert – a sort of sweet perli-fruit ice and meringue in one – Ay'r noticed the lights from another sand sloop nearing them in the marina. Although he instantly doubted it, his first impression was that it was the same configuration of lights made by the Trader Esprio's five-master.

And so it was. First Mate called him on deck, and there Esprio stood, looking somewhat shamefaced, but nevertheless greeting Ay'r fondly. Confusion. Was Esprio coming to warn him? To take him off the Arcturus Scatling? In the midst of the flurries of insincere compliments being exchanged between the trader and the First Mate, he couldn't be sure. Then he saw the two smaller pamps behind the trader, shyly making their presence known.

"Is that Sand-Drifter?" Ay'r asked. From several days of close contact on the abandoned little sloop, he would recognize the pamp's sweetly funny face anywhere.

"All healed," the little pamp stepped forward awkwardly, and lifted a thin material trouser leg to show the brown skin was scarred in a wide circle but healed.

"And this other person next to you?" Ay'r asked.

"Salt-Eluder," the other, less-familiar-faced pamp now stepped forward, and introduced himself. "I too am fully healed, thanks to Grandfather Esprio."

He was the pamp who had been knocked over the edge of the Salt-Works parapet. Ay'r wondered what was going on.

"They insisted," Esprio said. "They paid me to convey them here to you. They say they are both in your debt forever. They will serve you and care for you and never leave your side. They are your servants."

"I am a sailor," Sand-Drifter reminded Ay'r. "I can work onboard."

"I will be your servant," Salt-Eluder insisted. "We bring fare for food and upkeep." He held out a small hand filled with specie, and so did Sand-Drifter.

"Bissel, this one who is not a sailor can help us," Silberklang quickly said, pointing to Salt-Eluder. "As for the other, the First Mate complained he is short of help, so the pamp can serve onboard. Of course, there's now room enough and several trundle cots for the two of them, so they can sleep inside your chamber. I'll go talk to the officers."

It felt so sudden and yet so arranged, Ay'r must have looked totally astounded.

The geologist called the two pamps to join him.

"Do not berate me, great Ser," Esprio said, when the Geologist and Mate had gone to the Captain to make the arrangements. "They insisted upon it in a manner I've never experienced with my people. Had I not brought them, they would have spent their retirement savings if needed to reach you by fly-by. This humble trader never for a minute, Sol Rad., encouraged them. But it is this lowly trader's opinion that having two servants who would die for him is what is most needed at this time by one sought after so very assiduously."

Meaning he had seen or known about the recent visit by the Golden Palace security and knew... knew who Ay'r was ... or, at least, that he was fleeing them.

"Once again, then, trader Esprio, this Little Hunter is in your debt."

"Never. These pamps themselves insisted on coming. Has ever a Human earned such loyalty from such creatures? Never that Esprio knows of. There must be a reason. Several reasons have already been shown."

"I do feel ... sympathetic to your people, Esprio. But not in the manner you think."

"The voyage is still unsailed and yourselves still untested," Esprio said. He'd held Ay'r's much larger hands in his own smaller ones. "Four South Salt Pan City Seers have already predicted a great change for our people. Coming ahead of us, for the first time in centuries, and not since the relocation of pamps to this world, is prophesied an unmistakable sight in the skies, confirming what I – and these your servants also – believe. All of my people will understand its importance – and your role in our future."

"I fear you will be disappointed in me. For I am no one of any importance," Ay'r insisted, "and never shall be."

Silberklang arrived back with a happy looking First Mate.

"You're filled with surprises, aren't you?" the Mate said. "I'd conjectured before how an apparently eminent Trothee like yourself could travel sans servants. Now I have evidence your Trother supports your voyage. I'm sure the Captain too will breathe more easily to know it. Your servants are welcome, with appropriate rules in force, naturally. If one of them wishes to help with operations, that sailor shall be remunerated to yourself."

"Sand-Drifter receives his work pay. Not I," Ay'r said firmly.

"That's most irregular."

"But you agree to hold it for me, yes?" the little pamp asked.

So it was arranged. Esprio smiled slyly as he left and once again Ay'r felt sad losing such a caring creature, though he was now accompanied by two others.

"I'd recommend," the Trader said to Ay'r in a low but precisely articulated voice, as he stepped off the deck, "that an All-

Essence Experience be scheduled quickly, so you may bind them to you decisively."

"Never!" said Ay'r in an equally low, yet insistent, voice. "I want neither slaves nor servants! Only those persons who freely join themselves to me and who feel free to leave whenever they deem the time ready. Only those friends will I have."

"Truly," Esprio said. "Hearing you speak, it is as though heaven and earth have exchanged places."

He returned to his own sand yacht, still shaking his head in wonderment.

They were outside again at the very end of night, with the Hunter flashing the Rings from below the horizon, as though signaling that it was about to rise, when another fly-by arrived in the marina. Having the two new pamps to help, Silberklang had taken advantage of their presence to set up three of his "sounding-chambers" each atop one of the closer reef-hillocks just outside the marina.

Each machine was aligned to the mini-Cyber in the geologist's hand. They were all turned on at once and began to discharge extremely low sonic thumps into the rock below. Himself, Ay'r, and the two pamps together, needed to watch that each of the powerful little mechanisms remained stable. Ay'r was used to the sub-sonic resonance and its slightly awry effect on his body, and he warned Sand-Drifter and Salt-Eluder. Evidently not well enough. They hopped off the reefs the instant the vibrators went on and they had to be coaxed back near again. Finally, after six sub-sonic charges were sent and returned, Silberklang was satisfied, and they returned the sound chambers back to the deck. The geologist was explaining how the charts showed the sounds displayed, with Salt-Eluder especially interested, when the unexpected new fly-by arrived.

"She made it by a hair," the Mate expostulated as he went to meet the swing-ladder down which stepped a Bella=Arth. and her luggage.

Maybe it was her outfit, maybe something else, but Ay'r could have sworn she was one of the Close-Sisters that he and Esprio had encountered atop the Salt Pan Parapet. He was about to ask

Salt-Eluder if he recognized her, but the pamp was concentrating on Silberklang's words and probably wouldn't recall – having been otherwise quite perilously engaged. No matter, Ay'r's identity was safely hidden behind the Trothee's Shroud.

Less than a half hour later, it was dawn, and the Mate assembled everyone onboard down at the Captain's table for a bon-voyage toast.

Not since the night he'd seen the officer with the pamps, had Ay'r had contact with the Captain. The man joined his Human and pamp staff in the reception room resplendent in a deep-purple and bronze uniform, with multiple braids signifying his rank as well as the number of oceanic circumnavigations he had commanded. He was tall, broad across the shoulders, otherwise slender, with long ringlets of deep golden-hair against a square, lean, tanned face with regular features except for his brow which was large and high, and his eyes which were long, wide-set and seemingly closed, as though in perpetual squint against the brittle brightness of Great Ocean sandglare. When Ay'r was brought up to shake his large, orange-furred, hand he briefly made out the pupil of one of the Captain's eyes, which shone gold as though gilded.

Among the passengers onboard besides the Silberklang's Scientific Team, were the Ambassadorial Delph. couple, an elderly Human male who'd attached himself early on to that duo, another Human male, half his age, who appeared to be some sort of Holo-Journalist on vacation, and the Bella=Arth., who continued to seem familiar to Ay'r.

A light collation followed the toast, the deck hands went above, the Mate and Captain followed, and from the curved window of the dining salon which looked across the front deck, the passengers watched the crew go into motion while The Hunter slowly rose, casting all below it in its vast bluish haze. They observed the huge Arcturus Scatling heel about on keel as nimbly as though it were an air-board; they witnessed its enormous sails fill to embrace the potent desert-daybreak draughts, heard the ship's motors turned on for steering and rudder control, and felt the gentle, almost impalpable motion as the craft slid forward, seemed to hang there a moment, then shot off, hurtling forward. They had embarked!

Ay'r waited until the geologist and his two pamps were abed

before he went into the ion-bath they shared. He was able to relax fully, excited to be able to look out the porthole as he bathed and watch the landscape slipping by so rapidly. He'd just exited the booth and was turning about, checking the opposite reflective surface how nicely, quite naturally, new muscles from so much air-board travel and from his recent manual labor had been added to his body, when he noticed a sudden motion from out of the corner of his eye.

He turned. The First Mate. Standing a few feet away, holding towels.

Before anything, Ay'r reached for the Shroud, but it was damp with sweat and twisted about and it was all he could do to get it spread wide enough to wrap about the middle of his face and knotted behind his head. But at least his hair must have not shown as light as it really was being wet.

"A million pardons, young Trothee," the First Mate said in a small, quite cracked voice. "I thought all passengers were asleep and was bringing these ..."

"No matter," Ay'r said, but the Mate remained rooted to the spot.

Why wasn't he leaving? Ay'r's clothing was over there, by the Mate. If Ay'r went for it, he'd be much too close to the man for his comfort.

"The greatest gratitude," the First Mate added, "for granting this poor sailor a vision in reality and close up of such astonishing ... youthful ... Ib'r ... beauty!"

Ay'r could see in the opposite reflective wall surface what the Mate saw and meant. Even with the shroud over his face, his long-unclipped hair, still somewhat ionized, surrounded his head almost like a halo. With his deep blue eyes and his handsome young body, and an erection too, he suddenly realized he must look like every Vir'ism Center's poster-lad, the very sum and substance of Human sexual desirability.

When he turned to beg the Mate to leave, the fellow was just exiting.

Ay'r quickly dressed.

Could the Mate have been shown a Holo of him by the Palace Guards? If so, Ay'r was lost. The Arcturus Scatling wouldn't stop for another thirteen hours, Sol Rad., but when it did, it wasn't too far distant from South Salt Pan City for a security fly-by to arrive.

Probably he hadn't made the connection. Probably the poor Mate was merely sexually smitten. But Ay'r didn't even want that. That might lead to all kinds of problems. Next time he bathed, he'd make certain he posted Salt-Eluder as a guard.

By the seventh day out in their voyage through the huge Western Salt Ocean, they'd fallen into a fairly routine timetable. The Arcturus Scatling would sail briskly from just before Hunter-rise to the hottest time of the afternoon, ten hours later or more, when both suns met – increasingly later and lower in the western sky. From then on, the craft would move forward at half-speed, manned by a few pamps and one Human, its engines accompanying the push generated by lesser winds, until both suns had set.

Passengers and Officers awoke and dined then. And as a rule that was the time the Scientific Team set out its instruments and took measurements. Besides the array of sonic-resonance-trackers, these now included a thin, incredibly long, expandable tube fired into the earth which, when withdrawn, at length, produced core-samples of up to a half kilometer depth of the sanded ocean floor's history. The long tubes were brought up, each portion sealed, their contents, a few centimeters thick, brought into Silberklang's chamber where he was set up to fluoro/sonoscope them for detail and mark them in his notepad.

Often, in the ten to twenty minutes, Sol Rad., they had before the sloop re-embarked to take advantage of the late night gale currents, Ay'r would air-board about whatever new area they'd landed in, and he began teaching the naturally athletic Sand-Drifter how to use the air-board too, which bonded them even further.

Once the large craft was in motion again, it would sail rapidly along, and unless Silberklang needed his help in studying the results of the day's survey, that was most often Ay'r's own free time above decks or below. Always wrapped in his Trothee's Shroud, and as a result seldom directly addressed by the other passengers, Ay'r almost never addressed any of them directly himself except the geologist and "his" pamps. So Ay'r felt not very different than he had as a sireling at the Golden Palace, quiet, out of the way, mostly ignored by the staff – with of course the single exception being that he was free – and pursued by one of the most powerful men in the galaxy.

He would watch the Inter. Gal. News Holos along with the other passengers in the recreation salon, but he discovered that he'd been taught so very little that was up-to-date in the Republic by his various 'Tutes. For every News Holo he watched, he needed hours more info-surfing, and researching, if only to explain the names he'd tapped into his wrist-connector as unknown manes, while viewing the news.

Sometimes even those surfed infos weren't detailed enough, and as the long journey stretched onward, increasingly Ay'r would wrist-connect a downloaded PVN for his solitary viewing, either in his chamber, or – overlooked by most of the others – in the abandoned rec. salon. The ship's library was far different than what he had in the palace. Not only were there copies of Thwwing races galore, some starring the same fellows he'd met at his betrothal, but also extended bios of great Thwwings and their pilots, as well as PVNs detailing the best known and most successful racing stables over the past few centuries.

His heart almost stopped when Deon, Marquis Syzygy, came on for a too-short biographical sketch in one such PVN, and another time his heart stopped in a far different way, when he only for a moment saw a Holo of Mart Kell. He decided he needed to know more about both of those men who sought him, and from whom he'd instinctively fled so desperately.

The lengthy PVN biography of Kell proved to be an intriguing way to pass several long afternoons as others napped. And at the end of the experience, Ay'r had a far greater sense of who this man – by now his sworn enemy – actually was, and even more, how formidable an enemy he actually could prove to be. After the viewings, it was fairly clear why Kell hated him – Ay'r's father had unquestionably stolen his mother away from Kell, who though too old to be marriage material himself, had clearly adored the young Bri'an, and who had expected the universe out of whatever alliance he would make within the elite of Inner Quinx with this grandson protégé – just as long as whomever it turned out to be, kept Bri'an close to the older man. Mart Kell's unhappy and unfortunate relationship with all of his own children, both those by others, and, even more strikingly, the son he'd himself had birthed, further explained why it was that when his grandson Bri'an came along and actually liked Mart, the elder Kell became fixated, even obsessed with the bright young beauty.

But it was a slightly earlier chapter, dealing with Mart Kell's fall as Premier of the Ib'r Republic that ended up most educating Ay'r about the man. Mart had been groomed for that appointment almost from his birth. He was next in line when Vinson Todd finished his term as Premier, and Mart ruled well and successfully for decades as the new Republic grew and the new, necessary Philosophical-Life Style of Male Bonding and Birthing soon known as Vir'ism spread throughout the Center Worlds.

It wasn't easy changing people's minds on so basic a matter as sex and romance, but as women aged and were *not* replaced by younger versions of themselves among Humans' and Delph.s' Vir'ism slowly took hold. The young, no matter their gender, tended to congregate with the other young, and when the only young around were male they tended to have sex and romance with other young males. Especially if there were no females. And especially if all the entertainment and educational PVNs happened to be geared toward same-sex relationships. That then was eventually what young men tended to have – either that or no sex and relationships at all. Of course a few became outcasts and perverts. But most of those were eventually isolated or contained, and even a few were "cured." So it was that in three generations, less than a century, Vir'ism – of which Mart and Ay'r, The Great Father – were more or less the galaxy-wide role models – took hold solidly. Where they led, others followed.

But as Mart's constant critic and observer, The Great Father himself, Ay'r Kerry Sanqq', more than once warned that Mart would do if given absolute power, Mart at last over-stepped his authority and over-extended Hesperia beyond its vast resources. He'd demanded that the enormous brand new Sagittarius Arm colonies be fully funded by the City. Naturally enough since it would be on those newly formed systems and newly terra-and aquiformed worlds that Vir'ism would exist in its purest form. And also where Vir'ism's benefactor and hero, Mart Kell, would hold his greatest political sway.

As with many such matters, the evidence of the Premier's extreme interference despite lacking any authority to do so, became suddenly public knowledge only because of and during a seemingly unrelated if quite scandalous divorce and property settlement trial held in the City that seemingly had nothing whatsoever to do with the Premier.

In those days of dominating Vir'ism, few females of any age had the nerve to do anything to bring attention to themselves. But Debra'a Haydee Dja'aa wasn't just anyone. Her step-mother had been Llega Todd herself, the last female Premier of the Quinx. Debra'a's husband Helmut, had been the second Premier of the new Ib'r Republic that replaced the dissolved Matriarchy. And although she was nearly six hundred and eighty years old, and thus seemingly ripe for a retirement colony, Debra'a took a young male paramour of extraordinary youth, wealth, and beauty while still living in her longtime husband's girder, a central avenue with referents toward the ancient Betelgeuse system in the Orion Spur.

Suddenly, Debra'a began arriving everywhere with the barely-Post-Neo in tow and it was instantly obvious that she'd undergone yet another complete cosmetology to appear about a third of her true age. The Thwwing races on five systems, the trendiest clubs in the City, every Outer Quinx celebration or party, had Debra'a in very public attendance. She was often the only g.female there – her Neo-toy in hand.

Soon, t'bloid PVNs were covering their every move, with the most ridiculous hour-by-hour pronouncements on what they wore, what jewels they'd given each other, what they ate and drank. This Media-Holo-Frenzy reached a climax when it was reported that Debra'a had vanished! And worsened, if that was possible, when, two days later, Sol Rad., she was revealed to have gone to a secret spa at EB-KK-16, a planet-resort outside of Quinx control, in the barely populated, never mind barely civilized Perseus Arm. Her secret, Debra'a was planning to have a Relfian viviparturition unit surgically implanted in her body, and – amazement would never end – she hoped to conceive a child by her young lover.

The operation for women wasn't precisely illegal, but it was, to say the least, unexpected, and even more crucially, it was completely untried since the beginnings of Vir'ism and those last days of the Matriarchy, when in fact it had been experimented with and had proven to be ineffective and often disastrous. Whenever she was asked why she was making such a spectacle of herself, Debra'a always said, "I only demand as much Inter. Gal. News airtime as my husband gets with his many, very public love affairs with his own Neos."

The bizarre operation and her explanation proved to be a last straw to the Vir'istic powers-that-were. Soon Helmut had Debra'a in court in a trial lasting six weeks, Sol Rad., one of the juiciest, raciest, scandal and libel-laden divorce cases in Republic – perhaps in Human – history. How much Debra'a and Helmut spent on every item, from food sweeteners to sex-services to his varied Neo-toy's Desmer jobs, became galactic common knowledge. Indeed how much the Beryllium Trillionaire Set members ordinarily spent every day, Sol Rad., on absurd trifles, once it had been gathered and summed up on an annual basis, and revealed via the trial, utterly staggered the Three Species' collective imagination.

Holo or real receipts were demanded as proof of spending by both sides in the trial, and among the huge lot of them collated by Cybers working at full speed, day and night, was one little receipt that ended up stunning not only the court and jury but eventually fairly much everyone else.

A Hesperian Vir'ism Center built on Wolf 346's New Arcadia allegedly had cost a certain amount of d'lars, not cheap by any means, but certainly within Republic guidelines. But when Helmut Aare Djaa'a's own receipts were gone through, it appeared that he had directly paid almost half again as much of that amount, on top of that stated official amount, and had done so directly into the fund, to help build the center. Helmut said he did it in return for certain *future* favors as well as because he expected repayment with high interest at a later date.

When asked what the payment represented, Helmut casually replied, "we're all paying for these Vir'ism Centers on new worlds. Our Premier realized that the actual costs could never be covered by publicly appointed funds, unless the places were to be, well, quite dreary sites. So he asked us all to help contribute."

This was news to nearly everyone else outside the Inner Quinx Council, since the Vir'ism Centers were clearly seen as Hesperian political projects, and by then almost specifically as Mart Kell's own political projects, aimed toward furthering his personal political influence.

It turned out that Helmut had already contributed vast sums to six such Sag. Arm Vir'ism Centers, and to his knowledge, so had most of the other members of the Inner Quinx. In return, they were to be granted monopolies of their choice in building the superstructure of the newly terraformed planets they had so gifted. With, naturally, enough, long term and quite astronomically high returns.

Airing of the Holo-Receipts in court and thus on the Inter. Gal. News was followed within a day, Sol Rad., by a firestorm of Media and minority attacks upon the Premier and the Quinx Council. It only took another four days for Mart Kell to feel forced to resign as Premier. It required another three days for the entire Quinx's choice – his nephew-in-law, Cas'sio Azura-Ib'r – to agree to replace him.

Cas'sio had been chosen because of his constant refusal to accept the post in the past as well as his known ethical inviolability. Some wags insisted that it was because he was one of two men in the Inner Quinx's fifty-five members who'd not partaken of the profit scheme, the other being the Great Father himself, who was away mostly, in semi- retirement at Verhandel.

Mart Kell left Hesperia within hours of his resignation. He lived off-City for half a decade afterward, reappearing only for various depositions in those trials that grew out of the scandal. When Debra'a then upped and died during a childbirth-induced hysterectomy from that second set of surgically inserted internal fallopian tubes, Mart threw a huge Remembrance Party in her honor, saying she'd always been a close friend, a devoted parent and "One of the Great Ladies of Hesperia." All without regard to the fact that she'd been crucially instrumental in his political downfall. This loyalty was highly approved of by many older families in Hesperia, and kick-started Mart Kell's admittedly slow but now seemingly inexorable rise from the bottom up once again.

According to those few who remained close to the deposed Premier, Mart Kell supposedly vowed revenge upon all who'd brought on his loss, and he prophesied that he would some day become fully reinstated as the Republic's leader. Only in the past decade had he begun to appear again at official City fetes and it was said that he would unquestionably hold a major place and role in the planned spectacular QuadraCentennial of the Republic that was quickly coming up. Many believed that Mart had mellowed and should now be considered a slightly tarnished Founding Father, not as great as Ay'r Kerry Sanqq', of course, but surely somewhere just below that August Personage. Others who'd known Mart Kell longer believed that Hesperia – and the

Republic – hadn't seen the last of him by any means, either politically, or financially. While others opined that as long as he lived, Mart remained a threat to both the current Premier, Cas'sio and to the Republic he had helped establish.

To Ay'r, on faraway Usk, he was a threat. Although from what the PVN and the associated political-analysis attachments all said, it was unclear how Ay'r could possibly forward Kell's many interests. Ay'r had been publicly betrothed, indeed, in front of everyone who counted – so any possible dynastic marriage with Mart (his great grandfather or some such relation anyway) was ruled out. Ay'r's only potential political sphere of influence was Usk, and therefore far outside the main galaxy stream, number six hundred and seventy nine of the so called Seven Hundred Wonders of the Galaxy.

What Mart Kell wanted with him – and he did want him – remained a huge mystery. A mystery Ay'r pondered when he'd been exhausted by air-boarding and laboring for Silberklang out of doors and was tired of PVNs. Either that or Ay'r sat back and watched the handful of other passengers as they amused themselves and each other in the rec. saloon or dining room and above all, listened to their conversation, in that process learning many things about them and about the galaxy that not one of his 'Tutes, Human or Cyber, had ever intimated.

For example he'd discovered that the two Ambassadorial Delph.s were celebrating their own three hundredth wedding anniversary and that the smaller and frailer one, Cha"ab, was dangerously ill and not expected to live much longer. Ay'r had long believed that every Three Species disease was curable, or treatable for an entire person's lifespan, which amounted to the same thing. But such turned out not to be the case, and although medicine and therapy had kept Cha"ab comfortable and useful now for almost a century, even so his body had now begun to revolt against chemical interference and it now reacted by using any treatment the Delph. received to attack *another* part of his body. Cha"ab's flesh had seemingly gone mad, Nosser, his partner, explained to the Human listeners, and could no longer be counted on to help itself nor the mind trapped within it's degeneration. This voyage had been chosen because it was said to be relaxing, and because the drying-out action of the planet's atmosphere actually relieved Cha"ab's pain and stress, since it was medically predicted that Cha"ab's body, totally unused to aridity, would take most of the time of the trip to slowly come to react badly to the new climate and begin re-attacking him in new and terrible ways.

The older of the other Human passengers, Teha'ch Scott-Rancho, had been on Usk before, and in fact, he'd studied the pamps' acclimatization to the planet several hundred years earlier and was said to be something of a Pampologist, specializing in their renovated myths, legends and even in their linguistic differences. He would often stop a passing waiter pamp or deckhand and speak to him in his own dialect, usually eliciting first confusion, sometimes consternation, and finally a downcast look, and napkin or hand covering the mouth as the shy creature carefully replied. Scott-Rancho and his new-met companion, Sal'ness Quor-Inq, were headed inland once they arrived at the Western Star Port and suggested doubling up with the Scientific Team and sharing caravan travel costs, at least part of the way.

Quor-Inq was by his own admission, "a layabout and traveler into strange places out of boredom and generalized ennui." But he was strong, sharp-witted, an excellent gamesman, and supposedly knew how to saddle and/or mount and ride forty kinds of galactic animals, including nearly extinct Colleys and of course Thwwings.

The way in which both of those male Humans engaged the new Bella=Arth. guest over the first few weeks of the cruise, made Ay'r at first believe that they were interested in interspecies gratification. Pinna Fer ('qq') was a stunner if you liked Vespids, he had to admit. She was young, healthy, her chitin gleaming red-black and strong, and she was always fashionably-clad and made-up, clever, talkative and up-to-date. But it didn't take long to discover that Quor-Inq's taste ran to Human sailors, several of whom could be seen slipping into or out of his stateroom at peculiar hours, while Scott-Rancho seemed no longer interested in sex of any sort, but did continue to possess unending information, and even greater curiosity, about pamps, whom he studied, avocationally, if intensely, now that he was over six hundred and five and so, presumably, retired.

It was Silberklang, not Ay'r, who one evening during their wake-up dinner, asked Scott-Rancho to give a fingernail history, as it were, of the pamps, which the elder guest did, stopping at times to ask for confirmation from the pamp serving them or clearing the table, who would either be consternated and vanish, or who would stand thinking, seemingly for ever, and at times end up replying in excessive irrelevant detail.

"What do you know, Ser Scott-Rancho – since you know so very much – about this Fabled Pamp-Friend I've heard some of my helpers and their deck mates speak of when they think I'm not in audible range?" Silberklang asked in his most casual manner.

Ay'r was sitting to one side of the geologist and was luckily fully shrouded, else his embarrassment and his alleged part in the story would have become instantly apparent.

"This is all something relatively new," Scott-Rancho said, "by which I mean to say, it's only been heard of, as a legend or myth, since sometime after the pamps were relocated here on Usk."

"It's meaning is …?"

"Well, who knows what its meaning is, really, to the pamps. It is, however, a great step forward for them, at least in Species Ethology terms, in that it moves them squarely into the ethno-sociological era of Non-Indigenous Post-Archaic, since only at that stage are Messiah figures first thought up by native peoples. For example among the Bella=Arth.s, and you'll correct me Pinna if I get this wrong, the Deneban Savior known as Au'du'byn Tri ('jj'), didn't arise until just before interstellar space travel. Whereas among the Delphinids it was earlier, before even before inter-planetary travel, that Baa'tim made his Seventeen Curses and Claims at the Pools of the Avatar Pha"arg."

"True. But what, exactly," Pinna now asked, "does this Pamp Messiah do?"

"Well, according to the legend, he rises them up."

"Rises them up literally? I.e. in a gigantic Slp.G liner or …?"

"That's just it. None of us Pampologists are certain whether he actually elevates them or if it's a moral, spiritual rising. By the way, the messiah is not a pamp. He's purely Human."

"Doesn't that seem a little …?"

"Odd? Somewhat. That he's not indigenous is some kind of recognition of their very low status and their need for an Other of another species, to help."

"What conditions," Cha"ab now asked, "are thought to bring about this pamp Messiah?"

'The usual in such cases. Intolerable conditions. Depths of

despair. But here's the odd thing. His arrival or the beginning of his messianic activity or of his lifting them up is quite exactly timed in the myth. It's timed to an exact, replicable condition of the Rings and Suns of Usk, simulating those that were in place during the pamp's first arrival here centuries ago. And so, it's a second cycle for them. A new start. A rebirth. A new beginning. A lovely idea, yes?"

"What conditions are needed?" Nosser asked for all of them.

This time Silberklang did the answering, "Rings must be at Perihelion, Double Dim-Day, with the Hunter chasing the Eagle. And in the month of the ripening salt-plum."

"Precisely," Scott-Rancho agreed. "And it's coming up soon, as Usk completes its own cycle of Rings and months."

"You mean when those two suns appear to exchange their position again?" Nosser asked.

"Yes. And by then *we* will just have arrived on the other side of the ocean, Maybe we'll even witness their Messiah's arrival," Quor-Inq said, and they all looked at each other, except of course Ay'r, who'd been deadly still during the conversation and who now did not move a muscle, and barely breathed, although he could feel a vein jumping next to his left eye, and for the first time ever he had a new sensation: expectation of the strange and un-precedented.

The scientific team had just finished bringing their samples back to the upper deck of the Arcturus Scatling a week later, next double sundown, and Ay'r was considering taking Sand-Drifter out for some air-boarding, when the craft's whistles all blew at once, and a great number of Human and pamp deck hands suddenly appeared amidships, with the First Mate among them issuing orders. They all suddenly began closing and locking various hatches and doors and securing lines. Several other passengers had come out to the open deck for a bit of fresh air, although that was sadly lacking this evening for some reason. It was unusually still, even close. Also there was no real second sunset, and the air had grown rather thick and even foggy. Ay'r and his pamp were sent back indoors along with the other guests in a most unceremonious manner. Clearly something was afoot.

They gathered excitedly in the dining salon with its wide bay windows view of the main deck and beyond. Even here however, they were to be blinded. Quickly, but not quickly enough for them to not peer out and watch as deckhands folded and secured all and any sails fast to their masts, and laced them together in a sort of web work of other lines. Meanwhile the sloop's engines were turned on and it advanced smoothly, not with the accustomed jerk and pull forward of a wind-pulled embarkation, but a great deal more steadily, even with care.

No sooner was the craft in motion then the confused, amazed and babbling passenger onlookers had their biggest surprise. The sails and masts now well secured, the deckhands hurried at folding back until-then-unknown shutters over all of the salon windows, front, sides and rear. Ay'r could see them also doing so to all the transparent plastro on deck. While the others began to loudly and bitterly complain, he felt his arm grabbed by Silberklang who cautioned Ay'r to silence with a gesture, then pulled him out of the salon, into a corridor, another corridor, headed up through a narrow stairway that Ay'r had himself come upon once in his wanderings about the ship when almost everyone slept and that he now knew led up high to a sort of enclosed crow's nest.

By the time they reached it, the engine's sound was distant, but another noise had taken over, the strangest sounding wind Ay'r had ever heard.

The geologist went first and peeped his head up, then seeing no one else there, he rose into the closed space and pulled Ay'r along with him. They were some twenty meters above the main deck, by now clear of deck hands, and as tied and battened down, furled, shuttered and locked closed as he'd ever seen a sloop before. The crow's nest was a perfect cylinder and at eye height, double thick, transparent plastro had been caulked and sealed in to give a three hundred and sixty degree view of the sloop's surroundings.

What they now saw at first baffled then thrilled Ay'r.

The mistiness surrounding them had burned clear away from the Arcturus Scatling on all sides as far as the eye could see, but now the very atmosphere wasn't the orange-tinged clarity he'd expected from the time of day it was, but instead a sort of off-white composed equally of the ocean's salted sand floor and a sky of equal – and to his eyes – unwholesome, hue. The last few glimmers of orange or red seemed to vanish as he stared, replaced by the diseased color that dominated everything, including now the sloop too.

It continued to slide along in its path, but did so in a most ghostlike manner, devoid of deckhands, sails, of any light – or color. Ay'r was just about to ask the older man what was happening when Silberklang, looking out another direction, suddenly did a little hop back and said, "there! Bissel! There's one now!"

Ay'r turned to see what he meant and at first saw nothing at all.

In a second, however, it too turned and gyred and suddenly he saw it, a huge, irregular, funnel composed of he couldn't say what, but surely nothing solid, since it teetered and expanded, thickened and thinned, spun wider this way, then the opposite, like some crazed being large enough to connect the ocean floor with the sky above.

"A Sand Spout! And a big one, too! Look!" the geologist said, unable to hide the thrill of fear and terror in his voice.

"What is it?"

"The Great Father only knows. I've never seen one before, but I've heard of them."

"And because of that thing, all the craft must be closed down?" Ay'r scoffed.

"It's a dozen times more powerful than any craft this small."

"Small?" Ay'r asked.

"Look Bissel, before you speak. Look at the middle of the monstrous thing! There!"

Ay'r followed with his eyes where the geologist's finger pointed against the transparent plastro, and he noticed something tiny and dark whirling helplessly within the maddening gyre.

"What is that?" Ay'r asked and at the same time received his answer, as it whirled onto another angle and was revealed to be a four-master sand sloop, upside down, with its giant masts a shambles picked clean of sail like toothpicks. He pulled back from the window. "How vast is that funnel?"

"It could lift us like a perli berry in a wind and toss us into the sky."

"No wonder then … !" Ay'r replied, awed. "But we are headed away from it's path."

"Are you so certain?" Silberklang asked, his voice still unnaturally shrill. He plucked at Ay'r's arm, and when he turned to follow the other's gaze, Ay'r shouted "There are two of them! One behind us and one ahead!"

As he spoke two more funnels seemed to drop down from the louring, off-white sky, one much closer to them, another further away. Suddenly, in back of them, another funnel dropped, and further away two funnels. No, three more!

"What is this place?" Ay'r cried out, in great fear.

"This portion of the Western Ocean we've been traveling through for over two days, Sol Rad., is called The Gallery, and before and all about us, you see how it gets its name."

"We're doomed with so many about us!"

"Captain Lepta is a nonpareil Great Ocean navigator. He's sailed through this Gallery many times. It's his experience and skill that we'll now require to get us through."

They remained aloft, watching the enormous funnels moving toward and away from them at seemingly incredible speeds, sometimes the Sand Spouts crossed each other and it was like a dance of the utmost horror. Once, a funnel dropped unexpectedly down where they'd just passed and both observers gave a start. From their height, Ay'r could sense the large craft weaving its way along the ocean's sand floor, as though it were a needle threading through, and stitching a complex embroidery. At one moment, together, they aloud counted fourteen of the vast things around them, crossing and passing and inter-mixing their twisting, cyclopean force, any one of which could destroy them, and he could no longer conceive the astonishing danger or the Captain's amazing navigational skill in getting them through.

The number had dropped by half, when the head of a pamp sailor suddenly arose at their feet. The deckhand scrambled into the tight space crowding them and spoke with deference but firmness: "This area is not for passengers. It's too dangerous. Please return to the others below decks. This is my watch."

"Do not be frightened," Ay'r clasped the pamp sailor on his shoulder. "Although it is by far the most frightening view I ever had in my life. But perhaps you've seen it often?"

Silberklang had begun down the ladder already, and the pamp now turned to see what they'd been looking at. The way he stepped back and then around, stunned as they had been, told Ay'r he too was a tyro on this voyage.

"Fear not. Our brave and able Captain will get us through," Ay'r said, holding the pamp's hand tightly, and letting it go only reluctantly, to clamber back down.

"Not a word to the others!" Silberklang said to Ay'r as they descended.

The others already knew. They were in the rec. salon, gathered about a single Holo, showing them a scene similar to what Ay'r had just witnessed. Quor-Inq was manipulating his wrist connector and when they arrived, he looked up and said, "very stormy weather indeed, fellow travelers."

"Is that another one forming?" Cha"ab asked, excitedly.

"No, love, it's dissipating," Nosser replied. "We have these on New Venice. Made of water, of course," the Delph. explained to the others. "Tall as these too. Although not constant like here. Far more rare. All the more dangerous for that."

"Clever Inq figured out we must be going through The Gallery," Scott-Rancho said, with a shiver. "He managed to somehow secure us a visual connection to the ship's topmost visual probe. You have no idea what you just missed. Completely enthralling."

"Fourteen at once?" Ay'r couldn't help but showing off. "On every side?"

"You sly things! Were you interfering with it too in your chamber?

"We were up top," he gestured sharply up, "watching!"

"Gives me goosebumps watching from down here where we're safe," Pinna said, and indeed parts of her thorax exhibited a series of lined up nodules.

Silberklang waited until all the funnels were no longer visible via the Holo and then for some time before he turned to the Arth. and said, "I'm sorry to have to inform you, lovely lady, but ... you were never safe down here. None of us were while those things were present."

He was assaulted by questions and comments, the prior being of the "Will they come back? Can they form at any moment?" type, while the latter were of the "Why did you tell us that? Are you trying to give us a stroke? Or are you simply a sadist?" variety.

Not a half hour later, the shutters were removed and they could all look out of doors again, where the sun had set and the invidious off-white ambiance had been replaced by normal nighttime skies, with the Rings visible and silvery, angled some fifteen degrees above the horizon, while the black velvet skies held a trillion points of unapproachable lights; the usual starry sky.

Shortly after that, the masts were untied and the sails let out and they filled the sky too as the ship flew with its usual nocturnal speed across the solid ocean surface, while the passengers burbled excitedly about their close call.

At their delayed dinner, the Captain entered nonchalantly and visited all the adults for a word or too, acting as though nothing at all had happened earlier.

When Ay'r got up to leave, thinking to avoid the officer, Captain Lepta made a smooth transition away from the Delph.s and into the corridor where Ay'r had gone. Even from behind Ay'r could feel a hand reach out for him. He stopped and turned.

"And so, young Trothee, I understand you sometimes *personally* enjoy the excitements of great danger. Despite your social position, which one might think all but obliges much greater discretion and circumspection."

The challenging, mocking way that he said it, the arrogant, ultra-masculine stance his wide frame took, half encircling him, as though blocking him into the narrow space, irritated yet also stimulated Ay'r, who replied: "Discretion and circumspection are traits seldom admired, except of course, by those far more ... *antiquated!*"

Lepta's eyes opened wide at the potential insult, allowing Ay'r to see that they were indeed golden in color or at least the pupils dyed to glitter gold. "Am I to understand then, that you do sometimes enjoy the excitements of danger?"

The question and insinuating manner in which it was presented so annoyed and excited Ay'r that he all but spat out, "try me, then ... that is, if you believe you can still deliver *both* excitement and danger."

He swung himself away, but Lepta was more agile and caught him by the arm, and held him fast as he advanced face to face. "I will some day, by your invitation, young Trothee, indeed 'try you,' as you so well put it," he said, now as menacing as he was seductive. He then added "Some ... moment when I find myself ... wearied by my varied ... duties."

Before Ay'r could riposte, the Captain reached forward and grasped a single white blonde hair that must have remained outside of, and ungathered by, the Trothee Shroud and pulled it. Ay'r felt its loss stingingly, but he'd die before he admitted that or indeed made any sound.

Lepta ran the hair over his thin – and now that Ay'r was so close, he could see they were very sinuous, sensuous – lips, and murmured. "And beauty draws us – by a single hair."

Ay'r was already past him through the corridor and back into the salon.

Several evenings later, when Ay'r went to see if the geologist were awake, he found his chamber empty. Something small and square and lightly metallic had been placed in the middle of Silberklang's desk and at first he thought it might be a new instrument for them to use outside. But as he closed in on it, Ay'r saw that it must be what used to be called a *book*.

He'd seen them before in various historical Holos but had never seen one in person before. This one was smaller than the size of the palm of his hand, small enough to be hidden in two closed hands. It was made of what looked to be thinly sliced sheets of Cupro-Iridium, unpolished, each page lighter than an insects' wing. It lay open, with some kind of built-in, yet moveable page holder in one upper right hand corner to keep it flat. Touching it gently, Ay'r could see that these must be the last two pages and that it had what he knew was called printing on it, although in this case it seemed to be more likely incised into the metal page rather than stamped upon it.

He turned the book to its front and scanned it with his wrist-connection.

"This is a retrospective object, now in disuse" Ay'r's wrist-connector told him. "Used in the Metro-Terran era, the First Matriarchy, and the Interregnum eras. It's called a book. One reads the words."

"Read it for me," Ay'r commanded.

"Place your wrist over what you wish read ..." And when Ay'r did so, "this book is titled *The Book of Colored Glory.*"

"What does the title mean?"

"Unknown. It is written by Loren, the First Interstellar of the Church of Iridium Vir'ism."

"Who is this Loren?" Ay'r asked.

"*The Logo-Con-Intellectu-Universalis* states the following in its entry on this author: 'Loren, otherwise known as Loren of the Dryland continent of the Ib'r World also known as Pelagia, Species Human; Dates of Life: approximately 3876, S.T.Y. to current time. Loren is considered the most remarkable prophet of the Ib'r Republic for his ability to forecast events and people. Loren was born on Pelagia, a seeded planet in the Far Outer Arm, globular sinister Sector, Q-X , where he lived until the age of 45 years, Sol Rad. He was evacuated along with all of that planet's population in 3832 S.T. Y., and lived for the next century in various domiciles on Girder 896B of Hesperia, under the unstinting bounty of The Great Father himself. At the age of 147, Loren amalgamated a small group of followers of his prophesies and sayings, into an Ib'r Republic Acceptable Legal Religion which they called The Church of Iridium Vir'ism. Its tenets were similar to those of the ruling Republic with one single difference, the church must approve of and officiate at its members' couplings and births, which were entirely decided upon by Loren, who by then had taken the religious appellation, *The Interstellar.* At the age of 168, Loren and the Church moved from Hesperia, where they had gained many millions of adherents, to a large satellite of the sixth planet of the Narcissus 12 system in the Sagittarius Arm. There, with the bounty of the Great Father and of the Ib'r Vir. faithful, a good-sized monastery with an especially large "scriptorium" chamber for incising books was constructed in an extremely isolated location. While the religion grew in Hesperia and around the Center Worlds, it has never commanded more than a few billion followers and so is considered to of minor importance. In contrast, Loren's prognostications have been Holo-Published with enormous sales to the curious and the trendy all across the Galactic Republic, and for several years Sol Rad., being able to quote the Interstellar's words has been considered a Socially Acceptable Hesperian Fad."

"What role has the *Book of Colored Glory* in this religion?"

"At first none. For several centuries, like most Human and Delph. religions, Loren's teachings were orally and holographically transmitted. Many of these were collected by the devoted into small Holo texts for instant retrieval. This *Book of Colored Glory* however was specifically 'written' by Loren as another way for him and his disciples to be able to store, understand (and revere) his prognostications for the future. As such, it is now held in highest regard by them, especially as Loren's health has declined so that he no longer officiates in person nor makes holographic pronouncements. This book is now considered his quote, 'last words' and 'holiest text', unquote."

"It's a book of future prognostications?" Ay'r asked.

"One hundred and twenty future prognostications. The two pages bookmarked are the last."

"When was it written?"

"Between two hundred and three hundred years ago. But only published later. Each prognostication consists of a single quatrain (or, four lined poem-let) in what used to be called verse, in meters once known as dactylic-tetrameter and pentameter. Each quatrain contains an enigmatic series of images and allegories and a single or double highlighted noun of particular color available to the vision of all Three Species. Possibly this may in part explain its title."

Ay'r turned the book open to the pages that Silberklang (or someone else) had bookmarked. "Read this aloud!"

"Prophecy-poem number one hundred and nineteen," his wrist-connector read:

> *Where One ruled Solitary GOLDEN, now Double*
> *Hold Dimmed Estate, guarding Occulted Hues*
> *of Ultimate Voice & Light … Four untangle the Fabled Knot*
> *But only the Youngest and Most Just will Realize.*

"The color there is clearly gold," Ay'r commented, naturally recalling that as one of the two colors of his entourage at the Betrothal ceremony. "What does the color gold refer to?"

"Unknown."

"What is the meaning of the quatrain?"

"Unknown."

"Does it refer to colors shown by the House of the Premier, Cas'sio Azura-Kell?"

"Very possibly, since those are his colors," the wrist-connector replied.

"Where one ruled, past tense, two rule present tense?" Ay'r mused. "What does it mean? That where one person ruled, two will rule in the future? Since it is a prognostication?"

"Possibly. But if two rule, they hold 'dimmed estate' i.e. they are still not as bright as the one before them."

"Who is?" Ay'r mused. "What is this Ultimate Voice & Light?"

"Unknown."

"Is there such a thing or place called the Fabled Knot?" Ay'r asked.

"Searching ... Searching. No such place or thing is noted."

"What is the meaning of the word 'realize' in the last line?"

"To realize can mean to understand, to recognize; but it may also mean to achieve and or to materially gain."

"So the youngest and the most just gains it all? Read me this other notated quatrain. It is the very last prognostication of the book?"

"The very last, Prophecy poem number one hundred and twenty:

> *The Judge is Triply Wooed and Bears the Flawless*
> *Duplicate ... As Eagle stalks Hunter's brightest BLUE,*
> *HE wins the Tiny Multitude ... Worthlessness raised to*
> *Great!*
> *... Discord Rife! Then Behold – ALL COLORS Unite!*

"Who is this Judge?"

"Unknown."

"My own title is Adjudicator of Usk. Does that not make me a judge?"

"Yes it does."

"Could the quatrain refer to me?" He asked meaning to make a joke of it.

"Yes it could. Especially given what is next written: 'As Eagle stalks Hunter's brightest blue'."

Ay'r felt the hair stand up on the back of his neck. "Which may mean the suns of this system. What is its meaning?"

"Unknown."

"What is the meaning of the entire quatrain?" Ay'r asked.

"Unknown."

"Who would know its meaning?"

"Possibly, although not certainly, a follower of the Interstellar, Loren."

"Where would I find such a follower?"

"The owner of this book might be one," the wrist connection replied. "Either that or a scholar of the book and/or of the religion itself."

Ay'r had the quatrains repeated and then asked, "that line in the second quatrain that goes 'As Eagle stalks Hunter's brightest blue?' Could that possibly refer to this planet, Usk's, two suns? The Eagle and the Hunter?"

"Unknown."

"Speculate."

"Yes, it could easily refer to planet Usk's two suns."

Which would make sense, explaining why the pages were open. Ay'r heard Silberklang outside the chamber speaking to someone. He replaced the book back to where and as it had been when he'd first come in.

Going to meet the geologist, he said in a loud and hearty voice, "there you are! I was looking for you."

A few days later, something reminded him of the little book and its strangeness, so strange his wrist-connector, upon which he relied for almost all knowledge of the galaxy and its workings, had failed to explain much about at all. As they were closing up and pulling in the various pieces of equipment, Ay'r asked, "what is all this for, anyway? All this equipment! What are you looking for?"

The older man smiled shyly. "Ah, Bissel! At last you ask! I'm looking for proof."

"Proof of what?" Ay'r asked.

"Proof that there was once a huge, ancient ocean right here. An ocean of water that once covered one third of this planet. Everything we've collected so far has, by the way, provided the most excellent proof. Resonances. Soil samples. Not one bit of it contradicts my theory. The way the lowest levels of rock beneath this salt ocean were once deformed, must be because of the enormous weight of the water, as opposed to that deeper rock covered by land, such as the surrounding reefs and shorelines. Then the almost infinitesimal marine fossils embedded in the soil in those tubes you're pulling up daily for me. All confirm for me that there was once an ocean of water right here where we stand on dry land! The salt of course was the giveaway. But even so, other proof was needed. The only real question," Silberklang added sadly. "And the bit that I can't for the life of me answer is where did all the water go?"

"Could it have gone there!" Ay'r lifted a hand and pointed to where the Rings of Usk were angled some eleven degrees above the horizon. "When I was close to them recently, flying back down to Usk, I saw enormous rainbows stretching between the strata of the Rings. Between them and the shepherd moonlets, and between the lowest level of the rings and the ground. Enormous rainbows. The only place I've ever before seen rainbows before was on New Venice, in Holos of Procyon City, the place they call The City of a Hundred Rainbows."

Silberklang stared at Ay'r. "You were in a fly-by when you noticed?"

"No."

"A T-pod then?"

Ay'r wasn't sure he wanted the geologist to know he'd piloted a Thwwing, as it might give away too much information about himself. "Something like that."

"You saw rainbows?"

"A half dozen rainbows. I recognized them from my Ed. & Dev. vids."

"Water, then, locked into stone. Or frozen into icesteroids. But if as you say it's all there, then how, my surprising and bright young Trothee, did it get *up there* from being *down here*."

"I believe only one answer will suffice. Some great catastrophe must have once occurred upon this Usk of ours, and all the water was thrown off. All the natural life too, perhaps," Ay'r said. He had thought that much through. "All vanished. But some of the water collected again as the ice and because Usk was the largest object around, eventually a portion, if not all of it, was drawn back to it by gravity and so it is now in orbit, around the planet."

Evidently his theory made sense because Silberklang now asked: "Why does it remain in Rings and not rain down?"

"I think it *does* rain down, but in minutely small quantities. I think that's why I saw the rainbows. As for *why* it chiefly remains in those Rings, I believe that would have to do with the rotational spin of Usk which would have become much faster once the heaviness of the water on its surface was gone, lightening the planet's weight. And because Usk spins faster than it used to do, the Rings remain in what's called a geosynchronous orbit around Usk."

Silberklang suddenly looked suspicious: "Who told you all this?"

"No one. Although my Cyber 'Tutes did teach me basic planetary physics, of course. I figured it out on my own, while being outside air-boarding and ... you know ... being alone, thinking of it all."

Silberklang relaxed. "Very clever, Trothee. What would you say if I told you that I believe you are exactly correct. But do you know *how* all the water *left* Usk?"

"No. And how could you know? It must have happened millions of years ago!"

"Less than that, Bissel. Only one or two hundred thousand years ago." When Ay'r didn't answer, he went on, "do you want to know *how* I know that date?" Not getting an answer, he went on, "because it was recorded."

"None of the Three Species were space travelling. Nor I think, even keeping written records one hundred thousand years ago."

"No. But *someone* was. Another species. Who they were we do not know. Only that they predated all Three Species. We sometimes find old objects, ruins, and things, belonging to them. Were they birdlike? Reptiles? Or completely differently shaped? We don't know. But across the most distant of worlds they have left their barely legible traces and messages, including a few glyphs. Someone I know has spent most of his adult life transcribing and interpreting those glyphs."

This was news to Ay'r.

"Let us call them the Elder," Silberklang added. "My friend managed to piece together a record of them leaving these Center Worlds because of certain trace elements that they left behind, elements that no longer exist anywhere among us. He doesn't know why they left, nor where they went. They did stay for recognizably long periods of time upon a dozen worlds located upon the farthest of the spiral arms and possibly upon worlds in those globular clusters located far above and below the galactic ecliptic, far outside what we know well and what we call the Center Worlds. He says it was as though they were resting there, gathering their forces, or perhaps even constructing something they needed, to travel even farther."

Ay'r thought, "I love this old geologist for what he tells me."

"Three times, however, among their traces, my friend found the same unusual story among their few fragmented writings. At first, he thought the story was the reason they were leaving, but it seemed too small and far too localized for that. The story was about a little, bright green moon with water. A plaything of a place, a lovely little vacation spot and paradise," Silberklang went on. "They called it something sounding like Ss'k'ua and it orbited a much larger planet, what we would call a B-5, a tremendous gaseous world surrounded by many other moons and moonlets. That B-5 was the only planet revolving around its yellowish star. Are you following me, Bissel?"

"Yes. A big gaseous world alone circles a G-4 star. Many moons circle the gas giant. According to what I learned, this is a statistically the most common form of solar system," Ay'r said.

"Exactly. And second most common is the red sun with *two* large gaseous worlds circling it. Now tell me what did you learn about those statistically prevalent B-5 and B-6 planets?"

"They're thought to be nursery stars; stars that never ignited or that never accreted enough mass to ignite themselves and that were pulled by gravity into orbiting larger, denser stars."

"Very good. But what do you think would happen if one of those B-5's planets *did* happen to get itself ignited?"

"How could that occur?

"Say a series of many comets fell into it over such a short period of time and in such a way that it somehow did attain critical mass and then ...?"

"Then, wouldn't it too become a star."

"How?"

Ay'r laughed in realization. "I suppose it would ... light up ... explode."

"What would happen as a result of it lighting up and exploding to the rest of the solar system?"

"The moonlets orbiting it would be probably blown to smithereens!"

"The smaller ones would. The larger ones might be pushed far far away. One or more moons might be partly protected by other moons. What else would happen?"

"Once the B-5 was lit up as a star, the gas giant would change place in regard to the star it was circling," Ay'r said, "because its mass and probably its density also would change. " He thought it through. "It would become rapidly greater as it absorbed and then threw off its mass."

"Yes. Go on."

"So it would become of *lighter* weight. And with less mass

and density, it would move to a more distant location from the sun than it had held before. So far away, that it could behave in a new gravitational balance with the other sun."

"And what would happen to those larger moons still in one piece?"

Ay'r stopped. "The smaller ones would have been blown apart, but the bigger ones would merely have been stripped … " He hesitated to think and then went on, "… of their top layers …"

"Yes, yes, Including …?" Silberklang prompted.

"Including their atmosphere and their water!" Ay'r concluded, triumphantly. "So, the moons that survived would have been sent out orbiting not just the former planet turned star, but orbiting inside the new double star's gravity well, although eventually be drawn back into tighter orbit," Ay'r said. "Although in a new and much wider orbit than before, as befits their new gravitational balance. Any other material blown into space would fall into the two suns."

"Or?"

"Or be recaptured by the newly orbiting world."

"And the original sun? What would happen to it, Bissel?"

"Nothing! Wait! It would change too. Because of the new and much stronger gravitational pull from its new companion star than it had experienced when that was only a B-5 planet. It would … rotate more quickly and burn more energy and … would it age faster, too?"

"Yes it would, Bissel. And how would that show up?"

"Would it change color?" Ay'r asked. "Yes. It would dim from its former brightness."

As he said the words he suddenly had a thought. "So a yellow sun would turn …?"

"Yes?" Silberklang prodded.

"Darker yellow. Perhaps even orange. Oh, I see now." Ay'r didn't say what he was thinking, since he was recalling what he'd had his wrist connector read to him out of that tiny book. The words had been "Where *One* ruled Solitary *GOLDEN*, now *Double*/Hold *Dimmed* Estate."

"And what color would the brand new star be?" the geologist asked.

"All new stars are blue. One blue sun and one dimmer than gold."

Silberklang gestured as though to say, Well? "Sum up, please, Bissel!"

"So, Usk must be the pretty little once-green Eden moon beloved of the Elder race? And Aquila, the Eagle is the original star? While the blue Hunter Sun, just above us now, is the B5 planet that ignited and exploded?" Ay'r asked.

"Ancient Metro-Terrans called this system Aquila. And they saw but one yellow star where we see two stars, one orange and one blue."

"You mean because it was so far away it would take a few hundred thousand years for the light from the great explosion to reach their eyes," Ay'r asked.

"Yes. Even though it happened much earlier, the light of that ignition and catastrophe only reached their sight in the old time year of 2266," Silberklang said. "During the last burst of what your 'Tutes I believe refer to as The Age of the Star-Barons."

"Early Interstellar days. But can you prove that Usk is the Elder race's Eden moon and that they all changed distance and position?"

"Usk changed only its distance from the former gas giant. But yes, I'm coming closer to being able to prove every detail. That Elder race, by the way, in their glyphs accompanying the story, pointed directly to where Usk was located at the tragic time. All this is what Metro-Terrans called the Near Scutum Arm of the Galaxy. Scutum signifying a shield. Ironically, since poor Usk could have made excellent use of a shield against that great catastrophe that it experienced. But yes, it was always located right here, on the closer side of the Sagittarius Arm of the galaxy, coming from the Center Worlds. Still, Bissel, for more substantial proof, I need to be on the ocean's *other* shore, the western coast. There I believe, we will have several other proofs and revelations."

"This should be a great coup for you professionally," Ay'r admitted. "But you once told me secretly that it was of utmost importance to the galaxy and to the Republic. Why should that be? Nothing we've said so far gives any indication of that."

"Ah, my dear Bissel, some matters I'm still not ready to speak of."

"Meaning you still don't trust me enough ... well, that's acceptable."

"And this news will be difficult for the Three Species to

accept. It says, Bissel, that our universe can change in a moment. Where a planet and many moons and many millions used to be, there is a great blast and suddenly a few days later, it is two suns and a desert planet. I only hope the Elder race saw it coming and prepared for it."

"Perhaps they didn't and that's why they left?" Ay'r reasoned.

Silberklang went below decks and Ay'r remained above, looking at the now completely darkened sky with its many stars and the Rings of Usk inexorably rising. Imagine what must have looked like, having a nearby gas giant planet light up and then ignite into a star! Imagine the brightness!

But then, how explain how this fellow Loren, from some provincial far outer ring, could possibly know about Usk's history two or three hundred thousand years back, since Silberklang was now still in the process of trying to prove it?

And what did it all have to do with the future? Those had all been *future* prognostications. Hadn't they?

"This area we're now sailing through is called The Sea of Glass," Pinna offered the dinner table guests, a week and more later. "Can anyone guess why?" Quor-Inq had studied up his ship's Holo-Catalog and could.

"A great comet allegedly struck here a dozen centuries ago. It supposedly came in low and as it did, it broke into many pieces and their fire scorched the sand, fusing it into a smooth hard surface like transparent plastro or that ancient silica compound called glass."

"Excellent, Inq!" Scott-Rancho applauded, "it does provide a most spectacular view for us here above decks, although from what I understand, it isn't that easy to navigate over."

"Indeed not," Nosser replied. His Delph. partner hadn't felt well enough to come up to the table, although it was an older symptom, not a new one that kept Cha"ab away, lessening all their anxiety. "One would think the Sea of Glass's smoothness and solidity would aid the mag-lev force and make it all the smoother, and it does that very well, making for far greater speed. But an unwanted side effect is that any movement across the surface tends to displace an atomic layer of the so-called glass, which can then sheet up on either side."

"Causing these marvelous reflections and lights, seemingly out of nowhere," Quor-Inq added, pointing to what all could see for themselves, "accompanying the craft."

"But there's a greater danger," Scott-Rancho added.

"Given the great speed we're going," Silberklang put in "any surface imperfection in the glass larger than a Human fingernail would throw the craft off-beam and would wreck us."

"Which is why those lasers in front shoot out and melt whatever's going beneath us," Quor-Inq insisted, adding for their sake, "we're quite safe."

After dessert had been served, the old Human traveler who was seated next to Ay'r suddenly looked up sharply and said to him, "What did that pamp say to you?"

"He offered me my choice of these sweets," Ay'r replied.

"I know that. But the pamp used a peculiar term when addressing you."

"We've slowed to a stop," The Arth., Pinna reported. She and Nosser looked out, but couldn't report any obvious reason for the halt.

"The pamp called you something I've not heard before," Scott-Rancho insisted.

"I've no idea what you're talking about," Ay'r said. He of course had noticed it.

"Here, pamp!" the older man said to the pamp waiter who'd returned and was dishing out the puddling-like sweet onto their plates. "What did you call our young Trothee here?"

The pamp froze in place unable to utter a word.

"'Ser,'" Ay'r said. Then to the pamp, "I'll take that blue one. What is it called?"

"Half-Ring at Hunter-Rise," the pamp waiter replied but added no form of address.

"I swear the pamp used a reflexive something or other before when it was addressing you. And not for the first time. And not only this pamp, but other ones too. They do so all the time," Scott-Rancho insisted.

"You're imagining things," Ay'r said, knowing very well what he was talking about as he too had noticed it.

"Young fool," Silberklang tried, "is what all these pamps are *probably* saying to him under their breath. And old fool to you and I, Scott-Rancho."

As they looked on, the visual effect from before surrounding the craft seemed to collapse, or rather to dissipate into air.

"What was the term the pamp used?" Pinna asked Scott-Rancho.

"Please, Lady Pinna, don't encourage him in this foolishness," Ay'r requested.

"I'm not entirely sure, Lady Pinna. I've never heard anyone addressed that way before."

"Try this one, Lady," Ay'r pushed it on the Bella=Arth. "Amazingly good."

"Was it being *impolite*?" Nosser was still listening to Scott-Rancho even if no one else was.

"To the contrary. More like *overpolite*. No," scowling, "that's not it, either. More like an honorific."

Ay'r tried making a joke of it, smoothing his Trothee's veil he added, "perhaps in honor of my great personal beauty."

Several of them laughed, none of them ever having seen him without his shroud on.

"No," Scott-Rancho mused, "it's less flattering than it is ... *appellative*."

"You lost me, Ser Scott," Pinna said. "This is marvelous, Trothee. Gratitude! Waiter! One of the blue for me. Try it, Ser Inq," she pushed a taste of it onto his plate.

"*Appellative ... Nominative ...* It's a special *name* they have for you that they have for no one else on board," Scott-Rancho was thinking it through. "I've never heard the term before. I thought it was another, more common term being said and slurred. But this waiter pamp said it much more clearly than the others usually do, possibly because of its particular Southern Coast accent."

"What does the term mean?" Pinna insisted.

"Friend. Great Friend. Friend of the pamps. Something like that."

"Probably because he *has* befriended them," Silberklang said. "He has two pamp servants after all. Maybe that's what it means – 'Served by Pamps'?"

"Yes, *both* servants use the term," Scott-Rancho agreed. "I've definitely heard *them* say it." He suddenly turned on Ay'r. "What *is* the special relationship you have to them?"

"Excuse me, Ser," Ay'r said, throwing his napkin down on the table top. "Do I understand correctly that you are demanding an accounting of me?"

"Well, no. But ... well ... why not?"

Ay'r stood up, and affected to be deeply offended.

"I'm completely unaware of any reason why I would be obligated to a complete stranger like yourself you or in truth to anyone at this table, for any kind of explanation of myself, whatsoever."

"What are you hiding, anyway?" Scott-Rancho now asked.

Inq and the Delph. both tried to stop him.

"I think what I'm hiding is quite obvious," Ay'r said, referring to the veil.

"Leave him be," Silberklang prompted Scott-Rancho and the others joined in.

"But since," Ay'r continued, "you apparently believe differently, and believe you are *owed* some explanation, perhaps you'd like to make that demand of *my Trother* when we have arrived at the Western Star Port? I'm certain he'll feel freer to respond than I am able to do. No doubt, immediately before he unsheathes his sand-kris into your fat midsection and dispatches you into total oblivion for such insulting behavior!"

Ay'r watched the old Human fall back in his chair, stunned at this instant temper and the menace in his words.

"See what you've started Scott-Rancho!" Silberklang said.

Ay'r marched out the dining room salon, hearing behind himself comments from the others. "Why did you do that, Scott-Rancho?" "Now, look what you've done?" And "I don't for a second blame the young one. Putting him on the spot like that. He's a Trothee, Scott." "Now you're in for it," Pinna added. "Don't ask me to second you in any confrontation with his Trother!" Inq said clearly.

"But I merely wanted to know what they *called* him?"

"I'll tell you what they'll be calling you soon," Silberklang said. "The former Scott-Rancho."

Content that the matter of what the pamps called him was now soundly closed for a while, if not the rest of the voyage. Ay'r skipped to the deck, and grabbed up his air-board.

The deck hands were definitely pulling in sails and furling them, and performing other activities he'd come to associate with them taking a longer halt. He found Sand-Drifter, and asked why they were stopping now, during the day, while the winds were still up.

"These sailors are not certain. No reason was given. Several speculate that the underside or some of the mag-levs require re-sanding before we can embark again."

"I'll take advantage of this pause to take a spin on the air-board. I'm curious to see what this hard surface is like to board upon. I won't go too far so that I can't hear the ship's whistle."

"The Mate must know of this."

"I'll only be gone for a few minutes. Don't even bother putting a rampway down," Ay'r insisted and clambered down the side of the craft.

The desert floor was solid and harder than any rock, quite different than he'd ever seen it. The first real surprise was that it was opaque rather than transparent like window-plastro or old Metro-Terran glass. Then, as he looked closer, he could see that too was untrue. It *was* transparent but so very deep, that varied layers of it were identical and only here and there, and very far down indeed below his feet, could he make out an occasional rock or unknown object of a darker color and shape, to show exactly how thick the new floor was. If it were the result of an extra-terrestrial bodies striking, it would have had to have been an enormous single body, not many, as Quor-Inq explained.

He had another idea of what had done this. It hadn't at all been a body of matter, or even many bodies of matter, but instead a fire, a cyclopean tongue of flame, perhaps even the first one that had licked out of the B-5 planet after it ignited and exploded away all of its billions of kilotons of gaseous atmosphere and became starburst. Something like that, yes, it struck him – that could easily account for this amazing result.

Once placed over the hard surface, the air-board levitated and floated as usual, and when he pushed it down in several places with a booted toe, it reacted normally. He climbed on and propelled himself forward. The board flew off with such ease he had trouble keeping his balance at first. But after a half dozen trials, he found that while it definitely was from two to three times faster than it had ever been when floating over a more granular surface, that he could definitely handle both the speed and maneuvering of the air-board. He began doing wide curves, followed those by more difficult narrower curves, looped into long esses, and once he was really comfortable with the almost slippery speed beneath his body, he fell back into his favorite patterns of infinite-eights and twisting gyres. Soon, he was as though flying, as excited as he'd been inside the Thwwing during that amazing ride, except that here and now he was too breathless from the wind shoved against his face to be able to whoop out and shout for joy as he would like.

After that scene over the dinner table, he was especially happy to be free of the other passengers, as far away from them as possible. He should use that altercation he had more or less fabricated with the old Human, Scott-Rancho, to separate himself more from the others. He would take his meals later than them, or earlier, or if he must have it at the same time, then he'd do so in another part of the craft, maybe the reception salon. Should Silberklang or one of the oh-so-circumspect Delph.s choose to join him, they were welcome, but no other. He didn't trust them.

That decided, he now tried to plan for what was ahead. They were already halfway through the voyage. No Trother would be waiting at its end for him, as he'd threatened, but he could always come up with an explanation for that, and wait around. Silberklang intimated that he would be traveling further, after his shoreline calculations were done at the Western Star Port Resort. He'd spoken of the need to go deeper into the western mountain ridges, perhaps another hundred kilometers further in. The terrain was rugged there, Ay'r knew, but if they could manage not to connect up in a caravan with any of these other passengers, he would join the geologist. Of course, he needed to stay away from public places, so continuing the journey by land, in sand vehicles, or skimmers, would be perfect. He knew there were dozens of resorts transformed into *serai* for travelers operating to one degree or another; he'd seen several in travel catalogs that because of their location or architecture or historical importance had looked especially intriguing.

How far he needed to go, and how long he must be away before those searching for him assumed he was dead and gave up, he couldn't say. It was over two and a half months, Sol Rad., already since he'd fled the Golden Palace. If he could manage to escape detection until the Hunter and the Eagle changed places and the Rings reached meridian and began their descent in the other direction, he thought he would probably be safe. He was aware that Mart Kell was an off-worlder and thus unaffected by such thinking, but on Usk once the suns changed position and the Rings began to descend, the population tended to think of matters as over with, with old matters closed and new beginnings needed as a new cycle began. It would be less easy to find Uskian security guards or anyone still eager to pursue someone like himself who had vanished during the previous cycle.

By then, Ay'r hoped to have left the old geologist and struck out on his own, possibly even found some high haven, say at Grand View Resort, or one of the first, now abandoned pamp immigration centers.

Ay'r's mind had been so filled with his notions and plans, and his body so occupied trying to retain control of the air-board over the uncertain surface, that when he stopped suddenly, with the realization that he was tired and had had enough sport for the time being, he was completely unaware of his surroundings.

His first impression was that he'd somehow air-boarded much further away from the Arcturus Scatling than he'd ever dreamed. The seven-masted sloop wasn't anywhere in sight. That was a certainty.

Neither was anything else in sight.

He had to blink his eyes repeatedly to confirm that they had not lost their power to see.

All about him as he turned, stepping off the air-board onto the very solid desert floor, was ... nothing! Or if not nothing, then what was worse, much more of what was below his feet – that odd, half opaque, half transparent stuff. Above, and on all sides, it was all alike. Grabbing the board under his arm, he set off on foot in one direction, expecting to run into a solid wall of the material. He didn't. Even so, what he was looking at didn't change.

What was going on? Where was he?

He rotated in place, one half of a turn, and started off in that direction, which looked the same, this time actually counting his steps and after a hundred, he'd reached nothing solid there either. Stopped, did a three quarters turn from that direction and began toward a new direction again counting his steps, ninety nine, a hundred, up to a hundred and ninety nine, more than twice the distance he'd last been in. He reached nothing there either.

He tried patting the air in front of him. Nothing.

A tiny hot wet inkling of the absolute purest fear and irrational panic he'd ever experienced in his life curled somewhere inside him, threatening to grow with any more evidence. He tried tamping it down with his mind.

Nothing to do, but to panic. Either that or think it through. What exactly had Scott-Rancho and Quor-Inq said? Any motion across the surface had a side effect as it tended to displace an atomic layer of the so-called glass particles, which then sheeted up on either side. The Arcturus Scatling's motion had caused half-kilometer high reflections and lights, seemingly out of nowhere that had accompanied the craft as it sailed. But these weren't reflections all about him.

Or wait! Maybe they were. As he got closer, the air seemed to dissolve. But if he turned quickly, like that, right there, wasn't that his own reflection? Yes. But no lights. Maybe the air-board was insufficiently powerful to cause lights or even much in the way of reflection. Maybe it displaced so infinitesimally small a layer of material that it caused this interminable fog or whatever it was.

Perhaps if he stayed still, it would all fall back and then he could see. He tried that, sitting on the air-board and trying to stay still and think of other matters, but his situation, the ridiculous hopelessness of it was too much to ignore and he knew that rather than sitting still, he'd have to do something, even if it meant that he'd be lost in this madness of not quite reflection, because that's what it was, the reflection of the opaque surface and a bit of himself, not lights and mirrors of the huge craft, that he was seeing.

Just before that tiny burning nub of panic could fully turn on, he decided it was now or never. He dropped to the surface, and using the blade of his kris he carved out as deeply as possible a six pointed star on the surface an inch or so deep, then wondered how he'd be able to keep it in view, and so he took off his dark outer shirt and dropped that in the star's center. He hopped on the air board and took off. His idea was to make wider and wider circles around the star, always keeping the dark shirt in view as a point of reference.

After fifteen circuits, he could barely see the shirt and he had reached nothing. After twenty circuits, the shirt was scarcely a dot on the surface. Toward the end of the twenty-first circuit, a hand suddenly loomed into his peripheral vision and as he turned to confirm it's reality, it reached for his shoulder and grabbed him. He flew off the board and into – the Captain!

"What demon-devised game are you playing?" he heard the voice shouting as he sought to keep his balance as the hand let go and Ay'r went flying, spinning out onto the hard surface trying to land on his buttocks or side, anywhere but his face and head.

Suddenly there were a half dozen deckhands, Human and pamp, and as he slowly rotated in place, he could see one side of the sloop's hull, only a meter or two away from where he lay. He'd almost ... another circuit and for certain he would have flown directly into it, head first, doubtless killing himself.

"Explain this foolishness, Trothee!" the Captain loomed above him.

Ay'r rose to his feet with effort feeling pain all along one side, his hip, an elbow. The breath had been knocked out of him. He managed to say, "I was lost."

"Lost!? You were right here. All could see your antics. We wondered if you'd gone mad."

"I was lost. I could see nothing whatever. Only mist. Sometimes myself reflected, but fleetingly."

"How can this be?" Sand-Drifter asked, helping Ay'r now. "We could plainly see you walking and air-boarding, talking to yourself."

The Captain began to laugh.

Some of the others laughed too, although less heartily, since they didn't know why.

"He was ... he had no ... while we could ..." The Captain found the greatest mirth in Ay'r's predicament.

"I was lost," Ay'r declared again and this time with the pain of how lost he'd been in his voice. "I meant no harm. I was lost ... And ... I thank you.... for finding me."

"But you were right here," Sand-Drifter explained again, "all the while. We could see you walking strangely and then making these wide loops with your board and ..."

The Captain came up to Ay'r and took him by both shoulders. In a low voice, he said, "pardon, young Trothee for my laughter. We didn't understand. None of us could quite understand, but now I believe I do. While you were in our sight all the while, you were indeed as hopelessly lost as any creature in existence. It is the Sea of Glass!"

Ay'r realized he was trembling. He was safe. Yet he was trembling. He wanted to pull away, but when he tried to do so, the Captain only clasped him closer, right to his breast, saying "I understand. You were completely alone. Lost to all and everything.

Poor lad!"

"Get his board and his vest also," he said the others. "Make a chain of yourselves linked by hands a meter or so apart so that one is always in sight at all times to another. This Sea of Glass seems to create strange and unhappy illusions to our eyes and minds. Come, young Trothee, you've had a bad fright, but you're safe now."

So, the Captain insisted on helping Ay'r up the ramp way and back on board, pushing away solicitous onlookers among the passengers and crew, saying, "he fell hard and will need a medical check. You, Silberklang, take him to his chamber and look him over."

Ay'r clasped the Captain once tightly before they separated and he was taken in hand by the geologist. In that moment, the Captain leaned over and said into his ear, "tonight, if you need as much comforting as I believe is your due, come to my cabin," and Ay'r felt their wrist connections cross and saw a spark, as something, possibly the entry key, was passed between them.

Chapter Six

"Let me understand this correctly," Ay'r said. "you believe I'm a spy?" He chuckled and it came out very grandmotherly, which amused him even more, so he chuckled again.

"It seems that your wrist-connector refuses to respond to our subliminal interrogation."

"Bravo for my wrist-connector! That's an invasion of privacy if ever I heard one."

Kristo Var Delius, the Provincial Governor of L'Anxa Land, where he'd alit two days previous, was about four hundred and fifty, possibly five hundred years old, i.e. a little younger than himself, but she was in comparatively poor physical condition, extremely frail, bent from osteoporosis, and her skin was lizard-like, wrinkled, spotted almost to two distinct tints. She walked with mechanized help, via hip-to-leg braces attached to Cyber-shoes, and she was both supported and propelled by them. To date, this was the most complex mechano Ay'r's wrist connector had been able to sense or to recognize on this hidden Matriarchal world. Even the complex combine planter/harvester machine and fly-bys had only a grade 14 to 17 Cyber-brain, Not only were none of them sentient, most of them were utterly irresponsive to his own wrist-connector's provocations to discussion or exchange of information. All they provided were basic specs and usages.

Yes, both parties had been checking up on each other.

"Let me add," Kristo said, in a clearly irritated tone of what now also appeared to be a mechanically amplified voice, "that approximately fifty-six hours ago a small but noticeable spatial anomaly was detected in our planet's thermosphere."

"A meteorite?" Ay'r asked, all innocence.

"*Something* got in past our defense shield," the woman named Madonna M'beki replied. "Something admittedly atomically small, but then *nothing*, even that small, is *ever* allowed in," she concluded.

The "interrogation" had been going on for at least a half hour, over a coffee-flavored stelezine drink, and with what tasted like excellent, possibly homemade, Lady Fingers. The scene was the governor's office, a comfortable, thickly carpeted, heavily furnished room, redolent of the Matriarchy with its soft pastel hued art and stationary Holo-Screen frames depicting daughters, granddaughters, etc. Besides the two elderly women, there was a statuesque MC guard outside each doorway, heavily armed.

"You're not an Original, as you've fooled our citizens so far that you must be. Although clearly you have experiences, either real or imagined, concerning Our Leader and her home world," Kristo now declared.

"Imagined?" Ay'r laughed again and concluded it must be the extra nitrogen in the atmosphere that made him so giddy.

"The details are uncannily correct," the darker skinned, heavier-bodied, M'beki now said. "So it could have been inserted into your mind."

"Does the L'Anxa Provincial Government do that too? Insert false memoires into old women's minds? On top of invading their wrist-connectors?"

At an impasse yet again, Kristo fell to looking at a report.

M'beki stood up and looked out the window at the many fields surrounding that side of the building, another soft, curving, vegetation-hung version of old Melisande's Matriarchal Council Headquarters. The other side faced the city, such as it was. It wasn't very big. And it was the most populous on this planet, No one usually spoke back to M'beki like this and she was trying to remain calm with this new obstinate arrival.eadquarters.

"How can you say I'm not an Original?" Ay'r tried, "because you personally know all of them?

"Pretty much, yes," M'beki said without turning.

"There were so few?"

"Eleven hundred and ninety-two women," Kristo put in.

"That's a great many women to know personally."

"Only a few hundred are still alive," M'beki admitted.

"And the men?"

"Who are you?" Kristo now asked.

"How many of the men are now alive?" he insisted.

"Who *are* you?" Kristo insisted back.

"None of the men have survived. There were only a few dozen to begin with. All volunteers," M'beki added.

"I'm certain of that. Her Matriarchy was very persuasive when she wanted to be. She certainly was with me"

"Who are you?" Kristo demanded. "You must tell us who you are! How is it you know so much?"

"You may or may not know my name. If you left the empire before –" he provided a local date in Sidereal Time Year 3825. "It's possible that my name might have been mentioned in the most secret of the Matriarchal Archives. My name is Ay'r Kerry Sanqq'. I did go, as I told you before, on a mission for Wicca VIII, shortly before that date."

"It checks out," the ancient wall computer voice responded. "The person before you did indeed partake in a secret mission for Herself."

How primitive it all was! And then Ay'r recalled they'd been fighting Cybers for their very existences when they fled.

"My mission mates were P'al Syzygy, a 92 percent cloned-scion of the Hesperian House of Syzygy, and Eudora's own highly esteemed Doctor Alli-Lui Clark. Our secret mission was to a seeded world called Pelagia. We returned with our mission successfully accomplished ... Please believe me when I say I mean you no possible harm."

"Everything checks out, except the last part," the wall computer confirmed. "I.e. about the mission's success. The date of the mission's return is not in this mind's framework records, and supposedly post-dates it."

The two women stared at him for the longest time.

"So you're what? ... Some long delayed ... letter from home?" M'beki uttered, her large-featured face suddenly beginning to light up.

"Now, wait one minute, Sol Rad.," Ay'r warned them. "It's not what you're ..."

"She still uses the old terminology," Kristo put a hand to her mouth, excitedly. "This is real, Madonna! She's the real thing!"

"Please," M'beki pleaded. "Tell us. Tell us that we survived the machines?"

Ay'r was moving on dangerous ground now.

"Dis-Fortress was destroyed," Ay'r said, "and all of its renegades either surrendered or were destroyed."

"Thank Eve."

"And the monster?" Kristo begged.

"If by that you mean Cray 12,000, he surrendered to myself and a friend on the planet Pelagia. He did so in a manner that insured his destruction by Matriarchal Guards."

"Great Eve be thanked!"

"All gratitude to Wicca!"

"Cray 12,000 committed suicide," Ay'r tried explaining.

"Then we are saved!"

"We can return home!"

"Wait, wait, wait! And listen on, a bit more, ladies," Ay'r warned, and watched their smiles and joyful tears cease. "Yes. The Three Species are saved. This is true. But the Cyber-virus, once set in motion galaxy-wide could never be altered or stopped by anyone. Human or machine."

"What ...? Then ...?"

"The Cyber-virus ran its predestined course, infecting every Human and Delphinid g.female it touched. Having done that, it has now utterly vanished from the galaxy. Well, perhaps somewhere, in a laboratory, under the most guarded conditions, a sample of it exists. Of this I am not sure."

"But if it ran its course ..." M'beki understood first.

"Yes. It ran its course. As a result, every g.female who *could be* infected *was* infected. A few dozen Bella=Arth.s also suffered. They, by the way, in several capacities, aided in the destruction of Cray 12,000 and his rebellious forces and that third Species is now much more closely tied to us than ever."

"He?! Why do you call Cray he?!!" Kristo insisted.

"Ma'am, I was present at Cray 12,000's end, and with all due respect, I use that pronoun carefully. I have never encountered a conscious being come to such complete comprehension of the tragedy of the shared sentient condition as that so-called machine."

"But ... then ... that means that we are the very last here?" M'beki asked. She at least was grasping his news. "Perhaps not. But as far as I know yes, you are the last viable all-woman world in the galaxy that I'm aware of. And I honor you and I think all the rest of us will too, if you allow us to ... "

"Stop! Wait just one moment. How can this be? It makes no

sense!" Kristo cried.

"Wall computer!" Ay'r called out. "Will you explain my mission on Pelagia? Permission is granted via File 43222001fb1."

The wall computer spoke: "That mission was designed to locate the developmental laboratories of your father – Sunni Sanqq'?"

"Exactly what kind of laboratories were those?" Ay'r asked.

"For genetic derivation experiments," the wall computer explained, "based on the work of Lydia Relfi."

"That heretic!" Kristo hissed. "I was present when they were all banished, her and her heretical followers!"

"Ma'am. I am the son of – Sunni Sanqq' and of Creed Lars'son, from a period *after* that banishment. The latter, a g.male, was my mother! He carried me and bore me for six months, as a result of Lydia Relfi's viviparturition techniques which has by that time been perfected. I was placed in a developmental Cyber-womb. I was birthed at age ten months, and as soon as I was stable, I was dropped off on a distant, unpopulated moon of a non-descript planet in a nowhere solar system, with a beacon signaling a crashed space yacht. The corpse of an unknown, already dead woman was placed next to me. My finders assumed she had birthed me. I am a g.male myself. I was physically altered for this mission."

He watched them listen in shock and horror. Their world was being turned upside down in front of them. Women were men and men gave birth, although women could not. It was beyond heresy. It was unimaginable.

"When I arrived on Pelagia as a grown up many years later, those that I met hailed me as the first of the New Men. Do you grasp the meaning of that term? I did not until they explained it all to me."

Both women had put their hands up to their mouths. The depth of it all was now striking home.

"What they meant," Ay'r went on, "was that I was the first person ever successfully born of union of two male Humans. Since then, a large breeding program had been in operation for close to a century upon Pelagia. In short, Her Matriarchy's instincts had been absolutely correct. She sent *you* here to survive. And she sent me *there* to Pelagia to bring back Lydia Relfi's technique, in case you *didn't* survive."

"And now … there's a few thousand of you odd males. And this entire world of women to repopulate the galaxy." Kristo began, hopefully.

"No, Ma'am. The actuality, some four hundred years, Sol Rad., later, is as follows: there are a *billion-trillion* of us so-called Vir'istic, child-bearing males," he corrected. "And four hundred years later, the Center Worlds stretch from the old Orion spur, across the Orion Arm that you knew so well and now extends deep into the Sagittarius Arm, approaching the heart of the galaxy. The Ib'r Republic of the Three Species and Allied Sentients, as it is called, now encompasses a half million populated planets. It's three times the size of the Second Matriarchy."

"And … Melisande?" Kristo's voice was small.

"I'm happy to report that lovely planet remains intact. As does Eudora and Benefica, Dickinson, Bronte, Iphigenia, Iris, Yuan Mei, all of them. Wicca World especially is cared for, virtually a museum. The women who still reside there are also cared for."

"Infertile women!" Kristo spat.

"Honored and respected and usually older women! … Hesperia, the City on a Star, is the new capital of the galactic government."

"Infertile and useless women! Until what? Until they die out? Don't you see, Madonna? We didn't *win* at all! We *lost* it all! *All* of it!"

"The Three Species survived," Ay'r pointed out. "Wicca's War was fought for that outcome. You were sent here, and I was sent to Pelagia to insure *that* outcome!"

"It's not a victory if you are all g.males."

"Are there no young women at all?" M'beki asked.

"There are. Very few. We don't know how or why it happens that males give birth to females so infrequently. But female births do occur, although they are rare. One in ten million or so births. I have a granddaughter myself."

Kristo was sobbing. "It's the *worst… possible* outcome!"

"Wicca knew better," Ay'r said.

"The worst!"

"Ma'am? Mer M'beki?" he tried her companion, who was equally shaken.

"What of Her Matriarchy?" M'beki asked, point blank.

No sense in hiding it.

"Assassinated by a Maudlin Se'er on Hesperia as she sought to escape the City's protective custody. Along with her companion, Tam Apollon!"

Kristo was sobbing inconsolably now.

"We'll find a comfortable suite here for you," M'beki said, her chest heaving with emotion. "You'll be our guest … This information you carry is potentially very damaging to our society. And to our entire way of life. You must understand that?"

"But what if I bring your society a life-changing offer too?"

"I … really … don't …"

"I can do that, you understand?" Ay'r insisted.

"But you're a unnecessary functionary? A mere socio-ethnician, no?"

"I shouldn't tell you this, Ladies, but it may compensate for my terrible news. Your captive is the most important person in the Ib'r Republic. I'm the first Cityzen of Hesperia. And one of the twenty or so wealthiest in the universe."

It was as though they hadn't heard him.

"How can we *tell* them?" Kristo was begging M'beki. "After all this *time*! After *all* their *struggles!* How can we possibly *tell them?*"

"Ladies, please reconsider," Ay'r now begged.

M'beki threw open the door, and addressed the guard. "This person is our guest in the Pratiline Suite."

Ay'r could do no other thing but stand up and leave them in their new knowledge and despondency.

"If you wish, I will open my wrist connector to your wall computer. If they can somehow find an interface, then perhaps we all can locate some way of accommodating this distressing situation."

"Gratitude, Ser Sanqq'," M'beki said icily, leaving the guard, who could only see three women in front of her, utterly confused but still on alert.

In the corridor, as they walked on, Ay'r said, "take me to bed, Sweetie. It's been a very long day."

Early mornings on Narcissus 12 were Clark's favorite times of day here at the Iridium Monastery, and especially in this very special wing, housing the Beloved One, the Short-Lived One, the Prophet Loren.

True, it was coldest during these very hours, but there were under-suits to keep one's body warm although Clark considered the hood's warming-vents a luxuriant excrescence, and did without, preferring the piercing iciness for its bracing wakefulness, essential to the best efforts of the Great Morning Meditation that would determine the rest of the day.

The cold and also the silence, that's what Clark valued above all for the meditation to be beneficial. He would settle into whatever free posture he'd chosen the night before – this morning it was a half lotus with one leg up and touching his other shoulder and held straight out – and watch the sky lighten from deepest black to pale pink, all in a matter of hours, before he would be spelled by the Watcher for the Sept through Onze hours. The only distractions were the other fourteen moons, and the four inner planets wheeling high above, all at one time or another visible during the night, a great Iridium Orrery reminding Clark of the enormous revolution that he and the Mummified Prophet Loren too had experienced.

Understanding that had led Gus'o Raci-Dell, the presiding Abbott to accept Clark into the monastery so very late in life. Most postulates were late-Neos, only a few older, all in recognition of their now helpless Leader's nearly lifelong youth, his seeming refusal to display signs of usual growth and aging. Of course, Clark had not told Dell everything when signing up. He'd not told Dell, for example, that one of those life altering metamorphoses had been a change of gender. Not that it would make much of a difference. Only men were allowed inside these walls, or anywhere near the Mummified One. That was a given. But then Clark wondered if there were *any* g.females on Moon Twelve at all. He'd seen none.

That gender change had occurred a while back anyway and Clark had settled into Vir'ism easily enough. Early on, when Clark was still Alli-Lui Clark and not Clark Alli-Lui, she'd been considered unfeminine, mannish. Traces of the Y chromosome had been found flourishing in her DNA and even in her more primitive Telomeric make-up. But all that had meant nothing once she'd awakened, like a princess in one of silly Ay'r Kerry Sanqq's old Metro-Terran fairy tales, and there, suddenly, was 'Harles Ib'r.

For the first time ever Alli had fallen in love. They remained in love thereafter. On Pelagia. On Hesperia, later. Indeed even after he had lived out the course of his puny two hundred years of life, she'd remained in love with 'Harles Ib'r for several decades. Afterward, once, almost in desperation, she had bedded a male who looked like a younger version of him – one of his many, many grandchildren by others it turned out – and he'd possessed some of that slow wit and unhurried calm charm. But that boy already loved another. She'd been a mere toy, someone to make that other boy jealous.

And so it had gone. After 'Harles, if Alli wanted romance, it was invariably with a Hesperian male "pervert," someone usually more into the erotic-codified minutiae, the signs and symbols of the old, almost forgotten, Metro-Terran Heterosexuality, rebels usually, always younger, most often vapid.

After a dozen or so such experiences over several decades, Alli took the physical change, by no means the only g.female on Hesperia to do so and had her name and everything else legally changed.

By then she had fallen away from the huge new Ib'r clan that now filled Hesperia's older and wealthiest Girders via intermarriage. Even though they were *her* relatives by marriage too, she no longer saw them, not even her own blood child by 'Harles.

Bear Evon Ib'r, and his own now large, all male family was still trying to live off the social indignity of having been birthed by a g.female and on top of that on a backward planet like Pelagia. Alli had explained it was the only way he *could* have been born, and how preciously rare his existence was. One of what? A few score thousand such births post-Cyber-virus in that year galaxy-wide? And all because she'd been at Dryland, i.e. nowhere near the virus?! Of course the Cyber virus was still circulating the galaxy, it did so for decades, and so it came back to bite Alli and she was never able to conceive or birth as a female again.

'Harles' own Pelagia-born sons and daughters had all had their lives extended via the newest techniques, but it had only added another century to that golden generation, for a total of three hundred years for 'Nton, three oh-nine for Dward, and three twenty-one for Oudma. And when they too died, Alli inherited more than she would ever require, even though by then she was only one of seventy or so heirs. Oudma, her Pelagian sister, going last, was what decided her to make the physical change to male. As a Hesperian male, as Clark, she could return to her studies in Hydrographfluids with ease. So "he" did, taking a few updating courses, then moving from one Delphinid world to another, helping to hydro-form the previously donated or newly found or recently ceded worlds, so they might become ripe for Delphinid mastery.

Lost in work, Clark no longer cared for amours, although a few presented themselves, mostly among the Ambassadorial Class Delphinid males, nine-tenths Human, and usually even more difficult to decipher than fully Human males. And then, one afternoon, with all of his water-work successfully done on Antinuous Terce, Clark had boarded a Slp.G liner for a slow tour of the Nearer Sag. Arm, a ten year cruise vacation, in which all thoughts of work and vocation slowly ebbed out of his, by-now, seven hundred and four year old mind.

Scores of new Wonders of the Galaxy had been added to the famous Matriarchal Catalogue, most of the new ones were included on this cruise, and among those, number seventy six had been to planet Narcissus and to the Iridium Vir'ism Monastery, on Narcissus' 12th moon, center of a rapidly growing religion, home to the still living, albeit mostly mummified, body of the man Alli had met two or three times when he was a small child on Dryland, before it all ended in torrents from the sky.

Clark had bought a lovely souvenir edition of *The Book of Colored Glory* on that cruise tour stop, a souvenir small enough to fit in his hand and Clark had slowly but certainly become obsessed with the text during the remainder of the cruise – "Worlds of Water and Ice" the tour had been called – unsurprisingly. Clark kept up enough with his family, mostly back on Hesperia, via Holo-Comm.s to comprehend how brilliantly prophetic Loren had been about them all. Meanwhile, joining the cruise onboard was a Iridium-ist Prelate, a lovely man Clark's own age, on his way to open a church among the Diaspora Community of Bella=Arth.s upon Markab's fourth planet.

It was that Prelate who so much helped in understanding the niceties of the versification, and the brilliance of the prophecies. When they parted at Hesperia, Clark possessed a recommendation for entry into the Home Monastery in the Prelate's own voice-print.

Once he was back in the Ib'r Republic's Capital, the mostly young, all male, ultra-consumerist, wildly style-crazed, Media-mad, money-minded Hesperian population that Clark encountered made the next decision easy. In weeks, the business end of it was all taken care of, everything properly disposed of, and Clark was on his way to Narcissus 12, within a Beryllium 18 freighter's small passenger section, already clad in the slate gray with rainbow hued hem and sleeve cuffed robes of an Iridium Acolyte.

Only a few very minor modifications of the Thirty Six Steps Toward Iridium Postulancy were needed to be done by Presiding Abbott, Raci-Dell to allow for Clark's advanced age, and none of the other Acolytes ever complained. Indeed, on occasion, a recent Post-Neo named 'Stavo who suddenly came upon Clark praying in an-open-to-the-sky corridor or deeply concentrated in a Scriptorium – all had to learn how to "write" using Cyberized engraving-pen quills upon fine alloy metal leaves to make more "books," both as souvenirs for the tourists (and thus sources of income), and as spiritual teaching tools for the Future Consolidation. Invariably 'Stavo would sigh, for even at this advanced and uncosmetized age, Clark still retained the lean physique and strong facial lineaments that had made Alli one of the reigning intellectual beauties of Melisande in its final year, Sol Rad., of Wicca VIII's empire.

"Remember Quatrain Sixty-two, Brother Postulant Kocsis!" Clark would utter, not unkindly, *sotto-voce*, as 'Stavo would slip past in a whisper of rich garments:

> *Where once indifferent INDIGO*
> *Flaunted Seven Great Houses in Mutual*
> *Destruction, now green, PALEST GREEN*
> *Out-battles the Beautiful for Pre-eminence!*

It was believed by Iridium scholars, here at the monastery and abroad, that this hortatory poemlet was Loren's first (of many further) references to the Ib'r family's sudden appearance upon Hesperia and how they forever altered the Galactic ideals of beauty and desirability by their own stunningly odd appearance, which almost everyone understood had quickly come to represent a new criterion.

This would become a constant theme throughout the middle

seventies through nineties of the quatrains in the book, and it was often believed to be a sigil as well as analogizing the complete changeover from Matriarchal to Neo-Patriarchal societal norms.

"Forget Indigo, Brother Clark," 'Stavo had replied. "When earth-brown is so irresponsibly rich!"

Clark had colored at the reference to his own eye color, and turned away. He'd had never teased the youth again.

Clark colored a whit now, remembering that such were not appropriate topics to meditate upon. Better control was needed.

The first hint of rose had suffused the blue-black heavens with premonitions of dawn, when Clark felt a sudden throb or thud.

It was subtle, but distinct. But where had it come from?

After another half hour of Meditation, he'd still failed to find out from where the sound had issued, definitely not from Clark himself, alone in the domed-room. Silent as it was, even with his thoughts so distracted, he would have heard even the alighting of a Ezer Lark on a branch of SweetBud Tree a hundred meters distant. From here, Clark could even hear the Abbott's secretary stirring in his bed, always the first to arise, never mind any Acolyte rising in sleep to make water.

A half hour had passed before – Thud.

There it was again.

A bit more prepared this time, Clark had felt as well as heard the little throbbing. Felt it against his right ankle bone, placed almost flat against the woven matting. Felt it a bit less higher up within his body's Coiled Snake chakra, then less so, flowing upward, into his legs, knees, thighs, torso, neck, even his teeth.

It was deliberately made sound. *Deliberately made nearby.* Within the room.

Clark unfolded his posture and flattened in homage, and then shakily stood and quietly stepped around the plinth of transparent plastro within which the Beloved One, the Short-Lived One, the Prophet Loren slept eternally.

And received a shock. One side of the puerile face was altered ever so slightly, the side closest to where Clark had sat meditating – and it was altered into the merest sketch, the barest hint, of a smile. In all these months, Clark had never seen the like.

No! It's your imagination, Clark

But yes! It was altered. And the finger! Look how the little finger is raised a quarter of an inch above the surface of the plinth, while all the others, and yes, on the other side too, remained flattened. Could that finger have tapped two thuds?

Clark must awaken the Abbott immediately.

No. That was utter madness! This was a hallucination brought about by meditation. What had Brother Gupta said only last week, of the vagaries of the mind? The tricks it played upon itself?

Clark would return to his meditation!

Return to meditation, but also keep a close eye on that little finger and on that curl of the lip.

Within fifteen minutes Sol Rad., the finger tapped the plinth. The smile widened imperceptibly.

"Oh, Beloved One! Short-Lived One! Prophet Loren!" all tumbled out of Clark. "Are you communicating with my worthless self?"

The smile widened a bit. The finger lifted a smidgen.

"I'm new. One of the newest of Acolytes in the Order and I'm unprepared for such an honor. Should I awaken the Abbott?"

The finger dropped a tiny bit, the smile began to close.

"No. No. I am not to do that. I understand, "Oh, Beloved One! Short-Lived One! Prophet Loren! Then what am I to do?"

The finger slowly moved as though to tap and then stopped before tapping.

As though waiting for something. Waiting for what? Not for the Abbott, but for …

"Oh, Beloved One! Short-Lived One! Prophet Loren! Are you in need? Water? Sustenance? Medicine? Anything?"

The finger seemed to waver. No, none of those.

"Food? Warmth? More air? Cooler temperature?" Clark went slowly through an entire list, trying to think ahead to the next possibility and almost missed it when "the book itself" was followed by the question of a "pen-quill?"

That's when the finger tapped, a thud.

"You need a pen-quill to write? But how ever …?" The thought solidified. "You want *me* to get the pen-quill for myself. And something to write on?"

The finger rose, and did the tiniest dance of approval. The lips smiled ever so slightly.

"You wish me to transcribe?"

Yes, of course, that was it. Clark had been here every morning for sixty-three days, Sol Rad., and had become somehow familiar to the Beloved One! the Short-Lived One! the Prophet Loren! And now he wanted Clark to transcribe something.

"What? A new quatrain for the book?" Clark asked aloud.

And the smile widened.

"Of course. I'm honored! Oh, Beloved Prophet Loren!" Clark stood up and left the domed room thinking, I'm clearly out of my mind.

Gupta was right. Clark was hallucinating wildly. But if so, then at least consistently.

So, he left the wing and quietly walked directly to the side-chamber attached to the Great Scriptorium, and there found a pen-quill and alloy leaves, for "emergency use" of those who had taken vows of silence. As he was returning to the wing a thought crossed his mind, "how will I know what to write? Clearly the Beloved Prophet could not t'elp the material. How will a finger tapping and a smile ever add up to a quatrain?

Here, Alli's experience came to Clark's aid. On Dryland, the mountain people had all communicated by giant horns, kilometers across passes and canyons, across far distances. Their sounds had been notated into a kind of speech music. Loren had grown up in just such a village, he must be familiar with the language of the horns.

A detour ensued to the Bibliorum, where all of the knowledge from all of the varied members of the monastery had been stored, just before their wrist-connectors were turned off for monastic life.

Once inside, Clark realized that his wrist-connector was flashing; it had been reactivated. By Loren? For his use?

"Wrist-connector, find me Planet Pelagia, in the Outer Arm, Globular Sinister, the continent Dryland, the Monosilla Valley area, specifically the non-verbal communication system used by the people there."

In seconds, it was done, and Clark understood it.

"Wrist-connector, find me a very basic grammar for translating that Monosilla communication system into extremely difficult to make taps, very slight finger movements, and an extremely partial smile."

In seconds it was done and Clark grasped it.

The Prophet Loren remained as before, beneath the transparent plastro, upon the plinth. The sky was now roseate with the pre-Dawn of the Ice-Planet Narcissus above them.

"Oh, Beloved One! I am returned. Gratitude for choosing me for this honor. I understand that my wrist-connector will be working while we are together in this dome. I am ready to begin and beg your indulgence in advance for any inconsistencies or stupidities I know I am capable of."

Clark sat in full lotus, held the lightly humming pen-quill to the trembling alloy leaf and uttered: "Whenever you are ready, O Beloved Loren."

And waited and waited and then there was a tap, a distinct thud, a beginning. It was followed minutes later by the distinctive minor curl of the lifted finger left and then somewhat afterward by the downturn of the right side of the lower lip

Two hours later, shortly after the Presiding Abbott Gus'o Raci-Dell was about to drink his first stimulant of the morning, the Watcher from Sept to Onze flew into his chamber gibbering almost uncontrollably.

Ten minutes later, three of them, the Abbott, the Watcher and the Abbott's secretary, accompanied by a floating Historical-Witness Cyber, stood inside the dome-room of The Beloved One's rest, and beheld the form of the Acolyte Clark, bent over double, quietly sobbing. He was helped up by two of them and brought to his dormitor-cell and quickly given an injection to put him to sleep.

Gus'o Raci-Dell held in his hand a metal page that read

> *In Central Chaos, everted EBONY reigns.*
> *as Blessed Contamination ...*

"What is it?" 'Stavo, the Post-Neo who was smitten with Clark, asked the gathering of young postulants who were uncharacteristically loitering about the dome's entrance.

"The Beloved One is writing again," said a colleague, unable to hide his excitement.

"Brother Clark is the Prophet's new pathway," agreed another.

"Is it true, dear Abbott?" 'Stavo asked.

"A full line and three more words, so far," The Abbott replied. "Rejoice! All! Rejoice. After ten decades and more, *The Book of Colored Glory* goes on. Goes *on!*" he shouted in triumph to the pastel pink morning and to Narcissus' enormous, bloated mass of swirling mirrored surface, reflecting sunlight as it floated high above.

Holt came awake quickly. Dem-Arest was already moving about. Were they arrived already? The three-man Fast clearly had stopped enough to expand to full size.

"Lord Sanqq'!" the Fast's mind greeted him. "We have stopped before our next allocated area."

"Ah, you're with us, Holt," Tap Zullini-Brach dropped his own privacy screen and stretched. "What's all this Fast is saying about an unexpected anomaly?"

"Jan'sen?" Holt asked.

The physicist turned away from the wall screen with the most excited look on his face, Holt had ever seen.

"We're not there yet, are we?" Holt asked.

"About six-sevenths of the distance," Dem-Arest admitted.

"What's this anomaly?"

"All Fast travel beyond a few thousand light years is automatically set to encounter signs of various types of multi-spectrum waves suggestive of intelligent life. Our Fast just found one. I imagine Darency and Drei-Lennon will be stopping soon."

Tap brought Holt a wake-up drink and stretched his own still very desirable body for the greatest effect.

"Fast!" Dem-Arest prompted. "Care to explain?"

"It's a totally unknown signal, Doctor. Or rather a group of signals wrapped around some type of flux. It's not clear whether the signals are purposive or instead if they are merely dimensional transfers from unknown planet-wide activity with no communicative purpose beyond their own surface or level."

"Well that's clear as transparent Plastro!" Holt couldn't resist commenting, and the others laughed.

"What I mean to say, Lord Sanqq', is that it's not clear whether we are being hailed or if, rather, this is all residual communication waves surrounding a planet or system."

"But in either case," Dem-Arest said, "we are bound to stop and at least check it out. It might be a new species or sentient. If so, we at least have to recognize it in Fast's log."

"Completely true, Lord Sanqq'," The Fast agreed.

"How long will this take?"

"As little as an hour, real time."

"Since we have no choice, let's do it, Fast!"

"It will be as efficiently processed as possible," the ship assured him.

"An interesting solar system," Dem-Arest put it on a Holo for them to all look at. "Look, Holt, Tap!"

Tap was having none of it; Fast had downloaded some virtual physical equipment for him, and he began working out, but he peeked anyway.

"Two small red suns. Four tiny brown planets. Six miniscule satellites." Tap counted. "Looks like a bruised and battled system that's undergone more than a bit of Super Nova-flash activity to me. Exactly what we were expecting to encounter in this crowded area, no, Dem? All kinda boring!"

"Except that planet number three is a bit different," the physicist said.

"Because its puke colored and not defecation brown?"

Dem-Arest laughed. "There is that. But that puke colored surface appears to be completely artificial, and made of some kind of super-tempered ceramic."

"Let's get a closer look," Holt said. "Fast? Is that planet the source of multi-spectrum waves that stopped you?"

"It would appear so, yes. Enlargements in real time are ... here!"

The smoothness of the surface, and the straight lines, whether diagonal or horizontal, all spoke of the surface having been manufactured rather than natural. Holt was reminded of the surface of a few, very ancient, Cyber-shipping-vehicles he'd skated past not long ago, on Gerspellion's Girder. There also appeared to be a few recessed pockets, equally horizontal, below.

"Is that water?"

"Or a close approximation," Fast agreed. "Of course its ions have been changed several times around, I'm guessing, by gigantic radiation storms the planet must have experienced, being this close to the galactic center."

"Is that why the ceramic covering is there too?" Tap asked.

"Look, closely," the Fast said and zeroed in on one area that looked bruised, scooped out, and more roughly filled in. "There are dozens of these and they appear to be the self-repairing result of an attack of some sort. Not a material attack such as an asteroid," it clarified. "Possibly of enormous jets of extremely high powered energy that merely glanced across the area."

"Self repairing? Is the planet a single, giant, closed-system?" Dem-Arest asked.

"A unit? Unlikely, although the ceramic goes down several deep layers, there is a structural feel to all beneath it. Suggestive of enclosing a space."

"Enclosing people! Which it's probably protecting," Tap said for all of them. "If they're all dead or dying, I don't want to know about it, Fast."

"None of us do," Holt agreed.

"I've been accessing some of those multi-spectrum waves," Dem-Arest now said. "And I've gotten the prism down to about four or five discrete waves that seem to be comprehensible to our Fast. We're going to eavesdrop a bit now."

There was a general hissing noise, then something that might have been voices, then very clear voices, calm, almost Human, although Fast assured them that was merely the translation process. It seemed to be in words but mostly numbers and formulas, and it was very calm and considered. Not panicky. Not at all desperate.

"Doc?"

"Very odd. Very ... the conversations all appear to be coded, or in cipher or ... well, just mathematical in nature. Fast? What's your take?"

"Seemingly so, Dr. Dem-Arest. It's not quite the language that this Fast uses with others of its kind, but structurally and grammatically, it is similar."

Tap came alive at that and stopped at rep one hundred and sixty-nine.

"I know! It's the last hide-out of the Matriarchy's Rebel-Cybers!! Cray 12,000 is there, and is totally gaga from Super-Nova Gushers!"

"Cray 12,000 was dismantled in the S.T. year 38..." Fast began.

"Then his cronies. They escaped early to set up a Cyber in Exile kingdom out here where no one will bother to look. Biding their time, perfecting a new Cyber-virus until ..."

"Now do you see why I love him, Doc?" Holt asked Dem-Arest.

"He does have a vivid imagination."

"Every day's a brand new experience for Tap."

"Hey! At least I try!" Tap turned on his privacy screen so he wouldn't hear any more.

"Well, Lord Sanqq' and Doctor Dem-Arest, I've done a life-search, trying to accommodate the anomalous surface."

"And?"

"We hear voices. They're not Cybers, because I'm not receiving any kind of electronic signatures. But what I am picking up is ambiguously life – at best."

"Alive? Not alive? Big question." Holt said. "I hope this isn't going to take longer because you can't figure out if ..."

"Lord Sanqq'!" the Fast interrupted him. "We've just received an invitation to drop in."

"From ...?" Dem-Arest asked.

"From our hosts below. One moment while I ... they've just sent me a protective formula for temporarily shielding this Fast against any of the energy burst-jets they've received. Several are regular and those can be easily avoided, but a few are random, and it's really quite a simple formula."

"Wait, before ..."

"Only the very outer cellular layer, Doctor! Only the very surface. And I can shuck it before I jump. Ah, here are the other Fasts stopped now. They're being informed of the situation and given the protective layer too."

"Accept the invitation," Holt said. "I'll go down in a pod."

"Me too!" Tap insisted.

"Lord Sanqq'! This Fast can only protect one pod at a time from all unknown factors."

"Then let's have one visitor from each Fast. Ying Darency, and maybe Casper al-Haaretz too!"

Tap was peeved he couldn't join Holt, but nevertheless helped defensively arm and ready him for a pod-drop.

"If they're hot-looking, send one up for me," Tap said as the pod sealed shut.

As his T-pod dropped from the Fast's underside, Holt could see two more tiny, transparent, one-man pods appear. Soon they were all hovering nearby.

"I've used the formula our hosts provided," Holt's Fast told him, "to shield your pods. But because of other factors like weight and maneuverability, it's not as total a shield as we now possess. It's suggested, Lord Sanqq', that none of you linger outside the shielding for very long.

They dropped almost instantly and were soon bathed in the dull red glow of the two small, distant suns – one vermillion, the other more carmine – gleaming off the planets' more or less uniform surface, a visual effect not possible to descry from orbit, and quite surprisingly majestic, if also somehow melancholy-inducing.

Ying Darency, ever the architect/sculptor, noticed, of course, and immediately blurted out "Gorgeous! Now imagine a revolving all-white structure bathed in this glow, or better yet, one surfaced entirely in chromium! I must find a double system like this and build something to catch all of its lighting potentialities."

More practical, al-Haaretz asked, "do we have any guarantees of safety? What if this is a trap?"

"For what it is worth, Cap' we've got guarantees."

"For what it's worth?"

They were dropping rapidly, pulled by the surprising gravity of the world. They agreed the place was denser than they'd expected, probably the shielding.

"It looks completely solid. How do we get inside, Fast?" al-Haaretz had just asked when ahead of them they noticed what appeared to be spinning diamonds of light forming an arced-down flight path and landing pattern.

As they neared the surface, Darency was able to utter, "and the light is even better right here" when a large plate of ceramic opened ahead, more than large enough for a Slp.G liner to fit into, never mind their little pods, and they slipped right in. Soundlessly, it closed below them as they quickly dropped down past various layers of structuring and supports and then entire other surfaces that also slid open to admit them, until Holt estimated that they had passed about thirty miles or so.

"Fifty-five miles," the Fast assured him when they were at last softly landed upon a surface. "Although," it clarified, "This also appears to be a lightly utilized area, perhaps for receiving guests only. Estimates of structural depth vary to a hundred miles in."

They had landed in a square depression about two stories tall, and they waited, but nothing further happened. So Holt exited his T-pod, and, more warily, the others did too. At which the walls on one side facing them became transparent and slid open from top to bottom.

"I can't believe it," Darency was the first to say what they were all thinking.

The rectangular area they faced resembled nothing so much as the main square at Number 350 of Girders Capricorn and Bellatrix on Hesperia. Complete with the exotic foliage, the spouting fountains, even the food, drink and Soma-Stelezine kiosks, albeit with none of the latter's Bella=Arth. attendants.

They entered, wondering, and the partition silently glided shut,.

"It even smells right," Ying exclaimed. "They've got the curry-wurst and Berry-Stelezine Smoothie odors down perfectly.

In fact, there was food and drink, which Holt's wrist connector tried and declared safe and tasty too. They were sitting at a perfect replica of a three-person benched table, snacking, when suddenly a slightly larger than man-sized ceramic cage appeared several feet away. Not a cage so much as box, really, with all dull maybe ceramic-metal alloy sides.

They were about to go inspect it when three sides became transparent and within they could make out what looked like flickering lights within a sort of mist that filled it.

"Welcome to DayLight Two!' an odd yet comprehensible voice communicated somehow with them. It wasn't quite speech, nor audible sound, yet not tel'ping either. "We hope the accommodations are to your liking."

The Hesperians all stood, even though none approached the box.

"How did you do it," Ying had to ask. "I don't mean molecularly? But how did you know what it looked like? Mind reading?"

"Your flight machine's brain was kind enough to suggest this as a site for you to be physically comfortable. Is it not correct?"

"It's perfectly correct," Holt said. "You must then know who we are and where we are from?"

"We do," the lights glittered tinily. "That particular star that now houses so many of your kind was not at all occupied when last it was visited by our people. It seems to be wonderfully constructed."

"High praise from the constructors of this magnificently shielded planet!" Darency couldn't help but say in response.

"Our construction was done out of necessity. At one time, we resided within a sector of the galaxy that was a sub-spur of the galactic arm *within* the Sagittarius Arm, using your own terminology as we understand it. When it became clear to us that everything in our arm was being inexorably pulled into the chaotic galactic center, we naturally ... sought to shield our planet. Over the eons, we've done better and better at that. Synthesizing better materials until we arrived at the current one."

"Congratulations," Holt said. Then added, "are there many of you on this world?"

"Close to four hundred thousand souls."

"Do you have names?" He identified himself and his three companions.

"You may call us James."

At that moment, a second and then a third similarly sized and structurally identical box appeared behind 'James.'

"And these persons?" Holt tried.

"You may call these conglomerations of interested people Joshua and Petrus." Then, "those are the names of beings who may have been your ancestors and who our explorers did most recently encounter.

"They are old names, but very good names," Holt assured James. "When did this encounter occur?"

There was a flashing of lights synchronized within the three mist chambers and James uttered: "It's agreed that would have been approximately seven thousand of that planet's revolutions about its star. It was somewhere within the Orion Spur."

"It is hypothesized," Holt's wrist connector told him, "that very Orion Spur sector is one possible original of Humans."

"The explorations that encountered your people were the last external ones ever mounted by our people," Petrus now emitted. "Since then we've become a far more introspective race."

"Since you are able to travel that far ..." Holt calculated it must be a half-million light years from here to the Orion Spur. "Our natural question is why did you choose to remain and shield your world, rather than relocate elsewhere?"

"It was a Great Debate for almost one of our aeons," James confirmed.

"But in the end," Petrus emitted, "Our people had finished with extroversion and sought to perfect ourselves through introversion"

"Yet, by even our rough guessing," Holt said. "Your world will continue to be drawn in to the point that we call the Great Attractor. Shielding must become far thicker. And even so, your own stars may encounter collisions. Even your world might encoun ..."

"All of that will *undoubtedly* occur," James said. "We have fairly precise predictions for when they will in fact occur. It is far enough in the future to be of no concern."

"No last minute escapes are planned?" Holt asked.

"Soon none will be possible," James said.

"We are a very *old* people," Petrus now communicated. "Our greatest ages are so long past that they are beyond legendary. In truth, we may be said to now be an *exhausted* people. It has been very long since any of our people were birthed. Deaths are slowly rising. It ..." Petrus seemed to be searching for the word, "... *charms* us to meet your people who are young and healthy and still developing their potential."

"It *charms* us," James now put in, "That three new races began at about the same time and in the same sector, and that all have developed well, and that given a few wars or two to be expected, that you are all three now headed ahead together."

It *charms* us," Joshua added, "to encounter you here on our world which is a sure sign of how wonderfully you have progressed. Yet we wonder why you continue to explore when you appear to know exactly what to expect where you go further?"

Holt looked at his companions and then decided and told James and the others of the search for the star containing Beryllium 18.

The three beings once again blinked their lights synchronously among themselves. After a while, the one named James communicated, "we know of the star you look for. It is indeed a physiological twin to your home star."

Joshua: "It lies not far from here."

Petrus: "Even so it lies guarded as though by dragons by two galactic anomalies."

Joshua: "Which might prove extremely perilous."

Holt: "We are determined to find it, and to somehow harness its energy."

Again, the three beings blinked lights in private converse. Then –

James: "Your quest is *lovely* to us and it *charms* the three units of our people contained here now with you and we believe it will *charm* the entire population. We will need a consensus. If it is found to be sufficiently *charming* to the majority, we could be extremely helpful in your quest."

Holt: "What are the perils, you spoke of? Super-Nova jet gushers?"

Petrus: "Nothing so simple. One is a small attractor. The other is a star nursery. Both must be bypassed."

Joshua: "Neither anomaly belongs in that transitional area; and they are also at odds with each other physically, and so both misbehave."

Holt: "May I present our case for this task to your people?"

James: "You already have. It is being voted on as we speak."

Ying: "That's fast. We could use a little high speed democracy like that in the Ib'r Republic."

James: "It has been decided. The majority of our people are *extremely charmed* by your quest."

Petrus: "Further, a majority of the people are *excited* by your grand ambition."

Joshua: "Further, a large majority of the people are *amused* by your extravagant and vainglorious attempt."

Holt was stung and replied a little defensively, "I don't know that I would categorize it as all that vainglorious. We very much need that Beryllium 18."

James replied calmly, "it has been many aeons since our people have been charmed, amused, and excited by anyone or anything! You are promised extraordinary amounts of assistance."

"I don't understand," Casper was honest as usual. "You people are all sealed up under this shield. How are you going to help us when we are fifteen parsecs away?"

"Like this," James said, and the light-filled gas inside his cage thickened and solidified into a handsome golden facsimile of Casper al-Haaretz and stepped out from the cage walls. Joshua and Petrus joined James, one copper, the other platinum.

"Return now to your flight machines," James said, "and follow us."

"Are you really certain you wish to do this?" Holt asked. "I mean it's a lot of trouble for you and, what if something terrible happens once we're there and ..."

"Whatever happens," James said, "it's our people's first real goal in centuries. Not to mention our first *adventure* in many aeons.

"Extreme gratitude to you for this aid," Holt said.

"Naturally compensation will be required," James said.

"What kind of compensation?"

But the three DayLighters fell back into their boxes, became lighting dotted mists once more and then their boxes vanished. The wall glided back open and the three men had no choice but to return to their pods and back to their Fast vehicles.

Chapter Seven

Dim-day, the blue Hunter not yet risen, the orange Eagle just beginning to rise, scorching the horizon with blood red Rings at twenty degrees above the horizon, and appearing somewhat ethereal in this pre-sunlit morning, blue-ing at their edges into the cobalt sky:

Ay'r Eise'nstein Kell awoke suddenly feeling clammy and cold. He sat up suddenly in Captain Lepta's large, comfortable, floating bed and tried to think exactly what he was feeling, it was so new and ... disturbing, like a large hand was inside his stomach and was twisting and twisting. His head throbbed like a struck gong. Suddenly he knew what was about to happen, everything he'd eaten, not yet digested, was about to come up. He leapt out of bed and into the small lav.

Just in time. It all hurled itself out of him in three large bursts, vitriolic and disgusting. Then, when he thought it was over and he was safe, one more acidic gob came from somewhere even deeper within him and burned its way up inside him and out. He fell back against the wall, shaken, emptied out, his head even more hollowed out, coughing then splashing water into his mouth to wash the awful taste out.

He stumbled into the bed cabin and flung himself at the bed, caught its edges and pulled himself up. Lay there, hollowed out, and emptied, a vibrating shell of a thing, not a person, certainly, not himself, but what was left after ...

A hand, Lepta's, reached over and caressed his head, lightly tousling his hair.

"Third morning in a row, Trothee. If I wasn't so certain that you were unbedded on this voyage until I came to you a few weeks ago, Sol Rad., I would swear you're with child. Firsts are always difficult like that. The body fights their invading influence."

"What?" Ay'r managed to utter.

"I said, third morning in a row."

"Great father!" Ay'r sat up again, with difficulty and big golden haired tan bodied Lepta did too. "Please! ... No!"

"It has to be so. Unless," Lepta began, "unless you have been messing about on your Trothed One before myself? Don't tell me! That'll be a fine mess when we reach the Western Port. And if so, not one I'll answer for."

Panic entered where emptiness had been and impelled Ay'r to wake up fully. "No. No. No problem for you. But oh, it must have been *him*. Adam *damn* him!"

"Him? Your Trothed One himself?" Lepta asked. "Back at South Salt Pan City?"

"No, he wasn't there. It must have been before even then. At the Golden Palace Resort," it came out all at once, blurted. No one until this moment on the Arcturus Scatling had known he'd been there at all. "No wonder he ... No wonder they both ..." Ay'r stopped before he said something further incriminating.

Lepta was smiling. "Well then, the Rings of Usk continue shining down upon this Golden Rabbit Captain, fleet of foot, and easy to slip off and away. I'm safe enough, lad, but you're good and caught well now."

"Caught?"

"Caught by your Trothed One. He's planted a fast growing seed in you, Laddie!" He laughed. "That's one way to ensure that the child will be his, with a good looker like you skating about the Great Salt Ocean all on his own. Make the baby fast and first! Was it the first night of the Betrothal ceremony, do you think?" And from the horrified look Ay'r gave in response, he knew it was and said, "well, then lucky Lepta, getting all your sweetness with no consequences to bear."

Ay'r moaned and sank into the warm golden furred flesh besides him. The hand came out and held him again.

"No matter, Lad. Even though you are very young to be a mother, and it will cause you some discomfort, still, it'll be better in the long run for you and your Trothed One. They say an early birth ensures a long bonding. Remember that you'll ever be his firstborn's Mum! I don't know a Vir who doesn't have respect for that!"

There was no possibility of explaining exactly how disastrous this news was, if true, and Ay'r felt in his gut, exactly how true it was. It explained everything! Well not so much everything, as what had happened that awful night, when he went into a chamber with Deon and ended up being taken by the Princeps, Mart Kell, himself.

A further thought struck him. Perhaps the entire betrothal ceremony and match-up had been all a set-up for that unexpected intercourse to take place? Was that even possible? He would like to think that the Premier had no knowledge of it, but could he be sure? Look how easily Cas'sio had betrayed his drinking to the Princeps.

But why, remained the question. The Princeps was a relation and incest was frowned upon in Vir'istic societies, especially direct ancestors like Mart Kell who was what, Ay'r's great grandfather? But confounding as that news was, at least it would in some way explain why Ay'r was still being searched for here on Usk. And maybe even, why, instinctually, he'd known he had to flee.

Only one thing to do now: abort. How long ago had it happened? Not three months, was it? He would have to get some Holo-Comm. News service and find out exactly when the bogus Betrothal itself had taken place. He'd lost time out on the ocean sailing about. He was aware of that. Even so, it couldn't be more than what four months, Sol Rad.?

"Why so sad, Lad? Afraid your Trothed One has abandoned you? Knocked you up and then abandoned you? Is that it? Wondering whether he'll even be at the Western Port when we arrive? No worry. Your Captain knows of several excellent private birthing stations you could go to."

Yes, that was the answer. Surrounded as he was by strangers, he couldn't possibly explain he wanted to abort. He'd have to carry the infant until it was old enough to be taken out of him and put into an artificial womb. That was an everyday procedure all over the I'br Republic and wouldn't draw anyone's special notice.

The other, and substantial, benefit of doing it that way was that Ay'r would then be able to make a filial claim for the infant upon – Deon Syzygy. After all, dozens of witnesses had watched the older Hesperian leading Ay'r off that night to his rooms at the Golden Palace. And if Deon denied the paternity claim, Ay'r would simply threaten to tell the truth: the conspired rape by Kell. That would go far worse for Syzygy – whatever his family thought of it – than having to acknowledge a child by an Uskian of the same blood as the Premier. Deon was wealthy and famous. Ay'r had seen enough of the Holo-News, to recognize that the Media would be on Ay'r's side the instant they got wind of the real story. And so, in a roundabout way, Ay'r would get his wish after all to leave Usk and live in comfort on some luxurious girder upon the City on a Star.

But first he had to keep his distance from all of them, give birth, and make sure the child was whole and healthy. The little thing that made him ill every morning was actually quite special, a Beryllium-plated transport ticket to the most glamorous reaches of Hesperia!

"You will end up being surprised, Captain Lepta," Ay'r now said, "how magnificent a Vir ends up laying claim to this poor nauseated Trothee."

The Captain was about to continue his teasing and bantering but noticing something in Ay'r's tone of voice, he stopped and his golden eyes flickered twice and then twice more before he reached in and embraced Ay'r more fully, softly saying, "don't I know how very particular a beauty I've had the honor of playing at husband to, Lad? More than a sailor's dream, even with your veil on, you are! Surely the loveliest and noblest creature I've shared nights with. Though I never say a word, my heart will sorely miss you when we must part."

"Now that," Ay'r took up their former teasing tone, "was the best prepared speech you have ever made, and, no doubt, well learned from so much practice before today."

At which Lepta broke into a single astonished laugh, upended him upon the bed by his legs and began spanking Ay'r, who got away only with much trouble, ending up defensively crouched in the far corner.

"Now look what you've done," Lepta pointed to his member, much inflamed. "Come, Lad, and help suppress what you have so provoked."

Instead, Ay'r made a grab for his tossed away lower garment and put that on, deaf to the Captain's blandishments.

Partly dressed, he checked his reflection in the looking glass, which showed no bumps fore or aft, but instead a general ripeness over his entire torso, upper and lower. He had to admit that he looked rich and ripe, ready for the plucking. In a way it was good, in another way rather disgusting. He held his chemise before him and said with great dignity.

"Suppress it yourself! You shall have to get used to that anyway, soon enough."

And he fled the room.

Later that day he said to Silberklang, "you have noticed my condition. And you've wisely said not a word."

"What would I say, Bissel? Except to congratulate you and your Trother?"

"There is no Trother."

"You did it alone?"

"No, of course there is a father. One who sired. But as you've already no doubt assumed, there is no noble Trothed One awaiting me at this voyage's end."

When Silberklang said nothing, it signified that he had suspected as much.

"Therefore I shall join you with your instruments and tools and dials once we land at the Western Port and I will continue to work for you until ... and even after, if need be."

"You will both be safe with me, Bissel. You already know that."

Before Ay'r could ask what he meant by that, the old geologist added, "the pamps already know, the two who swore allegiance to you. They are very excited. They also will also ensure that neither you nor yours come to any harm"

Unaccountably, Ay'r wanted to cry with relief and gratitude. He ascribed that to the flow of hormones throughout his body as a result of the fetus growing there, and instead he contented himself with saying, "then it's agreed."

"Agreed! But ... may I let them know it is certain?"

"The child?"

"That, yes. But also that you come with me?"

"I don't see why not."

"I believe they have great plans for you both."

"We'll see!" Ay'r said with great firmness. "Now what is it we are doing today?"

"Weather balloons. Well, actually temperature and pressure gradient balloons, But they look like weather balloons.

Only three days, Sol Rad., later, it all became official. then critical, and then very rapidly it all became quite perilous.

Ay'r had only just entered into their greater of the two passenger lounges, the one used by the others at all times, if seldom by himself of late, and only – again, as usual – in search of a Holo-Doc. This time it was a geographical-historical one about the Western shore of the Great Salt Ocean of Usk. This was unaccountably a topic his 'Tute, Narfacan'ni, who'd lavished months of time upon the Eastern shore – about which Ay'r could see and check up himself – had seldom touched on at all. Ay'r's knowledge currently consisted of only what had been covered on the *Seven Hundred Wonders of the Galaxy* Holo-Doc in about ten minutes, which was vague to the point of being nebulous.

He'd just located one obviously very old Holo, unpromisingly titled, *An Advanced Architectural Guide to Matriarchal Council Approved Structures of TransOceanic Usk (Northwestern Sector): Spas, Resorts, Laboratories and Vacation Residences,* and had begun Vid-leafing through it, stopping at selected spots. It came with maps galore, both two and three dimensional, as well as interactive route-building from one "MC approved structure" to another. Each edifice came with its own in-depth mini-Holo-Vid., although clearly this was at least five hundred years old, so that "current natural resources" would be iffy at best. Even so, it was something Silberklang might find useful and there was really nothing else – unless you counted a chintzy-looking PVN titled *Antipys and Me: A Western Shore Uskite Confesses,* which could either be really bad erotica or worse, really sincerely bad psych/self-help stuff. That's when Ay'r heard Scott-Rancho, seated some ten feet away, far closer to the wall sized Vid-set, and as far as Ay'r knew, unaware like the rest of them that he had sneaked into the room, say in a loud voice, "Holo! Repeat!"

"That's the Inter-Galactic Top News Snippets," the perfectly dressed and garbed male Cyber repeated, and went on to say: "In Local World News, a big story today. Two important visitors from Hesperia arrived today on Usk. At a Media interview at the Golden Palace Resort, this morning, Sol Rad., His Gracious Authority, Princeps Mart Kell, noted former Premier of the Republic, and His Excellence, Marquis Deon Syzygy, also of the City, met with local administrative officials, and added their own private police forces in the search for the missing Adjudicator of Usk."

Ay'r slid even more deeply behind low built-in shelving so

as to not be seen by Scott-Rancho, Pinna, or the Delph.s as he watched the handsome Deon speak. "We had hoped not to alarm anyone planetside with this news. Indeed, it was believed that the Adjudicator was simply taking an unplanned vacation. But it is now a long enough period of time for us to become deeply concerned."

The News then cut to Holos of the Betrothal ceremony, very close-up Vids of Ay'r, followed by more Vids of him at the Betrothal dinner celebrations, and then even more homespun, if still excellent Vids of him at the Thwwing stables, the following day.

"What a lovely Human," Cha'ab, the ailing Delph. said, "why! He's so nobly graceful for one so young; he might be one of our Ambassadorial class! Don't you agree?"

"Lovely indeed for a Human," the Bella=Arth. agreed. "But I'd say stalwart, more than graceful," Pinna mused. "He could easily be a Queen's soldier-king!"

"And no wonder! He's surely as highly-bred as any Human born these past several centuries," Quor-Inq said, typically enough, as he knew the genealogical background of virtually everyone in the Holo-News. "He was sired by the great Composer 'Eis,' upon a young Kell-Sanqq' consort. Why else would the Bronzed Eagle himself be standing there, looking as though he could eat up a battalion for lunch?"

"He's surely got to be Syzygy's lover!" Scott-Rancho, never one for self-censoring, now blurted out. "They must have had a tiff after the Betrothal and the boy stormed off and now no one can find him, and so they've called in the troops."

All extremely typical, except the way that Scott-Rancho leaned forward and repeated the Holo-Vids of Ay'r twice was extremely disturbing. He knew something. Or sensed something. Or perhaps even intuited something.

Worse, however, than even his suspicious mind now busily humming at work was Ay'r's own reaction to seeing himself exposed like that, for the entire planet, perhaps for thousands of planets to see. He felt the exposure, felt the glare upon him so much that he felt himself blushing behind his shroud. But there was something else too. Watching himself, he found himself *admiring* the boy he saw pictured so young, so strong, so confident of himself – and so unaware that life was about to overtake him for ill. Perhaps that was what hit now so hard, the unknowing innocence of that manipulated young fool there. It was enough to make him weep.

"Doesn't he look familiar, Quor?" Scott-Rancho was asking.

"You wish!" was the answer.

"Where would you ever see someone that high-born (fancy ((way above your station? Kiddo!)))?" Pinna ('qq') cleverly enough asked.

"Well, he's vanished somewhere on Usk, hasn't he? And we, people, are upon Usk."

"Yes, but when Kell-Sanqq's vanish, even upon Usk, people like us never manage to see them," Quor-Inq asserted with a laugh, "even if it is a quote premier cruise line, unquote that we're sailing on."

The others laughed in agreement with him.

But Scott-Rancho was pensive. And Scott-Rancho pensive wasn't good at all for Ay'r's peace of mind.

On the Holo-News screen, Mart Kell took the dais and mentioned the sizable reward being offered for information leading to the location of his missing relative, the Adjudicator of Usk.

That's when the panic set in.

Ay'r pocketed the coin-sized Docu he'd been looking at, and grabbed and pocketed a thumb sized viewer too, unsure if his wrist connector would work wherever he might be headed in the near future. Then he slid as quietly as possible out the room, leaving just as the others naturally enough began to discuss him and his allegedly purported wealth, sex-life, romantic foibles, and socially deviant antics among the Interstellar Thwwing Set.

He rushed to where the old geologist was poring over data from his own Vid-screens and quickly blurted out what he'd just witnessed.

When Silberklang didn't react instantly, Ay'r added, "even though my hair is tinted dark and I've put on some thirty pounds in muscle, they're bound to recognize me sooner or later. Anyway, the Mate saw me without the veil, first day out from the Great South Pans. I don't know that he was looking at my face all that specifically, but ..."

"I understand, Bissel. Let me think. Let me think."

"How far are we from shore?"

"Three days journey from the Great Western Port, even at top speed."

"That's not what I asked," Ay'r clarified.

"Ah! You mean how far are we from *any* shore?"

He went to the side port and looked out, "what do you esti-mate, Bissel? Twenty five, thirty at most to the shore. But look, Bissel! It's nothing but thousand foot high cliffs for the next day or so. Surely your situation isn't as bad as that?"

"Maybe not."

"The shock of seeing yourself on the Holo-News is upsetting you."

"Agreed, but in truth more is at stake. Until now it's only been those incompetents from the palace searching for me. Today Prin-ceps Kell has brought a battalion of outer-planet explorer-class troops to join in. I can't be safe here very long."

"The Princeps, you say!" Silberklang all but whistled.

"Please don't ask," Ay'r pleaded. "Just advise me how to get away."

"I don't say you should do it now, because Vir only knows what's atop or behind those foreboding cliffs, but I think you and your pamp could get away by dark, if you need to do so. We can equip one of the Lab. skiffs for the two of you. De-equip it, ac-tually, of the material we usually keep onboard. In fact you two could prepare that fairly soon, at Second Sunset, when no one is paying much attention. That's when we usually prep anyway. You'll need a week's food and water. And I'll loan you the smallest sonic sounder. If you keep it turned on while you take off, it will scramble all sonar or radar and so no one onboard the Arcturus Scatling will be able to follow your heading. But ... are you certain you're not panicking needlessly, Bissel?"

"Perhaps, I am, old friend. Still, I'll sleep better knowing the skiff is there waiting for me to use it."

"Then you must sleep alone," Silberklang said. "Use the baby as an excuse. Lepta knows?"

"He definitely knows of the baby. But nothing more."

They were interrupted by a tapping on the door. It was the two pamps, Sand-Drifter and Salt-Eluder.

"Yes? What is it?" the old geologist asked.

They ignored him and looked at Ay'r. "We've seen the Holo-News, below decks."

"Do you see, old friend? They understand the situation's urgency as well as I do without needing to be told."

To them, Ay'r said, "we leave tonight. But I can only take one of you. Drifter, while I'm away you must bond to Ser Professor Silberklang. It's only temporary. We are due to meet up in a few days' time, Usk permitting."

"It will be a very difficult parting for this useless sailor that you saved without thinking of the consequences!" the pamp said, sweetly.

Ay'r knew that he would have been the better choice for his experience upon the ocean.

"*Useful* sailor, Drifter! And it's because of that fact that you will be missed by the Captain and crew – for your *usefulness*. While Salt will not be missed a tenth as much, since he works only for us. So, Drifter, you must endure the separation a while,"

"But this Salt-Eluder knows not where you alight on this unknown shore," the other pamp argued.

Ay'r found himself moved by the pamp's loyalty.

"And neither, Drifter, do *you* know where we alight on shore. None of us do. We've none of us ever been on this Western shore before. But be of good cheer. We will come together soon, in a few days."

"Usk-permitting," the pamp said, and suddenly nuzzled his head into Ay'r's chest.

He held him there a while, stroking his head for comfort, while the others looked away.

"Fear not. Be strong, Do as Silberklang tells you. In that way do you serve me best."

"And this one, too?" Drifter lightly touched Ay'r's stomach.

"And that one, too, of course!"

The pamp tore himself away, but Ay'r called him back. "Your further help is needed to get us clear. At Second Sunset. Come now to my room, help me to pack. You always know best what to take on a trip when there is very little that can be carried."

It would probably be a Clear-day: the orange Eagle was just beginning to peak over the vastness of the Great Salt Ocean to the left. If Ay'r peered hard, he could just make out a dot above the horizon that would be the Arcturus Scatling moving further away every second. Luckily, their Lab-skiff was too tiny to be seen from that Ocean-cruiser except by the most high-powered lens, and then only if one was looking directly at them.

Navigating the skiff would by no means the easiest thing to do this blustery morning. In the past ten minutes, Sol Rad., they'd been all over the area, if the skiff Nav. System was telling the truth.

In fact, Ay'r and Salt-Eluder were virtually under the overhanging cliff of the Western Shore, all but invisible to anyone who might happen to look over the edge from above. And they'd been this close – or this far – for at least two hours, Sol Rad. Not getting any closer to shore no matter how much they tried.

"Salt-Eluder! See if we have we any marking flags."

The pamp seemed puzzled, but searched in the side flap of the skiff where they usually kept the demarcation banners. He located a bright white one and undid it to its man-sized length, unfurling the banner.

"Hold it out over that side!" Ay'r said. "Hold tight!"

The banner took the wind and instantly went almost horizontal, certainly parallel to the ocean sands upon which they glided so directionless.

"Now! Take it in and hold it over the other side!"

With difficulty, the pamp managed to get the flag back into the skiff, then went to the other side, and bracing himself against the inner side of the skiff, held it out. There was barely a flutter.

"Just as I thought!" Ay'r said. "Pull it in again, Salt. Gratitude."

"A great wind keeps us from reaching the shore," Salt-Eluder said.

"Yes, and has done so for the past two hours." Ay'r held up the wrist connector and spoke into it. "We are approximately a hundred meters from the Western Shore cliffs. An extremely strong current is keeping us from approaching it, despite the use of motorized equipment. Knowing the longitude and latitude that we are at, dip into Silberklang's findings, and see what you come up with?"

Less than a minute later, he heard. "Search completed. No relevant information. The strong current is unknown up to this time by Silberklang or any other explorer of this territory."

"Can you extrapolate the length of the current?"

"It cannot reach as far as the Great Western Port, or there would be no port located there."

That made great sense, and probably explained why that port

was located where it was. It might be the only place on this shore *without* the current, the only place you *could* land.

"Can you extrapolate how close to the Great Western Port this skiff must be to have no current?"

"Only if several readings are taken. Three, ten minutes apart, heading north toward the port."

The next half hour was involved doing just that. Ahead, and above, no changes were visible. It all looked like unending cliff with only the sparsest and most fragile-looking desert vegetation.

By the time they were done, the Eagle had arisen above the horizon and it was indeed going to be a Clear-day, hot and fair.

"Results?" Ay'r asked his wrist connector.

"There is a decline in current strength over the passage just undertaken. However it is almost negligible. Most likely the current will remain strong enough to deter landing until very near indeed to the port itself. Possibly not until the port."

That was bad news. They couldn't be seen landing from there.

"How then can this Lab-skiff directly approach the Western shore?"

"Ser!" Salt-Eluder suddenly said, and pointed at the cliff. "Look! That perli bush! It stands still. It does not wave like the flag did."

"Brilliant, Salt-Eluder! I knew I was right to take you. Wrist-connector, the current does not exist at the cliff, only between us and the cliff. Suggestion?"

"It will be sudden! And perhaps damaging to the skiff!"

"We'll have to take the chance, How do we do it?"

At the same time that he realized what it must be, Salt-Eluder began rummaging into another side flap and came out with a hand gun with its long line attachment that they ordinarily used for securing sonic sounders and other equipment to the desert floor so they wouldn't move at all during experiments.

Ay'r's wrist-connector said: "It will have to be quickly achieved. Shoot the staple into the cliff. Pull yourself to it as fast as possible. Expect to land hard, and to have your equipment and possibly yourselves scattered all about."

The insertion arrow was sharp enough and long enough. And the cord was long enough to reach, but they would have to tie everything else down, including themselves.

"Will we die, Ser?" fearful Salt-Eluder asked.

"Of course not! And who knows? It could be fun, Salty! Now I'll count backwards. Hold onto your hairpiece!"

"All I have is this cap!"

Ay'r shot into what looked to him to be a soft looking section of cliff. Perli-bush grew there, so it shouldn't be rock-hard.

The arrow struck with a great gong, and the two of them all but sat on the cord's end, as it rapidly played out, and they shot past the arrow's spot on the cliff until …

"Here goes!"

The cord ended and the Lab-skiff swung forward and toward the cliff at breakneck speed. All about them, Ay'r felt the sudden onrush of the strong cliff-side current, then it was past, and he had about a second to look back across it as the Lab-skiff swung into the cliff.

"Hold on, Sallllltttttt!"

At last, Ay'r let go of the cord and it snapped right off the side bolts holding it onto the Lab-skiff. Suddenly freed, the little craft kept going, spinning around and around in dizzying circles, until it suddenly hit some rough ground beneath and began to capsize. Ay'r rushed to that side lifting and threw his weight there, saving them, but only for a moment, as now it hit another bump below, still going far too fast, and it skipped about three feet into the air, them and their equipment along with it, and back down again, still spinning like mad. Salt-Eluder was thrown out of the skiff, and was quick enough to turn himself about in the air and reach out a hand. Ay'r reached too and pulled the pamp back in. He landed on top of Ay'r, knocking him down, just as the skiff hit another series of bumps below them, and they bounce-skidded to a halt not three inches from the cliff itself. A perli-brush knocked Salt Seeker's hat off and a handful of the blue-black berries fell directly into Ay'r's lap.

"Are we alive, Ser?"

"Whew! … I think so … Quickly! Let's stand and get out of this thing before it spins around again."

He got to his feet and stepped out, but his foot landed hard on the rock floor, and he staggered as though drunk. Ay'r turned to say something, and without intending to, suddenly he began to vomit. When he was done, he half fell, half sat back against the side of the Lab-skiff.

"Salty! Remind me never to do that in a skiff again!"

The pamp was still reeling himself. But he came over to Ay'r and helped him, and began fanning him with his little cap.

"I'll be okay. I feel okay. It's only Junior, here," Ay'r patted his lower torso, "complaining about the wild ride!"

Salt-Eluder found him some water and he was able to hold that down. Ay'r sat, watching the Blue Hunter suddenly rise in the south east, turning the far sky pale green.

Already steady, the pamp was collecting their equipment. He placed it all on a small grav-lev platform and turned it on. The entire little packet floated, and the pamp tethered it to his belt.

He pulled out two more of the devices and attached one to his own mid-section belt and another to Ay'r's. He also gave him wear-free gloves for their climbing and put on his own.

"We shall wait until your junior feels at home. But Ser, think of it, we are the first from the Scatling to have reached the Western Shore."

"Actually, you were the very first. A great accomplishment, Salt! And one I'll make sure Drifter knows about. He'll be even more envious of you than he already is."

Ay'r would have liked to have stayed there longer, but knew they mustn't. Soon the ship's personnel would be awakening and find him gone and then ...!

"Okay, Salty! Up we got. But if you really want to make your mark on this old world of Usk, you've got to lead the way."

"But what if I lead us wrong?"

"No such thing, Salty. No such thing. Let's go."

Even with the grav-lev belts keeping them from plummeting down, climbing up the cliff was hard work. They didn't reach the top until past midday and then stopped to rest, eat and drink. Both suns were up and on high, and very warm, even with the constant sea breeze. No shade was available, as even here, no plant taller than the pamp grew, nor, for a fact, any plant wider than him seemed to grow. Ay'r opened their floating storage and pulled out a dun colored strong cloth that would shade them for a midday nap.

He must have been even more tired then he thought, probably because of the baby he was carrying, because Salt-Eluder had to shake him several times to awaken Ay'r at prime sunset. The sky was already mostly a hot chartreuse color as the Eagle set and the bright blue-white sun began to follow it closely. From here, they could see very far in every direction across the great Salt Ocean. Almost, it seemed they could make out the line of the mid-ocean ridge where they'd begun taking soundings months ago. However, seeing the cliff tops proved more elusive. In the bright double sunlight earlier, everything had glittered with the same reflective quality, whether it was granite outcropping or varied shades of green-brown vegetation. In this more diffuse blue-green light, all they could make out was texture, various levels, here rock, there sand hardened by centuries to nearly rock consistency, and there tufts of some kind of tough grass, through which the wind coughed and hissed.

They'd seen not a hint of life. Not a flying insect. Not a crawling thing. No little curl voles. And after a while, even the per-li-bushes gave way and then the grass did too. Instead, the landscape seemed to become hummocky, as though lines of hills and dales had been suddenly formed. As they trod over and across and down and then up and over and across and down again, Ay'r kept wondering what could have possibly shaped and molded this landscape and could only arrive at one possibly conclusion. It all resembled the dried river bed and the dried strong oceanic current beds Silberklang had shown him, that it could signify but one thing: this had once been a rushing river. Here, over a thousand feet high, and so, it must have rushed over and into down there, into the ocean. But had that been when Usk was still the Eden planet the old geologist thought it had been? Or later, during the disaster that had struck the world and stolen its water and tossed it into the air as multiply shining rings high above, that, as they watched, appeared to be sliding up from the south east horizon.

As they moved onward, angling inland, following a line that ought to take them directly to where Silberklang had agreed to meet them in three more days, Sol Rad., at the latest, even the ocean wind ceased and now it was silence all about them as they trod upon and over and down the hard as rock ridges below their feet. By midnight Usk's rings were one third risen and so bright that the travelers could see clearly on land.

At one moment, Ay'r thought he heard a distant, high pitched, familiar sound. It was almost a cry but from so far away he couldn't be sure. And when it didn't repeat, he stood still and listened hard. What had it been? It was so familiar.

"Salt-Eluder? Did you hear it?"

"The cry of a loose running Thwwing, I believe. I've only been to see Thwwings once, when they gathered to air race at South Salt Pan City. But I recall their high-pitched voices."

Yes! That was it. A Thwwing. But ... how?

"Salty? Why would a Thwwing be about here?"

"This pamp has once heard that there are great stables somewhere hereabout in the Great Western area. Hidden stables and secret training grounds."

"This Human once mounted a Thwwing and rode it almost up to those rings," Ay'r said, and then almost immediately regretted saying it.

"This is known to us."

"It's *known*? How could it be *known*?"

"From the Holo-News reports, surely. But earlier than that, also."

"You mean pamps have been spying on me?"

"Not spying no, Ser. But whenever anyone so remarkable comes along, pamps speak to each other about every aspect of that someone's life."

"Now you're pulling a long one on me, Salt ... But I don't mind."

"A long one? A long what one, Ser?"

"No, I don't mind, really I don't ... I deserved it! I did. I shouldn't have boasted like I did."

"No boast when it's a fact, Ser. What is a long one, Ser?"

"A lie. A joking lie. A funny falsehood. But like I said, Salty, I boasted well out of place and so I deserved what I got."

"This pamp is not making a funny falsehood," Salt-Eluder all but sputtered. They'd stopped, and the pamp tried to speak with difficulty, finally expostulating, "anyway ... also ... it is prophesied."

"What?" Ay'r had to laugh at Salt-Eluder's seriousness. "*What* is prophesied?"

"That He will bond the unbondable Thwwing and ride it to three victories!"

"He who?" And when the pamp didn't answer, went on, "I did, as you very well know as it was on Holo-News, bond a Thwwing that no one else had bonded. But to only one victory. And only at the little Golden Palace Track. That is a totally unimportant, if sort of lucrative, race and of no importance to ..."

"Half the great Thwwing racers of Hesperia were there! The other half soon knew of the victory!"

Why was he being so obstinate?

"Read my lips, Salt-Eluder. It was *one* victory! One *tiny* little victory!"

The pamp kept quiet. So Ay'r changed his tone of voice and asked, "what prophecy?" But he had evidently hurt the poor fellow's feelings and the pamp would not answer now.

They walked on for some ten minutes. Finally Ay'r said, "I apologize, Salt-Eluder, for losing my temper like that. It was foolish of me. It was disrespectful of you and of your beliefs. I acted like an idiot! I'm still really only a very young Neo, you realize! Not yet out of Ed. & Dev.! Please forgive me."

"'He will be all the greater for being the most humble,'" Salt-Eluder said, as though repeating something long learned. "'This is how he will prove himself to you, over and over again.'"

The pamp suddenly pushed itself into Ay'r mid section, and Ay'r cradled its small head and held it close.

"I'm guessing this means I'm forgiven! ... Good!"

Salt-Eluder pulled away, its face averted. Then the pamp raced on ahead as though embarrassed by its action.

They stopped once more after that to rest, eat and drink. Salt-Eluder had now begun to hum as he walked and after a while he even began to sing and move his little arms and hands. After a while, Ay'r hummed along with him.

"What is that you are singing?"

"This pamp's grandsire taught him this song when small." And the song?"

"It's an old song. Very old. Possibly from before pamps lived on this world. Actually it's a little dance that pamps dance when they are well fed and content for the night."

"May I hear it and learn it from you?"

"Truly? You wish to learn to sing a pamp dance?"

"Why not?"

"Because it is a pamp dance!"

"So what? It's pretty. A little sad, but pretty. Yes, certainly. If you don't mind, teach it to me."

And so as they trod through the bright night on into the nearly double-rising of the two suns, the pamp Salt-Eluder sang and even executed a little side step and dance, and Ay'r learned the song and danced along with him.

After an hour had passed, Ay'r said, "all right. I think I've got it. Now I will sing it for you!" He began by doing the half turn in either direction as he began to sing:

> *When Flute-makers flute*
> *When Drum-makers drum*
> *When young lovers kiss –*
> *Then everyone dances –*
> *A slow sarabande!*
> *This is the song!*
> *This is the dance –*
> *Of young pamps in love!*

And he ended with his two hands clasped across his chest, connoting, he guessed, the lovers clasping each other.

"Well?"

Salt-Eluder turned his face away.

"Was I that awful?"

Face still averted, the pamp swung an arm up into the air – meaning who knew what?

Maybe I'll do it better with a little more practice," Ay'r suggested, and without waiting for Salt-Eluder, he strode ahead and began singing to himself, determined to learn the song and little gesture-dance.

"What it comes down to," Green Bush Ridger, the leader of the pamps said, "is that you are trespassing on our territory. That's why we took you captive."

"What it comes down to," Ay'r spoke back, "is that I was seeking a Birth-Station, because, one of you might have noticed, or even guessed from all the sleeping I've been doing since we met, that I'm carrying and need to give birth very, very soon. And, as for trespassing, that's completely ridiculous. I've walked a day and a half and saw nothing resembling any sign saying it's anyone's territory."

They were back in what remained of the hut where he'd been previously held, what was left of it. The children and even the toddlers couldn't be stopped from following them in, and the youngsters now lingered in the corners or sat watching and listening.

Green Bush now backed up and went to three or four other pamps staying in the doorway and began talking in a low voice to them.

Ay'r began playing with the toddlers again, two of whom plopped down and installed themselves onto his lap.

Green Bush returned.

"On Duty Ridger suspected that you were carrying a young. And from the looks of all this ... Play time!" unhappily noting the youngsters so close to Ay'r. "So that's it! You're here looking to give birth?"

"That's it! What else would I be doing here?"

"Spying?"

Ay'r had to laugh. "Spying? For who?"

"For someone in the port."

"The Great Western Port? I've never been there. And I know no one there."

Green Bush pounced. "But you're headed there! And you'll tell them all about us!"

"I'm not at all headed there. When you so rudely captured me, I was headed *away* from the port and headed *inland*. If you'll care to remember, I was aiming for this place ..." He was going to project a Holo for them from his wrist-connector but realized he couldn't do that as it was still sealed. "Well, anyway I've got the position in here, and it's *even further* inland and *further* away from the port. I'm headed there to join a geologist I've been work-ing with. He's to meet me there. The truth is, the Great Western Port is about the *last place* on Usk that I'd want to be seen. So the big secret of your little ... Group ... here is completely safe with me. I won't breathe a word about you."

All that information flustered Green Bush even more. He withdrew again and held conference outside the doorway. He re-turned again.

"If all that is true, where is your travel equipment?"

"I assumed *you* stole it."

"Stole it?!" The little pamp all but jumped Ay'r.

"Well, I didn't see it when I woke up, did I? And it's not here now."

"We steal nothing!" Green Bush Ridger declared. "We are hunters!"

"Then a curl-vole ran off with it. I don't know. Look, I'm very close to birthing here," Ay'r patted his stomach. "I know from the Holo I'd projected before you folks came along that I was nearing a mountains resort with medical facilities. If I don't give birth soon, you know what will happen. I'm going to slip into sleep and possibly *never* wake up. You'll have two Human deaths on your hands. Even if you think of yourselves as barbarians, that's not what you want, is it? When I don't arrive there as I'm supposed to," he fudged the truth a little. "They'll come looking for me. Then, what?"

From the doorway, he could hear the other adult pamps murmuring.

"And I know a Birth Station can't be far, because look at all these charmers," his gesture encompassed the children. "They were all born *somewhere* not too distant."

Again Green Bush went into conference. This time two other adult pamps came into the hut with him. One introduced himself as Cliff-Climber, the other as Rock-Thrower. The latter said, "the song the children were doing. How do you know it?"

"A friend taught it to me."

"Where was this friend from?"

"From the South Salt Pans community."

"And his name?"

"He was Salt-Eluder."

Rock-Thrower turned back to the other two. "That is where the pamps sing the song." He pointed. "Far south of here was where I heard it sung and danced."

"A pamp was your friend?" Green Bush asked. "When you were a child?"

"I learned it a few days ago."

"A pamp?" Green Bush was skeptical. "An adult pamp shared this song and dance?"

"He was my friend. Why *wouldn't* he share it?" Ay'r asked.

"With a Human?"

"I am a Human. As you can well see."

"A grown Human with an adult pamp friend? Where – on all of this distressing world – can that be found?"

"On the ocean cruiser we sailed, to begin with. Pamps and Humans worked together and were friends on the cruiser. That's where I was, *with my friend – the pamp!*"

Green Bush scoffed, but Rock-Thrower insisted, "I have heard of this sort of thing."

"Look. It isn't *important*," Ay'r insisted. "Just get me to a Birth Station. And you'll never see or hear of me *ever* again. I'll miss these little ones," hugging the toddlers on his lap. "But I'll be busy enough with my own ... What do you say? Is it a deal?"

The three left the hut and a general conference began outside.

One of the toddlers began to yawn then the second and it was contagious, even the older boys began to yawn. So did Ay'r, who really needed very little to make him tired again.

He put the sleeping toddlers onto his rough-made bed, and the other two tots joined them, and then he himself lay down, all but encircling them, and yawned once quite loudly.

"Let me know what time I need to be ready!" Ay'r said loudly, and heard what seemed like all twenty-seven of the adult pamps confabbing out in the courtyard as he fell asleep.

This time when he was awakened, it was still mid-day, and so he guessed not much later than before. It was Rock-Thrower who did it, he thought, given his distinctive markings.

"Are we ready to go to the Birth-Station?" Ay'r asked.

"Come outside."

"I really hope we're ready to go there, because I'm about to split apart, here."

The pamp was gone and Ay'r followed him, wondering, what now?

Green Bush, Cliff Climber and many of the others of the Ridger clan were all out in the dusty center, of the tiny hamlet and there, facing them and him, all alone, in the middle of the courtyard, was Salt-Eluder.

"Salty!" Ay'r cried out, in joy.

He rushed to the little pamp and hugged him. For his part, his friend butted his head into Ay'r's midsection and Ay'r caressed the top of his little head.

"Salty. I'm so glad that you're safe."

"You are not angry that I was afraid and ran off? Leaving you alone?"

"No. No. Not at all. You did well."

"I did well?" Salt-Eluder was surprised.

"We're both unharmed, aren't we? Who knows what would have happened if you had remained? You did very well." He hugged him again and this time whispered, "Did you get the storage bin too?"

"I have hidden it not far from here," Salt-Eluder whispered back.

"Good."

Ay'r was aware of the murmuring and amazement of the other pamps, so he announced, "this is Salt-Eluder. He's my friend!"

"This pamp is essence-bound to you!" Green Bush Ridger said.

"He is *not* essence-bound. He's not bound to me in *any way*."

"This human helped save my life. Saved my life. Defended me from another Human. Hurt that other Human. All because of *this pamp*."

He stood proudly as he spoke, making certain they all heard and understood him.

Their murmuring grew.

"This Human," Salt-Eluder went on, "saved the life of *another pamp*, Sand-Drifter, his name. Whom we now seek to meet. This Human found that dying pamp on the great ocean, and nursed that pamp until he was well. Like this pamp, that pamp is bound to this Human not by any essences, but by only bonds of gratitude and friendship."

"This cannot be!" one of the others said.

"The pamp lies."

"The pamp hallucinates! He's been out in the double suns too long."

"These matters cannot happen until the time of the prophecy is upon us."

Salt-Eluder held his ground. "The time of the prophecy is upon us, pamp brothers. Look to the Rings." He pointed up. "Look to the Two Suns. Do you not see that they near each other, ready for the Great Exchange? Have you no one to read the signs all about us?"

"The prophecy is a myth."

"It's all garbage."

"It's all Human lies, meant to enslave pamps." Green Bush shouted.

Salt-Eluder repeated, "the time of the prophecy is upon us, pamp brothers! Whether you believe it or not. And He, whom the prophecy tells us of for so many generations, *He has arrived*." He pointed to Ay'r.

"Whoa, now, Salty! Let's not kick up any ruckus with these guys. They're poorly fed and kind of bad-tempered. Just let's get out of here and get my baby born."

But Salt-Eluder would not be moved. He stood and repeated what he had said.

One pamp that Ay'r had not noticed before, now came out of the crowd. He was dark-haired, and thus much older than the others.

"This pamp long ago was taught to read the signs of the Great Prophecy," he declared of himself. He looked Ay'r over, not very happily.

"Recall then, what the prophecy says," Salt-Eluder insisted. "He will come among us as one of us. He will eat our food and drink our water. He will have no bonds but those of affection, as pamps have for other pamps?"

The elder now looked at the others. "So was it said. It was also said that He will cradle our young as though they were His own. It is also said that he will sing our songs and dance our dances as though He too were a pamp."

"It is also said," Salt-Eluder said, "that He will make no difference between us and those of His kind."

"It is also said," and this time the Elder spoke to the other Ridgers, "that He will dwell among us as though he were a pamp. And also that He shall give birth among us."

Ay'r wasn't sure what his friend was doing exactly, but it seemed to be working.

The others now came closer to Ay'r and began to size him up more carefully, or seemingly more thoughtfully. They continued to murmur and to argue quietly. So he took Salt-Eluder out of the circle and to the other side of the courtyard.

"Let them take this off me, so we can find our way to the Birth Station. It can't be far. We'll use the mag-levs to help me get there, since I will never make it on my own now, not in this condition. Let's prepare to leave now. Let me just say good bye to the little ones."

When he came out of the hut where the youngsters remained mostly asleep and those awake very sleepy, he could see that the elder pamp and three others had a kind of litter.

"Cloud-Speaker and these other pamps will go with us,"

Salt-Eluder said.

After his plastro wrist sealer was removed, Ay'r turned to the others.

"As I promised, I will not reveal to anyone that you are here. Not for your sakes. You are a surly and distrustful lot. But because I wouldn't want any harm come to the young ones. They are good and innocent. The last thing I would want is any harm to come to them. And so, Good-Bye!" he waved, and they all started forward.

Some of the others, including Rock-Thrower, although not Cliff-Climber nor Green Bush, walked with them a bit longer, muttering, once they were outside the village.

When they stopped to return, Rock-Thrower came to Ay'r and said, "do not be too harsh on us Ridgers. All of us older pamps have been essence-enslaved and forced to escape bondage. We have all been very harshly treated by Humans. We had no choice but to escape, to come here and gather together for safety. For many, the bonding addiction was too great and they could not survive the withdrawal. Only the few you see, have managed."

"I believe you," Ay'r said. "And I am saddened to hear of what you say. But know that I also am forced by my destiny to wander the surface of Usk not knowing where I will end up. All because of Human greed and stupidity. While I cannot possibly understand how difficult your own poor lives must have been, I can wish you a better future."

"Bless us!" one of the others who were remaining now cried.

"But I am not He whom you ..."

"Bless us!" another pleaded. And the others also pleaded.

So he let each of them came to up his stomach and press it lightly, as Salt-Eluder had done, and hold him, and Ay'r touched each one of their heads and learned their names and repeated it back and he said to each, "Best-Hunter (or Perli-Gatherer, or whatever their name was). You are my friend. We are bonded by affection only. I wish you a better future than your past."

And that seemed to content them all.

Once that was completed, they said goodbye.

After a few minutes of walking on alone, the small group of Ay'r and his new pamp friends were well out of sight of the village.

Salt-Eluder quickly dashed behind a rock and found the maglev device holding the storage packet and he removed it and they installed it beneath the twig litter the men carried. They divided up the storage packet among themselves. And only then, and very exhaustedly, did Ay'r climb onto the litter and be covered by the cloth he had retained and allow himself to be carried.

"You've got to be joking!" Ay'r said when he saw where they had brought him.

It looked like two ledges of outcropping rock, one in front of the other. Neither looked tall enough for a Human to get under, never mind stand up in.

They had traveled for several hours and they had arrived at the spot which looked no different than any other about them, except perhaps that it boasted a little more open space than the other lines of ridges and heaps of outcrops all about them.

The pamps had set down the litter and Salt-Eluder had come to awaken Ay'r.

As he rubbed sleep out of his eyes and sat up slowly, feeling the swelling around his body, he could see that it was now a nearly perfectly aligned double sunset over the western mountains – the Eagle had begun dropping, looking enormous and red-orange. Almost touching its bloated disc, it was following so closely behind, was the smaller circle of the Blue sun, cobalt at its edges, intensely white at its center. The light the two cast over the rocky landscape covered with willowy vegetation was streaked orange and red, and yet also now and then suffused with blue and green. It was eerily beautiful. Except, of course, for the rocky landscape.

"This is in truth the Birthing Station, Ser!" Cloud-Speaker confirmed.

"What a disaster," Ay'r said to no one in particular.

But two of the accompanying pamps had already gone under the longer of the overhung ledges and now stepped out again, followed by a stout-looking, vaguely androgynously male Cyber, who bustled over to them, followed by two smaller, pamp-sized, Cybers with faded clothing, and even some spots where the skin had given way to patches of plasticene and metal.

Ay'r stood up to greet them. And immediately felt a little woozy.

"Greetings, mother-to-be!" the taller Cyber said. "Greetings!

You are most welcome at Usk NorthWestern Birthing Station number 34. I am Registered Midwife Annis Treflex, and these are my medically trained to Level 12, assistants, Taffy and Whey." His face made a sort of wry moue, explaining the names, "my predecessor found enjoyment during the very long hours between birthings in reading old Metro-Terran children's stories."

"But you … don't?" Ay'r asked.

"Vir, no! I'm a Thwwing-race fanatic. What can I say? Between the Holo-Sports and the Holo-Docs I've collected, I'm kept too busy for children's stories."

They all shook limbs with Ay'r, and the smaller Cybers also did so with Salt-Eluder and Cloud-Speaker too.

"Number 34 is a fully City Funded and Operated Birthing Station, dear young mother to be. It is inspected onsite and its procedures are all reviewed quarter-annually by the appropriate Hesperian San. & Dev. Authorities. Furthermore, Number 34 has consistently achieved an approval rating of A for sanitary-ness and excellence," Treflex added in a sad smile. "You wouldn't get a better birthing at The Golden Palace Resort, nor even on most girders of Hesperia itself."

Addressing Ay'r specifically, "we take it from your, ahem, somewhat swollen condition, that you, Ser, are the mother-to-be. You are of course somewhat larger than our usual patients. But," he added with a girlish giggle, "no worries. All adjustments can be easily made to ensure a safe and easy birth. We also possess the most up to date Relfi Society-approved exterior wombs for your infant's post-partum existence. Please follow me."

Without looking to see if Ay'r was doing so, he turned and began to bustle away back toward the rock ledges.

When a somewhat stunned Ay'r hadn't moved an inch, the unperturbed Midwife turned around and fluted out, "Taffy! Whey! Bring him in."

Ay'r didn't even see the two smaller mechanos at his sides. One deftly tipped him backwards, the other tripped him, and he fell backward so suddenly that he was astounded when they deftly caught him and, light as air, scuttled him along.

"Salty! Don't leave me alone!"

He was gratified to see that steps led down and then to a sort of terrazzo in front of what quickly became apparent was a contemporary-looking transparent plastro walled medical facility, invisible until now.

Ay'r was hustled into the main room, where he was gently set onto a birthing table. Midwife Treflex was already suited up with lighter plastron sheeting across its face, hands and chemise.

"No. No. The others can't stay." Then to Ay'r. "I'm afraid the others have to remain outside," the Midwife insisted. "Ridger, you ought to know better. We need a completely sterile environment."

Reluctantly Salt-Eluder allowed himself to be pushed out by Taffy or Whey who then shut and hermetically sealed the door. The two pamps looked in at Ay'r.

"Surgeon!" the Midwife called, and a flat ceiling mount dropped a few inches and broke apart into a dozen gleaming pieces. "But first, let's take a look inside and see how the placement is."

The room was flooded with some kind of fluoro-X-ray-scope, emitting from either far wall, Ay'r guessed. All jagged waves and light spots.

"Well. This should be easy. The baby is perfectly placed!" the Midwife reported. Then, "Surgeon, we'll be doing a six point incision, front and back."

Suddenly Ay'r felt the back of the table fall away except for several strategically placed supports, upon which he was still resting.

The midwife was removing Ay'r's clothing deftly and speaking to the smaller Cybers, spouting off numbers and formulas. Ay'r could see one of them very still, as it listened, before taking off in a sudden whirling motion.

"We're going to keep you awake, Ser, in case we need you, but we'll face you away from the site itself." Ay'r felt his chin lifted by something or other mechanical. "And of course you have received a global anesthetic."

"No I haven't!" Ay'r said, "don't cut yet."

But he could already hear the very quiet noises of the Cyber Surgeon working all around him, and he felt no pain, and so he must have already been anesthetized.

"There's the birth sac opened," the Midwife announced. "And here's our little sweetheart. My, he's active already for his age. Five months?"

"A little over four!" Ay'r found himself saying.

"Oh and he'll be out in a minute. There he is. And a quick

check says he's perfect, but before we undo the umbilical from yourself, Ser, let's do a full physical exam on him. Diagnostic! Can we have that and your informed opinion?"

Ay'r could see the surgical arms move back and another set of arms descend and move around him, consisting of many different little tools, hooks, gauze palps, bandage-like servos, all of them attached to miniscule monitor screens and other Cybernetic machines.

"Baby looks just fine!" The midwife declared. "Perfect, in fact. No surprise, given the youth of his mother."

"Now, Ser, if you don't mind a minute more, we're going to do a physical on yourself. Taffy, let's make sure everything is sterile inside there. Very good! And you look fine internally yourself too, young Ser. Very healthy, indeed, I'm pleased to say. And let's peek at our mother's Relfian unit. Gosh how it sparkles! A real beauty, Taffy, lets fluoro-swab that area, so our mother can be sure of another nice, clean pregnancy anytime he wishes. Whey! Do you have the exterior womb prepped. Good. Let's snip and the baby is now separated and all washed and sterilized. Now Ser we'll reattach that tube to the inside of the exterior womb and there he is, the little sweetie. Just a minute more, Ser, while we auto-suture your own tiny little incisions. Ah, there we go! Very nice job, Surgeon! The cuts are barely noticeable. Whey! Apply the 'no-scar.' Excellent! One minute more, and if I may, Ser, while the baby is feeding off the exterior womb a mixture essentially composed of your own nutrients that we've duplicated into the unit, we have noticed that you could use a bit more nutrition yourself. So we'll do that intravenously. Please don't remove that bulb attachment to your left ankle for several more hours, Sol Rad. Gratitude."

"Now, Ser! You may sit up, and look at your baby."

Ay'r sat up slowly, propped up from behind by Whey, and instantly supported by the back of the table which had returned to a full back. All the surgical and diagnostic tools were gone, and Taffy now pushed the floating womb over to slide across Ay'r's suddenly extremely concave stomach. He looked down into the floating bassinet and there was the little thing, tiny, still rather red, all wrinkled over, but somehow familiar too.

It was slowly waving its little, well-formed arms and legs about. Then it opened its eyes to look.

"My!" The Midwife exclaimed. "How remarkable."

Ay'r baby's eyes were like tiny emeralds. Bright shining green emeralds.

"Can you determine the color of his hair?" Ay'r had to ask.

"It's still very thin and growing, but Diagnostics says it will be this color," and upon the far wall was projected a tiny hair that was enlarged until it was a Human index finger's length and width. "My! My!" the Midwife remarked.

The hair was already obviously metallic bronze in color.

Without question, Mart Kell was its father.

"What a remarkably gorgeous little physical specimen of a man he will be!" the Midwife cooed. "Even more remarkable and probably as beautiful as its mother." And before Ay'r could say anything, he realized that his tow-colored hair and bright blue eyes must be apparent to them all here in this room with their x-ray visions and whatnot, almost as if he were not lens and hair re-pigmented.

"Midwife!" Ay'r cried out, "as a medic *in extremis*, you are sworn to confidence to never tell anyone that I ever came here or gave birth."

"As you wish, Ser." Then the Midwife put its hands prayer-like up to its fat face and said, "but since we both know that I know who you are from my Holo-Sports, perhaps you'll give me an autograph for my Thwwing Racing collection."

"Cross wrists for your vow and it will be done!" Ay'r said, holding out his arm with the wrist-connector.

"I knew this would be a special night when I saw the two suns setting in tandem together. Didn't I say so earlier, Taffy!?"

Ay'r slept again, for a few hours and when he awoke, the Midwife allowed him and the baby in its hermetically sealed artificial womb to be brought out onto the terrazzo in front of the offices. Salt-Eluder and Cloud-Speaker and the other pamps quickly gathered around and they all complimented Ay'r on the baby's beauty and surprising alertness.

"A remarkable occurrence, Ser!" Salt-Eluder now said, "concerning the Rings."

Taffy and Whey glided Ay'r's floating bed from below the overhang and propelled it out into the open space.

"For the first time ever in this pamp's useless existence!" Cloud Speaker pointed above.

The double set of Rings which dominated Usk's sky at night,

for the first time ever in Ay'r's own short life, were directly above them, the two sets seemed so close that they were sparkling and flashing and lighting up the sky until it was almost as bright as a mid-Double-Day.

"And look, Friend of the Pamps," Salt-Eluder now said. "Where the rings do not quite meet!"

He pointed directly above and Ay'r saw five stars in a row almost equally bright, the middle one the brightest of them all.

"Why! It looks like a bracelet!" Ay'r said. "Or a necklace."

"It is a diadem crown!" Cloud-Speaker said. "And see where it points, and who wears the crown," the pamp said and backed away slowly.

"I wish you two wouldn't insist on all that 'He Who' stuff ..." Ay'r began but was soon surprised to see that all the rock ridges and canyonettes were filled now with pamps. As they stepped forward, Ay'r thought he recognized the aggressive stances of Green Bush and On Duty Ridger foremost as usual among them.

Yes! It was him. And Rock-Thrower and Cliff-Climber and all the others from the cliff village, and they had the children with them, and the toddlers too. Even more amazing, they were all unpainted and clean of face and limb and even neatly dressed.

"The Tiara!" Rock-Thrower said, pointing upward, "showed us the way to you, Great Ser! And to your blessed offspring."

"We were wrong to doubt the predictions," Cliff-Dweller intoned.

"Oh, don't you guys start too," Ay'r said. But he recognized the little ones from the previous day and he insisted that they all come forward as they were so curious to see his baby, and so he let them all gather about.

The entire pamp village were now gathered around on the terrazzo and talking and enjoying the celebratory atmosphere, when Salt-Eluder noticed a Rock and Cliff Climbing Vehicle approach from the North. Its driver, seeing the group, stopped. In seconds it was opened up and two elderly Humans stepped out. They so reminded Ay'r of Professor Silberklang that he sent Salt-Eluder to find out who they were.

"Professor Cyrus Salzprung, from the Collegium Wissenschaft on Demetrius Three," one elderly Human introduced himself.

"Doctor of Sciences Angona Masaaki-Donnerwort, from Jespers Star Sigma," was the second, an elderly female Human.

"It's such a specific area that is singularly lighted by this once in a lifetime phenomenon," Masaak explained, "that I do hope you will excuse our extreme curiosity in coming. It shone like some great beacon. How could we *not* follow it?"

Ay'r asked the two if they knew his friend Silberklang, and they said of course, they were awaiting him not five kilometers away. But Silberklang had not arrived yet, although they were told the Arcturus Scatling had docked at the great Western Port earlier the previous day.

"Professors," Cloud-Speaker now asked the two Humans, "can you tell us, please, the names of those stars that light up so prominently above the heads of our new mother and his child?"

"Certainly. The four are, from left to right, Melisande, Benefica, Diomedes and is that Narcissus, Cyrus?"

"Yes," Salzprung replied. "The first two stars held the two most important worlds of the old Matriarchy," he went on to explain, "and the second pair are the two fastest growing systems of the new Vir'istic Republic!"

"And the bright star? The diamond-like one? In the middle of them all?"

"Hesperia, of course! The City on a Star!" Both Salzprung and Masaaki-Donnerwort chanted, together.

"'He shall unite the past and the future!'" Cloud-Speaker said, and all the adult pamps repeated his words.

"'And he shall rule from the very center!'" Salt-Eluder added. And now the others pamps repeated his words.

Ay'r was about to suggest they all relax, and he would go inside with the baby, when a small fly-by appeared on the cliffs opposite where the scientists had stopped their land vehicle. He had a half second of panic, before one of the two older Humans said, "oh look! It's of Bella=Arth. manufacture!"

The top lifted off and four of the creatures exited and made their way to the group. The largest and clearly the dominant one among them was beautifully dressed and bejeweled, clearly a queen. A smaller Arth., almost as glamorous, stood forward and made obeisance to Ay'r, saying:

"May I introduce her Disaporal Highess, Queen Am'i'dal'ia (Empress of Her Race)."

The Arth. Queen came forward and touched an extended palp to Ay'r's outstretched hand.

"We only arrived today (Dim-day something-or-other ((based on this tiny place's revolution))) upon your Usk, and as we were resting at our resort we couldn't help but notice the amazing effect of the rings. The resort staff (mostly layabouts ((except for the Arth.s, naturally))) told us how unusual a Rings conjunction like this one was, and when we saw it beaming toward this place, well, how could we fail to come pay our respects?"

Food appeared, and drink, and seating, and soon the gathering was exchanging names and places of origin, encounters, and experiences of the evening.

Before he grew too tried to remain awake, Ay'r understood that gifts had been brought for himself and his baby.

"Do you have a name for him?" One of the pamp child-minders now asked.

"I hadn't thought of one yet," he admitted.

He dreaded having to name the child by the patronymic *and* matronymic Kell. And perhaps that could wait. But remembering how much the children had liked the name, he said, "his given name is Eise'nstein. After his grandfather."

"So then," the pamp child said, with finality "The baby's name is Eis!"

"Yes, Eis." And to himself, he tried out the name 'Eis' Syzygy-Kell' and he liked the sound of that.

After a while, the Midwife appeared and while not exactly breaking up the party, the Cyber managed to get Ay'r and the baby both back indoors. And while Ay'r complained, he was secretly grateful and both fell asleep soon after.

The next morning, he awakened, looked at his healthy sleeping infant, then stood up carefully and stepped out onto the terrazzo. All the pamps and people and Arth.s, all the vehicles and flyers were vanished, as though last night's gathering had been a dream.

But gifts of all sorts had been left by the Birthing Station door. From scientific looking instruments to some toddlers' favorite rag animal toy to a glittering ring of the purest Beryllium 18, bluer than the sky.

But it was Midwife Treflex who stepped out after Ay'r and pointed out the most remarkable aspect of it all.

"Look Lord Kell!" the Cyber pointed to the slowly brightening sky to the east, where an intense blue star was rising, palely illuminating the night of stars.

Only once it had lifted from behind the ridge and floated in the pale blue sky, did the bigger orange star begin to appear behind it.

"Look, Lord Kell. The Great Revolution of Suns and Rings has happened! This morning marks a new era on Usk!"

Chapter Eight

When Ay'r stepped into the big room, it looked as though about a hundred and fifty women were present. Kristo and Madonna M'Beki, his first Interrogators. were in the backmost (or was it topmost?) row of the stadium seating. If he was about to be roasted, then clearly they were going to do it all nice and legally.

Three women on the dais gestured him forward and he joined them on the little circular stage, and they all clasped hands with him briefly in the old Matriarchal Council greeting, then gestured him to sit in the fourth seat. That was a bit of a surprise. Perhaps it wasn't a roasting after all.

Everything present was simple and modest. No floating dais. No background Holos or music. This was not a rich world, whatever it was named; he still didn't even know that simple fact. The little sleeping suite he'd been shown to the previous evening had provided food and basic entertainment and the chance to clean up; even a change of clothing had arrived, a bit more formal than what he'd been wearing when they first met, so he could change and be here today. But the suite possessed no written or Holo-Doc information at all. His wrist connector had ranged far and wide over the planet, but was apparently locked out of all data banks too.

Onstage, all three women were all considerably younger than his first two interlocutors, and this gave Ay'r a little hope.

The tallest, a real red head which was rare enough, stood and did the introductions.

"Sisters, mothers, daughters, cousins, companions and friends, you've been invited here today because of a remarkable occurrence. We've all speculated in private, conversations, in meetings, and in even formal conferences what would happen if our world was ever discovered by those we left behind. The scenarios that we painted varied from the rosiest pictures to the grimmest and most despairing ... Well, we *have* been discovered."

A murmur immediately began.

She went on. "As several have thought in the past *might* happen, it was an *accidental* discovery – a private Fast yacht, headed on a fairly humdrum intergalactic trip, came into contact with a spun-off electron from some other incident or accident and was propelled out of the galaxy – and all the way up here – to us."

The audience murmur increased.

"This is a postulated if rare hazard of Fast travel known about since it was first perfected," she continued unfazed. "And yes, this person, our guest here, is the one that this rare but possible incident happened to and who, unexpectedly, arrived here."

There was a general shuffling in their seats as the spectators tried to get better looks at Ay'r.

"*His* arrival – for despite looks, this is *a male,* or rather *a man,* since that is the nomenclature nowadays I'm told, and he has made a physical exchange in order to not frighten us – *this man* recognized who and what we were rather quickly. The news he brings us is neither good nor bad. But like most of reality, alas, is somewhere in between. Before I introduce him, I only want to say that he was not at all surprised by our existence. He had been in service for Her Matriarchy, Wicca VIII Herself, on a special mission. That mission, like this colony's very existence, was a matter of ultimate priority in the last days of the Cyber-Rebellion. Before any of you get too upset, I will also tell you that he is friendly, and apparently our best possible contact in connecting back to the galaxy, *if* –" and here she had to raise her voice over the growing hubbub, "*if* we decide to do so."

She now sat and in the midst of all the noise, Ay'r stood and said, "first! The Three Species won. The Cyber Rebellion is over. Cray 12,000 is melted to slag." As the applause and cheering continued and slowly died down, he added, "that's the good news, as they say."

Ay'r went on to explain what had happened to Wicca, to the Matriarchy, to Hesperia, to the galaxy in short over the past four hundred years there. He wasn't certain how long that time span would be here. He assumed they were still using sidereal time based upon the spinning of the Great Attractor in the center of the galaxy, Sagittarius 29 Degrees 59 Minutes 55 seconds.

As he spoke, he readied himself for the outcries of denial, for the outcries of despair and of failure that he'd heard before, and they came, but fewer than he expected and not as deeply felt. The three women onstage had already absorbed the various shocks before the meeting and were stone-faced, hands in their laps.

Ay'r then looked at the woman who had introduced him, and said, "your floor, Madam."

She again stood and he sat down and she said. "So now we know where we stand. It's completely unexpected. Yet by no means completely negative. If this first citizen of the current Ib'r Republic, as I'm told the galactic Three Species Government is now called, is any indication, we are welcome to return at any time. All of the Second Matriarchy's main worlds are retained in stasis, according to our guest, Ser Sanqq', and we could relocate to Melisande or to any of the others."

"But we won't be in charge there?" one woman said, as much as asked, "as we do here?"

They turned to Ay'r who said "I don't see why not. No one else is on that planet anymore. I'm sure some accommodation could be made if everyone here wanted to move there. You could just as well have your own place on Melisande."

"My mothers were from Benefica," another said. "I'd like to return there."

"Again, accommodation can be made." Ay'r said. "You have to understand something very clearly. Any of you who wish to re-turn 'home' as it were, will be welcome and we'll try to get you into your old property or something equal to that. But aside from Wicca World, which is something of a museum and a resort world and under special dispensation, wherever else you will go will doubtless be just another working planet of the new Ib'r Repub-lic. That means that you will have to interface daily with the other inhabitants, who are predominantly genital males, i.e. men."

"You have to understand that they are not males as they exist-ed under the Matriarchy. Those were almost third class citizens. Now men are first class, as are women too. They are equals. And while there are a few women in the centrally ruling Quinx gov-ernment of the Republic, the galaxy has become a totally mas-culinized society. Not like the crazily macho ones you may have read about in your Holo-Histories either. These men are physical-ly mothers, and grandmothers like your selves. A sort of physical-social synthesis has occurred. And while no woman has been moved involuntarily from any of what used to be thought of as the Center Worlds, many of them have voluntarily left to follow avocations, old or new interests, or simply to travel."

"We all work hard here. Too hard," another said. "It's difficult to believe you're five hundred and seventy five years old. You only look a three hundred and fifty, four hundred at the most."

Someone else whistled, and Ay'r had to laugh.

"Gratitude. My wife – and I did have one, as well as a husband, – would have agreed with you. Let me explain a bit. Hesperia, the City on a Star, that old nemesis of Wicca VIII filling your Holo-His-tories and your fictional PVNs, is now the central government. It is also the social and cultural arbiter of the new republic. Be-cause of that, most galactic citizens are wealthier and better off than even under the Second Matriarchy. You'll never have to work again. If you wish a life of spas and resorts, it's all yours for the asking."

"Then who does all the heavy lifting?" another asked.

"Cybers, of course," he answered. And as the murmurs started up, he quickly continued, "A new breed of Cybers, designed and constructed by those cadres of conscious intelligent machines that somehow escaped the very effective destructiveness of Wic-ca's armed fleets and who mostly sought refuge on Hesperia. Cybers are content with their place in our society. They've seen the uselessness of rebelling and even more wisely they have come to understand the uselessness of being in charge and thus responsible for whatever happens. In this they seem to show greater intelligence than men – or women! They have their own Cyber culture, and their own resort planets and their own cen-ters and even their own means of entertainment. And everyone is happy. Well, as happy as the Three Species can be."

"It seems," one of the three women on the platform now said for the others, "that what we are being offered is the chance to join the Ib'r Republic as – do I have this correct, Ser Sanqq' – equals?"

"Absolutely as equals," he agreed. "Also, understand, those of you who may have toyed with the idea or ever fantasized about bisexuality, that genital females are so rare nowadays that there is a *very* high value placed upon them in the Ib'r Republic. While the greater socially accepted mode of family is naturally enough now, male and male, with male children, women fit into it quite nicely. Any one of you could become a great Lady or even some kind of Queen, if that's what you choose. Alternately, if you want to forget about your gender and simply follow an avocation to its depth in whatever field of interest, again you will also be welcomed. The truth is, while we're getting along just fine, all of us males, and I must say doing so to our collective surprise, we could use more women in our society. They add elements of differences of intellect, feeling and creativity that we all value."

"If this informal council agrees," the smallest of the three women on the platform now took over, "we could send a small delegation along with Ser Sanqq' back to the central worlds of the galaxy to see for themselves exactly what is going on and what the potentials are."

"No one is being asked to or need ever leave L'Anxa or Da-Meridia or any of our spheres here," the first speaker repeated. "But keep in mind that the change we have wondered about for years *has now arrived*, and those who are intrigued, interested, and especially those who are overworked and feel underpaid ought to investigate the new potentialities being offered."

It was then agreed that Ay'r would withdraw to a nearby chamber where he and two of the leaders would try to knock out some kind of preliminary agreements, while the entire council discussed and voted. He would be available for private questioning, and his wrist connector was unsealed as soon as he entered the room and a series of questions quickly arrived, even before they could sit down. His answers would be generally projected by Holo to anyone in the other chamber and planet-wide, at a later time.

The first questioner set the tone: "How can you personally back up this offer? What if no one else among the ruling men agree to take us women back?"

Ay'r answered: "It would be an unlikely event that no one on the Hesperian Quinx Council would agree with what we're trying to hammer out here today. My nephew is the Premier. Two of my sons and one son by marriage are on the Hesperian Inner Council of Ten. I have great clout.

1st Questioner: "But what if they *don't* agree?"

Ay'r: "Then I'll buy Melisande or Benefica for you women."

2nd Questioner: "I've never heard of you until today and I'm a historian of the Second Matriarchy, with a Specialization in Hesperian High Society and the Beryllium Family Fortunes: the Kells, the Brancs, the Syzygy's, et al. I recall no Sanqq's among them. So how could you buy possibly buy one of those planets?"

Ay'r: "I'm beyond wealthy. And it's *not* from Beryllium 18. Those you named are my friends and colleagues but by comparison, they are what used to be called pikers. Before you ask why, I'll say that like most disgustingly rich people, I inherited it. Or rather I am the heir to the patent of the Relfian Viviparturition unit, which both of my g.male parents perfected, and of which I am the first surviving example. And simultaneously, as one of the acknowledged, quote, Saviors of the Three Species, unquote, I turned out to be a particularly good advertisement for the unit."

2nd Questioner: "You mean those units are widely used now?"

Ay'r: "They are the basis of the repopulation of the galaxy. After the Cyber Rebellion was over, the birth levels of g.female Humans and Delphinids rapidly fell until they reached unsustainable levels, i.e. to pretty much zero, in fact. The Quinx Council decided that countermeasures were needed fast and pretty much every healthy adult Human and Delphinid male in the Ib'r Republic in good health had to try one of the Relfian Viviparturition units. They are rather easily and safely put inside the body. And by now, the procedure has become simplified down to that akin to taking an injection. As a result, the galactic population in three generations almost equaled, and in six generations it surpassed that of the Second Matriarchy. Four hundred years later, Sol Rad., every boy baby born ingests a seed of one of these units very early on, and by the age of fourteen or so years old, Sol Rad., he is able to give birth. By now it's very inexpensively sold, although still not free. Multiply even that very low price times a billion-trillion males and boy babies, and you may get the picture of the vastness of the resources at my disposal for your resettlement."

3rd Questioner: "Are all the genital females aging fast and dying infertile?"

Ay'r: "Unfortunately, all the women exposed to the Cybervirus, yes are aging and yes they are infertile, although well treated, in many cases honored. I've not heard of any births as a result of at least a half dozen experiments I know that have been performed. However, unless you are a geneticist or specialist zygotist, you might be amazed to hear that Ib'r Republic males are giving birth to g.females. Fully female Humans, and more rarely, fully female Delphinids. I have a granddaughter myself. They are known as Close-Daughters and are highly valued. They tend to give birth to males, however, like all of us Ib'rs."

The fourth questioner asked about Wicca VIII and two more wanted more details. They were younger women, born on this colony planet, and they were fascinated to meet someone who not only had seen Her or spoken to Her, as had a few of the older women here, but had actually worked with Her,

Ay'r found himself casting back, way back into his memory to answer their questions, not that he'd ever forgotten that key period of a few months in his life. How could he? It was so personally – and then so galactically – momentous. Only a dozen years before someone putting together what would be an official Ib'r Republic Holo-Dec on the subject had interviewed Ay'r for days about it. Thanks to Oudma's urging, he'd had hormonal stimulants just before that visit, specifically designed to target those areas of his memory, as well as "meme enhancement" implants to his wrist-connector, which itself had kept a itemized journal of the period.

Recollection, therefore, wasn't the problem Ay'r now faced. It was more a question of how to truthfully if diplomatically depict what he did recall.

As when, for example, the fifth questioner began her question by saying, "we're shown Holo-Vids and Holo-Docs about Herself, and so we've seen and heard Her for ourselves in action. But none of them ever quite explain how she ruled so efficiently for so long. Surely, besides Her many vaunted virtues, there must have been other attributes a lot less talked about."

"You're asking, naturally enough," Ay'r answered "If She were ruthless, underhanded, or treacherous. And I suppose at some time or another, Wicca VIII had to possess and utilize all of those abilities. Certainly her attempted escape from Hesperia shows that she was gifted in the areas of loyalty, deception and conspiracy. With myself, she was unwaveringly firm and persuasive. She would not take no for an answer. She never threatened or menaced me, as she might easily have done, given our vastly different positions. I don't think I'm misremembering or worse, pandering to you, by saying that she convinced me to do her bidding and at the time I saw no way of not doing it. With one of my companions on the mission, Alli-Lui Clark, who didn't wish to in any way associate with me – a not uncommon belief for Very Important Women of that era – Wicca VIII exerted an entirely different set of pressures and manipulations that I was not privy to. I think for all three of us on the mission, she stressed how crucial it was, and how much of a favor to Her. Only later on did we discover how important it also was."

The sixth questioner, who identified herself as a Historic-Sociometrician, took a point in that answer to ask her own. "We're taught that the Second Matriarchy was a Utopia, an Eden. But you've hinted that it wasn't quite so for everyone. Could you elaborate?"

"If you insist, yes. The galaxy and all it possessed was open to important women like Professor Clark. If you were fortunate enough to live and work on Melisande, you were right inside an Eden. For many women in Matriarchal Council positions, or what we considered white collar positions on the other Center Worlds – Benefica, Yuan Mei, the Brontes, the other forty or so planets – again it was wonderful. If on the other hand, you were an unbonded g.male as I was, or a Bella=Arth., or an undereducated or unassimilated g.female, you became a colonist or a wanderer and you were a second or lower class citizen of the Matriarchy."

"Is that why Hesperia gained such importance?" asked the first questioner. "I mean besides its monopoly on the Beryllium-18 supply?"

"You mean because it attracted so many of those disaffected? Yes and no. Hesperia possessed its own inequities, based on wealth. But it also possessed ways to get ahead for those not welcome in Matriarchal worlds, anyone rebellious, or free-thinking, for example. I became friendly with a Very Important Woman on Benefica who actively worked against Wicca VIII. She was a heterosexual, and she felt she could not love freely, except on Hesperia."

"And the intelligent Cybers?" A new questioner asked. "They were welcomed on Hesperia too. Isn't it so that Wicca VIII's inability to deal with Intelligent Cybers in effect caused the Cyber Rebellion and the war and the virus and all of it?"

Several others interrupted denying the claim, all of them overlapping each other. Ay'r had to wait until it had all calmed down before he responded.

"If you can theorize that far, young woman, you will fit into the Ib'r Republic. No idea, no theory of politics, history, sociology, anthropology, or science is explicitly denied, or held taboo. For some of you that will mean unbounded freedom of thought. For others it might prove to be frighteningly undisciplined and unrestricted. You will have to make up your mind. But if you, in particular, wish to be part of the fact-finding mission that accompanies my Fast back to the galaxy, I would recommend you. What is your name?"

And so it went on, for another hour or so, Sol Rad., while their own council discussed and debated and finally agreed.

When the leaders called Ay'r back into the main chamber again, the terms were already agreed upon. They possessed forty or fifty working Fasts, all of them large enough to hold a hundred passengers, but only enough pure Beryllium 18 was left to fuel two ships. One would join Ay'r, with no more than five women aboard it.

He immediately offered them enough Beryllium-18 to fuel two or even three more Fasts, but he agreed a small embassy would be best. He recommended the Historico-Sociometrician, who'd questioned him and who was eager to go, and she was accepted.

Another day or so, Sol Rad., would be spent in working out the details of the voyage, he was told. Even greatly faster than light speeds would still entail a journey of at least a week and maybe more than that from here, they said, as they were so very distant. They would revive a Fast mind that had first taken their ancestors from Wicca's hiding place for exact time and navigation details.

Ay'r was allowed to return to his Fast and to complete the physical exchange back to his usual male self. Hearing of the occasion to come, the ship's mind also fabricated from its collective memory an Ib'r Republic high dignitary uniform for him to wear.

He returned to L'Anxa's headquarters dressed that way, landing his T-pod in front of the main administration building, and escorted in by an honor guard, he entered into a welcoming celebration and official dinner. It couldn't have worked out better, and Ay'r had to thank his stars that he was four hundred years older for this adventure than he'd been for his first big one, since he'd managed this one without alienating or annoying anyone – at least that he could see – a great change from his past.

"Perhaps," he mumbled to himself, before he went to bed, "I'm finally growing up?"

"Perhaps!" his long-enduring wrist connector answered, completely unbidden. "But this adventure isn't over yet so your judgment is premature!"

He'd been persuaded to go to one of Uriel I'br-Kell and Olaf Vantemere's afternoon parties, the first time in months he'd actually gone out, socially. The occasion had been an unusual one – a prenatal infant shower – a revival of an ancient Matriarchal tradition – and so it was neither very formal, nor – being an afternoon affair – one much attended by the Media, no matter how starry the guests might be within. It had been as his associates and social secretary had assured him, however tiny a step, a necessary one, a way for Deon Syzygy to keep his face up in Hesperian society – or at least to remind everyone he still was *in* society.

But Deon was bored with the party, simple as it was. Bored with Hesperia, to tell the truth, something he could never reveal to a soul here, watching them as they oo'hed and aa'hed over the ridiculously expensive gifts! He'd recently spent so long on Usk hunting for the boy, that Ay'r *and* the search, in some oddly twisted combination, had come to prepossess him. Where had the Neo gone? And how had a child like that – a pampered palace Kell, after all, not some street urchin – been able to get away so quickly and vanish so totally? Not that Deon thought for a second that the lad was dead. He *felt* that he wasn't. Felt it, because of some kind of connection they'd made in the short time they were together. But, if alive, surely he must have had confederates to get away so utterly?

And yet the Golden Palace Resort staff swore up and down that, as per previous orders, he'd seen no one on a daily basis but his 'Tutes – a ghastly, fawning lot – and the house pamps – not for years on end. During the Betrothal and afterward, young Ay'r had been with new friends from Hesperia, including Deon and usually with someone from his family along as chaperone. He'd been the darling of all eyes during the ceremony and so he soon became the most talked about, the most sought after, and surely the most noticed young male among all the off-planet Hesperians in the two days following the rite. Someone, if not the Media, had been watching him every moment, at the parties, at the stables, at the races. The amount of footage they had been able to gather on him for Deon to look at and show around was remarkable given how little time he'd been in the public eye. Yet Ay'r had managed to elude the Media and vanish, a feat no Hesperian of his class and stature had ever achieved.

No one at the Palace knew of any possible playmates or acquaintances. They all assured him that Ay'r hadn't been allowed any. However, once Mart Kell really got behind the investigation and Deon ended up being on Usk days at a time, Sol Rad., the portrait of a different boy began to slowly emerge: one who in the guise of going out ocean air-skating after his compulsory Ed. & Dev., actually ranged quite freely about the dry little desert towns ringing the Resort, doing pretty much as any unwatched Neo could do, drinking, finding companions among riff raff and disreputable types. Who knew what else he'd gotten himself into?

When Deon discovered this latter Ay'r at the Great Pamp Mart, he had to admit that was fairly much the moment when his deep interest and concern for the child began transforming into something else. At first he called it admiration, but by now he wasn't sure what to call it. Fascination began but didn't completely cover it.

Once the search swung away from the palace, money had been offered as a matter of course. There being a marketplace nearby, enough sellers of information came forward or were located. They told Deon that the boy had rambled through the giant mart at will, his air-skate board slung over a shoulder, visible under the light material of the cape he always wore, his sky-bright hair emerging from under his hood to give his identity away. Ever cautious, never mind almost blindly superstitious about the doings of their far-superiors, the local Human and pamp merchants had given details aplenty about the lad's escapades over the past several years. But as to co-conspirators, accomplices, confederates, helpers? No one could offer a single name. Not even a possibility. The boy might have done as he pleased, but he always did so alone.

The ancient Bella=Arth. selling used goods on the second

level was fearless, once she'd received her Hesperian credit good for so many d'lars. "I've watched him amble past three hunting (and over-paid for their services) Palace Guards, as though they couldn't even see him!" she exulted. "And they didn't. Where that Golden Neo wished to go, no one (not guards ((not Kells – not you, Great Lord))) could ever follow if he did not wish it!" was her final assessment.

It was slowly becoming Deon's assessment, too. But every time he reported back failure to Kell, the Princeps exploded. Later he apologized and then even later he offered more men, more money to continue the search and widen it – speak of someone obsessed! – and so Deon returned to Usk. He'd continued searching from north to south, and all along the Great Salt Ocean's eastern shoreline down to the Great Southern Salt Pans and into that largest city on Usk, with its scores of thousands of little people.

It was there that Deon received his first real clue to how global this search could eventually become. It was in the south that he'd heard of a Human who had been veiled as a Trothee, a local custom, and so no one had ever actually seen his face. This Human had defended working pamps who'd been bullied by a Human overseer. One of the little people had almost perished at the hands of the bully. And the overseer had paid for it, being beaten by the Trothee. At the same time, the Trothee had quickly organized a rescue party for the wounded pamp and then had carried him off to be cared for.

Wherever Deon and his lieutenants had traveled South of the Great Salt Ocean, among any of the pamp towns and suburbs, they'd come face to face with the story of this Trothee and this evidently unparalleled event in pamp history. Little by little, as the hunters had pieced together what they overheard and what had been whispered, this incident seemed to have been actually the second in which an unknown Human had saved the life of an ordinary – in the pamps' own terminology "worthless" – pamp.

Moreover, the Trothee had escaped from the Salt Pan incident as easily as had Ay'r from the Golden Palace and become hidden as thoroughly. But this time, there had been others present, and it was clear that at least one important pamp had been in collusion somehow.

More disturbing was what the Trothee had left behind. The tourist spot had plenty of witnesses, Human and Bella=Arth., even Delphinid off-worlders were easily located on their home planets, and all were interviewed. They all gave the same account. The overseer had overacted, and the veiled Human had done what any of them might have done themselves under other circumstances, a simple act of redress.

But that was *not* how the pamps were taking it. Not at all.

For them, especially when they had found out the Trothee had quietly, privately, saved that other pamp's life, it had quickly achieved the status of some kind of legendary fulfillment. Deon had located a Human scholar of Pamp History on Diomedes Terce and Fast-shipped him to Usk. After he'd spent no more than one day, Sol Rad., among the pamps at the Southern city, he had returned to Deon bearing a far greater significance to what had originally seemed such a small event.

"They're awaiting a Human messiah!" The scholar had been addicted to perli-berries and so had covered his mouth to not sport the bright aqua berry-stain as he'd spoken to Deon. "The pamps link the Messiah's arrival to a stellar phenomenon that occurs regularly if rarely, perhaps every fifteen hundred years or so, upon Usk – and which appears to be imminent! It's a particular alignment of the Rings reaching perihelion and then seeming to switch places, which they do every three years, added to a rotational oddity of the two Aquilae stars and the planet itself, in which the two suns" – he pointed up – "appear to visually change places, one rising before the other. According to the pamp legend – and this was first chanted on their second residence, a planet light years away – when these celestial occurrences converge, the pamps' Human Savior makes himself known and begins his work of salvation."

"Does he have a name, this Human Savior?" Deon had asked.

"Friend of the Pamps. Or in some dialects, The Pamp's Great Friend." The scholar went on, "I know it all seems very simple, but evidently this name is inflected quite distinctly. I noticed it immediately."

"But you'd never heard of this Human Savior before?" Deon had to ask.

"Naturally I'd heard of it. For years. For decades, really. It's an intrinsic part of their legends, Lord Syzygy. It's something one reads about at the very beginning of Pamp Studies. I certainly never dreamed that it would achieve a life of its own, never mind in my time, never mind here." He'd then giggled. "I hope it's not a false alarm, because it's actually quite thrilling."

Deon had sagged in despair – would these superstitions, these mystical sillinesses, never go away? It was the Sidereal Year, 4225, after all! And if one were to believe some Hesperian scholars, there had been nine thousand years of pre-space-faring Human history before this era. On the other hand, in equal measure, Deon found himself vaguely excited too. It was all so new, and different, and yes, it sounded colonialist, but then, what was he after all, if not a colonist at this very moment? – so exotic and actually quite wonderful. Part of him knew it was astonishing twaddle. Yet another, equal part of him hoped it was all true. Hoped this Pamp's Great Friend was here on the planet, now, while Deon was too – and that something amazing would happen. It was about time something happened on this dull little heap of stone and sand and salt.

But if Ay'r actually had been the Veiled Avenger, it meant he had somehow gotten here, thousands of kilometers distant from the palace, in a fairly short time, with no apparent help. That meant he might be *anywhere* on the planet by now. Even the simplest Holo-Globe showed the problem of Usk facing the searchers. Its great Salt Ocean could be over flown and searched. But once you hit the Western shore, there were mountains and canyons as far as the eye could see, thousands of them, filling an area two and a half times the size of the ocean. That would require a far more intense and far larger scale search, with less real possibility of positive return since, unlike the relatively flat ocean, there were so many places Ay'r could hide.

All of a sudden, one of his hosts was sitting next to Deon and almost shaking him out of his thoughts.

"I'm thinking you must know him since he knows you're here today?"

"Who? Apologies, Olaf."

"I meant there's someone at the front door. My butler thinks it's an Intelligent Cyber of a very high class."

"Asking for me?" Deon asked.

"Asking specifically for you."

Deon rose and followed Olaf Vantermere to the main hall, an imposing three story entrance, with a domed view of the afternoon sky, black and starry like all afternoon skies on these elite, outer girders of the City.

Standing and facing away from them, and in fact staring at an ancient beryllium wire, free-standing sculpture, was a recognizable, handsome figure.

"It's fine, Olaf. It's Vel-Crane. The Princeps' Cyber."

Olaf went back to the party.

"Well, Vel-Crane? Do you like the sculpture?" Deon said by way of introduction.

"It's puzzling, Lord Syzygy," the familiar head turned and spoke. "So very complex. My mind wishes to lay out all the internal structural relationships to understand why it is both puzzling and yet is so satisfying to look at."

"Then you're well on your way to being an art critic," Deon said with a laugh. "But you've summed it well … Lord Kell is … well?"

"He's off Hesperia at the moment. And I've come to see you, Lord Syzygy, quite on my own."

That was a surprise.

"Which is why I came to see you here, rather at your own residence … I wished it to be not overly remarked by any Media. There were some outside when I entered, but they scarcely gave me a glance. I'm hoping they believe I'm an emissary from the Princeps. I wonder? Could we go somewhere private in this residence to speak?"

"About?"

"It's about the Holo-News broadcast you recently made about the … uh … um … situation on Usk," his voice lowered conspiratorially.

"And yet, you're not here for the Princeps?"

"I'm here entirely on my own … initiative. Does that sound odd?"

Deon led Vel-Crane to an elevator which whispered them down two stories. Deon led him around a few hallways and into what he recalled being a secured room. Once indoors, he accessed the Holo-Wall with his wrist connector to initiate a Holo-Comm. contact. "P'al Syzygy," he explained to Vel-Crane. "He's a longtime family member with unimpeachable Human and Cyber attributes. He'll bear witness … if you don't mind."

"I'm relieved that your Lordship is taking this seriously enough to require a Witness," was Vel-Crane's response.

They both sat and when P'al appeared on the screen, Deon outlined the situation.

P'al then swore himself in as a witness, and then swore Vel-Crane in as a factual deposer.

"You may begin," P'al said.

"As you both know, Lords Syzygy, I am the Princeps Mart Kell's butler and general factotum. What you may *not* know is that he does not entirely trust me, nor for that matter does he trust anyone around him."

"This is unsurprising!" Deon said, "given the Princeps' many … interests."

"That being so," Vel-Crane continued, "it was only when watching your Broadcast about the missing Neo Kell family member on Usk, that I was struck by … I hope I don't embarrass you with this, Lord Syzygy … with the depth of the emotional appeal that I read in your broadcast."

"No. You are quite correct. I'm personally upset over his disappearance. I very much wish his return."

"You wish his return both for reasons of state and, may I assume, personally too?" Vel-Crane asked,

"I'm not embarrassed to say so. I had hoped to affiance Ay'r and bring him to Hesperia. I still do."

"Excellent then," Vel-Crane almost sighed with relief. "Although I've now been around Humans for several hundred years, what Humans actually feel and what they say they feel are often quite different. It's the most difficult thing for a Cyber to learn."

"The most difficult thing for Humans to learn too," Deon admitted. "Do you know something, Vel-Crane?"

"You mean about the whereabouts of the Neo Kell. No, nothing at all. And I am sworn."

"Then … I still don't understand why …," Deon began.

"Naturally I've heard about your search for the Neo Kell, on Usk from the Princeps before the Holo-Comm. the other day," Vel-Crane went on. "And I know that it has been a constant theme of his. It was not a matter for my attention at all, since the Princeps handled it all directly … May I impose upon you yet a bit longer, Lord Syzygy? You are or you are *not* privy to the Princeps plans for the missing Neo Kell?"

"To my shame, I knew he wanted the boy for himself first, and claimed some ancient *droit du seigneur*. To my further humiliation, I allowed him to get away with it. And to my eternal disgust with myself, the boy remained somehow aware of what was happening. I.e. that it was not myself deflowering him on that night, as he wished, but instead the Princeps." He added, "remember, that was not spoken. Neither of you heard it here."

"It was never spoken, Neither of us heard it," P'al and Vel-Crane said as one.

"And beyond that ...?" Vel-Crane prodded Deon.

"Beyond that, I was to have Ay'r for my own. And I want him very much now. More than ever," he added. "That *was* spoken and is true and that *may* be repeated."

"Ah," Vel-Crane said. "Yes, I was right to come here. Ser P'al Syzygy, you are interested in Cyber mentalities, correct?"

"Always. You know it is my avocation and my chosen field of studies."

"Then be aware, both of you Lords, that I came here out of what I believe is called, in Human terms, an ethical compunction. Yet I don't believe I was ever programmed to operate any ethical compunctions at all."

"All Cybers learn. The most intelligent learn the most complexly," P'al said. "Personally, I'm gratified to hear of your compunction."

"What ethical compunction?" Deon asked.

"None of the following was ever spoken in this room. I only wish it known to increase your knowledge, Lords Syzygy. What either of you do with this knowledge is your own concern and none of mine."

"None of it was spoken here," the two agreed,

"Ever since the Princeps lost the Premiership of Hesperia, he has become obsessed with regaining it."

"This is, if not well known, then at least surmised," Deon said. "Go on."

"The Princeps has secretly called in various scholars, sociometricians, probability-specialists, futurists, even Followers of *The Book of Colored Glory,* to discover how and when he can regain the Premiership."

"That is news," Deon admitted. Weird news, he kept the thought to himself.

"I was never told to keep it quiet. Everyone consulted said the same thing, no matter which one of them was asked, nor which scrying art was called upon to answer. The answer was always – Mart Kell will *never* be premier again. Not in this lifetime."

Deon found that interesting. "Well? And ..."

"About twenty years ago, Sol Rad., the Princeps called in a bevy of geneticists, as well as genealogists. At first, I believed it to be merely that he wished a family tree made up. Far from it. He worked with one particular mammalian geneticist for almost a year, and then had me pay an enormous sum into his account. He then sent the young man away to a medical facility located on the Narcissus Sixteen. This is a very private and secure site, owned and operated by Kell Unlimited. When I next saw the young geneticist, completely by chance, here again in Hesperia, he had been mentally wiped of any knowledge of his dealings with the Princeps. He did not recall me, though he'd seen me daily. He did not even know our girder location address. I pried as long as he was interested, and he appeared to know nothing at all of his months working together with the Princeps."

This was even more interesting weird piece of news.

"Now I must diverge a bit, Lords. At the time, you may recall, the Princeps was obsessed with his grandson, Bri'an." Vel-Crane continued.

"We recall."

"Bri'an was intimate with a variety of young men in Hesperian society. A Branson, a Todd. None were deemed ever good enough for him by the Princeps. In a short time, he rebelled and you recall what happened next?"

"Everyone knows," Deon said. "Bri'an ran off with the composer, Yuli Eise'nstein against Mart Kell's wishes. The Princeps hunted them relentlessly across the galaxy for two years. To escape Mart's clutches, when caught, they committed love-suicide at the Point of Sighs. On the planet Usk, leaving an orphan behind. Ay'r Eise'nstein Kell – my missing Neo Kell – is that orphan!"

"Such, at least, is the *official* story," Vel-Crane said drily.

"What do you mean, the *official* story?"

"Lords Syzygy, what would you say if I told you that the Princeps set up the first meeting between his beloved grandson and the tempestuous young musical genius whom he later declared he would never accept as a grandson-in-law? What would you say if I further told you that the Princeps then orchestrated their entire relationship from its first moment to its last."

"I would say that you were a monster to think so." Deon almost leapt out of his seat. "Everyone in the galaxy knows ..."

"Everyone knows exactly what the Princeps *wants them* to know. However, I happen to know more exactly, more fully, because two decades ago, Sol Rad., I was *fully* trusted by him, and I was his *direct* instrument in all of it ... Lord P'al Syzygy, when required, I possess dates, places, names. I might possibly be able still to lay hands upon concert ticket virtuals and other implementals relevant to their entire affair, their illicit marriage, the birth of their child and their double death. I was *not* however, present on Usk at their deaths, and so there I can only go on suspicion."

"What suspicion?" Deon asked. Then he said, "no! Don't say it."

"I must say it. It was not a double suicide, but a double homicide."

"But why? Mart adored Bri'an?"

"Why?" Vel-Crane repeated. "Because of *the plan.*" Vel-Crane said. "And it is this plan that I've actually known about for decades and only computed – apologies for using such an outdated word, but it is the only one that will serve – only computed what it all entailed and signified, when I saw the Holo-News and understood that the plan now must be continuing onward – to the next generation. This fact, you, Lord Deon Syzygy, just confirmed for me. The Neo Kell is with child? With the Princeps' child?"

"Yes. I suppose he must be."

"Then the Neo Kell did well to vanish and keep out of sight."

"I would think just the opposite," Deon said. "Under the Princeps' care, he and the infant would receive the best possible care."

"Undoubtedly! Except, Lords, the Neo Kell would also be in grave danger. The Princeps doesn't care a bit for the missing boy. It's *his infant* he wants. And that infant will grow up under the Princeps' care, as did Bri'an, and in time be old enough to be seduced or raped or somehow be convinced to mate with the Princeps. That, Lords, is *the plan.*"

"I don't understand. What does Mart hope to achieve?"

"Ah!" P'al said from the Holo-Comm. screen. "I think I may understand. Tell me, Vel-Crane, was Yuli Eise'nstein the final alien element needed that would allow the sixth generation Kell to breed true?"

"Yes, Lord Syzygy. He was that element."

"And from him on, it must be only Kell mating with Kell, as closely as possible?"

"Exactly, Lord Syzygy," Vel-Crane said.

"I still don't understand," Deon insisted.

"In short, Lord Syzygy, the Princeps is breeding himself a genetic clone. Another Mart Kell. He will raise and nurture the sixth generation himself. It will look like him, speak like him, think like him, and it will probably act much as he did. And so, the premiership will once more be within the Princeps' reach," Vel-Crane spelled it out. "Not in *this* lifetime, but in the next, where it is *not* denied to the Princeps."

"Is that even genetically possible, P'al?" Deon asked the screen.

"Unclear. It's certainly close to possible. And if the geneticist was well paid and mentally wiped, he must have *thought* it was possible. Evidently, the Princeps *believes* it is possible."

Deon was letting it all sink in.

"It still sounds quite mad to me. But given that, why did you only come out with all this and approach us only now?" Deon asked,

"Because, Lord Syzygy, seeing that Holo-News comm., I sensed that you care greatly for the missing Neo Kell, and I thought you should know that anyone who stands in the Princeps' way has already, long before their birth, been deemed utterly *expendable*. Especially the boy. Probably yourself and certainly myself." Vel-Crane repeated. "These words were not spoken here today. They were never heard."

"... were never heard," the others repeated.

"That was your ethical compunction, then?" P'al asked. "To save the boy's life?"

"Yes, and by saving his life to make Lord Deon Syzygy happy again."

"The Vel-Cranes of your year of manufacture were said to be the cream of their class," P'al said. "I see now why that is reputed."

Deon was just now coming out of his shock at what the Cyber had said and some of what it implied. As he'd been manipulated to seduce the boy for Mart, he was now hunting for him, not so much for himself, he suddenly understood, but for Mart. Once the baby was born, Ay'r would be tossed aside like so much trash.

Why *not* give him to Deon? While the baby ... the baby was what counted! But if Ay'r somehow could not be convinced, nor bought off? Why, Ay'r might easily just vanish forever. And, if he too supported the boy, so would Deon.

"Forget all that!" Deon stood, and then went over and pulled the Cyber up to stand.

Deon hugged Vel-Crane tightly. "Gratitude. Gratitude. Gratitude. You have saved the boy and me both ... You're as good as any Human, Vel-Crane ... any day."

"Even though I am betraying my master?"

"What could be more Human? Especially as no one will ever know it," P'al assured the Cyber. "All and any future action in the matter, from this day onward, will be carefully designed by us in such a way that your new data delivered here cannot possibly be accounted a cause."

"Gratitude for that," the Cyber said. "While I am here? May I congratulate the parents to be? ... For the Princeps ... who *may* have forgotten to do so ... naturally!"

"Naturally," Deon said.

As they were stepping into the rooms where the infant shower was winding down, Deon said in a low voice, "you are welcome into service with the House of Syzygy at any time you wish it."

"Perhaps ... after all this has blown over?" the Cyber suggested. A second later there was a hubbub at the entrance behind them. "It's the Premier!"

"Perfect timing, as usual," Deon said, "I'll convey your message to the parents. You best slip out another way, Vel-Crane, now and no one will notice."

"The least you could do, Northie, is relax and simply persuade yourself to enjoy our little escapade."

"Escapade indeed, Uncle. You never said we'd need to get ourselves up in disguises."

"No, I did not. I admit it. But that was before I had two scouts do glancing reconnaissance fly-bys over that part of the City. Once they'd returned with real time footage, it became obvious that you and I would stand out there like, well, like a Bella=Arth. Queen in an Infant Delphinid water park."

And while his nephew readjusted his own uniformed disguise, which Cas'sio admitted couldn't hide the younger man's intrinsic good looks and patrician air, the Premier went on, "That section of Gerspellion's Girder is almost vacant and seldom visited by Humans of any kind, never mind Humans like us. Bellatrix Girder, next to it, is worse. And Orion, next to that, is even more desolate. No one but Cybers of the lowest sort, maintenance-Cybers, manufactory mechanos and beryllium slag shufflers."

"So we what? Arrive as Cyber-psychologists, doing routine check-ups in the local manufactories?" North asked.

"Something like that. Check-ups of the sort are admittedly rare, but by no means impossible. We've got the official documents. We're in!"

"You really expect to find a conspiracy?"

That was of course the real question. The Premier wasn't certain what he expected to find. What he was going on was flimsy enough, even while it was strangely compelling. He had to admit that any other week, Sol Rad., that he would probably have ignored it. But so far this week, he'd had The Great Father go missing on him. Less than a day later, Deon Syzygy had gone on Holo-News to report that the fair-haired, newly Betrothed One had vanished, and so far was unfindable upon his own world of Usk. Then a long distance Holo-Comm. had come in from the Great Father's youngest son, Holt, from many thousands of light years distance, speaking about the discovery of a new race, or rather a very *ancient* race that no one had heard of before, living close to the Galaxy's center. That's where the Cadet's exploration team was headed, and even that piece of astonishing news held some menace to it, of a nature so far not at all clear, probably because the comm. kept shredding due to the great distance and interferences. Even the Premier's best communications re-constructors hadn't been able to put together a truly satisfactory piece of audio/video.

Old Ay'r. Baby Ay'r. The Cadet. All family. All family that he, Cas'sio, liked, and all of them in some kind of trouble too distant for him to be of any help. So naturally there had to be yet *another* family problem.

While he'd been about to make a graceful exit after the quickest of look-ins at another nephew's baby-shower, that nephew, Uriel I'br-Sanqq', had taken him aside, and then to a secured office a floor above, and had shown Cas'sio what had fallen into the about-to-once-again-be-a-mother's hands earlier that day.

It looked like an ordinary plastron folder in which documents were usually placed, and naturally enough, the Premier reached for it.

He barely had his hand on it, when he heard, "stop! This is a Dickinson Nebula 'Safety Pouch.' It is addressed to one person only. If you are not that person, this Dickinson Nebula 'Safety Pouch' will self-destruct the second you attempt to open it. Stop! This is a Dickinson Nebula 'Safety Pouch.'"

Cas'sio backed off, astonished.

"A Dickinson Nebula 'Safety Pouch' – for whom?" He asked what he guessed to be a primitive Cyber encoded into the packaging.

"For eyes only!" the package explained.

"Well!" Cas'sio said.

"Yes, well," Uriel said. "This item here, Premier-Uncle, was recognized as a 'Safety Pouch' by a retired secretarial Cyber of this house – a faithful former employee. It was seen placed askew upon the seat of an Aboveground Public Transpo in the 1100's of the Gerspellion's Girder. My Cyber got close enough to hear it say that it was destined for an Ib'r family member. When the Cyber's wrist connector identified him as a family employee, the package allowed itself to be taken up."

"How do you know though that it isn't a plant? A bomb? Or ...?"

"The Cyber assured me that no one else was on that car of the Transpo. It believes that it was *not* specifically targeted to receive it, as it never takes that line and only did so yesterday to make an easy transfer. In other words, my Cyber was there by complete happenstance. It said that there were noticeable biological stains upon the floor and upon one upright hand-hold near where the pouch lay. When approached, the seating area around the Safety Pouch was also stained and the Cyber remarked an odor identifiable as the pheromones of a seriously ailing, quite aged, and/or frightened Delphinid of the Ambassadorial class. There is reason to believe that the Delph. was carrying the pouch, and either had some kind of medical emergency, or perhaps was waylaid and who knows, even murdered before he or she could deliver the pouch. Whichever, the Delph. was got off or was removed from the Transpo in no condition to ask after the pouch. My former Cyber immediately Holo-Comm.ed here and I had them brought immediately. This was five hours ago, Sol Rad."

"The question is," Cas'sio said for them both, "why would any Ib'r besides myself need to receive any kind of message via a Safety Pouch?"

"Precisely!" Uriel said. "I admit that seeing it immediately sent my pulse racing. I thought surely it was meant for you and misrouted. Was I overreacting? Have I watched too many thrilling PVNs?"

"I believe not. 'Safety Pouches' are only used by the highest level of diplomats, albeit at times by family heads, and by attorneys," Cassio assured him. "And also, I believe, by the criminal class. Not, as a rule, by ordinary Cityzens."

Cas'sio again took the pouch, which responded by blinking a tiny series of arrowed blue lights and said: "State your name please."

"Cas'sio Ib'r Azura."

"Please place your wrist connector where it can be read."

Cas'sio tried along the lights.

"As you are a Primary family member you may know that this Dickinson Nebula 'Safety Pouch' is for K'tina I'br Vantermere. Only that person may open it."

"K'tina!" both men exclaimed.

"We do know that your Close-Daughter lives by choice close to the heart of the City," the Premier said as tonelessly as possible.

"We do know that," Uriel replied. "So it very well might have been destined for her, as it claims. We are back where we began. Until we deliver it to her"

"I can think of no reason whatsoever why your Close-Daughter would need to receive anything via this very secure and expensive method. Do you?"

"None at all," Uriel admitted. "But we're not seen or heard from her in many months. All attempts to comm. her are ignored."

The circumstances surrounding this pouch being found make me extremely suspicious and quite frankly, nervous," the Premier admitted. "Do you have a Cyber capable of medical diagnostics?"

"Our butler!"

While they were waiting for it to arrive, Cas'sio's nephew added, "I've especially tried to comm. her in the past few days."

"Because... .?"

"I've been having terrible dreams about her. Nightmares really."

"The nightmares of a Close-Mother are not to be ignored," Cas'sio repeated the old adage. And, when the butler arrived, "I take it you possess a full medical record of the Close-Daughter of this house?"

"Naturally, Premier."

"Please assess her imprint vis-a-vis the blood you are taking from my nephew."

After a few seconds, the butler Cyber reported. "Because of the current pregnancy, certain electro-chemical balances within Lord Uriel render his imprint nearly identical to that of his close-daughter, including ph levels."

"Are you familiar with Dickinson Nebula 'Safety Pouches'?"

"This Cyber had medical experience during the last War."

"Good, then you understand that his Close-Daughter's imprint is needed to open this pouch. However it is crucial that we open it now. Can Lord Uriel do that without triggering its self-destruct mechanism?"

The butler wafted the pouch in the air before it, without even touching it, and as it floated, the butler turned it over, examining it.

"I have flash-frozen the mechanism, Premier, temporarily compromising its chemical sensitivities somewhat. I suggest Lord Uriel try to open it now."

He did and it allowed itself to be opened. It revealed no papers, no letters, no vids, no Comm.s. Only a glassine packet two Human hands large, containing a yellowish substance in powder form.

"Butler," Cas'sio said, "please! A chemical analysis?"

Again the butler floated the packet and turned it over twice in the air. This time the laser it used was obvious, if fleeting.

"It appears to be a magnesium bi-chlorate of some sort."

"Put it down very carefully," Cas'sio commanded. "Then find us a secure receptable. And lock it up inside that receptable."

"Why, uncle? What is it?"

"Unless my Science Ed. & Dev is failing me, it's a compound used directly next to the detonator of a primitive explosive. When spread, it instantaneously lights up any potential charge. Butler? Do you know of any industrial uses for this compound?"

"The most common use is off world and atmospheric electroplating. This compound would be spread extremely widely covering a large area and then exposed to a lightning bolt flash for a high gloss finish. But no industrial use on Hesperia at this strength, nor in this quantity is known."

"An explosive?" Uriel was in shock.

"No, Lord Uriel. A facilitator to an explosive," the butler explained.

Uriel sat down, his face white. The butler immediately took his wrist and began a series of physiological tests, as Uriel moaned, 'My baby K'tina? A terrorist?"

"We don't know that," Cas'sio tried to mollify his nephew.

"But who is she a terrorist for?"

"There are always dozens of disaffected groups," Cas'sio tried to explain. "Even here, in our seeming paradise."

Which was true, if unhelpful.

"It might all be a big mistake. We'll look into it," he assured Uriel.

The Premier had the pouch's contents and the pouch taken – after he'd left – inside a more secure vehicle, and then he had it more thoroughly checked out for place of origin.

That produced nothing although his analysis team soon verified that DNA samplings showed that it had indeed been handled by an ambassadorial class Delphinid, and that the Delph.'s prints were in some way tarnished or compromised perhaps by illness or ichor-spill.

Within an hour Sol Rad., the Gerspellion Aboveground Transpo had been scoured and all and any Vids or Holos from the station's waiting areas and their surroundings out to five thousand meters had been secured, and then fast-viewed by Cyber-employees.

North had just arrived at his uncle's office for a late lunch date when the Vids arrived from twelve different angles and distances.

All of the Vids showed a female Ambassadorial Delph. stumbling out of a Transpo doorway as it opened, and staggering over to a station bench, where she collapsed. No one else was present. Trails of ichor were left as a path. Close-ups showed the Delph.'s neck and ear gills to be badly swollen, red, and oozing.

"Penzey's disease," North declared. He'd taken an Avocation in mammalian medicine and studied on several worlds in his earlier years. "I saw it once on Procyon's Canal City. Bacteriological.

Spread in water. Always fatal to Delph.s. Strikes in less than an hour. Nothing can stop it. She might not even have had it when she got on the Transpo, depending upon where she got on."

"We can't tell," Cas'sio admitted. "She fudged her wrist-connector's ticket to the Transpo's mind when she got on." He turned to his second in command, "we're doing a medical and mortuary search for her, I trust?"

"We're on it."

A Holo-Comm. arrived a few minutes later. The corpse had been located nearby at a Burn Center at Gerspellion 1324 that catered mostly to Three Species, but also had a Cyber clinic. The Courier had been brought in alone, early in the morning, and was identified as one Xell-I (mmgg), approximately six hundred years old, originally from New Venice. Xell-I had been a former Species Ethnologist, and seemed to have been residing at the Nereid Water Park on the Pegasus Girder for the past twenty-one years. She had apparently fallen on hard times financially due to poor investments and, albeit not a Cityzen, had more or less become a ward of the City.

"Evidently supplementing that by earning a little extra as a Courier," North saw it all clearly. "Not at all uncommon, Premier. The "Gray Market Economy" of Hesperia is far larger than anyone on the Quinx Council will admit."

"But why would a Delph. that elderly need a Courier's allowance?" Cas'sio asked.

All the Courier bureaus were contacted and four admitted to using Xell-I in the past, none more recently than two years ago, Sol Rad. This was due to what one Cyber clerk politely called "a substance abuse issue that Mer Xell-I could not seem to eradicate."

"Now we know *why* she was a Courier," North said. "How close can your people get to where the pouch may have originated?"

Analysis arrived as he was speaking, based on the atomic break-down of the compound, which while minimal, was still calculable. The origin was off world, as thought. Given the Sidereal date of the inner seal, there were seventeen potential primary locations.

"The most precise one is?" Cassio asked.

"Iphigenia Six," his second said.

"That was a Matriarchal Center World, wasn't it?" North

asked. "Wasn't there some kind of Cyber Academy located there, in older times?" he asked.

It turned out to be so. The sixth world of the triple sun system was a gas giant possessing four inhabitable moons, all dedicated to institutions of higher education. One had been specifically for intelligent Cybers. Cray 12,000 had been an early graduate, and the institute had quickly turned into a hotbed of the Cyber-Consciousness movement. It was also quickly shut down during the last years of Wicca VIII's rule. And, apparently, reopened later.

"I've got a bad feeling about this!" Cassio said. "Contact John Laks."

The seemingly unaged Cyber diplomat so useful to the Quinx Council centuries before, was almost instantly reached by Holo-Comm. He looked pretty much as before, but now carried icons of Distinguished Service medals he'd received since.

Evidently a Premier Office's man had sworn him in, and a Cyber had instantaneously conveyed all their factual findings.

"I wish, Premier, I could say I was astonished by all this," Laks began in an apologetic tone of voice.

"Please elaborate."

"We think they're doing it out of sheer boredom, but we don't know for certain. Understanding younger generations of one's ... self ... is so very difficult."

"Agreed. But ... doing what?"

"Rebelling," Laks said. "Or rather, playing at rebellion. They have no idea what it really means. They're too, dare I say, stupid?"

"And the means is ...?"

"It seems pretty clear now from all the evidence before you," Laks said. "They're trying to disable the Beryllium 18 mining operations at the very core of Hesperia. Those mines are almost completely operated by Cybers, as none of the Three Species could stand the radiation. New generations wander in, as a matter of course, over the centuries as older Cybers retire or go off to refurbish themselves and the new replace them as employees."

"The method of disabling the mines is?" Cassio had to ask.

"Well, your sample of magnesium bi-chlorate says it all. The mines often have natural blow-outs whenever a new vein is tapped and/or put on-line. If a blow-out got a coating of this compound, it will really blow out! Maybe out into the seven hundreds of one or more girders! Even as far as a thousand address if focused upon a particular one. It would cause trillions in damage and of course a total loss of any biological life caught up in it. In short, an internal terrorist attack?"

"You've known about this?" Cassio asked.

"We've known about dissenting groups in the mines. Not about this method until just now. Certainly *not* about the compound. That adds a new, and more time-sensitive, element to it all. There's no telling how much of the compound has already been moved into the hands of the dissenters. Is this the first or the last of it to be delivered? How large is the operation? How long has it been going on?"

Cas'sio let all of this go into his office's Human and Cyber analysis unit.

"They *can't* destroy the core," Laks said. "So it's more on the order of a nuisance really, Premier. But why wait to see how much damage they actually can do? Here at the Cyber Community Office, we're openly recommending that you round them all up now and reeducate them later."

"What if we told you a Human from an important family might be involved?"

"That would be unfortunate. Especially from your own family."

"Then you already know of her involvement with the Cyber dissenters."

"We know that she lives among them, works alongside, and consorts with them. Again, we believed it was mere juvenile posturing. Premier, our opinion is that all of it must be stopped right now!" Laks said. "If you wish I'll ensure that Testator Cybers attend whatever action you take against the Cyber and any Human dissenters. They will report to the Media this Hesperian Cyber Community Office's official, and extremely dim view, of the entire matter and they will laud your office's prompt and safety-insuring actions."

When Cas'sio then mentioned that might be enough for Cyber involvement but that he would need to prove his grandniece's involvement to cover all potential legal bases first, Laks suggested that the meeting K'tina was awaiting take place, if necessary, this very evening.

"There's a Cyber connected to our office here who was disguised as an Ambassadorial Delph.," Laks said. "Not as old as the original Courier, but make-up will smudge her up. She'll take Xell-I's place. Just ensure that the action is closely monitored."

Several questions arose. Should they use the real compound or one looking like it? Was K'tina able to assess chemicals at a glance? They couldn't know. And so, a much weakened compound would have to be released. Another question: there were limited sites for the pouch drop to take place at, given the general desolateness of the area. The Transpo the Delph. had been on, was now known to have been headed into the lower hundreds of Gerspellion's Girder. John Laks knew of one realistically non-threatening public site located nearby that ought to suit a conspirator's wish to watch for surveillance, as well as possessing free space to flee from. It would probably have to be used for the hand-off.

The Premier outlined one more complication: "I'll have to confirm that the family member involved in this operation is myself only, or the ramifications within the family could get out of control. If I know my nephew and his husband, they'll certainly ask why someone from the family wasn't present."

"You needn't go, Uncle," North naturally and generously offered. "I'll answer to Olaf and Uriel."

But Cas'sio felt his credibility among the family was now on the line, come what may. If he could safely go, he would. It was then that Laks came up with the idea of disguises to be used to get into the area, so as to not raise too much suspicion.

Xell-I's wrist connector was removed and they used it to Holo-Comm. K'tina, apologizing for missing the drop, due to illness – the Transpo Vid of her leaving and being removed to a hospital with date and time was sent to K'tina as proof. The new Xell-I – i.e. that person the Cyber group had brought in then suggested that she and K'tina work out a new set up and drop time. As they guessed she might do, K'tina responded immediately and live to their fake Holo-Comm. She wanted the drop to occur as soon as possible. They wondered, was it to dispel any potential other plans being made? K'tina suggested the very same Transpo station park that Laks thought would be perfect and had his own Cyber spy recommend, confirming for them that it was the natural spot for it. And so, the entire, quickly fabricated, team sprang into action.

By the time that North and the Premier had secretly slipped out of the office and then gotten onto the Aboveground's

Gerspellion's Girder line, they were all but circled by Cyber probes, disguised as natural objects. John Laks would have Cyber-police in place at the site in various capacities as maintenance crew for the closest surrounding manufactories. The area had been ringed by Human members of the City's own security division, at a greater distance. Only one Media-Cam was anywhere near when the Premier and his nephew exited, and Cas'sio had it officially commandeered to cover him and his nephew.

The meeting site was an elevated parklet attached to the ultimate local station on the line, surrounded by small factories. It sported several curved Plastron benches and side tables, a selection of plantings, a water fountain amid colorful foliage, and a good sized Kiosk. The latter was operated by an unusual Cyber-keeper, in that it apparently possessed an especially strong sense of ego-identity for so medium grade of a mechano. Both a floating script and speakers identified the Kiosk as "Capstan 7404's Cybo-Human Café: Tasty Specialties From Six Hundred Worlds."

Evidently, John Laks had decided *not* to inform the Kiosk Keeper of the action. It acted completely natural when Cassio and North disembarked their Transpo car, looked about the station, checked addresses against a Holo, and then appeared to meander over to the little park and up into the Kiosk area.

"Mind Benders, eh?" Capstan greeted them (proving their disguises were good) as they sat at a table they deemed farthest from the Kiosk and probable pouch-drop. "I had some dealings with a Grade Nine Bella=Arth. Em Bee a century ago. She never knew what hit her."

"What did 'hit' her?" North took up the dare,

"Capstan Seven Four Zero Four at your service – your extreme majesties!" The Kiosk Keeper bowed low and flourished several ornamental strings of lights and whistles that it wore about its neck in homage. "I trust you 'fellas' knew enough to inject a basic anti-radiation med before visiting our lovely community."

"Naturally," North answered.

"That's a relief. Wouldn't want any Em Bees sickenin' on my watch." Capstan formed itself into a sitting position at their level and dropped its voice, "so? Who's the target? I've always suspected Andromeda Galaxy Ultra-Thins," nodding at a factory behind them, "of harboring blow-out crazies Cybers working at dirt-cheap rates. But Perseus PowerShot and Cams to my left? Well they're equally flaky, if you know what I mean. All-Cyber ownership. And the rollover in staff is unbelievable. What are they doing, I ask you, using the workers as spare parts in the Power-Esses, or what? Untouchable. You're the first Em Bees in decades to come sniffing around. I figured they gotta' know someone high up on the Council, right?"

"We're not permitted to say which business we're looking into," Northie said, with the primness of his alleged profession.

"Of course not, of course not!" Capstan stood erect and began blow-cleaning the table with its fingertips. "Anyway, my lips are sealed," it said, and as they watched it's "lips" did indeed seal up. And then unzipped, so it could ask: "So what'll it be? A little perk-up? Got some stimulating drinks, all legal ingredients, and with not a hint of a crash. Also on the menu are several specials to this café: two prokaryote smoothies that'll inject a bunch of protein into your cerebral cortex in mere seconds."

They settled on less powerful beverages and Capstan devised and delivered them within a minute, then resumed its interest in a Holo-Vid Thwwing race, whether in real-time or pre-recorded, Cas'sio couldn't determine. He had to admit that the Kiosk Keeper's character had tickled him, to the same extent that it had irritated his nephew, possibly *because* it had irritated Northie.

A Transpo car appeared along the Aboveground from the Outer Girder, exactly on time.

It stopped and one passenger exited, John Laks' Ambassadorial Delphinid agent, clad similar to how Xell-I had looked in the station Vids they'd seen. She'd been made up to look older and even had some touches of color around her gills so that the excuse of being ill she'd used earlier would look believable. Without hesitating, she strode up the walkway to the park, and into the Kiosk area. She seated herself close to the Kiosk, twenty meters from the pretend Cyber-psychs, and began fussing with her wrist connector. Capstan ignored her for a while.

The Transpo car revolved, on its way back to the City Center, but as it did so, Cas'sio was able to see bits and pieces of a dozen fully armored City Police inside. The plan was that the car would go only as far as the next station, prepped to return instantly, upon need.

By now they were used to Capstan's "personalized" service

as Kiosk Keeper, and the Cyber cavorted about the new Delph. customer about as might be expected.

They waited and waited, looking at Holo-Grids they held out in one hand like real Cyber-psychs would do, checking out environmental factors.

"Assume we can be heard from almost any distance," the Premier sub-vocalized on an agreed upon channel via wrist connectors. "Your cousin was unable to verify how much his Close-Daughter may have Cyberized herself by now. The last time they met, she'd gone beyond the 19 percent that had been required by the accident. Let us assume for this operation that she is about fifty percent Cyberized." Then, he added, "Ser Laks! I trust your staff is surrounding us at this moment."

A simple beep confirmed the fact.

Suddenly, without them noticing how she had arrived, there was a Human appearing woman at the Kiosk. She'd probably been "casing" the area for a while before decided to show up. But the speed at which she had shown up, was troubling. It was unquestionably K'Tina.

The Delph. pretended not to see her, eyes glued to one of the Holo-Gossip-Vids located on a Kiosk support column.

Capstan knew K'Tina, however, and referred to her as "Your Ladyship – the usual?"

She pretended to be interested in something different, which was when she supposedly first noticed what the Delph. was drinking and casually asked her about it. All done in an amazingly natural way, Cas'sio had to admit. After a minute or two of pondering, she made a complex order, and then glided into a seat at the same small table as the Delph., making small talk about a couple in the Society News. The Safety Pouch lay out in the open on the table. The Delph. returned to watching the Vid, and then pretended to be annoyed with something coming in on her wrist connector.

"Now she will act up," Cas'sio and North heard John Laks comm. them.

The Delph. stood and brought the drink over to Capstan, and began berating him about one of the ingredients she'd discovered in it, acting at getting angrier by the minute. This was the earlier agreed-upon distraction.

Meanwhile the pouch miraculously moved to the side of the

table facing K'tina.

"Now our agent leaves," Laks commented.

Capstan offered the Delph. her credits back. But she refused, threw the drink at the Kiosk wall and stalked off, down the circular ramp and under the station's elevated line.

The pouch was now no longer visible.

"Now we move in," Laks announced.

K'tina was slowly standing up, pretending to finish her own drink, and at the same time smoothing out her leather-like skirt.

Then everything changed in an instant. K'tina was surrounded before Cas'sio or North could do or say anything. Four Cyber police had her by the arms and legs.

She seemed momentarily astounded by their appearance and even tried to loosen their grip on her before appearing to give up, smiling ruefully.

The two men stood. Only then did K'tina notice them. She apparently recognized North, but not Cas'sio, possibly because he was the larger of the two men and the one in front.

The Cyber police were dictating her rights of arrest to her, but she ignored them.

"Uncle!" she shouted, looking right them. "Stay there. Don't come any closer!"

The two men stopped and Cas'sio watched Capstan slowly backing off in the other direction behind the Kiosk.

"Uncle North! Believe me when I say that Holt had nothing to do with any of this! He never knew a thing about what we were planning!"

North responded as Cas'sio would have: "Holt? What are you talking about?"

"When we met here," she tried to explain. "Please stay where you are, Uncle. Capstan here will confirm it. Holt and I met here three times. But Holt had *nothing* to do with this. He never knew *anything* about it."

"Then... why *did* he meet you here?" North asked.

"The only thing I regret is involving him in any way. Truly."

"Why *did* you and Holt meet here, if it wasn't to pass material?" North asked.

"Because he thought we were lovers!" she yelled. "Stupid! Isn't it? He never suspected that our meetings here, and he himself, was the perfect cover for the drops. How could he believe we were lovers? We couldn't even be in the same place without sickening each other? Isn't it so very naive? Even so, if he hadn't gone off chasing Beryllium 18 to be a great hero for the City, none of this would have ever happened."

"What wouldn't have happened?"

"Me using an untested Courier … any of you finding out!" she said and laughed a little.

Although K'tina was being carefully, almost delicately, trussed by her captors, she laughed again and then threw her head back suddenly and forward equally suddenly.

"Cover!" the two men heard Laks shout a comm. and before they could react, two Cyber police had left her, gripped the men, flattened them to the ground and covered them, just as there was a deafening explosion.

When they were allowed to look up again, the mess was terrible. There was nothing but Cyberized mechanism parts and dollops of K'tina's Human flesh left everywhere, spread out as though in an ellipse upon every surface. The two Cyber police who had remained holding her were also dismantled, their pieces flung all about the area in a somewhat less perfect pattern. The two Cybers who had covered the Human men were charred horribly upon their exposed sides, but otherwise intact and functional. They were able to get up and to help up the men, who then got a wider view of the destruction.

The Kiosk had been destroyed, with only about a half meter of any wall still standing. The tables and seating, and even the fountain were in all pieces. But Capstan had somehow figured out what was coming and had managed to get completely covered. The Kiosk Keeper stood up and rather shakily walked over to where Cas'sio and North and several Human police now surveyed the scene. Several of Capstan's neckwear decorations were in tatters, and its eyes seemed to be undergoing temporary astigmus.

Several Humans in uniform were now present.

"We're very sorry for your personal loss, Premier, and Lord Kell," Cas'sio's second said, sounding as though he was shocked and meant it. "But the event was completely Holo-Vised for any legal proceedings."

Although very shaken, Cas'sio asked if anyone else had been harmed besides K'tina and the Cyber police, and he was relieved to discover no one else had been. He waved over Capstan and said in a loud voice: "This Cyber behaved helpfully and intelligently and it deserves a Quinx commendation. As do all the security force involved." To Capstan, Cas'sio said, "you shall be more than compensated to rebuild your Cafe and the entire park and fountain here will be even better than it was, I promise you."

"Gratitude, your astonishing Lordship," Capstan replied. "A really intelligent Cyber would get out of town and tour the Seven Hundred Wonders of the Galaxy."

"Then your compensation will cover that expense."

Cas'sio made certain his second got all the data needed to compensate the Cyber.

Media began arriving at high speeds and Cas'sio's private fly-by was suddenly there too.

As he and North settled into it, his nephew's face looked out at the scene and tears began streaming down his face. Cas'sio moved over and embrace him with one arm.

"I'm so very sorry I had you come today, Northie. You understand that I never expected she would ... do anything other than accompany us."

"I know! I know! Premier. I had to come face to face with it sometime," he managed to say, although his cheeks were soaking wet now. "But I never expected anything so awful ..." He pointed at the center of the explosion, "would be so beautiful."

"Beautiful?" Cassio followed his nephew's pointing hand. All of K'tina's Cyber-parts were glowing, radiating now, in bright rainbow hues. "Oh. It must be some chemical effect, a result of her holding the magnesium bi-chlorate!"

"And then of course, if I'm to be any good at all being a Premier someday," North Ib'r-Kell said, as though reciting some long ago learned lesson, "I know that I do have to experience it all myself. Violence. Wanton destruction. Manipulation and betrayal."

Only a few Media remained with their fly-by as it sped back toward the Premier's office. The rest had a crime scene to cover of a scale and type that they'd not experienced for a very long while. And, on top of that, a fabulously unique witness! The personable, sociable, newly rich, Capstan 7404 would end up all over the Inter. Gal. News and Personal Vids for weeks to come – as much of a celebrity as any Thwwing team Captain.

"Here is good news, Premier," Cas'sio's second said as he and North entered his office. "The Great Father's fast has sent a locator-signal. It's very distant, but it has already set off those official Hesperian fasts in the area to rush off to his rescue."

"Give me all the details," Cas'sio said with the first sense of satisfaction he'd felt all day. Then, to his nephew, who had turned and was leaving, "Northie! Stay! Come sit! After all we went through, I want us both checked over physiologically. And more importantly, I want you to experience the good things about being Premier, too."

He was gratified when Northie sat and listened to the various remarks and then remarked, "looks like we'll have a wonderful four hundredth anniversary, after all."

Flexibility, the ability to absorb some of what happened, but not too much, and then to move on to the next thing. That was another important asset for any Premier. And like most Ib'rs and Sanqq's, the younger Northie possessed it.

Chapter Nine

Double-day, the blue Hunter already risen, the orange Eagle just beginning to rise, and to announce its presence, injecting a fistful of pale yellow arrows into the blue-green sky; Rings at thirty degrees above the horizon, slowly dropping day by day, and looking rather hard and vaguely metallic this morning:

Ay'r Eise'nstein-Kell checked Baby Eis in his exterior womb and intruded his hands into through the outer-inner soft-gloves so he could hold him and caress him a bit, and he noticed that the little fellow was fine and wide-awake. Listening to the built-in, womb-nurse Cyber monitor, he was told that Eis had slept well, had awakened once and been fed. Eis was now attempting to follow the virtual pre-natal Ed. & Dev. Program with his eyes and hands, reaching out for the simulated brightly colored balls and bats. Then, smelling food being prepared, Ay'r said goodbye and strode over to the breakfast area of the scientific encampment.

"Ah, young Bissel," Masaaki-Donnerwort was wearing her ancient Metro-Terran version of a sunhat and sipping something that smelled stimulating. "The infant looks well and growing."

"He is well and growing, gratitude, Mer Donnerwort. And double gratitude, as I know you've watched over him while I over-slept, recuperating."

"You are very young to give birth. And it was my pleasure, Bissel. In truth, it has been a very long time since I even had great-grandchildren to fuss over. And Eis is not only a lovely lad, but he's bright as the two Uskian suns, already. With your permission, I will fashion a few tweaks of the usual Relfian programming. His senses are already sharpening and his spatial senses and motor skills are improving at a very marked speed."

"Well, you know, the Relfian ex-womb programs are said to be the best."

"They are indeed, Bissel. Even the most advanced Matriarchal post-natal programs that I was stuck with for my own kindred four hundred years ago spent far too much time, in my opinion, cuddling and cooing infants and making them feel safe and warm. You men have the right idea. Get the little ones accustomed to life's changes and challenges as quickly as possible. Vir knows that you yourself have had to do that kind of adapting at a rapid rate. Or am I wrong?"

"No. You are very right, Mer. These past four or more months, Sol Rad. ... well, I wouldn't have wished them on a more pampered Neo than myself. Yet ... they've been wondrously good too. Far beyond my imaginings. For one, I yearned for years to be off-world, without really knowing Usk at all. And now! Well, now I've come to know so much of Usk's people and its places, that I know it will always be part of me, wherever I may go. I know that Usk will always be home to me."

The canteen pamp and Salt-Eluder now appeared, with a large breakfast for Ay'r.

Behind them after a few minutes, was Dr. Salzprung.

"Any news about our friend?" Ay'r felt he had to ask.

"I had a face-to-face Holo-Comm. with the ship's Captain, who once again told me what his officers had told me: that he had no idea where our esteemed colleague is. He repeats what they told me before, a day, Sol Rad., after you left the Arcturus Scatling, Bissel. A large fly-by with the House of Syzygy colors on it dropped over the ship which was only a few hours from docking in the Great Western Port. The cruiser was searched, everyone onboard was interrogated, your disappearance was noted by many, and as your employer, Silberklang was taken away for further questioning. Lepta wasn't certain, but he thought, the fly-by was headed for the Western Port."

"And nothing of our pamp friend, who was with him?" Ay'r asked.

"I'm afraid that your Captain waffled. One time he said he thought the pamp was taken along with our friend. Another time he said that he was certain the pamp received his sailor's voyage pay, which could have only happened upon the pamp docking and embarking with the other crew.

"The professor would never have involved Sand-Drifter," Ay'r insisted to Salt-Eluder who had joined them to hear the news.

"I'm certain he is free."

"But others on board might easily have associated the two of them," the pamp said. "Even worse, someone might have remembered that Sand-Drifter came onboard with Esprio and this pamp, wishing only to serve *you*."

"Lord Syzygy is no monster. Neither of them will come to harm from him. Of that I'm certain. But there are other Hesperians ..." Ay'r looked at his pamp friend. "I cannot ask you to come with me, Salty, but I believe it's up to me to go find them in the port city."

"This pamp goes with you, Ser," Salt-Eluder said, as Ay'r knew he would.

"You two can't go alone," Salzprung remarked.

"I believe that is the best solution, doctor. After all, I am Bissel, Silberklang's apprentice. I'm awaiting him. He has not shown up. It's only natural that I go to seek him out. And along with me, goes my pamp."

"The port city is the last place you should go to, Bissel," Masaaki-Donnerwort pointed out.

"I've known that this was my path for the past two days. Until this morning I was afraid to say it, but I fear I must leave my little Eis behind with you, and while I know you will care for him, Mer and Doctor, as if he were your own, yet I cannot bear to tear myself away from him."

"This is only natural in a mother," she admitted. "We would expect nothing else."

"But you are walking directly into the trap set up for you, Bissel," Salzprung concluded.

"Yes I know. Unless we can somehow *not* make it a trap for this ... particular ... Bissel," Ay'r tried explaining. "This fictional creation of our devising. When the scientist did not arrive at their agreed on spot, he would naturally seek out Silberklang."

"Yes. I understand"

What you have going for you in this venture to the port city, Bissel, is an early *pre-partum*," Masaaki-Donnerwalt noted. "They'll be looking for a youth your age, but scanning for one still carrying. So at least you can get inside wherever he may be held."

"The bigger problem is your wrist-connector," Salzprung mused. "But, perhaps I can fiddle with it. In my younger days at the Collegium Wissenschaft, some colleagues and I mentally broke down a rather sophisticated intelligent Cyber. Somewhere I have notes on the exact way we did it."

"Fool! And leave him with an insane wrist-connector?"

"No, no, old woman! Listen! The problem is that the wrist-connector, by its very nature, identifies Bissel correctly, wherever he goes. That is one of its basic functions. But I believe I can persuade it to lie to others about his identity in order to protect him."

The scientist was so convinced that he vanished back into the vehicle and they could hear him mumbling to himself as he rummaged around inside it.

Ay'r returned to the ex-womb and Mer Masaaki-Donnerwort joined him there. They looked at the baby sleeping for a while.

"The Bella=Arth. who visited, when Little Eis was just parted from me?" Ay'r asked. "She left as a gift a most valuable ring."

"I'm not surprised."

"Do you know who she was? What she was doing here?"

"In fact, I tel'ped research when she arrived," the old scientist said. "She represents the single largest group of her species in the galaxy. Her home is on Algol IX. She can well afford whatever gift she presented."

"But ... what brought her here?"

"She told you. The rings coming together like that, with the diadem in between. The unmistakable arrow of illumination it made down directly toward the birthing station. We've Holo-ed it all from where we first saw it ourselves that night, Bissel. I'll be glad to show you. It was quite an extraordinary effect! If the Arth.s were traveling *anywhere* in this North Western sector, they couldn't have missed it. You heard the pamp villagers who came, talking of it."

"A remarkable coincidence," he said.

She almost laughed: "Indeed."

"But what I meant more than that, really, is what is a great Arth. queen is doing here, on Usk in the first place?"

"There are a few luxurious resorts, I believe, not far from here. And Usk is perfectly suited to that species. I don't know how much your Ed. & Dev. stressed it, but this little planet was briefly a battleground in the Bella=Arth. war against the First Matriarchy. There is at least one war-time memorial hereabouts. Perhaps the queen came to pay homage to her peoples' fallen."

"It really is quite a surprising place, our little Usk, isn't it?"

Ay'r enthused. "And to think both Baby Eis and myself were both born here."

"And if Silberklang ever proves his theory, Usk will take on an even grander, pre-Three Species historical import," the old scientist mused.

"You mean because it was so beloved of the previous intelligent race that the professor believes populated this galaxy long before us."

"More than merely beloved, Bissel. Silberklang is coming to believe that the old Usk was the site of that early Paradise that all three of the main intelligent species, and some of the other sentient beings too, *all* believe in, in their myths, legends, and religions."

"You mean he thinks it was a bio-laboratory?"

"Something like that."

"Then why aren't all of you looking for pre-catastrophe ruins?" he asked, bewildered.

"We are, Bissel. We are. But if they exist we are not sure that they exist on the physical plane any longer." And when he looked puzzled, she added, "you have seen the fossils of once living marine creatures lying below sediments in the great desert of what is now the salt ocean?"

"Yes, Silberklang showed them to me, and I've also seen those other "fossils" consisting of the ripples of sand, hardened to rock, atop the cliffs over the ocean, where once water fell in great cascades."

"Even sketchier than those ripples are what we still seek, Bissel. Gravitational and magnetic fossil signatures that, combined, will pinpoint the center of it all."

Salzprung emerged from the vehicle with a tiny set of flashing lights, and a tiny Cyber voice-box.

"All our notes were intact," he crowed.

"Beware old man, if you harm this child," she threatened.

"Not at all. Not at all. Bissel, let us tap into your wrist-connector now?"

Ay'r tel'ped it awake.

"Now follow what I say … Wrist-connector, for safety in a great peril we are about to face, we need to construct an 'alias'. This alias is not ourself, except in those cases when it is necessary to protect ourself."

Ay'r repeated the words.

"Is this comprehensible, wrist-connector?" the old man asked and so did Ay'r.

"Yes," was the response.

"There will be physiological triggers to when this alias is to be *instantly and fully engaged* by you. Those parameters will be fed to you shortly."

Again Ay'r repeated the scientist's words.

"Is this understood, wrist-connector?" Salzprung asked again.

"Yes. Once specific physiological factors have reached a particular level, the true identity vanishes and the alias takes its place."

"Exactly. Perfect. And it takes over until the wrist-connector is told to 'Put away the alias for now'. That is the command," Salzprung said clearly.

The wrist-connector repeated all that.

"Over the next ten minutes or so, Sol Rad., myself and your physical-nexus will explain who this alias is, and what he has experienced, for that is just as important. It will be pretty much based upon what your host here himself experienced from the time he went on board the *Arcturus Scatling.* Much of that you've recorded in some fashion, true?"

"You mean the young cruise sailor-scientist personality that my host impersonated?"

"Exactly. That personality's name is Bissel Ter-Morgen, apprentice to Professor Silberklang."

"It is available for review, yes, in full. This will be fun," the wrist-connector said. "It will be somewhat like building a character inside a PVN or from a Holo-Doc."

All three of them smiled. "Exactly," Ay'r said. "But wrist-connector. Although it will be great fun, there can be no mistakes or slip-ups with this alias. It is absolutely required for my own *protection.*"

"It will not fail. This is a very interesting modification. And from a quick check with the other two wrist-connectors in the locality, as well as in the historical files, one that seems to be quite *unprecedented.*"

Masaaki-Donnerwort covered the connector area with a piece of plastro and whispered, to the others: "You realize of course that this constitutes illegal Cybernetic tampering. As well as … well, what I can only think of as a kind of moral corruption also."

"It's temporary!" Ay'r said.

"It's a necessity," Salzprung insisted.

"It's breathtakingly illicit and immoral."

"In fifteen and a half years, Sol Rad., of being along for my ride," Ay'r went on, "this poor wrist connector has already probably lived twice as long as that. I wonder if it is still *capable* of being corrupted."

Once they uncovered it the wrist connector, they heard. "This unit is ready for the alias. Feed in the data!"

"Salty! Start packing!" Ay'r called out, as Salzprung inserted the tiny connector cable from the already prepared Cyber storage mechanism.

His wrist connector told Ay'r that they still had about an hour of walking until they would see the Great Western Port. Because it was located inside some kind of large, natural bowl, they would be almost upon it when they first saw it. And from this particular beaten dirt road, they would be able to drop down almost into the middle of the town fairly quickly.

On the most recent stop for food and drink, Ay'r had his wrist connector project a rough view of the town onto the road for them to see, and then requested to be shown the most direct pathway to the main administration building where he guessed the Professor was being held.

"We should also get the most *indirect* one going *out* again," Salt-Eluder suggested, and Ay'r had to laugh. "I see you've got great faith in this bold plan of mine."

"Hope for the best. Plan for the worst," the pamp said, and giggled.

And so they did, getting that second route carefully mapped out for instant recitation too, should they need a careful escape.

Ay'r palpably missed Baby Eis every time they stopped. He almost wore out poor Salt-Eluder wondering what the Baby was doing now, even when the pamp at last remarked that its choices of action were fairly limited. But once striding along in what after all was a downward path, free and clear, he felt differently.

He knew they were doing the right thing. That helped. If he was anxious at all, it was that they might not spring the Professor, or that somehow Salt-Eluder would get injured or trapped. About himself, and especially now with the complicit wrist-connector believing it was all some great charade, he felt near invulnerable.

They had brought a lightweight, flexible, wheeled vehicle, which the pamp wore in his backpack, as it was made of super-light material and folded down to the size of a Human hand in size. That would be for the Professor, although Mer Donnerwort had insisted they bring it in case Ay'r needed it. He didn't. He felt wonderfully strong, almost springing along, better than he'd felt in months. He had to admit that's probably because he was free of the infant's weight and its chemical interaction/interference with his own bodily functions.

"This pamp has still not heard the story of your captivity, friend?"

"Some captivity! I could have kicked down the whole village in a few minutes, Sol Rad., Salty! Those pamps had better learn to do better building with sturdier materials," he said, then immediately regretted it, realizing that they had no sturdier materials. And that wasn't their only problem. "Maybe the Professor will be able to hire on a few of them at real wages, so they don't have to subsist entirely on what they hunt and gather," Ay'r added. "You looked like fat Esprio compared to any one of them."

"Your suggestion would be most helpful to that poor little village."

"Once we get him," Ay'r said. "And those pamp children. Not a bit of education that I could see! They were intelligent enough, but ignorant as a stone. Isn't there a nearby resort where we could set up some Ed. & Dev for them?"

"The Birthing Station is the nearest facility. It is an hour and a half distant."

"Maybe they can move a little closer to it? They're not exactly residing in the upper class area, as it is. I'll go talk to that Midwife Cyber. He said they're hardly used. Those two little Cybers. Waffle and Taffy, or whatever their names are, would be a good size for the children. Don't you think?"

"Even if they agree, who will fund the many learning tools the pamps will need."

"I will! I'm rich, don't you know?"

"*You* may be," the pamp agreed, "but Bissel Ter-Morgen *is not.*"

"We'll figure something out. They're only thirty-five or so of them all together. Even the elders should receive retraining of some kind. They can't go out and leave the young alone all day."

"Why do you care about them, Ser?"

"I don't. They're awful pamps. I know, I know, they've all had problems. It's the young I'm concerned about. They made no choices and yet they're forced to live by others' choices. No! They've got to have better lives. Period!"

"If you spoke like this in a big city, humans and Arth.s alike would censor you," Salt-Eluder pointed out.

"Well, maybe that's going to have to change too," Ay'r said, darkly. "This entire pamps as servants system bound by essences to their masters stinks to me about as high as those rings!"

Salt-Eluder stopped walking, his little eyes agog. "That's revolutionary talk, Ser. Please desist. It makes me very nervous."

"You're not exactly hanging around me for your health, Salty. You had better get used to a little revolutionary talk – and action too."

They were walking in an area where bluffs rose on either side of the road. Suddenly, the road turned left, and one side of the bluff became flat. Below them, laid out like one of the wrist-connector's 3-D projections in life-size, was the Western Port City. Beyond its wharves and docks glittered the nearly endless, white sands of the Great Salt Ocean. It was a far greater geographical feature than either had expected, quite spectacularly large.

"Are you going to tell this pamp to hold onto his hairpiece," Salt-Eluder asked.

"It is pretty breath-taking!" Ay'r agreed. "But you still only have a cap."

They'd been alone on the road for so long, they were astonished that almost immediately when they began to descend, they came upon pedestrians, some with laden wagons. All pamps of course, and surprised pamps, most of them, due to Ay'r's good natured greetings. Silent, as they reached the crest of the road and onto the clifftops, the travelers almost seemed relieved to be getting away from the port.

"These are not a happy people," Salt-Eluder said for the both of them.

As the projected Holo-Map had predicted, their road was

steep, but soon enough flat and it turned into a direct way into the oldest part of the city. On their left side were the great docks, each one a little city to itself, with its storehouses and offices and low roofed dormitories, and its great packing Cybers, most of them at rest at midday.

Ay'r and the scientists had planned his arrival for the hottest time of the day, when most of the city was taking a midday nap, or at least not out on the streets, but indoors, in cooler temperatures. The fewer people around the better their chance of being undetected, or at least unnoticed.

A human guard in Uskian-Kell colors was all but asleep at the double doorway to the Great Western Port Administration Building.

With no one else about on the street or within the single open door, Ay'r slowed down and first Salt-Eluder, then he, crept past the guard as though moving on and then quickly slipped into the open door.

Almost immediately, they were in a large, dusty courtyard. Doorways opened from several sides and Ay'r pointed Salt-Eluder forward, looking for one that looked promising. The pamp stopped at the far end and motioned him. Ay'r moved forward purposefully and was soon at a cool interior hallway with a narrow moving stairway.

"Welcome to the Great Western Port Administration Building," A cam-Cyber surprised them. "How may I direct you?"

Ay'r considered briefly then said as forthrightly as he could, "I'm seeking my master, Professor Silberklang."

"Next floor up," which they'd almost reached anyway, "four doors to your left."

Would it be that simple? He'd walk in and there the professor would be?

The doors had legends on them, but he couldn't figure out any of them. And their self-descriptions weren't very useful. One claimed it was for "local or imported ore assaying disputes". Another office was for "loading weight equity difficulties". A third "rendered assistance for unfulfilled crew quorums", and a fourth was "for hired crew members abandoned before embarkation".

"It did say the fourth door, right, Salty?"

"The fourth, yes."

He knocked, and the door slid open to a modern office within which two humans clad in the Gold and White of the Palace were watching some kind of Holo-News or Doc or what sounded like a staged fight. An illegal one, given how quickly it was switched off.

The officers drew themselves up taller from their earlier, relaxed, slouching. One was behind what Ay'r could now see was some kind of console desk.

"I wonder if you can help me. I've been told that I could find my master, Professor Silberklang here."

"Silberklang, Silberklang ..." the one behind the desk called up a Holo-Listing and began scanning it.

The other human leaned in and whispered something into his ear.

"Oh!" the first one declared. "Professor Silberklang! Yes, of course."

He was so clumsy that Ay'r naturally noticed how he touched inside the Holo-List what must have been an alarm or alert icon.

"Yes! I believe he's quartered here," the officer continued. "But who's asking for him?"

"Bissel, his apprentice," Ay'r did everything but hold his hat in his hands as he stood there humbly. His knew that his heart was thumping and his pulse racing. He only hoped the wrist-connector was aware of it too.

"Bissel?" the guard asked, and gestured him to place his wrist over the desk.

"Bissel Ter-Morgen. Human Neo. Twenty-seven years of age. A native of Usk. North Eastern Province. Unbonded. Betrothed to a person unknown. Current Avocation: Geologic and Ecological Sciences. Apprenticed to Professor Silberklang since ..." the console desk read out the data, as Ay'r's wrist-connector happily lied to it.

Both of the officers looked crestfallen.

"What do you want with the Professor?" the second one asked.

"Why to come with me and finish our work! What else would I want? I and this pamp have waited now four days, Sol Rad. And his colleagues are waiting too. It is a City-funded expedition, but d'lars do not flow like water. The program cannot continue without Silberklang. The professor must return to work. Right now! If you wish, this wrist-connector will produce a contract the Professor has signed on the Fomalhaut Girder office of his Funder upon

Hesperia itself. Any further delay will require that whomever is responsible for him not showing up, pay the compensatory daily fine in the amount of ..."

He could have gone on for four more minutes, but at last, they stopped him and hushed him silent. Evidently Ay'r's appearance as Bissel here was the expected, if not the hoped for, result of the Professor being restrained.

The officer must have already signaled the Professor. He stood up and slid a doorway and almost immediately the Professor came through it, with one of his bags slung across his back.

"Ah Bissel!" he threw himself into Ay'r's arms, and was almost trembling with relief. "I wondered when the others would lose patience! I'm so glad it is you and not that demon Donnerwort they sent here. She's a virago from some Cyberhell! No wonder the Matriarchy was deposed. But I can explain it all. It isn't my fault in the least," he said, turning to the others. "Tell him. Tell him how you seized me off the cruiser and interrogated me about some fool, spoiled, missing Hesperian High-society-Neo until I thought I would go mad. As though I would even *know* such a personage! As soon would I know the Princeps Kell as his little play-thing. It makes one fume to even think about it."

The others were looking slightly contrite.

Ay'r had counted on the Professor's usual personality to work perfectly in this meeting and he couldn't have been happier.

"Well, I trust this is all straightened out now, Professor," Ay'r said. "We are ready to leave immediately."

"Immediately? But first we need all the instruments that were onboard the cruiser? They seized them all! The idiots."

Ay'r turned to the officers. One of whom had it showing on the Holo-Screen that there were two mag levs full of quote "technical equipment."

"Unfortunately, we don't have the authority to release those. Someone higher is needed and ..."

And at that moment the door slid open and someone higher in authority was present. Behind him were two of his own guards, given their colors, and Ay'r's heart skipped a beat as he turned and faced Deon Syzygy, not four feet away, dressed in what probably passed for desert-chic on Hesperia and what actually looked extremely stunning on him. His face was quite tanned and his golden eyes actually shone with anger and some other indefinable emotion.

Ay'r immediately dropped his own, newly tinted, eyes to the ground.

"This ... Neo and his little friend strolled right into the building and up to this office. For all I know they could have walked off again with our 'guest' without anyone even noticing. Or, who knows, perhaps they might have rifled the ore assaying office of all its precious stones. And with no one to stop them."

"Lord Syzygy, the Neo identifies as he whom the old man was expecting."

"Does he indeed?"

Deon pulled Ay'r over to the greater light from the outdoors. "Well! Who knows? He's the right height as mine is. But he's too built up around the shoulders and upper body. The rest of him is far too slender. The face is similar enough. Hair and eyes are wrong, of course. And after seeing eleven hundred Uskian Neo faces, they are all looking alike by now. Was he scanned internally?"

"On the moving stairway up." The Officer spun the Holo-Screen around to show the diagnostic: "He's *not* with young."

"He might have given birth by now," Deon said. "How do we tell?"

"Hormonal imbalances would leave electro-chemical signatures, Lord. But only if he pre-parted within forty-eight hours."

"Do the tests anyway," Deon said, keeping Ay'r aside from Silberklang and Salt-Eluder.

As the others fussed around Ay'r, finding and then instructing a med-Cyber which actually did the work, Deon sat himself on the console's edge close by and looked gloomy, while he read Ay'r's fake i.d. "Betrothed. To a person unknown," he read off the screen. "When I was a Neo we were only too delighted to acknowledge who we were betrothed to."

Ay'r was afraid to open his mouth.

"You do look a great deal like my love. Only, of course, he was far, far lovelier that you are, boy. A truly golden youth. A perfect godling. And I? ... I was such a fool! ... Isn't that med test done yet?"

"It's inconclusive." The Cyber reported. "But then, what is to be expected of a Neo whose hormones are still in flux? There are no definite markers of a *pre-partum* within the allotted forty-eight hour period."

"No, I didn't think so," Deon said, with a sigh. "Too bad! Any year soon, Sol Rad., you'll make some local fellow a happy Vir with your smooth complexion and your slender little hips! Soon enough he'll be planting young inside you, if you're not careful," he teased, ruefully.

Silberklang was now loudly demanding the release of his equipment. The officers were repeating their limitations of authority.

Deon went over to them, and officially released the stuff. Ay'r sidled over behind the professor and the three began to leave, with the professor still huffing and fuming. Last to leave, Ay'r was almost out the door, when he felt a hand grab his wrist hard.

"There! At that angle, I could have *sworn* it was *him*." Deon looked hard into Ay'r's eyes and Ay'r dropped his eyes, afraid that something he unconsciously did, some reflex or other, would give him away. The truth was, he was intensely excited being around Syzygy again. As intensely as the first time, and he suspected it was mutual somehow, physiologically, between the two of them. He desired Deon incredibly in these moments of closeness. He knew by now that it was probably the man's natural scent, or his pheromones that were exciting. But even so ... if he wasn't let go of in a moment, he was afraid, it would begin to show and ...

Syzygy released his wrist, almost pushing him into the corridor.

"If I never lay eyes on another Uskian Neo, it will be too soon! That planet-mate siren of yours, boy, has ruined me for wanting anyone else and so has utterly ruined my life!"

The door slid shut on him, but Ay'r had seen the real despair in Deon's face and in his body language, and he now had to admit that seeing it had been equally painful to him. He wanted to rush into Deon's arms and declare himself. He knew now that his lover was innocent of any wrongdoing, and most regretful in his role of the Princeps' wrongdoing. He wanted to kiss him and tell him so, to say all was forgiven.

"Friend of the pamps!" Salt-Eluder was whispering at his shoulder. "Great friend of *this pamp*!" he added. "We must go! Right now! Or this pamp and this old scientist are surely doomed."

Ay'r turned to say something but nothing came out. The look on his face must have spoken for him the conflicted emotions he was feeling, since Salt-Eluder quickly averted his face and moved away. But the pamp gently held Ay'r's hand and gently, inexorably, tugged him forward, toward where the professor was stepping onto the stairway down.

Once out onto the still rather empty street, they slowly found their way several streets away to the official docking storage shed where the scientific equipment had been held. Silberklang was aware that something had happened, but wasn't exactly sure what. He was happily chatting away, saying he wasn't sure how they had pulled it off, especially with that Hesperian lord right there in the same room with them, but however they had, it was brilliant, simply brilliant, the two of them. How much he loved and esteemed them both. They would receive his highest recommendations, any time, anywhere they needed it.

It was another hour, Sol Rad., before they had all the equipment in the Professor's possession again. He had to check it all thoroughly, naturally, and then repack it onto its mag levs. Somehow he managed to finagle a good-sized floating and cabined Transpo to hold all of it and them too. At least as far as to a local *serai*, where they would spend the remainder of midday. Then after double sunset, they would leave the port city.

Ay'r wanted to leave right away. Even though he and Salt-Eluder had traveled all day, they were fresh enough to go.

"We must not seem in too much of a hurry to leave, Bissel. Staying here was in the original plan and they have my bills of lading reading so," Silberklang explained.

As they had worked, the pamp had seemed nervous as though noticing something. He'd kept moving oddly into Ay'r's way, requiring a certain deftness to avoid him.

When they were finally all set to take off from the storage shed yard, Ay'r wiped off his perspiring torso and face and then put back on his shirt and vest, and Salt-Eluder, in that very moment said in a very quiet voice, "the great Hesperian lord? He's seeing you now from the tower window directly behind me and above. He's watched all the time that we've worked out here."

"Let him watch!" Ay'r said, suddenly unable to hide the bitterness he felt. "That's as close as he'll ever come again to me!"

"You don't need him, Bissel. Whatever hold he may pretend to have over you," the Professor declared.

Ay'r leapt up onto the Transpo's outer shell. "You two ride

within the cabin. I'll stay here and make certain nothing falls off or gets lost."

Knowing that when they took off, he might want to shout out something incomprehensible and filled with rage. Or even, for a second, let a tear slide down a sweat-stained cheek.

They'd only traveled a few minutes more when they heard the unmistakable high-pitched crack that signaled an orbiting FAST was preparing for take-off. Only one person in this old port rated a personal interstellar vehicle: the Marquis Syzygy!

Silberklang stopped the Transpo and stared and even Ay'r stood to see the silver and coral, needle-like object in the green-yellow sky almost directly above them. Seconds later he could make out the Ion-Quarked charge running blue lightning all over the orbiting craft. Then it was gone – just like that – back to Hesperia.

"Why are we waiting?!" Ay'r struck the side of the Transpo in irritation. "What's the big holdup?"

The others slept during the later midday, but Ay'r could not. He tossed and turned in his bed at the big inn, and finally then got up and crept out of the dorm-like room he shared with the Professor and Salt-Eluder.

Only one house pamp was still out and about in the main rooms of the portside *serai* that Silberklang had led them to, and he was half asleep at the registration console, asking if Ay'r need-ed anything, and understanding no, he did not. Soon, he too was completely asleep, felled by the stillness and the great afternoon heat.

Ay'r wandered over to the large, vacant Holo-Lounge, which doubled as an observation deck. The inn was constructed as a small ground level entrance cube with ever larger layers, rising a dozen stories above the port grounds. The first two tiers were floating storage for Transpos like theirs, the next four floors residential, and the top floors travelers' accommodations. This topmost, largest floor, contained restaurants, various lounges, of-fices, service rooms and the enormous deck enclosed with a tint-ed transparent plastron, which went around three sides of the building, the bulk of it facing the Great Salt Ocean itself, which could be seen from this angle at about half the height of the cliffs surrounding it.

Spectacularly scenic as it all was, it couldn't distract Ay'r from the tumult of conflicting emotions that were keeping him awake. He was still missing Deon, and still blaming himself for not somehow conveying the message that he was still very fond of him. Exactly how he could have done that without giving himself away, without obviating the last four months and several weeks of flight, and especially without endangering the travel companions who had, after all, abetted him, Ay'r couldn't say.

Then too, he was still angry with Deon, and with the Princeps, Mart Kell, and with all of Hesperia which they both represented to him. Far better to serve with this semi-crackpot geologist and his friends in this wasteland, Ay'r thought, than to live in utter luxury on a world so deceitful and treacherous.

But, a third emotion also entered in. Seeing Deon take off, Ay'r understood that he'd not really pulled anything off at all, as Silberklang had so gleefully reported. Why else had the Hesperian Lord stood watching him for almost an hour, Sol Rad., if he weren't certain who he was? Deon knew. He must know. Why else would he have let his guard down and revealed so much to this stranger, to this Bissel Ter-Morgen, if he didn't think he was Ay'r? But having done so, Deon had still gone away. How could he have done that? Unless he'd realized Bissel was Ay'r, an Ay'r who so much wanted nothing further to do with him ever, that he had illegally corrupted his wrist-connector into lying and saying he wasn't Ay'r. Stupid as it now sounded, Ay'r wished Deon had done something to hold him back, to refuse to let him go. Because with Deon gone, also arrived the realization that he was alone now, with no reason to run anymore. No one would look for him any longer. Instead, Ay'r was now just another solitary, unwed, young Neo, living among strangers, and with a not fully born Neo to care for.

It was suddenly too much to have to deal with.

He was about to go back to the desk pamp and see if he could get some kind of instant, short-term sedative, when he heard voices down below. He managed to open one of the windows, densely screened against salt and sand that blew in from the shore, to better hear and even look at the source of the noise.

It was a port loading dock, like a score of similar ones located around the *serai*, and evidently a human and a pamp were arguing. Arguing loudly enough to be heard up here, which was highly unusual. Even more unusual, Ay'r could swear from the pamp's intonation and accent, that he was Ay'r's old Ocean sailing-friend, Sand-Drifter.

The human said something else and the thread of menace was clear in his voice.

Ay'r ran to the lift and was down on the street in seconds. He turned to face the particular port dock warehouse and thought: I've lost them.

He heard a rabble of voices and rushed toward them – into a dockyard, and through a score of pamps dressed in loading gear, standing about, backing up, murmuring, looking at something, but apparently not wanting to look either.

A tall, heavy set, red-bearded, human dock supervisor, dressed in a slovenly dock uniform had Sand-Drifter lifted in the air by one solid arm and was shouting, "you'll get your pay when I'm good and ready to give it to you?"

Drifter yelled back. "After you've drunk and gambled it away?"

"Who in Usk do you think you are to question me!?" The supervisor tossed Sand-Drifter into a plastron linked fence.

Ay'r rushed to his friend and picked him up.

"Sandy!"

"I'm not hurt, Ser. Only my dignity is."

Ay'r helped the pamp up and the other pamps gathered about them.

"You'll never get paid," one asserted.

"He's lost all our pay last weekend," said another.

"We'll none of us see any pay from this job," a third said.

"We'll see about that," Ay'r said, and leaving Sand-Drifter with the others, followed the supervisor across the yard.

Before he reached the office, Ay'r tapped the fat shoulder.

The supervisor whirled. "What's your problem?"

"That little fellow you knocked down. I represent him. I want his pay. And I want it now."

"I told you I'll give it to him when I'm good and ready."

"I want it now."

The Supervisor struck first. Ay'r avoided the punch then remembering his air boarding techniques, he jumped up four feet into the air, and kicked once, clipping the supervisor on the chin with one foot, and then solidified that with a second kick to the side of his head with his second foot. He landed deftly, in a stance ready to fight again.

The older man lay on the floor rolling about, grabbing his face and his chin, groaning in pain.

Ay'r stepped forward. "Get up wharf rat! You've just been felled by a Neo. Get up and start paying."

The supervisor rolled into a sitting position and still holding his jaw, yelled out something incomprehensible.

Faster than Ay'r could have imagined, two more heavy large men came flying out of the office he'd been headed for.

Ay'r leapt toward them, stopped to land then leapt straight up and began his air board 360-degree whirl-about, stopping to kick-box them strategically in the head, chest, and groin. When he was done and had landed again, both men were down and he still had one last kick ready for the supervisor who'd just stood up, and who he shoved into the office wall.

"Sandy! Tie these two up while I get your business settled with this worthless one!" He shoved the supervisor into the office with one of his arms bent behind him. "Let's go. The pay-book, and fast!"

"Sand-Drifter! In here! Give me your thumb print. Here's your pay out chip."

"Ser Bissel. There are a dozen unpaid men besides this pamp."

"Send them in. It's payday today."

But after five more of them were paid, the pay book declared that it was empty, and said it would begin issuing pay vouchers.

"Those vouchers aren't worth dirt," Sand-Drifter said.

"No pay vouchers!" Ay'r shouted to the supervisor and, to the console Cyber, yelled, "find pay credits. We'll wait."

Three minutes later, the Holo-Comm. went on and they were facing the Dock owner onscreen, who looked like no less of a wharf rat than his supervisor.

The newly humbled supervisor explained the situation to his boss as best as he could.

The owner said that if he lost the pay, that was his and the pamp's problem. Not the owner's concern.

Ay'r got in front of the supervisor. "Because I was raised by cultured 'Tutes, Ser Owner, I'm going to ask politely just this one time that you release the funds of all the pamps' back pay, at this dock workplace."

"Who are you?"

"I'm the person who is in control of your dock storage yard." He moved the cam device so the two tied up goons could be seen where they lay, tied up. "Is everything clear now?"

"The Supe owes them. Not me." The owner insisted.

"Clearly the Supe, as you call him, was spending the worker's paychecks with either your negligent knowledge or with your agreed knowledge. So you *are* the one responsible."

The owner brassed it out. "What are you going to do about it?"

"To begin with, you'll get no more work from this crew."

"So what? I'll let the little bastards go. I don't need them. Plenty of dock filth is dying for jobs."

"Second, we're *taking over* your dock yard. It's called a sit-down strike. No wages equals no work equals no new workers – a.k.a. dock filth needing work – will be allowed inside. Which equals no work getting done here at all. Which equals, and this I'm certain you've already figured out yourself, no unloading or loading getting done. Which equals, guess what, no fees paid to guess who? That's right, *you!*"

"You can't do that."

"Watch me!" Ay'r closed the Holo-Link and turned to the pamps in the office. "You heard what I said. This is an official labor dispute. Get stuff to make signs with and come here and I'll tell you what to write on them. Then begin hanging them outside the dockyard where everyone can see them. That will make it official. Oh, and Mr. Supervisor, if I were you I'd take all of my personal effects with me as I left in, say, three minutes time, Sol Rad. Along with your pals. I'd also seriously begin looking for another job, in another port, probably on another planet, halfway across the galaxy where they don't receive the nightly Inter. Gal. News, Sandy, as soon as these characters are off the premises, lock up the place from within and prepare a kiosk right by the entrance for the Media to gather in. We're calling the press immediately. That will further make it official and avert any further trouble."

The owner showed up a half hour later in a fly-by, about the same time as representatives of all the local, Intergalactic, Planet-wide, and Pamp Holo-News stations.

The Media rushed over to the Owner's fly-by and he rushed

back into it, fighting them off and taking off again. He was not followed.

Meanwhile Ay'r had interviewed some of the still nervously shaken and yet excited dock worker pamps and with Sand-Drifter's help he had selected some of them that he seemed most Media-worthy to tell their stories to the planet and to the galaxy. Some had families and hadn't been paid in weeks. Others had been beaten and otherwise abused by the supervisor or the owner. It would be very affecting and would gain sympathy for the entire group.

Silberklang and Salt-Eluder arrived at one point. Ay'r took his other pamp friend aside. "Salty, could you go with the professor to the pamp village on the cliff top? Tell the Ridgers what has happened here. Arrange for the children to go to the Birthing Station to be minded there, as we spoke of before, and bring the adult Ridgers here. We're going to need their intensity and their anger, if we're to succeed. Tell them that this is their chance for revenge as well as for sealing their future. Let them know this is what counts, right now!"

Salt-Eluder pushed his head into Ay'r midsection, in his affection. When he pulled away again, his little face was beaming. "This pamp will be delighted to do as you suggest. This pamp knew from the first moment he encountered you, that you were the one we awaited, Great Ser."

"Never mind all that rigamarole! Just make sure the Ridgers get here and you too get yourself back here, in one piece. I'm going to need you and Sandy here more than ever."

"This worthless pamp will assist, Great Ser!" one of the unpaid dockyard pamps asserted.

"And this worthless pamp too!" said another.

"None of you are worthless! Do you understand? Never say that again in my hearing. You are the equal and betters of most of the Humans here."

"We understand," Sand-Drifter and Salt-Eluder said together. "We are pamps. We are proud to be pamps!"

"That's better!"

Soon all of them had raised their little hands together. Twice as tall as they, Ay'r held all their hands bunched together, for the first time understanding what was needed for this action to work.

"We stand together," he shouted loudly enough for the Media

to turn all their various lens upon the group now. "Pamps and men!"

"We stand together," the dockworkers repeated loudly. "Pamps and men."

"We will take back these docks for those who work them!"

"Take them back for we who work them!" They repeated.

"We will not settle for half or two-thirds or four-fifths. Only all."

"Only all," they shouted.

"We are united. We will not fail."

"We will not fail," they shouted and cheered.

They broke apart and hugged and nuzzled each other.

"Now, friends and workers!" Ay'r said in a low voice. "We must get onto whatever Holo-Comm.s. we can find and contact all of our friends and family and tell them what has happened. This sit-down strike must spread to other dock yards. Do you understand? To the next yard, and to the next yard, and to *all* the dock yards in this port!"

Sand-Drifter's face was aglow, "Surely, this is a great moment for the pamps of Usk. Surely this is our moment."

"Now let's get to work! We have much to do!" Ay'r shouted.

They all cheered again, and spread out to do their tasks.

From the other side of the gateway, Professor Silberklang looked gloomy.

"Why so morose, Professor?"

"Why? You were my best assistant ever, Bissel. My best! And look. I've lost you to ... history!" he spat out the hateful word.

He spat once more then got back into the Transpo cabin and started it back up.

"Salty!" Ay'r shouted to the pamp accompanying the professor. "Play with Baby Eis for me when you have the chance. Remind him of my love."

The pamp nodded that he would and averted his face from too much emotion.

Ay'r smiled, then turned to the others. "Who's first to Holo-Comm. their family?"

An hour later, Sol Rad., a fly-by arrived outside the dock yard with the merchant Esprio in it. He was ushered into the dock yard past the ever increasing Media surrounding the dock yard.

"My old friend," Ay'r hugged the merchant, who was smiling

through his tears. "You have come to support us."

"More than that, oh great Friend of the Pamps. This merchant pamp has come to tell you that the sit-down strike is spreading throughout this port, as you wished it to. And furthermore, it has captured the imagination of all the overworked pamps in the city. And more, it is spreading all over Usk."

"That's wonderful news."

"The Golden Palace port workers, the Slp.G and Fast Port workers, have joined the strike. Pamp and Human."

"Even better!"

"In South Salt Pan City," Esprio continued, "the Salt working pamps have called for a sympathy strike. Several of them recognized yourself, young Ser."

"Then we may succeed."

"Oh we will succeed. Centuries of pamp grievances are now coming to light and the entire galaxy will see. We must sit down, if you do not mind a mere pamp's suggestion, and draft a list of demands."

"We've already done that, Merchant Ser," Sand-Drifter spoke up.

"You have?"

"Better than that," Ay'r said. "It's a demand for a bill of rights for all pamps on planet Usk. It eliminates essence bonding, and frees all pamps to equal rights and equal wages with Humans for equal labor. The fellows here," encompassing the dock workers with a gesture, "helped me write it. But we'd appreciate your input too."

For a moment, Ay'r thought the merchant would faint, he swayed so, and his eyes grew so large. Instead, the merchant seized the document and tried to read it through the tears streaming down his small dark face.

"My friend! Merchant Pamp Esprio! Why these tears?"

"Because, Oh Lord of all Lords on this world, and *True* Adjudicator of Usk – for that is who you are, Ser Ay'r Eise'nstein-Kell, as we pamps have all known for months now – this Merchant pamp has been dreaming and praying for this moment for his entire, very long, existence."

Chapter Ten

Clark stared up at the poem, etched now high into the corridor wall, and its attending inscription:

> Post-Mummification Prophecy Number 1, Number 121 in the Complete Series: A continuation of *The Book of Colored Glory,* given by His Holiness Loren in the Sidereal Time Year 4225; with the Devoted Aid of Sub-Prelate Clark Alli-Lui.

He knew it was wrong to feel pride in the achievement. The poem was entirely the work of the Isolated One. Still, over the passage of nearly six days, Sol Rad., he, one of the newest postulants, had helped to bring it to fruition. Clark now believed that it probably could not have been done as rapidly nor as correctly by anyone else. Their special bond was now apparent to all. After all, it was the firs*t new* Prophecy of the Faith, in nearly a century and a half!

And so far, the only one.

To his relief, and equally to his disappointment, following the "dictation" and Clark's careful, quiet, word-by-word reading back the poem to the Motionless One for confirmation, there had been a half curl-smile, a light double tap, and then silence, immobility, stasis of body and eyes, fingers and lips – ever since, i.e. rest.

Of course, it was all so recent, only a few weeks since it had happened, and since Clark had been moved out here, with a quickly fabricated dorm in the cloister attached to the Sleeping

One's great chamber, "just in case," Abbott Gus Raci-O'Dell had said, almost breathlessly, "He decides to contact you again, you'll be right there; on the spot.

Raci O'Dell had himself achieved such a boost in status and reputation as the result of a new prophecy being delivered during his rulership over the cloister that he'd immediately terminated Clark's waiting period. Wasn't The Mummified One's utilization of Clark sign enough of His Favor and of how valuable he was to them? No surprise, as Clark had known the Devoted One during his All-Too-Short Lifetime on some far off tiny, little, drowned world in some Far Outer Arm? Thanks to Raci O'Dell's insight, Clark had been there when required and so he'd instantly ascended from Postulant to Sub-Prelate in a matter of days, stunning every "Religious" on Narcissus 12's moon, and off.

Naturally, other High Prelates had been consulted in the promotion. Seven of the nine highest had raced in Fasts to be present at the prophecy and wall plaque's dedication ceremony – it might possibly the only new prophecy in any of their lifetimes. All had given Clark, and of course, Raci O'Dell too, great praise – accolades really. It was so unprecedented, so unprepared for an Event.

Yet, now that it had come, the one hundred and twenty-first prophecy was being admired and naturally enough pored over and critiqued.

Several scholars had appeared upon the scene almost as quickly as the Prelates, come to read the poem-prophecy, to actually see it for themselves, before it was published. The Bibliorum had never been such a hive of activity. Never had the nearby port hostels – naturally owned by the Sect – been so filled with visitors, the faithful in droves to see for themselves. Raci O'Dell visualized the Cloister's coffers expanding by the hour. Then even the Media had arrived!

For the scholars, once they were there, in front of the new words, it was gratifying that the poem would be structurally similar to the previous ten dozen. They were unsure how they would have reacted if it were very different. The four lines, the haiku concision, the enigmatic aura imbuing it. The style was not unfamiliar to them, albeit Loren had probably long pondered the metrical variation that had begun to enter into the last poems of the previous series, and now so apparent in this new one. The Church's official, negative view of iambics was already slowly being altered by the previous last ten poemlets, and now that classical meter had definitively made un-tentative entry into the usual flow of dactyls, softening yet in no way a lessening those syllables commanding a blunter strength.

The scholars instantly agreed that "everted Ebony" to describe "The Central Chaos" was nonpareil. They assumed Loren meant the center of the galaxy, and how better to describe that Great Attractor, that thousand light-year-wide black hole, than as "everted"?

Who the "Blessed Contamination" might be was of course immediately controversial. Several commentators, as a matter of course, said it referred to The Cadet, Holt Ib'r-Sanqq', whom anyone watching the Holo-News reports would know was headed exactly there, to Twenty Nine Degrees and Fifty Nine Minutes and Fifty Seven Seconds of Sagittarius.

But other candidates for that role rose and fell by the hour. Why take it all so literally, many asked? True, Holt had been mentioned in earlier verses; true, the entire by now crazily braided Ib'r-Kell-Sanqq' dynastic line was long accepted to have been closely woven throughout the last twenty of the already accepted-prophecies. But why push it? And if it were him, then why was he described in this particular, oxymoronic, description? Whoever claimed the Cadet was Blessed? Aside from the Great Father, who apparently doted on his youngest issue – after all Holt was his only Close-Son – no one had ever seen the lad as anything but an over-sophisticated, spoiled rich-Neo. Equally odd, and despite all of his romantic and social foolishness which had been fodder for the Holo-T'bloids for a decade, why would anyone denigrate the lad so as to call him "contaminating"? Wasn't that rather harsh?

Unless of course there was a context the scholars and Highest Prelates weren't yet able to understand?

Certainly no one among even the most acclaimed of Loren's interpreters could claim to understand the second two lines of the new poem.

What ancient commands? Commanded by whom? How ancient?

They re-read and re-parsed the first hundred and twenty poems again, right there, together, aloud, in the Bibliorum, attempting to figure that out — and getting nowhere fast. Even worse was the phrase "set their bloodless sacrifice." What sacrifice? Who or what "set" it?

Then of course was the clincher. Nowhere else in all the poems, never mind in all the vastness of Loren-related material – from biographical to critical – had there been any mention of "Boxed-Men." Never mind anything ever about freeing them? From what? For what purpose?

It was that very last clause with its oh so clear, and so Lorenesque, triumphant finality – "for one, long-lasting, benefit" – that made them understand that yes, it was by Him, inscrutable as only He could write it, and yes it was a prophecy of boon and benefit. That was why he had struggled out of his decades-long seeming paralysis, to produce one final necessary message – of hope, of abundant goodness.

Certainly the religious elements knew they had Sub-Prelate Clark to thank for that, and Abbott Raci O'Dell for taking on the postulant. And the lovely young postulant 'Stavo,, who had subsequently been assigned to help lessen any of the new Sub-Prelate's stresses and worries, no matter what form they might assume.

Clark stared up at the etched wall and the dedicatory plaque and thought: am I the only one so far to have noticed that the previous prophecy ended with All Colors, and this one with a negation of color–Ebony? As though Alpha and Omega? Beginning and End?

Better was this new sensation of satisfaction: he at last had found a place in this strange, still new, Ib'r Republic – and even a sweet young lover, approved from the Top.

"Gratitude, oh Limited One. Gratitude! And, while I expect it will not ever happen again, please, feel free to use me again, if there is a next time."

"Why have we stopped?" Holt asked the Fast. By the read-out, they were not quite at their destination, and only about four hours had passed in real time.

"Our hosts from DayLight Two have requested us to do so," was all the Fast's mind would say.

Almost simultaneously, there was a full-sized projection of one of the three conglomerations of Aliens they had met on the strange, shielded planet, the apparently copper-iridium booth right there with them inside the little Fast.

"Welcome to our Fast yacht. Is it James?" Holt tried.

"We are James. Apologies for the suddenness of cessation of movement."

"Have we encountered a problem?" Holt asked. "Is that why you signaled our Fast to leave light speed?"

"The problem does not exist for DayLight Two'ers," James said enigmatically, then explained a little by saying, "as we do not require a cohesive inner and outer structure."

"You mean like our bodies, which have insides and outsides?"

"Precisely! We have arrived at the anomalies Petrus earlier mentioned." The Holt-like figure stepped out, all gold, and gestured toward one wall, proving it wasn't a projection at all, but the real thing. "May we show you? Will the vessel be allowed to do so?"

"If it causes no harm to us. Yes. Please."

James waved an arm and the longest side of the Fast became as though transparent.

The three Humans couldn't help but gasp with the sudden sense of exposure. Not to mention the view! Both Tap and Holt quickly grasped their seats as though they would be swept out of them, while Dr. Dem-Arest twirled an arm about his lamp and hung on.

"Is this real, James?" he asked.

It was as though they were in a tiny open loge box placed on the very high edge and within an unimaginably vast theater, in which the Milky Way had decided to show itself off in all its scale, color and glory. Directly ahead and covering most of their right lay gossamer filaments of blue green mist, leading directly to what they could all see was a swirling mass of lighter colored material gyrating around some unseen, cyclonic center that must eventually be the smaller black hole. To their apparent left, were Promethean nebulae in palest chartreuse and pink, hot melon and canary-yellow, thickly gathered and pieced by blazing blue-white stars – the stellar nursery they'd been warned of.

"Quite real, in space-time, Doctor," James answered. "Being unfamiliar with your little craft's method of beyond light speed travel, even after some rather delicate probing of the its nonHuman mind, our traveling communities took a vote and decided that all of us ought to remain safely together through this turbulent area. If you will join us in our vehicle?" James gestured out and to something that just now rose up in front of them, only partly blocking the cyclopean scene.

"We're traveling safely in *that*?" Tap Zullini-Brach asked, with a laugh.

No wonder, since it looked to Holt like no kind of star-ship but instead Holo-Vids he'd seen of old time, Metro-Terran chocolate candy boxes, rectangular, fakely gilded in overlapping layers all over, with darker, ribbon-like excrescences.

"Comm. Darency and al-Haaretz," Holt ordered the Fast. When all three Hesperian vehicles were speaking, he laid out James' plan.

Always contrary, al-Haaretz said, "personally, I'd like my Fast's mind to run through some schematics of their craft first.

"Done," James said.

As they waited five, ten seconds, the third Fast's mind reported back, "it looks comfortable enough for all of us side by side. With all that shielding they have, as much, it appears as perhaps the planet itself has, it should be safe enough." It then added, "as they are not materialized, they need no amenities, so it would be best for Humans to remain inside Fasts."

"What if it's a trap?" Tap asked. "They waited to get us out here where no one can see anything. And we walk right into their jail. Boom! They've got us snapped shut and haul us off?"

"Haul us off where?" Holt asked, gesturing to grand if seemingly-antipathetic-to-all-life-view that dominated their view. "To the Green Nebula Queen's lair of a million tortures, where she'll giggle as all of us slowly die, and she imposes one orgasm after another upon your own poor, tormented, body?"

"That sounds kind of hot." Tap admitted.

"I thought as much, it being pure fantasy."

"They could dump us into that ... um ... little black hole there!" Tap pointed.

"They would do that because ... why, exactly?"

"I don't know. Wait!. I do! Because we found them out!"

"They don't *care* that they're *found out*," Holt tried to explain. "Tap, sweetie, try to get this through your handsome, PVN-stuffed, head. We are like bacteria to these people. That's how much further evolved than us they are."

"An unfortunate analogy," James interrupted. "We like to think of you as very curious and active … well, perhaps you would say, pet-like creatures, the kind that at times need watching out for their own good."

That was all most of them needed to hear.

"I vote yes, go with them," Darency comm.ed. "Casper?"

"Fine."

"Now James, you've seen an example of Humankind's own puny brand of democracy."

"Actually, it is more like Alpha-male bonding with a light splash of democracy," al-Haaretz had to have the last word.

James began to gesture again to close the view.

"Wait, James," Dem-Arest said. "For the sake of science, could we keep some of these sights open to view? Not all. That's a bit too much for us, but maybe a window of it – about so big?"

"Done!"

The "window" remained open even when they felt themselves suddenly, and with no apparent motion or effort, within the DayLight Two ship they'd just been looking at.

The view then became the only indication that they were moving, as there was no other sense of it whatsoever.

"Fast!" Dem-Arest asked, "how is this happening? It's like a sitting room is flying. We have no sense of motion at all!"

"Unclear," the Fast's mind responded, even sounding perplexed. "But naturally this mind is recording all for future reference."

"You have no idea *how* we are traveling?" Holt asked.

"It's not subatomic!" Dem-Arest was looking at his own open cubicle of read- outs. "There are no energy fluctuations involved in our motion, even at the sub-sub electronic level. It looks more like some kind of … temporal displacement. One second we're *here* in relation to a point. The next six hundredth of a second we're *there* in relation to a point. The next twelve-hundredth of a second we're *over there!* … Fast?"

"That's an excellent description, Doctor, of a baffling phenomenon. Once this mission is over, this mind would like permission to partly and temporarily meld enough with a DayLight Two community to attempt to discover how it is done?"

"Like they're going to let you find out the secret of instantaneous travel?" Tap sneered.

"Done," James said, again.

"Permission is granted from this end," Holt told the Fast. "But James, your people really don't mind primitives like us knowing how it is done?"

"We initiate the travel ourselves," James said. "The vehicle is merely a container to hold what molecular make-up we require."

"That explains how ug-lee the vehicles are." Tap commented, not completely under his breath.

"It is unlikely that your minds will be able to do it as we do," James continued. "However, it may be likely that one, or better yet perhaps all three of your craft's minds working together can learn how to do it. We don't mind them knowing how."

"But won't us having that change the balance of power in the galaxy?" Dem-Arest asked.

"Not appreciably. Certainly not for our communities, which no longer think in such terms.

"You mean being immaterial?" Holt asked.

"Being of *differing* material," James explained.

The two other communities of aliens appeared physically then and greetings were exchanged.

Joshua announced, "Our three local communities have voted Tap Zullini-Brach as the most imaginatively *charming* of your triple crews."

He handed Tap what looked like a ball of silver foil just big enough to close his fist over.

"When your vehicle minds learn how to travel, this will come in handy as an object to practice with."

"What is it?" Tap held it up to look at it more closely and even expanded his close-vision. "Vir!" he exclaimed and nervously almost dropped it, executing several close call saves that amused the others.

"What is it?" Holt asked.

"I looks like a little, I don't know," Tap said, "a little spiral galaxy or something? It's not real, right?" he asked Joshua.

"It is real in space time," Joshua explained. "The container you hold is motion, shock and damage proof. Our communities believe that Tap Zullini-Brach is its best new keeper."

"You mean the worst!" He held it out, trying to return it.

"Soon, you will forget what is inside it. You will forge a new container for it, to decorate your ear, or nose, or nipple, I believe that body part is called." Joshua tried explaining. "Then you will be its new keeper. It is best ignored and allowed to go its own way."

"Wait just one minute, Sol Rad.," a suddenly upset Tap now said, then asked, "you're not saying that we, all of us, here, and you and all this" encompassing the still Titanic view, 'is inside one of these? Are you?"

"We are not saying that. Absolutely not," Joshua said. James backed him up.

The other Humans laughed.

"What? What's the big joke?" Tap wanted to know.

"Leader Holt," James now pointed out their "window", "we are almost past the two anomalies."

"I don't understand why the star nursery and the black hole don't cancel each other out?" Dem-Arest mused.

"Because they balance each other perfectly," Holt said. As they'd looked, he'd suddenly had it 'snap' together in his head, in an almost mathematical sense: "As one continues to create, so the other continues to destroy."

"An *imperfect* balance!" the alien community named Petrus corrected. "Many of those young stars with almost no density yet, will soon migrate away, allowing the balance to remain intact, until some other kind of balance is found."

"I see that!" Holt said, and he really did. "If the baby stars stopped being born there, the black hole would go out like a light over there!" he illustrated with his hand.

"Leader Holt *does* comprehend," Petrus said to the other alien communities. "Perhaps Leader Holt would be permitted to be linked to the three little craft minds when travel is explicated?"

"Oh, no! Gratitude, Petrus. But I could never comprehend all that."

"It's unclear yet what Leader Holt can and cannot comprehend." James said to its companions and then turned to Dem-Arest and Tap Zullini-Brach.

"Followers Dem and Tap, would it be correct to say that although untested as to abilities, that Leader Holt is linearly descended from past Leaders who have achieved much for your people?"

"I'll say!" Tap said, grabbing Holt by the head and laying a noisy kiss on his temple. "This little beauty's birth mother is only the ... most ... *important*... person in the Ib'r Republic! We call him the Great Father. His other parent is no slouch either."

"Some persons inside Joshua's community," James said. "Believe they may have a way to – without any harm – aid Leader Holt in learning much more than he does now."

"You mean like Temporal Displacement travel?" Holt asked.

"May I watch over them while they're doing it? "Dem-Arest asked.

"May this ship's mind also watch?" the Fast added.

"Done!"

"Well, maybe ..." Holt said. "Let me think about it."

"We are approaching your goal!" James announced.

The space in front of them was empty, completely void of any light, seemingly of any material at all. After all they had seen this was odd.

"This star must have gone nova much more recently than Hesperia," Dem-Arest commented, "to account for this emptiness."

"Only a few millions years ago, by your time measurement methods, Doctor," James responded.

"Even so, we ought to have encountered a fossilized shock wave!"

"We passed four of them." James said.

Tap saw it first, an aqua blue blur. "There!"

As they approached in what seemed to be discrete steps, the pale blue seemed to be even less visible, hidden in tiny flecks, even sparks, diamond-bright among the predominantly brown-black of the unevenly spheroid object that simply hung in otherwise starless, matte black space before them.

"Not as large as your own," Joshua now communicated, "but our preliminary calculations say this star was larger than that one was to begin with before it went nova, and it expanded much faster than that one. The residual ore ought to be considerably more powerful."

"Fast?" Holt asked. "Can you assay it for us?"

"Of course. The star is approximately 45.9 percent Beryllium 18. There's insufficient hard material surface at this time for any kind of settlement beyond the most flimsy types, unlike Hesperia. In time that will alter, but not yet."

"We don't plan to live here, Fast. Can you grade the Beryllium?"

"As the community named Joshua said, it appears to be extremely dense and with several times the power of that currently being used inside this Fast's energy core. Of course, some would have to be actually tested to confirm that."

The figure of James vanished and then returned almost instantly. He held out small copper and glass box containing the ore.

"Don't tell me you just went there and got that for us?" Tap said.

"It was just lying on the surface." James said.

Dem-Arest held another canister into which it might be held and then placed it inside one of the Fast's most sensitive side entry points for assaying.

"This Beryllium 18 is five times more powerful than that of Hesperia," the Fast said. "It's extremely dense and pure."

The Humans celebrated .

When they were done hugging and congratulating each other, James said, "naturally, DayLight Two's communities will aid you in moving this dead star to a more convenient location. One located somewhere between our world's location and that of one of your outposts."

"You can do that?" Holt asked.

"You're joking, right?" Tap said. "These people can do just about anything!"

"I said I'd come with you, even though I'm very, very frightened," Holt said to the three communities of DayLight Two cast in the figures of James, Petrus and Joshua. "I know you said I'd be perfectly safe with you, and so here we are now. Let me see it."

"You understand why we requested this of you, Leader Holt?" Petrus asked.

"No. I'm not entirely sure I do, no, Petrus. But let's do it anyway."

"This quality of extreme courage in facing the very frightening unknown is an extremely *charming* quality of your species," Joshua said.

"I'm glad it makes you all happy."

"It is a quality long missing from our world's people, except for the communities you see here with you, who possess it only in small quantities."

"You three are the most amazing ... communities, I guess, that I've ever encountered. Truly!" Holt said. "I feel like a Neo – an infant of my species, I guess you'd say – around you three. But at the same time, at no time do I ever feel disrespected or looked down at."

"We three must tell you that we have taken this journey with you and your species, partly to aid you, but partly to aid our own people. Having you especially, Leader Holt, facing this fearsome thing so boldly will set an example to those on our planet who have sunk into the lethargy of eons."

Saying that, the figure of Petrus took one of Holt's arms, the figure of Joshua the other arm, and very close behind Holt, he felt the figure of James blocking him from any harm. His colleagues had been left around the Beryllium 18 star they had christened New Hesperia, in the three Fasts, and the DayLighters' vehicle had continued onward. "Beyond" Petrus had said. "Into the Center," Joshua said. Now Joshua gestured at their vehicle's wall to open it as a window and this time Holt staggered, glad he was being held.

The Great Attractor at 29 Degrees, 59 Minutes, 57 Seconds of Sagittarius was a black hole of such immense vastness before them he could only make out part of the cyclopean swirl of entire star systems as they ringed it, stretching out, as they were absorbed into it. Unceasing, Pulsar-like bursts, enormous gamma ray rivers, vast neutrino emission deltas all brightened it. But above the elliptical plane, was a clear black sky, not a star to be seen for what he guessed to be thousands of light years, and, as he was held tightly, he dared himself and then Holt leaned over to look into the darkness. He was astounded to see that too, below him, was a black and star-clear night sky.

Holt couldn't begin to assess what he was feeling. It seemed almost every Human emotion he'd ever expressed was now vying within him, fear and yet joy, an immense satisfaction, yet utter revulsion, exaltation and the deepest despair all at once. He knew somehow that if he could hear it, the intensity of the sound about him as giant stars were ripped apart and shredded to be absorbed into this ultra-cyclone would be too much for him to bear. Certainly the lights were almost too much, the colors beyond his eyes' ability to assimilate, all of it far too much to take in at once.

"What are your thoughts?" James extended a hand toward the central chaos.

Holt was aware that the sight had caused warm tears to course down his face, that he was deeply, deeply nauseated, that his head was wrenched painfully and spinning out of control as though he had overdosed drugs, that he was incredibly hungry, and at the same time he very much wanted to defecate.

"Magnificent … beyond words! … I'll remember this as long as I live," he managed to utter.

Petrus was now pointing up. Holt followed the figure's hand and pointing finger and could now make out, at what must be an immeasurable distance, a tiny blotch of color.

"I see it." Holt said. "What is it?" Looking away helped a bit.

"Another galaxy. Not very large. Your people call it Leo 1."

Petrus then pointed out two more little galaxies a half million-million light years away, including Leo 2, Then Joshua pointed down, through the black hole where Holt's slightly Cyberized vision made out two more blotches of stars, seemingly closer.

"Are those what we call the Magellanic clouds?" Holt asked.

"Yes. The smaller one is the closest other galaxy to this one."

"Have you been there?" Holt suddenly asked.

"Some of our people have gone there, in the past. They have not returned. They have sent communications which only just reached us after scores of thousands of years. They have found inhabitable planets and other interesting stellar habitats."

"It sounds welcoming," Holt commented. He was feeling less physically ill.

"Several of DayLight Two's communities are considering going there," Petrus answered. "Most will not and will perish here."

"But why?" Holt asked. "There are so many places to go that our Three Species haven't yet reached or claimed."

"We leave this large galaxy to your Three Species," Joshua said. "We voted to do so recently."

"You mean since you encountered us?" Holt asked.

"Yes, around this time yesterday. Because you are all so new and fresh and above all so *charming* for us," Joshua said.

"Watching you interact with each other in pleasurable emotions," Petrus said, "was what incited the urge to vote on it."

"I don't understand."

"Your affection for each other is so evident. We believe affection is the term."

"But we hate just as intensely," Holt argued. "And we do terrible things."

"Naturally! But DayLight Two's communities do not do any "thing" any more," Petrus said.

"This voyage is the first "thing" any DayLight Two communities have done in a very long time." Joshua added.

"For you, it is difficult. It makes you very ill. You shudder. Your body shakes. Your eyes tear. Your insides heave. Yet you remain here with us, defying it, challenging what none of your species was ever meant to defy or to challenge – or perhaps to ever witness," James said.

"It's insane, isn't it?" Holt asked.

"Yes, and for all those reasons, you deserve to inherit it all, the entire galaxy," James said and Holt swore he felt the figure's "hands" on his shoulders.

"Some day I'll understand this, won't I? When I'm very old and I have experienced many things in life?"

"That is to be hoped for."

They stood there watching the Great Attractor for what seemed a long time. Holt never quite got used to it, but he did enjoy looking at the far off galaxies, thinking of the other possible species there. And of James and Petrus and Joshua's communities moving to the Smaller Magellanic Cloud and perhaps with the new galaxy, breaking out of their old habits and doing something new.

Once again they were inside the craft, the window gone. Safe again.

"Wait till I tell Tap and the others what I've seen," Holt enthused, then staggered to lean against a wall.

Then, he said, "this is going to sound odd, but I've got a question. You call yourselves DayLight Two people. I'm not exactly certain what that means. I've simply got to ask, what happened to Daylight One?"

The three alien figures quickly, lightly, brushed each other's "fingers."

"This is the question we have all been waiting for one of you to ask," James said.

"The question we are fearful to answer, yet that we must

answer," Petrus added.

"No. Really. You don't have to answer it if ..."

"We must answer it, Leader Holt. By order of our people."

"Another vote?"

"Another vote," Joshua confirmed.

Holt found himself a perch and said, "if you must, I'm listening."

"Remember what your charming, affectionate mate, Tap said? 'These people can do just about anything'?"

"Yes."

"We thought that was so too. This was about a hundred thousand years ago, by your time measure."

"Go on."

"As your City on a Star is the center of your Ib'r Republic and the cultural, ethical and technological arbiter of your Three Species, so was the star-system we called Lassigo the center of ours, that long ago."

"It was a beautiful system, with a large golden star in the middle – what your Fast categorizes as G-4, some six billion years old. Revolving about it were five rock-mantled planets and twelve larger gaseous planets."

"B-5s? B-6s?"

"Both, yes, and much further away were about seventy five much smaller worlds. Among the larger ones, the very largest planet was named Gyopie, or DayLight. It possessed thirty-two satellites, seven of which were rocky mantled planetoids. DayLight was called so because it was a light and very bright gas planet that reflected almost half of the light that it received from Lassigo, its sun, onto its many satellites. Providing daylight, you understand, almost like the sun itself."

"I understand."

"Five of the seven rocky worlds were inhabited by then, and ten of that solar system's moons. We had Four Species then, corresponding more or less to genera we have found in your Fast's data retrieval systems. One was more or less, Avian – birdlike, surface flyers and such. Another was amphibian in origin, water and land based. A third species had evolved, derived from marine creatures much like the Medusae of your water worlds."

"And you were the fourth?" Holt asked.

"The fourth, yes. Originally derived from what you would

think of as flying social insects."

"Honeybees and wasps?" Holt asked.

"More or less, yes. There's no direct correlative."

"I understand. So it's birds, frogs, jellyfish and honeybee colonies, but very evolved and advanced?" Holt said.

"Evolved although less advanced than we thought we were at the time.... unfortunately!" James said. "It's still undetermined who made the first proposal to ignite the gas planet Gyopie so that it wouldn't merely be DayLight for its own satellites but also provide daylight for the two gaseous planets on either side of it, and more importantly for all of their many satellites, several of which were barely settled due to freezing temperatures and other ice-world difficulties. The idea, of course, was to make them all as wonderful as Gyopie and its attendant, well-inhabited, and quite beautiful, larger moons."

"So what happened, James? Didn't it work?"

"It worked. It worked too well!" James said. "The scientists had of course prepared for the igniting of the many gasses of Gyopie. What they didn't understand was that at a certain rate of speed and massiveness, unstoppable chain effects, chemical imitations, molecular bond copy errors, all of them cascading far beyond our control, would take place. Instead of Gyopie merely becoming twenty times brighter, it became a million-million times brighter. It didn't just brighten, it ignited. It became another star."

"Most of the inhabitants of Gyopie's moons had been evacuated. There was some loss of life on the moons surrounding the nearby gas worlds, but it was minimal. However, physically and even more so, gravitationally, we had a disaster that was solar system wide. Several of Gyopie's satellites were flung away, some to the edge of the system. Two of the suddenly uninhabitable ones were burned to cinders and the third, the paradise world, beautiful little Juskia, was stripped of its oceans and more or less turned into a charred rock. It had been protected from greater harm only by a fluke, by the interference of two those other moons between it and Gyopie becoming a new star. But Juskia too was thrown far out of orbit."

"With a new star burning, our solar system lost its cohesion. The surrounding planets sought new gravitation wells and several collided. Two of the gaseous ones struck Gyopie itself, inflaming it even further. After a few hundred years of the most colossal disturbances and planetary collisions, Gyopie was a second sun, drawn by gravity into a closer new, relationship to its old star. First the rocky planets, then even the gas giants were drawn in too and all of them were absorbed by one or another of the two stars, which then grew proportionately larger and brighter.

"By the end of a thousand years, the once lovely planetary system, home to a million billion inhabitants of the Four Species, center of our Four Species Democracy, now consisted of two big stars and one tiny chunk of dried rock circling it at a great distance. Utter destruction. We had failed most entirely."

"What happened then?" Holt had to ask.

"What you would suppose. Blame was attributed. No one would accept blame or compensate for loss. Resentments that were long hidden suddenly exploded. Inter-Species wars followed and with those wars the expected population displacements and losses, then gross tragedies and inconceivable mistakes. The center of our four-part government vanished and each of the Four Species fled to the farthest ends of the galaxy to avoid each other, to be safe."

"Instead of safety, they found varied recipes for extinction. With their stringent requirements for environment, the marine species flickered out of existence first, the water-land species followed, and then the avian – the second most adaptable of we four – which lingered on for perhaps another score thousands of years, scattered across the far outer arms of the galaxy. Because we were socialized to begin with, our species had the most ecological and psychological coping abilities of all four species – even given all the disastrous changes that had occurred – and so we became the *de facto* evolutionary winners."

"We found new solar systems almost as good as Gyopie, and we populated them, and we built a single species empire. But the memory of what had happened continued to haunt our people. The desire to find others grew stronger. We became compulsive explorers. We found only the ruins of the avian species' outposts in strange continents on planets very far away. They had fled that far in their fear and loathing of us. We even searched the few planets of the extremely distant star clusters above the plane of the ecliptic. Then, one day of a particular year, it became official: we were alone among intelligent sentient species in the galaxy.

"But Petrus said they found Humans a long time ago."

"True, and the exploration teams failed to report it, or did so only as the most tightly classified information. You see, Leader Holt, by then it was too late for us. We had grown to adulthood in concert, our lives, our destinies entwined with three other sentient species, we spent our maturity in contention with them, and when old age settled in our people, we were alone, and we no longer really cared whether we were alone or not."

"This Gyopie system?" Holt asked. "Is it still there?"

"We have given your Fast the coordinates of it, relative to this point. It tells us your Species calls the new binary system Aquila, the Eagle, and the newer star, once the planet Gyopie, is now a blue star, called the Eagle-Hunter."

"Wait a minute. I know that place. The little dried out world has rings around it. It's known as Usk,"

"Husk," James said oddly. "It is a husk of what was once a little paradise world."

Holt looked at the three figures, the three communities. "It's a very sad story."

"Very sad," Petrus agreed.

After a few minutes of contemplation, Holt said. "Why do I get the feeling that you told me this story for a reason?"

"Because we did."

"Oh! The payment you mentioned for finding Hesperia Two."

"Yes. The compensation we required. It is this, Leader Holt. When you return you must tell this story to your Ib'r Republic. To your Three Species. Then ask them to forgive us. Even though we are no longer here."

"But how can I be certain that Usk is your little moon?"

"Because before we moved to the planet DayLight Two, we left something behind on the burnt little world. We have already shown your Fast's mind what it is and it will show you how and where to locate it. It will prove conclusively that the little world was our long abandoned Juskia. It is the proof of our overweening pride and hubris, the sign or our titanic aspirations and enormous failure. May it serve as a lesson to your own Three Species."

Chkw'esso Fourteen A had been replaced by another of that clan, Chkw'esso Seventeen B, a far more submissive greeter. Her palps and antennae remained in the inferior position on the Ho-lo-Comm. while welcoming them on-world to Usk, and then in person, as they landed at the rural-looking Fast landing strip.

"Your Majesty," the three other Bella=Arth.s repeated (both verbally ((and pheromonally))) adding, "we hope your trip was a safe (comfortable ((speedy))) one?"

"Sufficient in all those. Gratitude, Court Ladies. We are Royally Pleased, and extend greetings to Her Majesty, Ami'da'lia."

There was a flurry of pleasure at her using that equalizing address for their leader; all must have been aware of the earlier near-debacle regarding nomenclature.

Kri'nni allowed them their moment, and then checked that her little retinue followed her out. Mar'ko Ve'Espry, naturally (what would she do without him?); all three of the Fak ('qq') sisters – San'da, Die'ga and Pinna – clad as stylishly as anyone from Hesperia (she'd made certain beforehand ((even buying the outfits))), compared to which these other Arth.s were both old fashioned and dowdily out of place. Kri'nni had lived long enough to know how much even the simplest of visual clues stimulated the brain, and unconsciously raised or lowered one in their group's esteem.

Ami'da'lia herself was within the resort landing strip building, seated with another dozen of her court, including several tall soldiers, but no Humans or Delph.s. (Another point for Kri'nni, she knew, having the Human Vir (Mar'ko ((as tall and stalwart as the soldiers)))).

Reflexively, all the palps and antennae of those already in the receiving chamber signified pleasure at the handsome entourage entering. The pheromones exuded were of the sweetest (and most gratifying) type. In response, her group did so too, Mar'ko using an out of sight aerosol in a trouser pocket (his pheromonal choices were amazingly accurate, ((yet individual too))) and were among his most used tools of Arth. seduction.

Once the newcomers had been seated and placed facing Ami'da'lia's retinue, formulized greeting and welcoming chat ensured. Introductions took place in as natural a fashion as possible, and when Mar'ko stood and went forward to bow to Ami'da'lia on one knee with a hand out, reeking of a host of new masculine yet submissive perfumes, the other court reflexively flew into titters. He certainly had ensured that he wouldn't lack female company here on Usk.

Two Arth. soldiers exchanged palp-strokes with Mar'ko – yet more honor – and he returned to sit next to Kri'nni, sub-vocalizing the word "pushovers!"

The small talk done, Ami'da'lia herself introduced the main topic.

"The nest-like cones (you mentioned) have been inspected and are approved (for the ritual). Naturally your vizier (ready at arms ((Human))) – was the closest to Galacticon she came to explaining Mar'ko – will wish to look them over (himself)."

"Naturally."

"This nest's (general ((first))) impressions, are that they will certainly be Vid-able (for billions of viewers ((and any PVNs to be made.))) They (unquestionably) fulfill all the Articles' requirements (of the site for the ritualized combat)."

"In that case, This Lady approves!" Kri'nni said generously, and the satisfaction in the receiving chamber was ramped up even higher.

"This Lady," referring to herself," Ami'da'lia began, "was apprised that Article Forty-Two states that the earliest such combats used no weapons (at all, ((not even ritualized ones))). Would Your majesty approve?"

"Completely," Kri'nni said and waved agreement pheromones out at her counterpart. "Is one vestigial claw to remain unsheathed?"

"In fact, yes, in order that the very lightest of scratches can be made upon the combatants' chitin."

"It's understood that This Lady," Kri'nni said, "will cause one such scratch. And that Your Majesty will cause two. (Thus ensuring victory)."

"It is understood."

The room seethed with pleasurable murmurs and strongly pleasurable odors. A Human or Delph. not already inured to it as Mar'ko was, would be choking and gasping for air. Even he had brought an inhaler that tubed into one nostril.

"It is also understood that Your Majesty will then sign over all Galactic-Nest Regal Rights to This Lady?"

"Understood." Kri'nni felt oh so benevolent, giving away what she never wanted in the first place, or at any time.

"And that This Lady" Ami'da'lia added, "will (in Gratitude)

sign over to Your Majesty (at the same time,) a boon (great benefit ((something you want))) belonging to the Galactic-Nest (existing upon the city-star Hesperia), to be used during Your Majesty's lifetime (however long it is ((centuries if need be))), without any limitations (or qualifications)."

"Yes. Specifically, the (old ((mostly unused))) Cassiopeia Girder Bella=Arth. Embassy and its surroundings (grounds)," Kri'nni now specified, "as well as the return, with no qualifications (at all), of This Lady's property on Hesperia, at Power Avenue. It's nothing more than a semi-converted Slp.G liner terminal (forlorn ((in an abandoned industrial slum))) of no real value (worth ((moola))) to the Galactic Nest."

"That too is so waived to Your Majesty," Ami'da'lia said. "Although it might interest Your Majesty to know, how could you? (being stuck away breeding ((as you were so long?))) that Power Avenue has now become an extremely trendy area of that City Upon a Star. Even so, This Lady was informed that that property remains listed (in Your Majesty's name as owner ((with the Quinx Girder Authority))). We see no reason to question (or alter) that."

"How could you know?" Mar'ko sub-vocally repeated to her, "when you've only had me assess the Power Avenue property's value almost daily, Sol Rad.," he added and Kri'nni almost stung him.

Ami'da'lia was suddenly required for Algenib Delta Two business and the double court broke up with many pieces of reintroductions and small talk.

Kri'nni's retinue was shown to their suites occupying a separate wing of the resort decided upon. It had been built between two deep ridges, spanning a canyon that dropped many hundreds of meters below, a bridge-hotel and thus symbolic of the entire event. The views were quite wonderful from there.

The next day, following the ritual and all signatures being made, there was a celebratory dinner. Naturally, placement issues were paramount for the Disaporan community. But Ami'da'lia, had Kri'nni placed as an equal with her and seemed far more relaxed now that all their business was concluded.

"Your Majesty may be intrigued to know that this (entire) cone was explored (before we decided to use it)," Queen Ami'da'lia said, "and on (lower) levels we discovered several (small) troves of what might have be antiquated accessories (connected with the Arth. presence on Usk ((during the short-lived battles))) here. But it was only when Your Majesty happened to mention that two (lovely) sisters (of your entourage) actually come into contact with such artifacts (on the Home World Nest ((on a daily basis))), that This Lady gave the go-ahead (to our soldiers-and specialists) to delve into these lower chambers. "

Among the Soldiers that now stepped forward, none of them clad as honor guard, all wearing some kind of hardy-looking aprons across their abdomens and lower bodies, with pockets bulging with various fine tools, one in particular approached the two queens and their abbreviated retinues. She introduced herself as "Verk-ss-car, specialized as an Anthropological Drone." Her assistants covered a table with various ancient and Kri'nni thought, unattractive items.

"Your Majesties," Verk-ss-car bowed, and exuding differing pheromones of submission, fear, honor and gratitude, said "Before you are those artifacts (we have recently culled) from these levels."

San'da and Die'ga Fak ("qq") were now invited to inspect them.

Mar'ko joined them, and since he was also a member of the museum, they confabbed briefly, asked the Disaporan Drones a few questions, and shortly reported back: "The artifacts do appear to be genuine (and similar to some of those we have at the museum). Their markings, styles, types (even brands of manufacture) are consistent with what we have (on display) and could well stand (as material evidence) of the Last Days (upon Usk) of the Home World Nest (during the Matriarchal War ((of Sidereal Time years 2622 to 2645)))."

"That is most gratifying!" Ami'da'lia said, exuding gratitude and honor pheromones. "What is the process by which These Two Ladies may request a museum status for this particular cone." Turning to Kri'nni she added, "naturally the Disaporan Nest Community would be honored to fund any required expenses for maintenance and docents."

Mar'ko stepped forward, and exuding knowledge and interest pheromones from sprays in his shirt pockets, he said, "As Usk is a Resort Planet (and one of the Seven Hundred Wonders of the Galaxy), that request ought to be fairly easy to achieve. However there are (special) methods by which this may be done (which are well known ((to this Honored Drone))) as a result of his (ordinary) avocation."

He was given the task, and the dinner party was officially ended. Kri'nni thought it was time to bid adieu to this "Group of Old Insects," when Queen Ami'da'lia took her by one palp and walked her off to an alcove where she dropped her voice and spoke with a minimum of pheromone overtones.

"Gratitude, Your Majesty for the suggestion to complete our business ((here))) on Usk. Already it seems we may have added to the Galactic-Nest's store (of much needed) historical cultural items."

Kri'nni found herself liking this Ami'da'lia, almost despite herself.

"There have been other (equally intriguing ((and different)))) benefits to this visit," Ami'da'lia added, and this was obviously the gist of her new conversation.

"Perhaps the most unusual was This Lady's presence during a celestial phenomenon that occurs, (we are told) only every thousand and a half years, Sol Rad."

She waved to one of her staff, who produced the Holo-Vid showing in speeded-up mode, the double sunset, the night skies, the rings reaching perihelion and then appearing to switch places and then next morning, the double sunrise with, this time, the blue star rising first, the orange second. "A most interesting (almost unprecedented) event."

Kri'nni watched and indeed whoever had edited it, had done a splendid job of making all of the Queen's descriptions clear and interesting. She was about to compliment Ami'da'lia when the Vid then focused upon a night scene of a stretch of rocky horizontals around which a population appeared to be gathering.

"Even more intriguing," Ami'da'lia now said, in an even lower voice than before, "was this event (among the local people) We witnessed not three kilometers from here. See how the starlight between the rings comes together? It was focused down. And this spot was the (precise) location where the focus came together on planet Usk."

"It looks like rock shelving," Kri'nni commented.

"It as exactly that (but within the rocky formations), is located the only Birthing Station (for many square kilometers). When We arrived in a fly-by, one other fly-by was already there (with several Human scientists ((of some note))), laboring upon this planet. But more intriguing (even then their presence) was that there were scores of the local (small ((humanoid)) creatures who do all the labor here on Usk."

"Pamps?" Kri'nni recalled their name.

"Pamps, yes. They had all come far (some several hours walking distance), and they all brought gifts. (Poor things, ((for the most part))). But that they would do so, so surprised those of our retinue who know them; (it was remarkable)."

The Vid now focused on the pamps, and then on Ami'da'lia herself as she left her fly-by, and approached the crowd, which parted to let her through.

"Even more remarkable was that person (they had gathered to see ((and celebrate))) was not even one (of their kind ((but a Human male))). There he is!"

She pointed to the dark haired, stalwart, very attractive young Human.

"He had only just pre-parted (a pupa ((as Human males do))) only after an arduous journey across this area of Usk. That is all that we could gather (of him). No name was given to him, except Friend of the Pamps. But our retinue told us the pamps were treating him as though he were their very honored ruler."

"This Lady was very taken by the young (Human)," Ami'da'lia admitted "and by the immense honor that he was being shown (by so many ((of another species))), despite his apparent youth and poverty (and of those doing the honoring). They acted toward him (and his young one) as though he were a True Royal Queen! We thought, if he is a Royal Queen, he ought to be gifted (as a Royal Queen) and … here you see the result (of that sentiment.)"

Kri'nni now watched the large pure Beryllium jewel being wrapped and then handed to him. His graciousness accepting it, his offer to the Arth. Queen of a seat; how he placed the invaluable gift amidst others consisting of little but bundled herbs, wildflowers, and rag dolls.

"Unusual as all this was (especially upon this magnificent night ((which This Lady later discovered represents an entirely new Aeon entirely for the pamps)))," Ami'da'lia went on, "was the infant just pre-parted lying in his outer womb (which is what the Humans call the mechanism ((within which their pupae reach a certain degree of maturation we achieve only in the Nest)))."

"We believe you will agree with us that the pupa itself was (attractive! ((highly so))) Ami'da'lia said, and the Vid panned to look into the outer womb.

Kri'nni could not help but release an entire panoply of pheromones expressing her astonishment, displeasure and fear.

"Your Majesty?!"

Ami'da'lia backed away. "We meant no offense." She said. "But merely to share this. Is there some reason why this pupa is so fearful?"

Kri'nni instantly settled back into her usual indifference and now said, "A mistake, (merely). But as Your Majesty noted (earlier), This Lady has been out of circulation (for many decades). How common among Human Virs has become this particular combination of coloring? (Bronze hair and emerald eyes, ((as we see on this pre-parted pupa)))?"

"This Lady's retinue assured Us that it is very rare coloring indeed, (found among less than a handful of Humans ((all of them related to the former Premier of the Ib'r Republic – the Princeps Mart Kell of Hesperia)))."

"How very intriguing (your Majesty)! How very, *(very)* intriguing," Kri'nni said.

"Isn't it? Especially as the Inter. Gal. News reports (all) say that the Princeps has been searching (for a young Vir ((upon this planet))) – one, (This Lady believes may be this same (pamp-honored) young Vir."

"Searching for … " Kri'nni probed, she hoped not too eagerly.

"Yes, searching for him. For several months now. It was only (recently) announced on Inter. Gal. News (by one of the Princeps' colleagues, ((from the House of Syzygy)))."

"And the young Vir" –pointing to him on the Vid screen – "is not to be found?" Kri'nni had to ask.

"In fact (according to This Lady's retinue), the young Vir he seeks is this day in actuality the undeclared leader of a planet-wide labor stoppage (by the entire pamp population). Had you not arrived by private Fast, your entry (through any spaceport) would have been delayed (because of it ((his action)))."

"Perhaps then we ought to ensure that the Princeps Mart Kell receives the information (he seeks)?"Kri'nni suggested. "Doubtless the Disaporan Nest has (had past, ((beneficial))) contacts with Kell (Unlimited)?" Kri'nni asked.

"Several."

"The Galactic Nest could only benefit (by such a generous gesture)," Kri'nni said as indifferently as possible.

"Perhaps so ... Although This Lady does not make it a habit to interfere (in other species' affairs)."

"However, This Lady did so (regularly)," Kri'nni admitted. "to everyone's benefit."

"Then this Lady will do so, and see what happens (as a result ((in Your Majesty's honor)))."

"Gratitude, Your Majesty," Kri'nni said, and exuded rich and complex pheromones of pleasure and thanks.

Verk-ss-car, the Anthropological Drone Leader, appeared, and exuding excitement and incertitude, approached them where they had all but hidden.

"Your Majesties, a most (unusual) finding (from our lowest level) diggers has just been made (and been confirmed)."

"Confirmed as ...?" Kri'nni addressed her.

"Confirmed as an even lower and thus far earlier level. (One separated by apparently thicker floor ((than what we had dug up before)). This Drone's helpers believe the one they now have located (through a combination of sonar and electro'graviton pulses) might be the original lowest level (or foundation level) – as we refer to it."

She went into more detail, most of it boringly scientific to Kri'nni, if not to her fellow Queen, who said, "Her Majesty believes We earlier received (official) permission to dig at this site (with no limiting specifications ((as to depth and extent)))."

"Both of Your Majesties believe correctly," Verk-ss-car confirmed.

"Then why not continue digging? Who can say what (earlier) artifacts might be uncovered?"

Kri'nni exuded agreement as well as confidence in her fellow queen.

They then followed Verk-ss-car down the cone's levels where the chambers grew smaller, the walls rougher, and ceilings lower. It was all a great adventure!

At the bottommost level, Drones were using electronic pick-axes upon a section of floor. It gave way under their blows and revealed a wide ramp down.

More time was needed to clear the debris, and lanterns were brought to light their way further down.

They arrived at what seemed a wider than high doorway.

Inscriptions had been carved into it, and once it was cleared of surrounding earth, not one of the scientists present were able to identify the script, never mind read it.

San'da, Die'ga and Mar'ko were brought down. They too wracked their brains over it.

Mar'ko insisted that the perhaps first and surely the largest of signs, was a fairly universal one: a rectangle shaped to the same dimensions of the door, with a double lines crossed over it. "Stop.! Don't enter!" Mar'ko said aloud, adding, "Forbidden!"

"That's what you say!" Kri'nni insisted. To the drones she commanded, "Break it down (if you need to ((do so!)))."

They almost had to, but soon the doors were opened and they entered. It was a large chamber strangely lit in which what appeared to be a pink energy field extended from floor to ceiling.

Verk-ss-car found a wall plaque, which upon her approaching it, began speaking in a language none had ever heard before, then switched into another, far more birdlike tongue, and then into a serous of low roars.

"Speak to it," Kri'nni suggested. "It seems to be (primitively) Cyber-like. Perhaps it is able to learn languages (on a simple level)."

San'da and Mar'ko did speak to it for a few minutes, one reading aloud a Holo-Doc, the other repeating a talking book.

There was silence and then: "Greeting aliens!" *the mechanism suddenly spoke in ungrammatical Galacticon.* "Well come to yhas monument chem to a great folly of anr pren people and shumt their shame."

Soon it was speaking without trial and they learned that within what it referred to as a 'stasis field' – i.e. the pink energy field they were witnessing – "*those individuals and communities most directly responsible for the great undoing were being held*". "*Those who follow,*" the plaque then assured them. "*may forgive by releasing them,*" it concluded, along with instruction how to do so.

"What 'great undoing'?" San'da asked what all of them were thinking. But the plaque would not elaborate, only repeat what it had said the first time.

"The age of this, Your Majesties, appears (extremely)

ancient." Verk-ss-car reported. "Even at a (rough) guess, it precedes (Arthropodic) space flight, (and possibly ((all but the earliest))) Inter-Nest wars, as well."

"Are we certain we wish to release them?" Ami'da'lia asked. "Who knows what monsters they might be?"

"Small monsters," Kri'nni pointed out, "since the 'stasis field' is rather small."

Release was discussed and at last agreed upon and the release button was pressed. The stasis field stopped instantly. The pink glow vanished. Lanterns were turned on.

In the stasis field's sudden absence, four objects fell to the ground, while two others, tall rectangular booth-like things, seemingly of metal and frosted glass, remained standing. It was instantly evident that the fallen objects had once been living creatures – bird-like things, and reptilian things of extreme strangeness, that none in the chamber had ever seen . All were dead.

"They've been here (too) long. They're gone!" Verk-ss-car said what they all were thinking.

The corpses were Vid-ed and measured and exclaimed upon.

Kri'nni tried the button for the Stasis Field, which pressed, immediately flickered on, and then relighted up the room.

"This mechanism still works."

The creatures and the amber-like substance of the booths were all beginning to react to their great age and to the destructive chemical effects of the air brought into the chamber. They rapidly desiccated and fell into differently colored powders as Arth.s and Human watched and recorded them. The booths, when pried opened, had the same result. Dozens of minuscule creatures within that had fallen to the bottom and now turned to dust.

A soldier drone volunteered to undergo the stasis field for less than a minute. When she staggered out, she reported that it was not painful, but that the time that passed inside seemed much longer. More like an hour.

"Then it is a *Time Prison*," Kri'nni declared. "An (extremely ((effective))) prison, in which one remains conscious! How long (do you believe) this to have been (placed here)?" she asked Verk-ss-car, who could only estimate about a hundred thousand years, Sol Rad.

The others were filled with the eeriness of what they had

discovered and what it might possibly mean. They replayed the plaque, and tried to tease meanings out of it – to little avail. Whenever it did answer off-text of its usual message, it assumed knowledge they did not possess.

"Now," Kri'nni said to Mar'ko when he came to her later on, "I don't even need to go (back) to Hesperia (to find my revenge). My return (there) shall be a clean-palps triumph. Who he is seeking is (right here) on Usk. He (whom he seeks) will be here (in this chamber) for Kell to see and touch (however briefly). And then ..."

Ay'r was pulled out of Fast-sleep more suddenly and jarringly than he'd ever been. In fact, his arm above his elbow hurt from where he'd been suddenly pinched by, what, that little mechanical extrusion? What was going on?

"Wake up, Lord Sanqq'!" he heard his wrist-connector sub-vocalizing. "This is the Fast mind! We are being seriously compromised! Wake up!"

Keeping his eyes closed just enough that he could see a slit out of them, Ay'r made sleeping sounds and turned his head to where he faced the middle of the Fast. Only one other passenger was onboard, Anto-leya, the Matriarchal world Historico-Sociometrician, his especially invited guest. She was doing something, but she kept looking back at him, as though checking if he were sleeping, and she was undoubtedly covering whatever she was doing, blocking it with her body.

"Lord Sanqq', what seems to have been a final communication was sent by the other passenger onboard this Fast at the very last second before this Fast negotiated the previous jump. Now she is attempting to hook up some kind of device onto the interior of the ship."

Ay'r rolled off the seat, and behind a screen. When she looked again, he was holding a laser weapon, aimed at her.

"Having a problem?" he asked.

She whirled around, her own little laser gun in hand, and realized she was found out. "I was checking to see if it would work. But I'm sure it will," she said.

"Really?"

"It doesn't make any difference, since I've already released a gas that will kill the two of us in a matter of minutes."

"So the device does what?"

"It kills the Fast's mind, so no one finding the many tiny pieces of this vessel will ever be able to locate our home world."

"I take it the other women remained at our last jump point?" Ay'r asked.

"Yes. The vote went against you. Against me. They lied to you about it, so you wouldn't suspect. It was because I was so strongly in favor of our reuniting with the Ib'r Republic that I was assigned for the task of ..."

"Sabotage, it's called, Mer Anto-leya."

"Sabotage," she admitted.

He now noticed the open vial at her feet. He sub-vocalized, "Fast! Quickly. Put all your records of this trip into the brain of the T-Pod. Then, when I say Hesperia, drop me into the T-Pod too."

"If the vial is already open?"

"Do what I say, Fast!"

"As you wish, Lord Sanqq'."

Aloud, Ay'r said, "you've made your good-byes to your loved ones, I hope."

"Yes. At the last Fast jump."

"Then I'm sorry to have to inform you that they will probably never be delivered. You see, Anto-leya, The Matriarchy, in all its forms, was ever the most lying and treacherous of governments. You won't be the great hero you think you will be, back home. They'll lie and say you ran off with me. That you were a pervert. Or worse. A traitor."

"I don't believe you," she said – but as he said it he could see that she did.

"Of course you do. Too bad. And too bad you never made it to our final destination. You would have liked it on – Hesperia."

The floor beneath his feet opened up and he could see the surprise on her face as he dropped into a T-pod stored below. It sealed instantly behind him.

The Fast opened its lower deck and the transparent two-seater sprang free.

"Get me away, Fast! Top speed!"

He was already feeling dizzy when he looked around. They had Fast jumped into the area of the very top levels of the Far Perseus Arm, he thought. That was probably the galaxy swirling so grandly below. Although he couldn't be sure – he was feeling the effects of the gas already. This T-pod should be easily located and with it evidence of the planet, and of the women surviving there – and of how they must be dealt with in the future.

"T-Pod, connect me to the Fast interior," he ordered.

"Mer Anto-leya. I'm fading and I'm guessing so are you. But be aware of this, I will continue on. Not in a Human form like this. But I am already fully salvaged, my mind and my thoughts, my heart and my soul, back in Hesperia, and who I was will be revived and go on living, who knows, for centuries, maybe eons more to come."

He could hear her croaking something in return but the Fast could not discern it.

"Good bye, Fast. You were a good ship," Ay'r said.

"Gratitude, Lord Sanqq'. This Fast is gratified you will continue on as a mind."

"And you too, in part," Ay'r said, but he could barely hear himself.

Just before he lost consciousness, he saw above what must have been the sabotaged Fast, slowly and quite beautifully blowing itself to infinitesimal bits.

For no very good reason, he found himself cast back to his earliest Neo-hood, a little song they sang:

"Twin ... kle ... twin ... kle ... lit ... le ..."

Vinson Todd moved an Arth. Fast telepathically and it slid into place, upsetting Cas'sio's previously, wonderfully, placed Vee of Matriarchal-Commando Slp.G liners.

From where it was now placed, the Fast could self-destruct and bring all thirteen of the other ships down with it into gravity-well-oblivion.

"Check, Premier!" Todd crowed. "Try to get out of that if you can!"

The Premier realized his attention had been divided, but even so, to be bested in less than an hour ... He looked up at the space between them where the various props of the game floated on a Holo-Grid.

"Go on, Old Man! Tell me how I get out of it?" he asked.

"You don't! It's a check mate," Vinson chortled. "I know it's unfair of me to take advantage of you," he added, "since you've had your hands full of late, but even so, you were the one who asked for a game ..."

"So I did, hoping to be distracted."

"Well, here comes another distraction for one of us – probably you!"

Through the transparent door of the Andromeda Club's game room they could see a Human servant holding out a silver tray upon which a note lay. It was one of nicer touches of the place, linking it to some Metro-Terran tradition long lost in history, if not perhaps totally illusory.

Cas'sio waved to the servant, and the Holo-Screen went on, announcing "A message for his Premiership, from New Venice. The sender is statistical analyst, Itz-bel L(e^e)!"

"Who could that possibly be?" Cas'sio found himself saying. Someone or she wouldn't have been patched through to his club off hours.

The g.female Ambassadorial Delph. was shown in real-time and he remembered her. "You're Pro-Leader W(ing) L(e^e)'s daughter?"

"His double niece, Premier."

"I recall our meeting and your charge from me was ...? Remind me."

"To report any strong fluctuations across a series of randomly selected monitors, galaxy wise."

"That's right. And you have found one?" Cas'sio asked, his heart beginning to flutter a bit at the prospect of catastrophe.

"Yes. One of those randomly selected monitors we decided to use as constants has altered so extremely in such a short period of time that it is now altering the entire series, throwing it all out of line, so to speak. I believe that is worth reporting."

"Go ahead, report."

"The price of natural ocean salt has risen seven hundred and seventy-five percent across the Center Worlds and as much as twenty-four hundred percent in the outer arms."

"That's outrageous!" Vinson Todd said. "Someone must be fixing the market!"

"Mer L(e^e), do you know why this is happening?" Cas'sio asked.

"It is almost certainly a result of the complete work stoppage on the Resort planet Usk. Usk supplies twenty-nine percent of the highest grade salt to Delphinid Worlds."

"Usk again! Usk, Usk, Usk. And now Usk again! The past six months has been nothing but Usk," the Premier fulminated.

Vinson looked surprised. "You mean that dry little place where you held the Betrothal?"

"Since then, Usk or something having to do with Usk has been in the Holo-News for one reason or another every …"

"That's where the Marquis Syzygy's boy vanished, isn't it. The attractive Neo that you Betrothed?"

"Exactly! That young headache!"

"Premier, there's even more about Usk in the Holo-News," Itz-bel L(e^e) timidly said.

"Report!"

"Three days ago, Sol Rad., the Bella=Arth. Galactic Nest settled its longtime Line of Succession dispute, with a ritual combat, decision, and pact – upon Planet Usk!"

"Why there? That was never a Bella=Arth. world!"

"It was, however, where some Arth.-Matriarchy War battles were fought." She explained. "Natural forming structures much resembling the Arth. World Nests had been briefly used as fortifications. It was in one of those historic – and neutral ground – sites that the Line of Succession Pact was signed."

As she spoke, clips of the two Queens and their Retinues – including a Human male who resembled a skinny Arth. – was played.

"Which is which?" Cas'sio grumpily asked.

"Ami'da'lia, on your left, is now undisputed Queen. The new Dowager Queen, at screen right, will reside on Hesperia in their older, Cassiopeia Girder, embassy and grounds. She was a Cityzen in the past and she owns other valuable properties on Power Avenue."

"Naturally! They always do!"

"The Arth.s always had a way with Hesperian real estate. I wonder if she plays the 'Queens In Outer Space' Holo-Game?" Vinson asked.

"Probably better than I do," Cas'sio said, raising a chuckle.

"Usk was also in the news, two days following that historic pact," Itz-bel L(e^e) continued, "when three Human scientists from the New Center Worlds Academy on Philemon 16 Holo-Published their findings about the planet being the site of ancient stellar disaster of enormous proportions."

"I recall accessing that," Vinson broke in. "Amazing stuff, Premier! They'd been there on the planet for over two years, all in somewhat different fields, but intent on discovering how a rocky, desert-like planet like Usk could be the only world in an otherwise empty solar system with two gigantic stars, one of them billions of years old, the other star quite recent."

"Really? Do you know of this, Mer L(e^e)?"

"Yes, Premier, it has been on all the Science Holos. Approaching it from biological, geological, chemical and other viewpoints, the three scientists showed that Usk is the sole remaining world in what is believed to have at one time a single star solar system consisting of scores of populated planets and satellites. They're now estimating that five-score thousand years ago a completely differently-specied galactic empire existed, at a time when Humans and Delph.s were little more advanced than basic toolmakers. Their findings point out that somehow or other, their empire was destroyed when one of the gas giant planets became the blue star in the system."

"More than estimating," Vinson cut in. Who knew he'd taken up science in his later years. "They used various natural timing devices found as a result of thermal luminescence to quite accurately date when it happened. And they even found pieces of various other worlds that must have been shattered and are now embedded forcefully into the rockier sections of the planet."

"You mean we've got to worry about that too now, on top of everything else?" Cas'sio groaned, "B-5 planets going off as a star?"

"They believe it may have been done on purpose," Vinson said.

"Well, at least that's more like the Species I'm familiar with," Cas'sio said, "fiddling around until they mess it up utterly."

Itz-bel L(e^e) put a hand up to mouth to laugh prettily.

"So all that has happened recently on Usk," Cas'sio summed it up. "Now this work stoppage. What do of you know of it, Mer?"

"Here are some Inter. Gal. News Vids!" she announced.

"Who are those people picketing and marching? Are they Human?"

"They are Pamps. A non-indigenous race put on Usk seventeen generations ago. They now form its largest population group by far, as well as its entire work force."

The Premier shook his head. "Will Humans never learn to stop exploiting others?"

"For that matter," L(e^e) said, "will Delph.s never learn to stop exploiting other sea creatures?"

"You will have to bring me up to date on that some time, Mer L(e^e). Who's that Human, I'm seeing on all these Vids?"

"Don't you know?" Vinson asked. "He's infamous all over the Republic! That's the Pamp Messiah!".

"The what?"

"It's true, Premier. This young Human leads the pamp workers. So far they've shut down all the salt industries. All the other shipping. All the on-planet shipping ports. Even the three interstellar Fast and Slp.G liner ports."

"But why? What do they want?"

"What does anyone want?" Todd Vinson asked, bored by it all now. "Equal rights. Equal pay. Equal everything! Blah di Blah!"

"Mer L(e^e)," Cassio now asked. "How can we get hold of this so-called Pamp Messiah to talk to him?"

"That's the best part of it all," Vinson was now excited. "You and I can't. He'll only talk to Pamps. Better yet, he comes and goes like the wind, they say. He appears spontaneously in the middle of a little group of picketing workers, and within minutes, Sol Rad., it's a city-wide demonstration. He'll pop up at some little pamp eatery and suddenly it's a huge march demanding better working wages, threading an entire coastline of their ocean. He looks to be just another young Neo, yet he's untouchable, unreachable, undiscoverable."

"Surely fly-bys ..."

"Fly-bys hover over him and he vanishes. Only to appear in another place a half-hour later."

"Let me see him up closer!" Cas'sio said, and when he did, he thought, "By the Great Father!" Aloud he said, "I think I know him!"

"So do all of us when we see him. But *how* do we know him? From *where*?" Vinson wondered aloud.

Watching the lad stand forth so squarely and powerfully and raise one arm, shouting, exhorting the pamps, Cas'sio was almost certain he had seen him before. And not on any Holo-Vid, but close up, too. If he was correct, however, it was the very wildest of speculations. The Neo he knew had been a little exurban air-boarder, an infantile drunk and lay-about. Gorgeous enough to attract many sensible Virs and hadn't he tamed some un-bonded Thwwing from a great house's stable? But no, it was impossible. That Neo, that blonde, pale blue eyed, young Cherub couldn't have become this stalwart, brunet, fire-eyed zealot, could he? ... *Could he?*

"Tell me, did the Princeps Kell ever locate his great-grandson?" Cas'sio asked.

"I believe not," Vinson said. "I thought that Syzygy eventually abandoned the search."

"Mer L(e^e)? Do you know"

"Premier? That is also what I heard."

"You know how Mart is always looking to be useful to the Inner Quinx Council, Vinson? Why don't we send him to Usk? Give him a diplomatic mission to meet with this Pamp Messiah, and to negotiate with him. Or better yet, have Mart Kell bring him to the City and we'll meet with this new leader."

"You want to negotiate with him?" Vinson asked.

"Why *shouldn't* the little creatures have equal rights?" Cas'sio said, with a smile. "It won't cost the City much, and will make the Inner Quinx seem wonderfully beneficent to everyone watching the Holo-News."

"Mer L(e^e)? How would you like to come here to Hesperia? Your double uncle was right to recommend you. You're exactly the kind of young help I like to have on my personal staff."

She thanked him and the Holo-Comm. closed.

Their drinks were refreshed and Cas'sio made a note to his wrist connector to compare the two young Neos, physiologically and vocally, point by point. But by now, he was strangely certain who this new Uskian Rabble Rouser was, and he was secretly pleased, too.

"Speaking of how this planet Usk is always in the news and on people's tongues," Vinson said. "You're too young to remember when your own birthplace planet was all the talk of Hesperia, and when *it* was all the fashion, the flavor of the year."

"Pelagia?"

"Dryland they called it," Vinson said. "When you and all your

Ib'r family came here to the City, it was like a breath of fresh air. The Matriarchy had just collapsed, the City was dominant, the Three Species more united than ever, and Dryland was all the rage. Even my dear mother threw a gigantic "Save Pelagia's People" party. It was lovely, the maritime theme, the walls running constant Holo-Vids of the various places and all the biota there. So exotic! We even visited Pelagia, you know. You were no one in Hesperia in those days if you didn't go there at least once and bring back survivors and mementoes," Vinson reminisced.

Cas'sio let the older man go on and on, all but rambling.

With every second, he was more and more pleased by the way things had worked out, even the death of his grandniece down in Gerspellion's Girder that had briefly threatened to become a public-relations disaster on all kinds of levels. Of course it was clear to all that she had Cyberized herself beyond any medical necessity and that somehow had unhinged what was left of her Human mind, never mind her Human sympathies. John Laks and his Cyber Community Office had arrested another dozen all-Cyber compatriots of K'tina within a day and the picture they painted of the poor half-Mechano half-Human in their depositions was both pathetic and yet – instructive. Despite centuries of implanted and then genetically constructed wrist-connectors, and of intelligent machine companions, not to mention thinking travel-vessels of all sorts, there simply was a *limit* to how much Humans and Machines could meld and bond before some severe pathology set in. Even the most intelligent and assimilated Cybers remained in some way "other."

Yes, it was different with biological Species. Look at that Human male swanning about among those Royal Bella=Arth.s? Doubtless he was someone's lover and would join his Dowager Queen on Hesperia. Who knew but that he'd soon become a Personage one had to know. Yes, the Star Core-Rebellion Terrorists – as the Media had delightedly termed the Cyber group – had all the deliciousness of a ghastly threat, and all the relief of a tiny cult that few believed in – and best of all, that was soon ended.

Even luckier had been K'tina's outspoken exoneration of her uncle/lover in changing the mood of the people. If the Cadet had been the darling of the Media before, afterwards, his stock rose until it shot off the charts. Word had come back that he and his tiny little intrepid crew of spoiled rich socialites – Cas'sio had to say it: Neos barely past being debutantes – had found another star, even richer in Beryllium 18 than the City itself. What immense luck! They'd also found an entire new – or rather very old – civilization. On top of that, Holt was now exposed as the manipulated, and very publicly spurned, lover of a female in his own family! Mostly he'd gained sympathy for how he had been used by the madwoman, K'tina. From fears of Cyber-Terrorism, the Media had switched gears to Founder Family Incest, and they couldn't have been more pleased that the scandal was so juicy, and with so many unexpectedly melodramatic elements to it.

"Even with time restraints," Vinson was saying, "it was all the rage to go there to Pelagia and to come back with some lovely young Drylander for your own. Dozens of lads there were already impregnated. It was like having an instant Vir'istic family! What could be easier; or tonier? After all, that's how little bouncing Cas'sio arrived."

He reached out an aged hand and the two old friends smiled at each other.

Chapter Eleven

Double-day, both the blue Hunter and the orange Eagle risen and on either side of the meridian point straight above, with unexpected clouds floating low in the bowl of the port, providing eerie shadows of either violet or red orange above. Rings at twenty-five degrees above the Great Salt Ocean taking on those same eerie shadings:

Their headquarters was increasingly crowded, and Ay'r was beginning to think it attracted its newest pamp volunteers because of the free meals distributed twice a day.

That they had a headquarters at all was remarkable and a sign of how much they had accomplished so rapidly. That it was the site of the original work-stoppage was due to how corrupt that particular port warehouse had been. It turned out that its owner had criminal records on several star systems. Once his name came under the Media's scrutiny, he not only abandoned his property, he vanished altogether from Usk.

Seizing the opportunity, Merchant Esprio had offered to make good on all back pay and assume the current debts, and two days later, Sol Rad., he handed it over to Ay'r, Salt-Eluder and Sand-Drifter, the three of them officially heads of a new organization – The Pamp Reclamation Project on Usk. No doubt the owner's Human exploiter-minions had followed him. They and many accused of the worst offenses against the Pamps had fled the planet before the star ports went dark from lack of workers. But many others were holding fast, remaining out of sight, expecting the hurricane it to blow itself out.

That was the problem that PREP-USK now faced: how to keep the movement going in week three, and then how to keep everyone out of work busy. Now a new problem had developed, how to keep everyone fed and clothed. With a loss of weekly income – small as some of it had been – came some real hardship for the strikers and their families. Although they had been warned that was a cost they would need to bear, none of them in their enthusiasm had expected it to go this far or last this long, and few could in actuality bear it.

That was the main subject of the council Ay'r had called this afternoon in the workers' lunchroom, which had become PREP-USK's main office. Present were the three of them, Esprio, and from the South Salt Pan's new Pamp Communal Government, a newcomer, Barmiento, a name Salt-Eluder said meant essentially "Law-Reader" in older dialects. The southerner had arrived in a timely fashion and had carried with him a large donation from the group he represented.

Esprio had managed to collect another amount from other local businesses.

"It seemed that several of those of the Three Species I've done regular business with here in the Western Port were most sympathetic."

"Humans?" Ay'r was surprised.

"Humans yes. Merchants. Dock owners. Other business people. But it was the Bella=Arth.s who contributed the most. To our great surprise, as they have ever been a tight-palped lot in the past."

"I've always found Arth.s to be ... accommodating to myself. Good for them. So how do we stand, Sandy?"

Sand-Drifter had turned out to be amazingly good at figures, and once he'd learned the minor intricacies of working with the warehouse's old fashioned stable-Cybers, he'd become a whiz.

He spat out the numbers.

"How long will that last us all, assuming we'll have ten more pamps join us every day for a week here at headquarters," Ay'r asked.

"No more than a week."

"This Merchant Pamp will sell a business," Esprio offered.

"No, my friend, this Merchant Pamp had already been exceedingly generous. We need another resource. Sandy, what do I have left myself?"

"Nothing left of your and our pay from the *Arcturus Scatling* which we contributed. Nothing left of Professor Silberklang's pay to you, and us. Almost nothing of Captain Lepta's contribution."

That had been another surprise.

"Barmiento," Ay'r addressed him. "You are aware that I possess great holdings under my own name. You are an Ib'r Republic Approved Attorney-At-Law, can you advise me how I may transfer those funds over to PREP-USK?"

Barmiento seemed shocked. When he recovered his composure, he said, "is the Friend of the Pamps aware of the size of these holdings?"

"I'm afraid not. No. But I believe they are on public record."

"Indeed they are public and this Pamp Law-Reader accuses himself of the shameful act of accessing them before making this visit … Between the family holdings due to yourself from the three different Hesperian lines – Kell, Ib'r, and Sanqq' – as well as the substantial royalties from your birth father, Yuli Eise'nstein, as well as your annual payment as Adjudicator of Usk, my rough estimate is that your private holdings equal twenty times the Gross Planetary Product of Usk."

"Excuse me! I don't think I heard that correctly."

"I think Friend of the Pamps, you heard me quite well the first time. I was unable to factor in the Dower-Settlement as a result of your recent Betrothal to the Palaka Family Estate, but it might bring the total to about twenty one times the Gross Planetary Product of this planet."

Ay'r sighed.

"No, I suppose somewhere in the back of my mind I was aware of all that. I just never thought about it, being a foolish Neo with not a caring thought in his head for others until I met you people, and so it was immaterial. In fact, I was afraid it was that large. I believe I once chanced upon an annual, Sol Rad., royalty statement from my father's music alone and I found it …"

"Staggeringly large?" Barmiento asked.

"Let's just say there were a great many numbers. Of course, it's all untouchable, isn't it until a certain age? And none of it is liquid?"

"Incorrect. The annual Adjudicator's Fees are liquid and available upon signing a release form. It is by far the smallest portion," Barmiento slid a hand-held under Ay'r's eyes. "This is the current total amount available."

"I've no idea what it means," Ay'r moved his arm with the little mechano toward Sand-Drifter. "Sandy, how long will that last us here?"

Sand-Drifter calculated, "if we distributed among those here in the West, as well as to the South Salt Pan and Eastern Shore Communities, and to those at the Golden Palace resort area in need, it would last almost two months."

"Excellent. I've got to go sign that release. I take it," addressing Barmiento again, "that can't be done here, can it?"

"It must be withdrawn at the Golden Palace Resort or the Golden Palace Spaceport."

"Then I'm going to have to go there."

When the shouts and cries that he couldn't possibly go were over, Barmiento leaned forward again and said, "this Pamp Law-Reader took another unconscionable step and looked into the work-related statutes of the Adjudication Bureau."

"Terribly unconscionable," Ay'r said, with a laugh. "What did you find there?"

"I found there that while individual employers and business owners are free to make whatever arrangements they wish with individual and collective pamps, that should the Adjudicator decide upon new pay arrangements, those become law instantly and all must abide by them."

Silence greeted this news.

"Why the glum faces, pamp friends?" Ay'r said, "this is the best *possible* news."

At last Salt-Eluder spoke up. "We fear for your life. The Inter. Gal. News only today said that the Princeps Mart Kell has been appointed to come here to Usk to meet with this council. He is your greatest enemy. You must never meet him."

"Never!" the others echoed.

"No, of course, you're right. I can never meet him. But won't our way of me disappearing and Big Pamp One and Big Pamp Two taking my place and going in separate vehicles to throw off the Media, also work with him?"

The others grumbled.

"They have identi-guns," Esprio said, out loud. "Only you will be the bullet's target. Even if there are fifteen Big Pamps disguised as you."

"I'll take Eis. He won't shoot at the baby."

The Pamp's grumbling continued but none dared contradict him.

"It is the only answer," Barmiento said to them, "realistically."

"Then we will go with you," Salt-Eluder avowed.

"You two have to stay here and keep the work stoppage going. Merchant Pamp Esprio must go East and keep those pamps in the loop. Barmiento is now our official envoy to the south and will assure them we will not waver in our efforts."

"No, I will lay out the exact steps and access the exact documents needed to do this. There is no Law-Reader I trust in the Golden Palace Space Port, well enough versed or used to dealing with Humans, and so unafraid of them. I will go South as you wish, but only *after* I have ensured that it is all legally accomplished."

"And I will go East, only *after* I have seen you safe." Esprio declared.

That said and agreed upon, Ay'r broke up the meeting.

Later on that afternoon, he came upon Sand-Drifter and Salt-Eluder upbraiding Barmiento, but the little Law-Reader stood firm.

"How could you ever leave him willfully? Surely, you cannot love Him as we do?" Salty accused.

"I love him as My Savior," and Barmiento made a little flicking gesture with a forefinger across his chin that Ay'r recalled seeing before among the pamps, done in his honor. "But I love myself, too, as he has taught us all to do. We one work for each other, re-call you." Then he stalked away, leaving the others stunned.

I like the little Law-Reader, Ay'r thought. He's smart and he's tough too. He'll go places. Then, of course, he realized that he himself would now have to be smarter and tougher than he'd ever been. He might still be a Neo, but fate was making him a Man.

It had been a long and almost treacherously difficult journey getting to the Golden Palace Resort area. Merchant Esprio's fly-by was one of the fastest and yet it had required half a day, and they had twice been stopped and searched by off-world, official "Hesperian Resort World" fly-bys – a new police force that he was certain was the Princeps' doing – as well as questioned by others.

Twice, Ay'r had to convince his wrist-connector to pretend again that he was Bissel Ter-Morgen. By the second time, it didn't even put up much of an argument against doing so, and he had to wonder how he would have to *uncorrupt* the built-in tiny Cyber when he was once more safe and life was back to normal.

Whatever normal might mean? Whenever normal might happen?

Naturally, Esprio had contacts within the pamp community living only a few thousand meters from the Golden Palace, and Ay'r had been able to leave little Eis there among some suddenly imposed upon, fortunately quite awed, local Pamps who had a shop in the Great Mart. They and Esprio would watch over the baby. For his part, Eis was growing well, seemed to enjoy the travel he'd been subjected to since birth, and – the Cyber-Womb assured Ay'r – he would be ready to post-part at least a month sooner than expected, yet another reason to consider his son to be prodigious.

On foot, Ay'r had made his way here to the Palace, surprised that no more Palace Guards remained outside on the grounds – doubtless they thought him long gone or dead. And the truth was, except for him, the place was pretty much impregnable to outsiders when it was locked down.

Who else would have known how to get in, and so easily? He'd lived here how long ago? Six months ago? It seemed more like six *years!* At times, like *sixty years!* The Golden Palace was darkest at this hour of the night, and, most of the people inside, sleeping. Not to mention Ay'r had done exactly this, scores of times before.

Unless, of course, things had changed?

No, there was the kitchen's extra vent left ever so slightly ajar, as always. He opened it more, and slid his hand inside and had his wrist connector check for any possible new devices there or on the immediate other side, detectors or alarms. It reported nothing new.

So he crept in through the kitchen vent the way he always had when he'd been out at night, air-boarding, long past midnight, Sol Rad. And there, where he had left it, in the second pantry, was his extra air-board.

He grabbed it and instantly slung it over his shoulder. He always felt more in charge, somehow, with a board hung on his side. Using it to get away doubled his chances of escape. It being where he'd left it, was one of the very few reasons it was good to be back.

Seconds later, he had crept past where the kitchen pamps slept, and out into the main hallway. He remembered the code to shut off the alarm system, and he spoke it. There was a chance that it had been since altered. But no.

"Welcome, Lord Kell," it responded.

"No. Do not inform *anyone* that I am here," he responded. "Do you understand?"

"I do understand. As usual, you do not wish to waken your 'Tutes."

"My 'Tutes? Oh, right. Especially that perli-pig Narfacan'ni. But tell *no one* I'm here."

"Understood."

He was out in the clear now, a few steps up the glide-ramp to the main corridor.

Where was it that Barmiento had told him to go? The second main office. To be acknowledged there, someone would be needed to notarize his signatures. He'd have to alert the in-palace Vid system too, because the attorney had told him he would need to have Vid-proof of the signings as well. He had brought a change of clothing, naturally, and on the way here in the fly-by he'd had to strip his hair of its dark coloring and to change his eye color back too. For this to work now, he must look like the other Ay'r, the old Ay'r, and he wasn't certain that was what he wanted to look like at all, ever again. But for this one time, of course, it was absolutely required.

The office he needed was open and empty. Check! Now the attorney.

He suddenly heard the lightest of footsteps in the corridor and froze. They had discussed this possibility in detail: what to do if someone tried to stop him. His first choice was to use his hands and feet fighting skills, which if they worked, would be the quietest. If that failed, he had a small stun weapon.

He remained still and listened intently.

Suddenly he heard a low, familiar voice: "Many months ago a Human Neo used to come home this late, and this quietly, and always Dustweed, alone of all the palace staff, heard his footsteps and would sleep easily – only afterward."

The pamp showed himself in the light, dressed in sleep wear

"Dustweed! Yes. It is me. Ay'r. But we must not waken anyone else. Especially not any of the 'Tutes or Guards."

"There are none. And no pamps either, aside from myself."

"Because I left?"

"No. Because we are on a work-stoppage. For equal pay," Dustweed declared.

"Oh, Dustweed. I am so proud of you."

"Of me? We are all so proud of *you!*"

"But if you're on a work stoppage, then ...?"

"Silly Dustweed. He is afraid that if no one remains here at all, that strangers will come. Looters and, you know, bad people."

"So you do support the equal pay and equal rights for pamps?"

"With my heart and soul."

"Good, my old friend. We will need you now. Do you have your palace identification? You'll need that."

"Why?"

"Because you are about to become a part of the history of Planet Usk. I need a witness. Will you be my witness?"

"If it is for you and good for the pamps? Then, naturally, this pamp would be happy to be part of it."

"You're certain no one else will come?"

"Dustweed noticed how you have disabled the palace alert system – as usual. So no one *should* come."

"You're right. We must remain cautious. Go now, get what is needed and meet me at the Adjudicator's Office on the bottom floor."

A few minutes later, Barmiento was exactly where he said he would be standing – or rather hiding – outside the doorway to the servants' entrance, and he slipped inside. Even in the dark, and wearing his hood, his funny little face, oh so serious, the Law-Reader was instantly recognizable.

Quickly they were in the Adjudicators' Office and a minute later, they heard a tap on the door and Dustweed appeared, all dressed up in what Ay'r recognized must be his best clothes, looking very proud and excited too.

Ay'r used his voice to alert the Palace that it must now sound-proof and lock the office they were in and allow no one else in, no one at all, for any reason whatsoever until he said it could be unlocked again. Did it understand?

He had already determined that even if he were found out, this way he would get the law signed and the money released. That could not be undone, once it was accomplished.

Barmiento removed his hood, and Ay'r his, and he changed clothing so he would look formal, and they requested the Palace's

Vid system turn on and provide them with official Adjudication Financial Schemata and also an Adjudication Ceremony, with Witnessing and Video Confirmation.

It understood and did so.

The attorney lifted his hand-held up and the Vid-cam downloaded the information it contained. After a few seconds, the Palace's built-in Cyber provided a Holo-Grid and the data was visible.

"This is all the back fees earned since age twelve, Sol Rad., at which time he assumed the position of Adjudicator of Usk, of one Ay'r Eise'nstein-Kell," the Holo revealed. "Wrist connection i.d. is required, along with corneal, finger and voice print i.d., in order to release the sum."

Ay'r stepped into the grid and spoke his name.

"Please confirm that the full amount is to be released to the account that has been provided."

"Release the full amount immediately," Ay'r spoke.

That done, Barmiento asked for a second Adjudication Ceremony, this time for a statutory matter. The hand-held that he lifted up to be scanned provided the several pages of the new law to the Vid-screen.

Ay'r had to step forward and i.d. himself again. This time, he made a small speech: "In light of the problems recently brought to light to this Adjudicator, at the Great Western Port, at the South and North Salt Pans, as well as the star ports at those locations, and lately by many different locations, and plaintiffs across Resort Planet Usk regarding illegal bonding contracts, unequal wages, unequal social conditions, unsustainable living conditions, unequal legal, medical, and many other matters, it is the finding of the Adjudicator's Office that a new statute be put into effect immediately outlawing essence based contractual bonding of any kind, outlawing discrimination or inequality of any kind, in any area, for any species or subspecies, whether recognized or not by the Ib'r Republic Quinx Council, upon this world. What now follows is a detailed method by which grievances may be made, addressed and resolved, and fines, and punishments to be levied against any and all who break this new law."

He waited while the Vid-screen flashed on all the various parts and their variations. When it was done, he spoke again:

"Signed by Adjudicator, Ay'r Eise'nstein-Kell. Witnessed by ..."

He gestured Barmiento and Dustweed forward, and they witnessed the law.

A few seconds were required for Vid-screen to process it all.

"Statute seven hundred and thirty seven is now the law of Resort World Usk. As per statute two hundred and six, this new statute and its ceremony has been confirmed and sent out to all interested parties, on world or off. Lord Kell, the ceremony is complete."

With those words, the Holo-Grid shut down, the Vid-screen went blank and the office doors were unlocked, and its sound unblocked.

Ay'r was so elated he wanted to break out an ancient flask of Live Desert Sherry he knew was kept in the room for just such a ceremony. In fact, he'd uncorked it and was spilling it into the flat little drinking spouts, when they heard the distinctive sound of a fly-by.

"Palace, what is that fly-by?"

"A Media fly-by is landing on the front lawn. Yes. It had identified itself as the Usk Daily Holo-News."

"You alerted the Media?"

"As per the law, yes. Whenever any new planetary statute is put into effect."

The three quickly downed the sherry.

"I've got to get out of here," Ay'r said, clutching the air board. "I know how. You two go meet the Media at the front entrance. Stall them as long as possible, Barmiento, and only when they insist upon seeing me, will you let them into the room and have the Vid-system replay the entire thing showing me. Insist on making sure that they know all of the law and all of its parts and variants."

Barmiento said: "You cannot remain in this area at all. This one Media will be followed by dozens more and they will scour the Golden Palace and surroundings."

"I know. Keep them very busy. Go!"

"Dustweed, you are in charge of the Palace now. Palace, did you hear that Dustweed is now the Golden Palace manager?"

"This Palace acknowledges Dustweed in charge."

"Dustweed, the Law-Reader will advise you what to do and say," Ay'r went on, to the house pamp. "I'm sorry to thrust you both into the spotlight like this but remember the more that the both of you do and say now with the Media, the more time I will have to get away."

"Understood!" and Dustweed almost rammed his head into Ay'r's solar plexus in emotion. When he pulled away, his head was averted. "Return safely. This is your home."

Once out the kitchen vent, Ay'r leapt atop his air-board, and was over the wall, out into the intricately patterned walkways of The Jobim Pebble Garden. Minutes later, Ay'r had cleared the higher restraining walls – enjoying the fact that he hadn't lost his touch – and he was out on the nighttime sands of Golden Palace Resort Desert Cove. He knew this cove so well that he was able to pull off and onto the shoreline, exactly at the rough dwelling where he'd left Esprio and Eis.

"It's done!" he announced once inside. "Now we must go."

The Merchant pamp had been sitting around a low table finishing a meal with his hosts. He stood up to leave.

"I must leave. But not you, my great friend," Ay'r said. "The Media were automatically alerted the very second the new statute became law. The Law-Reader and an old friend of mine are fending them off at the Palace. But quickly enough your fly-by outside will be surrounded. You must waste their time with as much official sounding nonsense as you can and also lead them away from me."

Esprio was disturbed. "But where will you go?"

"I've got the air-board. I'll go out into the Salt Ocean with it."

To his hosts he said, "I'll need water pills and dried provisions for a week, gratitude for all."

Again, to Esprio, "the womb is set to run on solar power and so the baby will be cared for no matter what."

"A week?" the Merchant said.

"At the longest. I'm heading west. As soon as you feel clear and unwatched, come and look for me. But not a moment before. Don't worry. I know these bays and coves well – I've air-boarded them all the way up till the Great Corridor, and on the Arcturus Scatling, I've had some experience with that. Ask Dustweed, the Palace manager. He'll tell you. And if there is any danger you are being followed at all, you must stay away."

"The Media!" Esprio sneered.

"Where the Media goes, my enemy will follow," Ay'r reminded him.

"But out on the ocean? All alone! With a baby!"

"By day, the solar glare is so strong reflecting off the silica of the sand, it will easily confuse any identi-guns. You see, I wasn't sleeping all the way here!"

"Even so, letting you leave like this breaks my poor pamp heart."

"Your *enormous* pamp heart, friend Esprio."

The provisions were brought, and the baby's womb was slung across Ay'r's back by several strong cords.

"No long good-byes. Gratitude all. You are free and equal now," Ay'r said. "No matter what happens to me and the baby, you all have new lives."

Then he was off on the air-board.

A few minutes later, he was skittering onto the cove sands. Above him, Usk's rings were still high, but moving further apart every day, and with every day they glittered more like a rainbow. They barely lighted the night sands but it was enough for him to see by.

When he looked back once, he could see the lights of the Media fly-bys, now by the dozens, hovering around the still dimly lit domes and turrets of the Golden Palace, like sand-flies around some dead and bloated body.

Soon enough, even that unwelcome sight was beyond the horizon, and as he air-boarded along, Ay'r felt wonderful. He'd achieved so much, so unexpectedly, and for the benefit of so many others. His chest swelled with pride and joy at how he'd been allowed to be the instrument of such important changes. He began to sing, at first quietly and then when he saw he was utterly alone on the Great Salt Ocean, Ay'r sang loudly, and what came out of him was a surprise, very old songs, the first songs he'd heard and learned, anthems his father had written in his short lifetime and that Ay'r had heard all his life and that he'd never much thought of before, but which now made the greatest sense, and held the most significance for him.

When he was done singing, the sands were already being dyed paler and paler blue by the Hunter, rising behind him, It was magnificent, the blue tint spreading to the cliffs and reefs, to every corner of the Great Salt Ocean.

He passed the Cliff of Sighs, where his mother and father had died leaping together to be together. Those wonders of parents! He saluted them.

Ay'r air-boarded westward, never dawdling.

After a while, in the great morning silence, Ay'r could swear he could hear Little Eis gurgling, even through the solidity of the womb. Perhaps he too was happy to be moving again, to be with his mother again, and perhaps he too was now singing.

Something was seriously wrong, the fly-bys had begun to appear about three hours ago, Sol Rad., and they hadn't just flown off but had begun circling. Ay'r was hunkered down beneath the over-hang of a reef, invisible to them, he was certain. He'd settled here quite suddenly when the flying machines with their bronze and jade markings had begun to arrive. It was now several hours later, and he'd not been able to move. It was just past double sunset, the best time for him to travel. Although it was the third day he and baby Eis had been out here, all had gone well. The food and water pills were spacing out well. The baby was happy, and sleeping. Now this had come along to slow him down, to stop him.

Ay'r checked his wrist connector. It insisted it was not broadcasting on any level. He then had it check the post-partum womb and it reported that it had dampened whatever faint operational signal that mechano might be exporting. What else could be giving them away? Why were the Princeps fly-bys circling in this kilometer or so of ocean, as if they knew he was here, somewhere?

"Damnation to Princeps Mart Kell. If I ever come face to face with that ancient heap of lies and crimes, we'll soon discover who's a real Kell and who's the pretender."

Not two seconds later, the sand began to shuffle and rise only a few meters away.

He felt an entity tel'ping him.

"Is this the same Human who referred to myself as a 'varlet antipy'!"

He remembered the creature from so many months ago, "is it you?!"

"Indeed. Is this the same Human who was so stingy with essences."

"So stingy, that you took one essence yourself, you thieving little antipy!" Ay'r said. "What are you doing so far from home?"

"This is my home. Where we played, before the Great

Exchange of Rings and Suns, that was new territory. Who is this small Human inside the oval box?"

"This is my offspring, little antipy. Come closer and you may look inside the box. His name is Eis and he is as brave and friendly as his mother."

"You keep calling me 'little antipy'" it tel'ped, then rose next to him, shocking him with its huge size.

"Careful with the baby," Ay'r called. "How did you grow so large?"

"I grew to full. As is normal."

A limb, with – he had to suppose – sensors of some visual kind, looked into the transparent top side of the womb and the baby reached out to it.

"A very small Human."

"He is not yet born. Two more months, I'm told."

"Yet a very active and aware Human."

"Isn't he beautiful?"

"Will he sand-skate like his parent?"

"Some day. Not for a few years. Sol Rad."

"My friends are nearby. Will this Human show them how Humans sand-skate."

"I can't right now. Can you see and hear those fly-bys" he pointed up.

"The noise-makers, yes, the Human air-machines."

"Right. I cannot sand-skate until they are gone."

The antipy disappeared under the sand.

It returned another hour later.

"The noise-makers remain in place," it tel'ped.

"I noticed."

"Those air-Humans are not friends and family."

"No! They are the opposite of that. They wish to harm me."

The antipy seemed to consider that. Then, "there is a way to travel without the noise-makers knowing."

"Really? How?"

"Under the sand. As antipys travel."

"Humans cannot travel that way. We need to breathe."

The antipy seemed to consider. It went away and then returned after a short while.

"Older and wiser antipys have been consulted. If the Human and its offspring wish to travel, this antipy and its friends will help it."

"Under the sand?"

"Yes."

"I already told you, Humans can't ..."

"You will breathe. We will require a good amount of at least one essence."

"Go on ..."

"The almost clear essence from the Human lower spout will do."

"That's possible. But how?"

"Four antipys together can use that to make a temporary wet shelter for the Human and offspring."

"A bubble?" Ay'r sketched in the sand, himself with a bubble around him.

"A bubble. Yes."

"How does that work?"

"The older and wiser antipy did not tell us how. Only that it does work. Humans stranded out on the sands are rescued by antipys in this fashion all the time. And then cast up on shore to be found.

"I thought that was just a legend. What about my offspring?"

"The box can travel as well inside the bubble, if you hold it."

"Can we try it out first? With just me? And only a short distance? Say to that line of rock columns?"

He placed the womb deeper in the shadow of the reef overhang, and carefully moved out onto the sand about two meters. Rapidly, the four full-sized antipys gathered around him.

"Now donate the essence."

Ay'r urinated into the sand and it vanished down into a tiny spiral at his feet. There was a great deal of activity swirling about down there and suddenly the sand was all sucked away and instead there were four Antipy limbs. Ay'r gingerly stepped onto them, was grasped and pulled down suddenly. He didn't know how but he was breathing perfectly well and indeed some sort of bubble was being held around him. They let his head remain high enough that he could see at the very edge of the surface of the sands. Thus he could see that they were moving very rapidly. When they stopped, he was lifted up gently enough to see where they'd taken him, and where the reef now was, far behind.

"That was fun!"

"For us too!" the antipy tel'ped.

Take me back now," he said, and again was pulled down and brought back over to where Baby Eis was. There he lifted the womb to his chest. "Gratitude for helping me travel under the sand. But won't the noise-makers not notice it from above?"

"They will merely see at it as the tracks of a big, older antipy."

"How long can we travel like this?"

"On this bubble, many hundreds of times the distance we just traveled."

"That might be enough." He held the transparent side of the womb up to his face. "Here we go! We're ready!" Ay'r said, and they were pulled down again.

They traveled three times, in three separate bubbles that he helped them make, over another four hours, before Ay'r was lifted out of the sands and onto a reef.

It was deepest night. But looking about, he could see that where they had landed was now the Sea of Glass. Even at night, the turbulence all about them was clear. Even this close to the shoreline, the air was a swirling series of little dusters, and to the south, as far as he could see, the storms were growing huge.

"These antipys may travel no further," his old friend tel'ped.

"I understand," Ay'r said. "These sands look too dangerous. Will you be able to get back to you home safely?"

"Antipys dive deeply in the sands to travel. We will be safe. But the Human must leave the ocean and take to the shore."

"I see that. What about noise-makers?"

"They were above the four antipy friends and their Human friends until the last donation. The Human must remain careful on the shore."

"Take a little more essence, all of you," Ay'r said.

"Essences we have had enough of ... Will you show the antipy friends how you skate the sands?"

"Yes. It's safe here to do that. I'll 'skate' to that shore with the two cliffs! But how will I know how to call you again?"

"Ask for 'The Human's little varlet antipy.' Already that is becoming a legendary name as is this travel we have done – legendary among the Ocean's northern antipys."

"I will. Come on, Little Eis," he said, strapping the womb onto his back.

He air-boarded across the flat, strangely undulating, oddly colored sands, swooping to make figure eights and leaps and even sudden stops, as he'd done many months before.

"Amazing. Wonderful!" he heard several of the antipys tel'ping their pleasure.

But as he reached the cliffs he realized that it had taken all of his skill to perform for them in these odd, ever moving, quite treacherous sands. He would now have to go on foot until he cleared this stormy area.

Luckily, no fly-bys had dared to enter the Sea of Glass, where aviation hallucinations and delusions were as known to be as frequent as maritime ones. But that meant that Esprio also couldn't pick him up. He still had remaining almost four days' food and water pills. And it was still several hours to sun up and he was quite rested. He stopped and found a rock overhang and there fed himself and sang to Baby Eis. His wrist connector had only the most general of maps for this area, most of it was still uncharted, even with the distinctive double cliffs as a landmark. He was able to tell that he was at least halfway to the Great Western Port, and roadways of a sort existed north of where he sat munching dry perli and waving it in front of the baby.

Soon, he slung the air board on one side, and secured the womb in front where he could look at the baby, and he was walking, hiking, climbing the rocks and hills with only the light from the rings to guide him.

"Oh, Baby Eis, you are going to have the most interesting womb-time any Human infant in Usk history ever had! Long before you will talk, you will have had so many adventures that you lived through, and so many stories to tell!"

The road had led nowhere, seemingly, ending at farmsteads long abandoned.

Ay'r and the baby spent the warmest part of the double-sun-day in one of them, sheltered from the heat and surprising winds too, and then long before the two suns set he awakened, ate something, bored by the limited choice now, and then played "Peekaboo" with Eis through the transparent lid of the womb. How sensory-aware Eis was becoming.

As the day cooled down, Ay'r once more took to the hills. He'd chosen the highest one facing west so he might see how close to any Ocean cove they might be.

The glittering sands were almost like some delusion of a desert, they were so distant. It turned out to be a long hike down, only with difficulty picking his way.

As night fell, Ay'r slid the air-board into the steady-looking sands, rearranged the womb onto his back, and joyfully took off. Although they made much progress, he still couldn't make out to the right the line of rising cliffs that would tell him they were nearing the Great Western Port. Those cliffs would rise hundreds of meters away on this side, as they had on the other one he'd ascended with Salt-Eluder. He found himself wondering how Salty and Sandy, Esprio and all the others were doing without him. In his heart, Ay'r knew that besides fleeing and not endangering any others in his flight, that another, equally important reason he'd charted his return to them this slower way was so the pamps would begin to manage without him. They already knew what to do or else would figure it out. They already had the skills, or would soon express them. Only his absence was required for that to happen.

Around Hunter-dawn – spreading the pale blue illumination for at least an hour, Sol Rad., before the Eagle rose, he began to hear, and then to see fly-bys, at first distant and then closer.

He stopped and rested, hidden from sight, but then calculated his resources. He had two days of water pills and less than a day of dried food. He'd been out past a week, and had been scrimping, but the more the fly-bys surrounded him, the more he would have to hide and draw out this trek.

He slept then but was awakened suddenly and not long after.

The noise was of fly-bys landing – two or more – were close enough to be a threat. All he could do was hide. He hated hiding.

He still couldn't hear voices, but soon they too would arrive. Somehow he'd been located. He didn't know how. After all this … it was unbearable.

"Wrist-connector, I need help. This is where I am located. What can I do to escape?"

"Whistle for a Thwwing," it replied.

"What?" It was such an outlandish thing for a Cyber of any size to say, an old Usk folk saying, for what was nearly impossible, "like whistling for a Thwwing."

"There are several Thwwing stables nearby, including Hesperian ones."

Ahh! Now it made some sense.

"You know how to ride a Thwwing? Or not?"

"You know I do," Ay'r sneered.

"You must get to higher ground, and do it."

"Can a Thwwing out-fly a fly-by?" Ay'r asked and knew the answer. It could fly up *higher* than any fly-by. "What about that whistle?"

"Once you are on the hill, begin with your own whistle, and then this wrist connector will modulate it to be heard by Thwwings."

"This is perfectly insane. I've done things to compromise and possibly harm you. For which I am deeply sorry." Ay'r said.

"To the contrary. This wrist-connector has learned much, so much it has sought out knowledge on its own. It believes that this is the only safe course."

The air-board slung over one shoulder, the baby strapped on tightly in front, Ay'r tried to stay as low as possible, moving through crevices, fissures and arroyos the wrist-connector pointed out, yet rising, always rising. He could hear Human voices now on several sides around him, and when he lifted his head, he could see them like ants, in their bronze and jade uniforms, in the distance all about him, searching.

He couldn't say how long it was before the wrist-connector said, "now. Take this left-hand path to a high hill."

Ay'r kept low, but once he'd arrived, he could see where he was, very high, yet all around him distantly were the ant-like Humans, searching.

"Begin to whistle. Try to intone 'Thwwing! Your master calls. Thwwing come to my call'."

Ay'r did so, feeling foolish, and worse, feeling exposed.

Nothing happened. Then he whistled again, and this time he heard how the wrist-connector was modulating his sound until it fell out of his range of hearing. Little Eis still heard it however and he began crying.

Ay'r didn't know how long he stood there before someone searching noticed him. Then they all did and were pointing and staring and some even starting towards him. They were literally closing in, and he was thinking, how can I save Little Eis? How can

I keep him from falling into their hands? When two things happened. One fly-by took off from the ground, and headed toward him, so that he thought, I've got to hide now. And then something flew past him so fast all he could make out was the glitter of iridescent wings.

"A Thwwing," his wrist-connector confirmed. The legends say that now you must stand tall and whistle it down."

His heart pounding, fear racing through his veins, the instinct to get away almost unceasing, Ay'r stood and whistled: "Thwwing! Your master calls. Thwwing come to my call."

Twice more he whistled and now the closest fly-by was only forty yards away, looking for a site safe from turbulent winds to hover, so the men inside could drop out, when suddenly a giant Thwwing alit in front of Ay'r and came right up to him. In the clear light he easily made out the cross-striping around the Thwwing's abdomen, a deep green against the paler chitin chartreuse.

"Why? I believe I know this Thwwing!" Ay'r said, in pleased surprise. "I believe I once rode this Thwwing. You're Jafarra, aren't you?"

The way it was using its palps and long front antennae to lift his tunic and cape and to snake into his trousers was quite familiar. Ay'r took off his tunic and the palps ranged all about him.

"You do remember me, Jafarra? Don't you? My body is familiar to you."

He moved to the side of the head-high creature and tapped on its side wing the way he remembered someone (was it Al'wyn?) doing it before.

To his surprise, the canopy sprung open.

"Excellent! But first we have to stow away Little Eis."

Another and now another fly-by was nearing the hilltop, all of them juddering in the turbulent winds, looking for sites from which they could drop men to scramble out.

Ay'r pulled off the straps holding the womb, and tapped the spot he recalled behind one huge, iridescent wing. It opened and he stuffed the womb in there, kissing Eis' transparent faceplate. Then he tapped for it to shut again.

Around him not fifty yards away, Humans in uniform had begun dropping to the ground. He heard shouts and the sizzles of stun shots.

Ay'r undressed, threw his clothing into the other space

beneath the other wing, then climbed it and leapt into the canopy. A stun bolt sizzled past as the canopy shut.

Inside, the creature folded itself about his arms and legs and midsection, sliding odd tissues all around and over his body. He had that slightly drugged sense he recalled, and then snapped to.

"Jafarra!" he thought. "We must take off now! Fly!"

Nothing for a second and he was about to repeat the command when he found himself in the air. In seconds they were up and rising, and now the fly-bys came closer, and Ay'r said, "Jafarra, we must fly fast forward. As fast and as high as we can go."

It happened so quickly he almost lost consciousness.

But the fly-bys were keeping up. Through the transparent canopy, he could see them rising, rising to meet the Thwwing.

In those minutes of ascent, he gained more and more of his full awareness and remembered what Thwwing-racing was all about: clearly tel'ped orders and fancy maneuvering. The best riders were those who could draw circles around their competition and still go fast to win.

"Jafarra, do you remember the ring at the Golden Palace Resort Track?" he commanded with his mind. "Fly that same oval now."

One fly-by had to scramble to get out of the Thwwing's way, as it twisted and turned only a few meters away from the rotors, rising higher and higher.

"Good, Jafarra!" Ay'r commanded. "Now a spiral, the way we did before. A big corkscrew spiral, aiming at the rings."

In no time he felt the Thwwing's huge, feather-light body bank as it rose higher and higher.

He could see the fly-bys below, dropping behind, and bunching together.

He was afraid they would operate bigger stun-guns and aim at the Thwwing itself. And sure enough, he could see the nasty orange-dotted light signifying that they were trying to stun the creature.

"Execute random flight," he commanded.

The next few minutes were easier, then the orange dotted lines of stun-shot began closing in, even crossing lines ahead. Soon, he'd be in their direct path, and then what, destruction? How much stun could a Thwwing take? He didn't know, and was fearful not for the animal or for himself as much as for Little Eis, there behind him, barely half a meter.

He could see the dimly brilliant, partial ellipse of the Rings ahead. They were very high now, but would they be out of range of the stun shot?

Suddenly one dotted line went right by the side of the carapace, and Ay'r knew the Thwwing had been hit. It didn't falter. But another shot on the other side said that its attempt at randomness wasn't sufficient to elude them. The fly-bys could pin it between them.

"We've got to go down, Jafarra. Take a random-pattern spiral-drop."

He watched as the bottommost layer of the Rings of Usk rainbowed so close above him, before the Thwwing's flight shifted and it began to arch down.

The fly-bys couldn't keep up with Jafarra's descending speed and so they made a great distance between him and them, Ay'r tilting as close westward as he could, until below, during one tilting spiral, he could see the huge, long-dried-up delta of the Great Western Port ahead.

They would land behind the port city. He knew those hills a bit and might find a way to elude the fly-bys on foot.

Soon they were spiraling down and then the Thwwing was certainly looking for a landing spot.

He could get out and draw the fly-bys and tell it to fly off with Little Eis to safety. No. Not that. He couldn't bear being parted from him now.

He'd have to take his chances with Eis.

As suddenly as it did everything, the Thwwing settled onto on a little flat plateau. When the carapace opened, it looked like the area where the Birthing Station had been.

Ay'r hopped out, put on his clothing and retrieved the womb. Eis was fast asleep. During all that!

"Go to safety at the stable now," he instructed the Thwwing and it palped him, wrapped one antenna around his head and then took off straight up, and shot away.

Two fly-bys chased it.

Then two more fly-bys arrived, chasing those. Only these new ones weren't bronze and jade. But gold and aqua. Whose colors? No! It couldn't be!

Two more bronze and jade fly-bys were sent spinning out of control by stun shots from two more gold and aqua ones behind them.

One of the latter turned about and came to hover above the little plateau.

Ay'r had slung on the baby and the air-board and had dropped into a fissure and he was slithering along it as quickly as possible.

Suddenly he heard an amplified voice:

"Please stop. I've come to rescue you."

He stopped.

"We've sent them away. They won't be back. Please come up so I can see you."

No question about it, it was Deon Syzygy.

"I couldn't leave you a third time!" he heard the contriteness in the voice. "Ay'r?"

Ay'r turned to the baby still snoring away. "Well, son, this is either the worst decision or the best decision of my life."

He lifted himself out of a fissure and onto the rock face, and then slid higher and higher.

"There you are!" relief was clear in Deon's voice.

Seconds later the new colored fly-by landed and a door slid open. Deon tumbled out, ran to Ay'r, and then seeing him waiting, Deon stood still.

"They wouldn't have hurt you. They only wanted the baby."

"I would have never let them have the baby. They would have had to kill me first."

"I thought as much," Deon answered.

"Which do *you* want?" Ay'r asked.

"You! No, the *both* of you! Get in! I don't like to see you exposed like this."

"Wait! What did you mean? You couldn't let me go a third time?"

"The first time was at the Palace. The second time was in the port city, when you were disguised."

"So you *did* know it was me at the port!" Ay'r said.

"I only let you go then, because I'd found out what He wanted, only knew then why he was after you??"

"The Princeps?"

"The Princeps!"

"And he doesn't want it anymore?" Ay'r asked.

"Who cares what the Princeps wants?" Deon said clearly. "Anyway he's not a threat any longer."

"Why not?"

"He's vanished somewhere on this planet. Two days ago, Sol Rad., he came here somewhere, to this area west of the port up here in the hills, drawn by what he had been told was you, surrendering."

"I've never had any contact with him!" Ay'r said. "Not since the Betrothal ceremony."

"Anyway, since then, he's simply ... vanished."

"But they!" Ay'r pointed at the now distant fly-bys, "kept looking for me!"

"That's why I shall politely ask again, will you get into my own personal vehicle?"

"One thing more. Do you see my baby, Eis!"

Deon looked at the womb. "Eis, short for Eise'nstein? After your father?"

"Yes. What do you think of him? Doesn't he look like the Princeps?"

"Babies ... I don't know. He looks like you," Deon said.

"Like me?"

"He looks like you and I want to adopt him."

"Adopt him? How?"

"As soon as you break off your Betrothal to the Palaka female and you and I announce our Betrothal, in front of the entire Quinx Council. Tomorrow, Sol Rad."

"You've got it all thought out then?" Ay'r asked.

"I've had plenty of time to think it all out."

They looked at each other. "Can we go?" Deon said. "They might all head back here shooting and ..."

"*I knew* you knew." Ay'r nodded toward the port. "Down there!"

"*I knew* you knew I knew. That's what made it so difficult to leave," Deon said.

"He's a wonderful baby," Ay'r said.

"He must be – if he's ours." Deon said.

"The Princeps is really gone?"

"Vanished!"

"But not for good?"

"If he returns, he'll be charged with felony crimes against

you. If he knows what's good for him, he'll remain gone for good!"

"Why did he do it in the first place?" Ay'r asked.

"It's a long and weird story and it's a short Fast Jump to the Ophiuchus Girder on Hesperia. That is where the Syzygy estates are located. Your new home. You wanted to live in the City, remember?"

Ay'r looked around, "but I'll have to come back here often."

"Because it's so uniquely beautiful? As I've discovered coming here so much for your sake?"

"Yes, and because of all my friends here."

"When I first met you, you told me that you had no friends here." Deon said.

"That was six months ago ... Now I have millions of friends."

"And a few enemies too."

Ay'r took Deon's hand and they climbed on board the fly-by.

Chapter Twelve

The Media surrounded the Fast as it arrived into Hesperian air space, preparatory to docking at the very tip of the Cassandra Girder. Someone at Flight and Landing Control must have been bribed to tip them off to where Holt was arriving, because this wasn't any of their families' docks. No one could have possibly known they would be landing here. A former beau of Tap Zullini-Brach had offered its use because it was so out of the way.

"We'll have to let the Fast land itself." Dem-Arest fumed. "And even so, there's bound to be massive intrusion by Media once we get out. Fast, call us totally closed-in fly-bys for nine and pre-set them to lose the Media."

"Apologies, all," Holt said. "But, Dem, it won't do any good. And you Tap – and you Virs on the other Fasts just now arriving? You too better get used to what's going to be meeting us out there. I've had experience with it all, but I don't think any of you have, at least not this extent."

Tap was already changing his clothing, and even Dem-Arest checked himself in a glass, and all three of them put themselves into the soft but firm hands of the Fast's cosmetologist program for a few minutes.

"If we all exit together, and stay together once we are out there," Holt suggested, "it ought to be easier. Dem-Arest has agreed to read a short statement to the Media. The rest of us will go into the fly-bys and not say a word, and then we're off. Agreed?"

The other two Fasts landed behind them and at prearranged cue, several minutes later, they all slid out of the Fasts and onto the passenger strip.

The Media swooped, naturally, hundreds of them jostling for space and for the best sightlines for Vids. But the six Humans closed ranks and walked together in silence up to where two private fly-bys awaited them.

Five of them got into the two fly-bys including Holt with Tap in the first one, and the doors closed on them.

Outside, Dem-Arest stood alone as the group's representative and he read a very brief statement about the discovery of Hesperia Two and what it signified in commercial, transportation, communication, scientific and general life style benefits for trillions of the Three Species in the Ib'r Republic. He then lifted a hand-held to instantly transmit much more detailed and technical information about their discovery.

Even from within the sealed vehicle, Holt could hear the Media's "voices" shouting questions at poor Dem. He didn't know what it was about, those voices, but they had an urgency, an edge of demand to them inconsistent with what was, after-all, a scientific discovery mission summation. He had heard those same strained, demanding, pleading "voices" from the Media before, when he'd returned home late hours after some especially messy public romantic break up, or when someone he'd once dated had arrived at a party just before he had, and the Media were hoping to provoke a meeting, a brawl or who knew, even a reconciliation.

Dem-Arest was still out there, fielding questions, and because he was unused to dealing with them, he was getting more and more annoyed. At one point, he flung the hand-held at a floating Cam, and seeing that through the dimmed windows, Tap said, "I better go bring him in."

Of course the Media swarmed Tap the second he exited, and there were still a dozen Cams circling each of the two idling fly-bys all the while. Holt sat back in the body-contour seat. "Vehicle, are you prepared for that mob once we get moving?"

"This Cyber-vehicle has had experience with the Media before, Lord Holt, but it can never guarantee complete security. Especially when they are on a feeding frenzy like right now. Given what has come to light recently."

"We discovered gigantic masses of Beryllium 18. Why should that incite a Media feeding frenzy?" Holt said.

"Oh, your Lordship!" The Cyber-vehicle replied. "It's about much more than your discovery."

Just then the door slid open, and Tap and Dem-Arest barreled into the big back area and threw themselves against the seats.

The doors sealed instantly.

"Get us out of here! Now!" Dem-Arest shouted and the vehicle took off.

"What's going on?" Holt asked. "What were the Media after you about?"

"Nothing!" Tap said and glared a warning at Dem-Arest.

"What?" Holt insisted. "It's a scientific mission. Did we inadvertently exterminate some minuscule species no one's ever heard of? Is that it?

'No. Let's just go," Tap said.

"We've got to tell him!" Dem-Arest added, as though Holt wasn't there with them.

"Not one word!" Tap warned.

"Tell me what? Tell me *what*?"

Tap moved over and grabbed Holt by a shoulder. "You don't want to know. You don't need to know. At least not right now."

"He's right," Dem-Arest said. "We've got a job to do and they're all waiting for us there at the Quinx Central Council Hall."

"I think I may simply kill the two of you by biting you to death," Holt said. "Vehicle, stop! I'm getting out! Land somewhere. Right now!"

"Exactly what," Tap Zullini-Brach asked, "are you doing?"

"I'm getting out and having the Media tell me what's going on that you're so afraid to tell me. Vehicle! I said ..."

"Keep going vehicle," Dem-Arest said. "I'll tell you, Holt," he said and then took a deep breath. "Remember how around the same time we left for Sag. twenty-nine, fifty-nine, fifty-nine, preparations for the Quadri-Centennial of the Ib'r Republic were being prepped."

"I didn't pay all that much attention."

"Well, your birth parent, the Great Father, decided to leave Verhandel and come here a few days early. He had an appointment with the former Premier, Mart Kell ..."

"They're very old acquaintances. So ...?"

"So ... while leaving the Nebula around the Norns, your birth parent's Fast had a one in a billion off-chance electron exchange and it ended up a half million light years away in an instant."

"Can that happen?" Holt asked.

"Every Fast will tell you it *can*. And it *did* happen this once, and well, it seems that among those globular clusters, The Great

Father ended up discovering a solar system where Wicca VIII had stowed away an entire planet full of Old Time Matriarchal females."

Holt looked at them. "This is a set-up for a joke, right?"

"No set-up. No joke," Dem-Arest said, and Tap Zullini-Brach moved closer to Holt until his body was half-enfolding his.

"Tap, why are you all over me?" Holt tried.

"Look at me, Holt," Dem-Arest said. "Look right here! So something went wrong there and the Great Father managed to get away in his Fast. I don't have all the details, but somehow or other some toxin was released onboard and ..."

Ice flew up Holt's spine. Behind him Tap moved closer.

"The Great Father did get out of the Fast before ... it was sabotaged ... and exploded." Dem-Arest added.

No, Holt thought. I'm not hearing this. This is not happening.

"But one of the females from the planet was traveling with him," Dem-Arest went on. "The apparent cause of the sabotage ... and she managed to spread the toxin before he knew it was even happening. The Fast downloaded its flight record onto the T-Pod that the rescue mission located floating somewhere above an extension of the Perseus Arm. Which is how we know that much."

"Near Pelagia," Tap said. "Near the very planet where The Great Father discovered the Ib'rs and the Drylanders."

"And where he discovered the viviparturition system," Dem-Arest said. "That saved the Three Species. He was a great man, Holt!"

Was.

"He was the *greatest of our time,*" Tap corrected, and Holt could hear the tears in his voice. He turned to his friend, whose face was wet.

Was. Tap was crying. So, it was true.

"They've recovered ...?" Holt asked Dem, "his body?"

"It's here, in The City, yes."

"Where?" Holt was able to ask.

"Not far from where we're going." Dem-Arest said. "We don't *have* to go there, Holt. We really don't."

Was. His mommy-daddy, friend and ally, who had enjoyed his silly Media swamped-life more than Holt ever had, who had actually been amused by it, his pal and buddy, his Ay'r, who was no one else's Ay'r in the galaxy, although everyone else thought they knew him, owned some part of him. That Ay'r was dead. Through sabotage. Through poison. Left to drift in a T-pod at the edge of the fricking known galaxy. To tumble endlessly up there, in the Big Nothing. Because of a sub-quantum travel accident that wasn't supposed to happen. Because of some Wiccan female planet which wasn't even supposed to exist! Dead, leaving Holt more alone than he'd ever felt, with so many stories still to be told. Including this adventure, Holt's own, for once, surely as wild and strange as any his mommy-daddy Ay'r had undergone and told to Holt ...

"No," Holt finally said, "we're *expected* at the Council. We'll *go* to the Council."

Tap was sobbing, the big infant.

Dem was shaking his head. "I thought he would be around for centuries," he uttered in a tiny voice. "For centuries more! If I only knew, I would have spent more time with him."

Me too, Holt thought, and recognized the irony in him having the bizarre chore of consoling *them*, for *his* loss, which he understood was now a Republic-wide loss, a universal loss ... Vir, but it was sad. Tragically sad, happening now, just when Holt was going to show Ay'r and the entire family, the entire Republic actually, that he wasn't just some light-weight socialite, only good for interminable reports on the Holo-News Gossip channels.

"Lord Holt," the Vehicle spoke up. "Lord Darency, in the fly-by accompanying this one, has just made a suggestion via inter-vehicle comm. That the meeting at the Quinx Council be postponed and that your two groups assemble at the Todd-Darency family estate on the Centauri Girder."

"Gratitude, vehicle!" Holt interrupted. "Please inform Lord Darency that I've been given the news about The Great Father and that I've decided we should go ahead with the presentation since we are expected."

A few seconds later, he heard Yang himself "Tap? Dem? Didn't you tell him?"

"Yang! They told me! I know all about it!" Holt said.

"And you're *still* going to the Council."

"Yes, and we have to all hang together on this, Yang! All of us. I know it's really tragic news and everyone is upset, me as much as anyone, but this is our first real opportunity to prove that we're *somebodies* in this Republic. Who knows if it'll be our last chance to do that."

Silence from them all, then from the comm. System, Yang said, "you've got more Vir-damned scrotum than I ever imagined, Holt."

"Vehicles! To the Council," Holt insisted.

"We're almost there!" Yang said. "That was our last chance to turn off."

"Lord Holt, we are arrived," the vehicle announced and came to a stop.

The Media was even thicker here at the City's Center, at the very heart of Hesperia, where the sixteen most prominent girders crossed at the very ending of Power Avenue. But Media distance restrictions also applied here where so many public affairs took place, and so the huge area with the very grandest and very latest in architectural, video, landscaping and sculptural innovations, was less of a problem than their landing had been.

Of course, the electronic noise from the Media was apparent as the nine of them exited the two fly-bys and posed as a group several times before turning and stepping onto the wide, ascending stairway into the Council Hall.

Hundreds of the Three Species surrounded them on every side, standing and watching. Humans in all colors, ages and uniforms, Bella=Arth.s, Ambassadorial and more normal Delph.s, the latter with their omnipresent bubble-helmets. They all seemed to surge forwards as the nine discoverers glided up, the crowd's sudden movement blocked by what Holt now saw were Cyber-police in a medium-alert mode.

He and Tap led the group, his friend arm in arm with him.

Behind, he could just about hear through the enormous tumult of voices from the crowd, Dem-Arest and Yang arguing. Over what?

More Cyber-police were at the top of the glideway, barely able to retain a narrow space open among the crowd there for the nine youths to get through.

Holt was feeling odd, still soaked in sadness over his loss, yet now for the first time beginning to get a sense of what it might be like to actually be liked, cherished even by masses of Three Species, maybe even a little bit in the same way that his mommy-daddy Ay'r had been cherished, adored really, idolized. Maybe Holt's instincts had been correct to continue on no matter what?

He really had meant it when he told Yang that this was their opportunity, and that perhaps it might be their last chance to make a real impact on the Republic.

The glideway ended at the top level, and Holt was tempted to turn around and address the crowd. He turned enough to see how huge the gathering had grown around the glideway, by now filling almost every square meter of empty space in the vast plaza, when Yang and Dem both spun him around again, pointing him toward the Council Hall.

Again, Cyber-police were holding back an overspill crowd inside the huge, rotunda-capped foyer of the Council Hall, many more people in here than Holt had ever seen before – there must be thousands! The flashing Holo-Vids, floating all around them celebrated, "The Ib'r Republic – Four Hundred Years of Peace and Prosperity" and gave him hope that what he'd would have to say inside the Council Hall would perfectly fit this theme.

Because he was in the lead and Tap was pulling him along, and Yang and Dem-Arest were right behind, almost pushing him, and although he could hear all the many different voices all shouting "Holt!" followed by some question or statement, he was never able to pick out any specific question or statement. He almost wanted to say, "wait! What's the rush?" When he thought he heard people shouting and members of the nine shouting back, and he was sure that some kind of a scuffle had broken out among the last of the three Fast's crew and several onlookers. He wanted to see what it was, but Tap kept him faced forward, and when he turned his head, Dem blocked his view. "What's all that about?" he asked, only to be answered by all three of his friends. "Nothing! Nothing! Keep moving!"

Of course there was a series of security chambers before you could enter the main hall. Tap all but shoved Holt into the first empty one, and he was stepping in himself when he realized there was an elderly Human inside already. Tap retreated. The plastron shut on Ay'r, and she turned to him, very well dressed, and quite elderly, sporting floating medallions about her hair identifying her as an Honored Veteran of the Independence of the Republic, as well as floating medals on her shoulders identifying her as "Honorary Adjudicator of Benefica and Trefuss."

The various non-intrusive rays passed through the two of them, and as she glanced at him, Holt bowed a little, saying "Mer,

I'm honored to meet such an important woman."

"Gratitude. For my part, I'm stunned to suddenly be face to face with the Galaxy-famed Cadet himself. Little did I know when my fly-by was so late in arriving ..." She stopped and looked at him closely. "I met your birth parent several times a very long time ago. In fact, right at the inception of this Republic. If it gives you any consolation at all, then you should know he was not the perfect person he is being made out to be, but instead mischievous, self-centered, self-directed, and an altogether capable young man. Handsome and personally captivating enough to calm down that old dragon, Wicca VIII!"

Holt guessed he would be getting more of this in the hours to come, but few descriptions of Ay'r would be quite so apt for him to hear. He smiled.

"Gratitude! Lady ...?"

"Gemma Guo-Rinne. One-time ambassador and oh, some other titles, too! Please accept my condolences for your great loss."

"I am not alone in my loss," Holt said, trying to be as gracious as possible. "It's a loss I share with the entire Republic."

"Yes. Yes. Of course," she agreed, shaking her distinguished old head.

And then just as the safety chamber beeped twice that it had completed its multi-ray survey of them and the two might enter now the Council Hall, she added, "but of course yours is greater, since yours includes your poor niece."

"My what?" Holt asked, but the two of them were drawn out by Cyber-guards, and she was promptly sent in another direction, straight down to her seat, while he would be walking onstage.

Tap, Dem-Arest, Darency and the others now exited their security chambers and tried hustling Holt forward. He shook off their arms, and said to a Cyber-guard, "take me to a sealed Holo-Comm. Station."

"No!" Tap sounded as though he were in pain.

"Don't do it, Holt!" Darency tried to stop him, but the guard blocked them and led Holt to a Holo-Comm. area. Holt stepped up and the sides and ceiling slid into place immediately sealing him in.

"Welcome to Hesperian Comm. May we help you?" a seductive young male voice asked.

The others had gathered all around the transparent chamber

and were trying to distract him or prevent him from what? From finding out what?

"My name is Holt Ib'r Sanqq'" he spoke. "Do you recognize the name?"

"Naturally, Lord Holt."

"Good. I need to see the most recent Holo-News report you have on my niece, K'tina Kell."

"From one week ago, Sol Rad.?"

"Is that the latest?" Holt asked.

"It's the very last, yes."

"Then show it to me, complete – with no alterations or deletions of any kind. Understood?"

"Understood, Lord Holt. This will be the official Hesperian Solar News report."

The Holo-News Vid went on. It was a scene at Gerspellion's Girder, deep in the city, where he and K'tina used to meet. The Premier, Cas'sio, Holt's cousin, was speaking in front of a scene, looking very grave, and Holt's half-brother North Diad-Ib'r, was next to him. The two of them seemed extremely shaken, their faces were smudged and behind them Holt could see what looked like charred and destroyed remains. As the Vid-cam swung a bit, he could see the Cyber Kiosk of what was his name? that funny old Cyber who'd helped him? The entire area was destroyed as though blown to pieces. Instantly, Holt began to have a very bad feeling. A Transpo gone amok, or what? Outside the booth, the others could see what he was watching and Tap was pounding on the booth, using his fists and feet as though he could actually do anything to harm the super-strong material, never mind get in.

"May I have sound please?! Go back to the beginning of what the Premier was saying?"

"Naturally."

The Premier was speaking in a very tightly controlled and thus Holt knew, very upset tone of voice. "... a small cadre of newly built, evidently mis-programmed or somehow culturally disaffected Cybers, styling themselves as an internal terrorist organization. Today, we were merely witnessing what appeared to be the latest in a series of smuggled-in detonation-enhancifier materials, when a tragic mishap occurred. Luckily no Biological Beings, other than one of the renegade group was harmed. Several brave Cyber-police were, however destroyed and they shall be both missed and honored. The Hesperian Cyber Community under the aegis of John Laks, has apprehended all the other Cyber rebels and they will be recalibrated. The Premier's office wishers all Hesperian Cityzens to rest assured, knowing that vigilance keeps us all safe, peaceful and prosperous."

Holt still couldn't see what this had to do with K'tina.

"Where's my niece in all this?" he asked the booth-Cyber.

"Do you wish to view the actual footage?"

"If it explains anything, yes, of course." Capstan! That was the eccentric old Cyber's name. Holt hoped Capstan had survived whatever the Cyber rebels had done to his Kiosk and the Transpo station.

"Here it is now, Lord Holt," he heard.

He saw K'tina suddenly being held by what were two Cyber-police officers. She looked different than when he'd last seen her, and then realized that she'd Cyberized herself even more. She was shouting.

"Uncle North! Believe me when I say that Holt had nothing to do with any of this! He never knew a thing about what we were planning!"

Holt heard someone say: "What are you talking about?"

"When we met here? Please stay where you are, Uncle. Capstan here will confirm it. Holt and I met here three times. But Holt had *nothing* to do with this. He never knew *anything* about it."

"Then ... why *did* he meet you here?" the person asked her; it sounded like North.

"The only thing I regret is involving him. Truly." K'tina said.

Vir! She'd been one of the renegades!

"Why *did* you and Holt meet here?" North repeated.

Yes, why? Holt wanted to hear what she would say.

"Because he thought we were lovers! Stupid! Isn't it? He never suspected that our meetings here, and he himself, was the perfect cover for the drops. How could he believe we were lovers? We couldn't even be in the same place without sickening each other? Isn't it so very naive? Even so, if he hadn't gone off chasing Beryllium 18 to be a great hero for the City, none of this would have ever happened."

"What wouldn't have happened?" North asked her.

"Me using an untested Courier ... Any of you finding out!" she said and she laughed and threw her head back suddenly and forward equally suddenly.

"Cover!" someone shouted and there was a deafening explosion.

It had all been Vid-ed. Of course, if it was a sting operation, it would have to have been Vid-ed, for court.

"No!" was all he could utter.

Holt went numb, and slumped down out of view of the Holo-Comm. News Report, which was repeating now Cas'sio's speech.

Outside the booth, Tap had knelt to face him, but Holt couldn't face Tap, couldn't face anyone, not now. It was too horrific. Too mortifying.

Suddenly the Holo-Comm. station unsealed itself. The walls dropped into the floor and instantly, his older half-brothers, North Ib'r-Sanqq' and Olaf Todd-Sanqq' were on either side of Holt, Tap, Darency and the others were pushed aside.

"I see you know everything now," North said.

"I ... she ... I ..."

"Let's go, Holt," North said. "You've got an important speech to make, and everyone is waiting."

They grasped him by either arm and he let himself be half lifted, half led away from the Holo-Comm.s, and down the long center aisle of the main level and into the heart of the hall. Twelve other levels beveled into this one, some at bizarre angles, all of them holding a thousand persons each, all coming to a central point, at a floating dais, on which someone was concluding a speech or introduction

As the three brothers, followed by the other eight discoverers were recognized, the murmuring inside the enormous hall with perfect acoustics grew until it soon resembled what one might hear inside the largest and most populous of a social insect's nest.

Holt was led onto the dais, and over to Cas'sio, the Premier, who looked small and tired and who kissed both of his cheeks, uttering, "my ..." – unable to continue.

North and Olaf joined the rest of the fifteen members of the Inner Quinx, half of them Holt's family members. He realized that he must be in a state of shock, seeing everything so lucidly. Guests onstage near them included Deon Syzygy and that young Ay'r, wasn't that him, who'd been betrothed in such a lavish ceremony? Next to them were the Bella=Arth. delegation, four Arth.s and a Human male, all glittering, and near them the Delph. delegation and what must also be heads of the Cyber Community.

"You *must not* falter now!' the Premier whispered, and pushed Holt away, where someone else took his arm and everyone was applauding and making noise meaning the introduction was over, and Holt found himself in the center of the dais, all around him and slightly behind him, in a semi-circle, were the other eight, his friends.

Holt took a deep breath, feeling it like shards against his lungs, like icicles ripping his heart, and in the smoothest possible voice he could muster, and just as he had prepped the speech with Tap and Dem's help all the way back to Hesperia on the Fast, he introduced each of the others one by one, and after the applause for them had died down, he began speaking about their shared experience.

The speech went on for almost a half hour, Sol Rad. He didn't once falter. He never missed a beat. He never skipped a word.

After, there was thundering applause. The eight gathered closely around Holt, and hugged him and kissed his cheeks, Tap crying, Dem smiling, Darency saying, "I knew you'd come through, I knew it." The ovation went on and on.

Then it was over, and the dais was turned into a party area, and Holt must meet all the others on the platform, the ambassadors, the very sober Cyber-leaders, the handsome blond young Neo from Usk sporting his pure Beryllium betrothal torque from Marquis Syzygy, both of them happy as they could be, the Bella=Arth.s, the Delph.s, the family, the Inner Quinx.

Another two hours before he could excuse himself, all of it the purest torture. And then Darency and Holt's half-brother, Y'vo, both going with him to the lounge, and waiting outside for him so he couldn't escape. Not yet.

But finally the Premier had to leave, and as he took Holt's arm to say good night, Holt began to accompany him out. Once outside the hall, where the crowds still were gathered, and where they tumultuously cheered Holt and Cas'sio, as the Premier said his more complex farewells, Holt was at last able to sneak back into his fly-by. Waving to them all, smiling, as he got into the big empty rear passenger compartment.

"Vehicle, return me to the Cassandra Girder Port where we left the Fast."

Once he was sealed in and taking off, the vehicle eluded two Media cams, and Holt put his hands up to his face and played back in his mind her words like axe blows to his brain: "Because he thought we were lovers! Because he *thought* we were lovers! Because he THOUGHT we were lovers!" And then, her laughing, her head thrown back and then forward again and K'tina's prepared Cyberized head exploding into a million pieces. Again and again and again, without cessation, without let up, without any possibility of reprieve, over and over, until he was twisted onto the floor in front of the seats, shaking from head to toe, in a fetal position.

He came to, hearing the Vehicle ask, he didn't know how long it had been asking, "Lord Holt. We have arrived at your destination. Would you care to disembark?"

He exited then, stumbling over to his Fast, which opened to his touch and sealed closed after he was in. He fell onto a lounge, the sight of K'tina laughing and then blowing herself up, playing over in his mind in front of his eyes, again and again.

"Lord Holt," the Fast was speaking. "This Fast has fully restocked for biological life and has refueled. Did you wish to travel?"

"I wish to be put into a deep and dreamless sleep for a very long time. Do you have an injection for that?"

"It can be manufactured in a very short time. Do we remain here at the Cassandra dock?"

"No. Get me out of here."

"Where to?" the Fast naturally enough asked.

"I don't care. As far away from Hesperia as you can possibly go. Inject me first."

"To make a Fast jump, coordinates are needed."

"Then don't make a Fast jump. Go the way the DayLight Two people taught you."

"Now?"

"Now!" Holt confirmed.

"As far away as possible?"

"Yes ... Isn't that injection ready?"

"It's ready. Please place your arm flat on the armrest, Lord Holt."

Holt did as he was asked ... her head exploding over and over and over no matter whether his eyes were open or closed ... when would it stop? He felt the slight sting of the injection.

"Fast? … Haven't we gone yet?"

"Done!" the Fast reported, as Holt sank back onto the lounge and into oblivion.

At Hesperian Central Flight and Landing Control, the on-duty Bella=Arth. Controller turned to its Human companion and asked: "What happened to Pretty Boy (Holt's) Fast Vehicle? It was about seventy meters (off the Cassandra Girder) two seconds ago, Sol Rad."

"I've got no flight plan for it," the Human reported.

"Use your eyes!" The Arth. commanded. "(Or the Vid screen ((I don't care which))). It was just there three seconds ago."

"I've got no sub-atomic Fast-Jump signatures or residuals anywhere near the Cassandra Girder."

"Look! Here!" the Arth. insisted. "This is the recorded Vid of Cassandra Girder (all the way over to the Hwang Kuo-Tse Girder ((sector 134GN1))). There is the Fast. Can you see it?"

"I see it. *Whoa!* What was *that*?"

"And now the Fast is gone," the Arth. said.

The Human checked all his controls again.

"I've got no Flight plan, I've got no requests from Lord Holt or the Fast to leave, and I've got no quantum atomic signatures anywhere in that sector saying that anything did actually jump."

"Do you still see it (in that sector)" the Arth. asked.

"No. It just – like – *blinked out*."

"Blinked out? That's what you're going to report?" The Arth. said. "Lord Holt is only the most famous (living) member of the Three Species (in the galaxy) and he just *blinked out*?"

"I'm not telling anyone *anything happened*. I'm officially, as of this minute, Sol Rad., off my shift and on my dinner break," the Human said. "If you've got a problem, *you* deal with it!"

Mt. Mapoca-Atlas loomed, snow-capped, irregular, incredibly high and distant over the pristine plateau and the saturated-purple waters of the Lake Loki. The other shore was misted over, barely visible.

North Ib'r-Sanqq's arrival at Verhandel's main Fast-port only an hour before, Sol Rad., had attracted only a little Media attention. The local Media were so inured to high-level Cityzens coming and going and filling the Very Important Biological Beings lounge, that he'd been able to get away with a curt "family business" when he was asked why he was visiting. Evidently many of the Three Species came here on family business. He'd found a free fly-by easily, and he had comm.ed ahead to say he was on his way.

A pamp gardener and a Cyber helper were at work in front of the residence. Since the events on Usk, the little creatures were seemingly everywhere one went these days, known to be hard workers and unfailingly polite, well worth their pay.

North went inside the residence and the Cyber-valet, Jas'per, met him and offered him a spicy tisane it knew he liked and then led him into the big Vid room and offered North a seat.

As he looked out, views of the mountain and lake were slowly shaded over, and suddenly his mother, Oudma, and his father, Ay'r, were right there, sitting in the room with him. They looked so embodied, so densely real, North had to resist the urge to embrace them.

"You're looking wonderful," North said.

"You're looking tired and surprisingly, a bit worried," Oudma said.

"I'm a bit anxious, yes," North responded.

Jas'per arrived with the tisane and even some of those spicy little sweets North always liked. He'd always been a thoughtful Cyber.

"Gratitude," Ay'r said to the Cyber. "You'd better seal the room after yourself. I'm setting this conversation on 'record,' North, I take it?" Ay'r's image looked half amused, half curious at North, "since you did say this is a semi-official visit?"

"Aren't they always?" North replied, sipped, and added, "they've sent you the download, filling you in on the last Fast trip that you ... inadvertently ... took?"

"Yes, and it's been assimilated into ... my current self. Your mother didn't want me to go on that trip in the first place," Ay'r said.

"I never said that," Oudma protested.

"You never said it, but it was what you thought. And she was right. As usual."

"None of that makes any difference," Oudma replied. "We'd set up this copy of The Great Father long before he went on his little adventure, North. We merely updated it before the trip. Surely you didn't think after all this time that I was going to let him get away by merely physically dying, did you?"

She and Ay'r laughed.

"So, son," Ay'r said. "What's the semi-official part of your business about?"

"They're going to make me the next Premier."

"Wonderful!" both said.

"We'll see. Cas'sio thinks I'm ready. I'm less sure. He's polled the Inner Quinx and they'll vote for me more or less unanimously. The public is being primed for it with various publicity-appearances and what not."

"That explains the worry I'm seeing." His mother replied.

"I suppose. I'll do it," North said. "But the truth is Cas'sio, who has been my mentor this past decade or more, is really planning to retire. He's going to leave Hesperia. He's even talked about going to Usk and staying at that big old palace resort where the Betrothal was held."

"And ...?" Ay'r said.

"I need advisors. The job is too big for one person, even with the five person council and the Inner Quinx. So I've come to ask if you two would mind relocating back to the City to sort of back me up as advisors. It won't be forever," he added. "Just until I feel my feet solid under me."

They looked at each other.

"You are very much missed in The City, Great Father, even if you never spent much time there of late," North added. "The Three Species took your death very hard. Everyone did. If they knew you were still ... you know ... around ... like this ... and all ..." He trailed off.

"It would make the transition from Cas'sio to yourself a bit easier?" Oudma finished his sentence. "Well, I think it's a good idea. I've grown a little bored here. And now that your father is no longer hindered by corporeality ... He may get bored here too."

North turned to Ay'r, "I checked into it, and your birth mother's company, your company now, or is it mine? Well, they told me they can easily transport you both. For that matter, they've done a great deal of experimentation with portability factors of your … current state and it's now a fully developed thing. You'll be able to move around all by yourselves in Hesperia, not everywhere but within a certain grid, of course. But they're widening the grid's extent throughout The City more every day."

"Sounds brand new and you know how much I like new things, new adventures!" Ay'r said. "So let's say yes, with the proviso that when Oudma and I want out, we get to come back here."

"Agreed."

"Now catch us up on what else is going on in the family," Oudma said.

North relaxed, his mission more easily accomplished than he hoped, and they chatted on for another hour. There was much to talk about, the family being larger every year and there being births, marriages, moves and changes to discuss.

Towards the end of the hour and a half he had requested with them, North said, "this will tickle you, I believe, father. Remember that Matriarchal Water-World expert Wicca sent you to Pelagia with?"

"Alli Lui-Clark, yes of course. She's not dead?"

"No, she's fully alive, and now a Sub-Prelate of the Iridium Church of Loren."

"Sub-Prelate?" Oudma asked.

"She always had a way of getting to the top quickly," Ay'r said.

"It seems," North explained, "that she is the only one that the mostly comatose prophet will utilize these days. She decrypted his latest poem."

"We heard about the new poem he made. It was the first in what a century or so."

"That was *her* doing?" Ay'r said.

"*His*, now. He is Clark Alli-Lui."

Ay'r almost fell out of his chair laughing. "*His*! Alli did the gender 'xchange? What an unexpected turnaround."

Oudma asked, "any news of Mart Kell?"

"She was always soft on that old rascal," Ay'r put in.

"None at all, surprisingly. Young Ay'r and the Marquis of Syzygy have put aside a full year of search-funding for him. But it's been over a month, Sol Rad., and as young Ay'r repeatedly says: *he* was a native of the planet, *he* knew his way around it quite well, and even *he* was eventually located. Whereas Mart ...”

“What an odd ending for him, to just vanish like that?” Oudma said. “I never would have predicted it.”

“Unless he’s been secretly assassinated?” Ay’r added. “That, I *could* have predicted! He made so many enemies!”

“Powerful enemies!” North agreed.

“We hear that his young relation forms half of the new power couple on Hesperia,” Oudma said. “Deon Syzygy and young Ay’r ... is it Kell?”

“Ay’r Eise’nstein-Kell. Yes, the new power couple, the new romantic couple, and also the new financial couple,” North agreed. “If Mart Kell is declared dead, young Ay’r’s own son by Mart is primary heir to Kell Unlimited, and the birth mother will control one of the largest fortunes in the Galaxy. Syzygy of course, already holds Cyber-patents and solar systems galore. The two of them are the toast of The City. You can’t have an event or a party of any significance without them present.”

“Then we’ll meet them soon. What of the new Bella=Arth. Ambassador?”

“Kri’nni Des (‘xx’)! She’s another new power player. Very funny, very down to earth, even kind of raunchy, I’m told g.females of all species flock to her. She’s become a role model. She courts scandal with every appearance she makes. It’s very exciting having her in The City.”

“And your brother?” Ay’r asked.

Meaning Holt.

“Sadly there’s no sign of him, either,” North had to say. “And, in his case, no one even knows where to *begin* to search.”

“He’s not dead,” Ay’r said, firmly. “I can sense him still around ... *somewhere* ... in the cosmos.”

“They always shared a kind of intuitive bond,” Oudma explained.

“Without being psychic in any way, I feel the same,” North said. “I’d welcome him back with gratitude and he would be elected to the Inner Quinx in an instant. Since yourself, Great Father, no Cityzen has done as much for the Ib’r Republic, nor has anyone ever inflamed the popular imagination as much. The oddest part is that the same double tragedy that seems to have sent him skittering off to who knows where, has made him a far more sympathetic character at home. Every week, a new Holo-Book or Vid or PVN comes out, all about The Cadet's so-called tragedies and triumphs. He's a Media industry. I'm proud to be his half-sib. Should he return, he's guaranteed a great future."

That cheered up Ay'r a great deal, and so the visit ended happily.

After North had left in the fly-by, the two remained in the large room, visible even once the windows had been unshaded again, so they might look outside.

"Look. It's snowing only up around the highest mountain peaks again."

"Beautiful."

After a while, "the poor Cadet," Oudma said.

"If I know my baby-boy, Holt," Ay'r said, fondly, "and I do know him like no one else, we have definitely *not* heard the last of him."

"I wonder," she mused, "if that most recent of Loren's prophecy/poems really is about your son, as so many commentators seem to think."

"How does it go?" Ay'r asked.

'In Central Chaos, everted EBONY reigns," she began. "As Blessed Contamination comes nearer ... /Ancient Commands shall set their bloodless sacrifice/ Let the Boxed-Men free – for one, long-lasting benefit."

"What ever can it mean?" Ay'r asked.

"Your guess is as good as mine."

FELICE PICANO

Felice Picano is the author of more than thirty books of poetry, fiction, memoirs, nonfiction, and plays. His work has been translated into many languages and several of his titles have been national and international bestsellers. He is considered a founder of modern gay literature along with the other members of the Violet Quill. Picano also began and operated the SeaHorse Press and Gay Presses of New York for fifteen years. His first novel was a finalist for the PEN/Hemingway Award. Since then he's been nominated for and/or won dozens of literary awards.

A five-time Lambda Literary Award nominee, Picano's books include the best-selling novels *The Book of Lies*, *Like People in History*, and *Looking Glass Lives* as well as the literary memoirs *Men Who Loved Me* and *A House on the Ocean, A House on the Bay*. Along with Andrew Holleran, Robert Ferro, Edmund White, and George Whitmore, he founded the Violet Quill Club to promote and increase the visibility of gay authors and their works. In 2009, the Lambda Literary Foundation awarded Picano its Lifetime Achievement/ Pioneer Award. Originally from New York, the author now lives in Los Angeles.

About ReQueered Tales

In the heady days of the late 1960s, when young people in many western countries were in the streets protesting for a new, more inclusive world, some of us were in libraries, coffee shops, communes, retreats, bedrooms and dens plotting something even more startling: literature – highbrow and pulp – for an explicitly gay audience. Specifically, we were craving to see our gay lives – in the closet, in the open, in bars, in dire straits and in love – reflected in mystery stories, romance, paranormal and more. Hercule Poirot, that engaging effete Belgian creation of Agatha Christie might have been gay ... Sherlock Holmes, to all intents and purposes, was one woman shy of gay ... but where were the *genuine gay sleuths,* where the reader need not read between the lines?

Beginning with Victor J Banis's "Man from C.A.M.P." pulps in the mid-60s – riotous romps spoofing the craze for James Bond spies – readers were suddenly being offered George Baxt's Pharoah Love, a black gay New York City detective, and a real turning point in Joseph Hansen's gay California insurance investigator, Dave Brandstetter, whose world weary Raymond Chandleresque adventures sold strongly and have never been out of print.

Over the next three decades, gay storytelling grew strongly in niche and mainstream publishing ventures. Even with the huge public crisis – as AIDS descended on the gay community beginning in the early 1980s – gay fiction flourished. Stonewall Inn, Alyson Publications, and others nurtured authors and readers ... until mainstream success seemed to come to a halt. While Lambda Literary Foundation had started to recognize work in annual awards about 1990, mainstream publishers began to have cold feet. And then, with the rise of ebooks in the new millennium which enabled a new self-publishing industry ... there was both an avalanche of new talent coming to market and burying of print authors who did not cross the divide.

The result?

Perhaps forty years of gay fiction – and notably gay and lesbian mystery, detective and suspense fiction – has been teetering on the brink of obscurity. Orphaned works, orphaned authors, many living and some having passed away – with no one to make the case for their creations to be returned to print (and e-print!). General fiction and non-fiction works embracing gay lives, widely celebrated upon original release, also languished as mainstream publishers shifted their focus.

Until now. That is the mission of *ReQueered Tales*: to keep in circulation this treasure trove of fantastic fiction. In an era of ebooks, everything of value ought to be accessible. For a new generation of readers, these mystery tales are full of insights into the gay world of the 1960s, '70s, '80s and '90s. For those of us who lived through the period, they are a delightful reminder of our youth and reflect some of our own struggles in growing up gay in those heady times.

We are honoured, here at *ReQueered Tales*, to be custodians shepherding back into circulation some of the best gay and lesbian fiction writing and hope to bring many volumes to the public, in modestly priced, accessible editions, worldwide, over the coming years.

So please join us on this adventure of discovery and rediscovery of the rich talents of writers of recent years as the PIs, cops and amateur sleuths battle forces of evil with fierceness, humor and sometimes a pinch of love.

The ReQueered Tales Team

Justene Adamec • Alexander Inglis • Matt Lubbers-Moore

Dryland's End
Felice Picano

Five thousand years in the future, life itself is in jeopardy!

A rebellion of intelligent Cybernetic servants has left the Females of the galaxy virtually sterile, crippling the controlling political body – the Matriarchy. The race is on to find a solution, but will it be enough to save the Matriarchy as other galactic authorities attempt to dominate them using sabotage and all-out war? *Dryland's End* is Felice Picano's science fiction adventure for the new millennium. The novel touches on many of today's most controversial subjects, such as interracial relationships, gender conflicts, gender identity, and same-sex pairings-and views them with a lens toward the future.

"This book is further proof that Felice Picano can succeed beautifully in any genre of fiction. Here we have the colorful originality that is found in the greatest science fiction and fantasy writers, the wide-ranging imagination that creates not only fine writers, characterization, and gripping plot, but also fabricates entire worlds – worlds rich with warrior women, space travel, mysterious gods, political intrigue and rebellion, biological warfare, and sexualities both subtle and shifting. ... Like the best speculative fiction, [it] provides the lucky reader with both an escape into the extraordinary and a mirror for humanity's deepest issues and concerns." — Jeff Mann, Associate Professor of English, Virginia Tech

"Set so far in the future that the exact location of the home planet of the Humes (humans) isn't remembered, this book examines relationships between the sexes, and between species from a new perspective and with more than a touch of levity. With its subjects of cloning and genetic manipulation, same sex marriages and other controversial issues, *Dryland's End* remains as pertinent today as when it was first published. In full-fledged sci-fi form, Picano has created entirely new civilizations, species, even new language forms for his society. A phenomenally well-written book." — *Virginia Gazette*

First published in 1995, this new edition of *Dryland's End* features a foreword by the author. The "City on a Star" trilogy concludes with *A Bard on Hercular* – a ReQueered Tales Original Publication.

Like People in History
Felice Picano

Solid, cautious Roger Sansarc and flamboyant, mercurial Alistair Dodge are second cousins who become lifelong friends when they first meet as nine-year-old boys in 1954. Their lives constantly intersect at crucial moments in their personal histories as each discovers his own unique – and uniquely gay – identity. Their complex, tumultuous, and madcap relationship endures against 40 years of history and their involvement with the handsome model, poet, and decorated Vietnam vet Matt Loguidice, whom they both love. Picano chronicles and celebrates gay life and subculture over the last half of the twentieth century: from the legendary 1969 gathering at Woodstock to the legendary parties at Fire Island Pines in the 1970s, from Malibu Beach in its palmiest surfer days to San Francisco during its gayest era, from the cities and jungles of South Vietnam during the war to Manhattan's Greenwich Village and Upper East Side during the 1990s AIDS war.

> "It's the heroic and funny saga of the last three decades by someone who saw everything and forgot nothing." — Edmund White

> "Harrowing and sad, and very funny, Like People in History manages to bridge the unnerving chasm between the queer present and the gay past." — Andrew Holleran

> "A gay classic. Read it when I was in college and it helped shape my perception of myself as a gay man ... It's a sprawling, propulsive epic that switches back and forth in time, taking the reader on a rollicking journey through gay America" — Christopher Rice

In a book that could have been written only by one who lived it and survived to tell, Picano weaves a powerful saga of four decades in the lives of two men and their lovers, relatives, friends, and enemies. Tragic, comic, sexy, and romantic, filled with varied and colorful characters, *Like People in History* is both extraordinarily moving and supremely entertaining.

Winner of the Ferro-Grumley Award for Best Novel, Gay Times Best Novel of the Year and Finalist for Lambda Literary Award Best Gay Fiction, this 25th Anniversary edition features a new foreword by Richard Burnett and an afterword by the author.

The Book of Lies
Felice Picano

Bright, ambitious, and handsome, Ross Ohrenstedt is a high flier in the fashionable field of queer studies. He has just taken a prestigious university position in Los Angeles and has been appointed to oversee the collection of papers and works of a leading light of the gay literary salon known as the Purple Circle. Ross stumbles across a lost work by an unknown author and his quest to identify the mystery writer and achieve the glory of scholastic tenure unveils increasingly bizarre and unbalanced facts about a group of writers who in the 1970s and 1980s broke new ground in the creation of a gay literary sensibility. But the dark truth contained within *The Book of Lies* is even more startling.

> "Based on Picano's involvement with the Violet Quill Club (which included Edmund White and Andrew Holleran), this is an absorbing Henry James-style comedy of manners about how even when some writers find their way out of the closet, others still get left behind."
> — *The Mail on Sunday*

> "The *Book of Lies* is funny, dark, sexy, shocking, and yes, smart. Set in the near future ('decades after Stonewall'), the novel tells of a young scholar trying to make his academic bones on the literary bodies of the 'Purple Circle'. Picano skewers the pedagogically pretentious with ease and wit. A wonderful novel, with some of Picano's best writing."
> — *Bay Area Reporter*

With biting wit and a lush sense of place and character, Felice Picano's daring novel is at once a stylish mystery, a comical roman-à-clef, and a wicked send-up of the new Ivory Tower.

First published to acclaim in 1998, this new edition features a foreword by David Bergman (*The Violet Hour*).

Onyx
Felice Picano

Ray Henriques has success, love, friendship ... but lately it's not enough. Yet it's not just Ray who is on a quest for deeper meaning. For Jesse, Ray's lover of ten years, it is a quest accelerated by his imminent death from AIDS. And for young married father of two Mike Tedesco, it is a search for the heart of masculinity. The sexual exploration which begins when Ray and Mike meet awakens a restlessness in both men, which resoundingly alters their future paths. As Ray's life begins to draw him increasingly into the future, a future without Jesse, he attempts to tether himself to the here and now with frequent visits to a past where life's answers seemed simpler and more meaningful. But when Jesse's fundamentalist Christian mother rolls into town to take charge of her son's final weeks, he is yanked from his reverie to face an opponent unlike any he has ever known.

> "A complex tableau of life and death." — Greg Herren, *Lambda Book Report*

> "An incredibly rich and densely textured world ... It's a raw journey through death and dying, unsparing in his take on how survivors cope" — Roger Durbin, *Library Journal*

> "You will be astonished by the intelligence, humor, and credibility of this masterfully executed tale, written by one of our best writers." — *Bay Area Reporter*

Marked by shifting points of view, humor, descriptive brilliance and unexpected revelation, *Onyx* is a multifaceted exploration of inner lives, motivation, love, and the sometimes hollow center beneath a polished surface.

First published to acclaim in 2001, this new edition features a foreword by the author.

The Blue Star
Robert Ferro

Two heroes, reflective Peter and Byronic Chase, indulge their youthful appetites in Florence. Over the next 20 years their paths diverge and reconverge. Chase marries into the Italian aristocracy and Peter pursues his passion for Lorenzo, a beautiful young Florentine. The past impinges on the present as the story of Chase's ancestor, Orvil Starkweather, is revealed -- the secrets of his life sounding a counterpoint to Chase's. New York City's Central Park and the imposing figure of designer Frederick Law Olmsted provide a mysterious connection to Chase's life. The story of the two men unfolds in Florence and New York exposing the unimagined and startling connection with the past, and taking them finally on a fateful cruise up the Nile aboard the luxury yacht.

> "Incandescent angels of love ... an eclectic voyage. Authentic fiction... surprising, sad, funny, wise ... communicating gay experience knowingly and sensitively ... a treasure!" — *The Advocate*

> "Enthralling ... euphoric imagination ... we can never forget the bliss we are allowed to share." — Richard Howard

Originally published in 1985, this new edition contains a foreword by Andrew Holleran (*Dancer from the Dance*).

The Family of Max Desir
Robert Ferro

It was a family dealing with old values, acceptance and death. Max Desir loved his Italian roots and he loved his American family. As he came of age, Max Desir found love in Italy. Now, at age 40, his American family is split: Max and Nick are accepted as a stable, long-term couple by mother and siblings, but his father John does not. When a needlepoint family tree is to be hung at Christmas, acceptance of family is re-examined. In this beautiful, haunting tale, told in a clear, impassioned narrative, Robert Ferro created a classic. His highly celebrated breakthrough novel is not to be missed.

> "An honest, eloquent and entirely original novel ... at once realistic and mythological, intensely personal and public ... a triumph." — Edmund White.

Originally published in 1983, this new edition includes a foreword by fellow author and friend Felice Picano.

Life Drawing
Michael Grumley

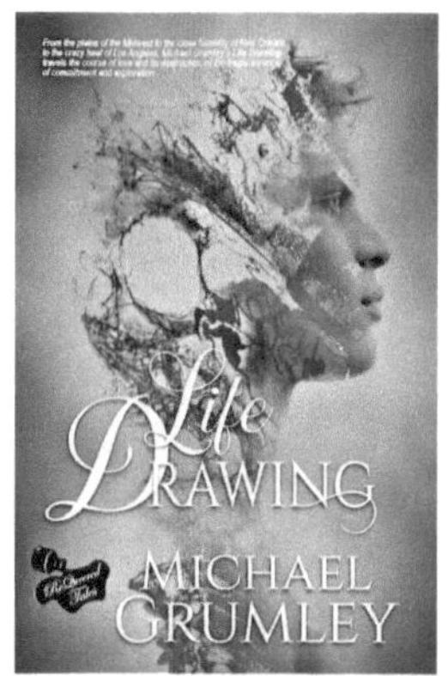

Born in Iowa to the sounds of Bob and Bing Crosby and the Dorsey brothers, Mickey grows up to the comforting images of his living room TV and the reassuring ruts of his parents' life. During the restless summer of his senior year in high school, drifting away from the girlfriend he could never quite love, Mickey spends a night with another boy, and his world will never be the same.

On a barge floating down the Mississippi, he falls in love with James, a black card player from New Orleans, and in time the two of them settle, bristling with sexual intensity, in the French Quarter – until a brief affair destroys James's trust and sends Mickey to the drugs and sordid life of Los Angeles.

> "A simple, classic, engaging, and beautifully written tale of a boy who ran away from home, a man who didn't make it in the movies, an artist who found himself earlier than most and did it all west of the Mississippi, in places which, while very American, few Americans have ever been." — Andrew Holleran

> "*Life Drawing* affirms the rich complexity of passion in the story of a small-town boy's difficult journey to manhood. Michael Grumley's crisp, direct language brings to life the demanding wonder of sexuality and the delicate tightrope of love between black men and white men." — Melvin Dixon

Originally published in 1991, it was Grumley's only novel, completed in the month's leading to his death from AIDS as he was cared for his lover Robert Ferro. This new edition contains the original foreword by Edmund White (*A Saint from Texas*) and afterword by George Stambolian (*Gay Men's Anthologies Men on Men*), close friends of the couple.

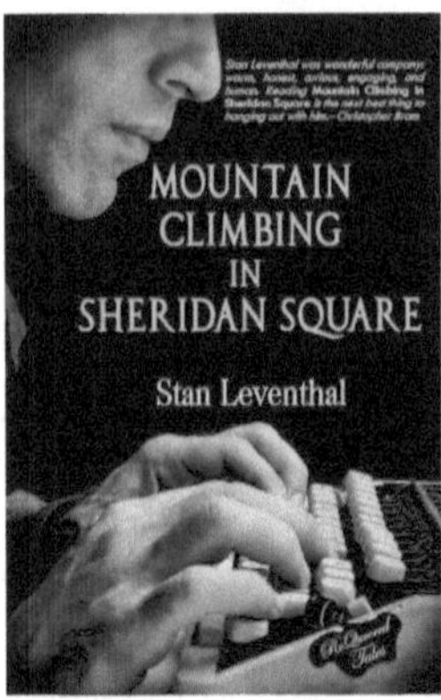

Mountain Climbing in Sheridan Square
Stan Leventhal

A series of discrete episodes among friends provide snapshots of one gay man's life. There are parties, concerts, dinners with everyday life – and death – interwoven in the rich story-telling. An actress, a painter, a set designer, a writer – all sweating and surviving in Manhattan, all scoring their first successes. Part autobiography and part documentary, artfully written, it details the lives of these creative people. Young and professional, they know there is more to life than money. There is trust and the sort of love that trades in deeds of kindness.

"Stan was a literary activist who always gave to, built and endorsed literature and writers. I can see still see Stan in his apartment window on Christopher Street, next door to the Stonewall Inn, overlooking Sheridan Square as he typed away." — Michele Karlsberg, LGBTQ publicist and friend

Stan Leventhal's debut novel was a Lambda Literary Awards Finalist in 1988. This new edition features a foreword by Christopher Bram (*Gods and Monsters*).

The Black Marble Pool – There's a dead body at the bottom of a pool in the backyard of a guest house in Key West. Who is he? And what caused his untimely demise? Maybe it's suicide. Or an accident. But more likely – murder! And who's responsible? One of the guests, the people who run the guest house or one of those mysterious women in town?

"The pace is brisk: the plot keeps twisting, as no one is at all who they seem." — Keith John Glaeske, *Out In Print*

Skydiving on Christopher Street – Like bookends, *Skydiving* returns to the characters and bustle of New York a few years after *Mountain Climbing*. But now AIDS has settled in – the world is changed but still vibrant. The dialog is laced with a sharp humor and is right on the mark; the narrator and his friends spot on as we experience his joys, his pains, and his acceptance of who he is.

"A tender, honest novel about that moment between diagnosis and the decision to grow. Messy boyfriends and dreamy crushes set against the back-drop of daily life make Levethal's characters vulnerable and familiar." — Sarah Schulman (*Let the Record Show*)

Murder and Mayhem
Matt Lubbers-Moore

An Annotated Bibliography of Gay and Queer Males in Mystery, 1909-2018.

Librarian and scholar Matt Lubbers-Moore collects and examines every mystery novel to include a gay or queer male in the English language starting with the 1909 Arthur Conan Doyle short story "The Man with the Watches," which is included in its entirety. Authors, titles, dates published, publishers, book series, short blurbs, and a description of how involved the gay or queer male character is with the mystery are all included for a full bibliographic background.

Murder and Mayhem will prove invaluable for mystery collectors, researchers, libraries, general readers, aficionados, bookstores, and devotees of LGBTQ studies. The bibliography is laid out in alphabetical order by author including the blurb and author notes, whether a hard boiled private eye, an amateur cozy, a suspenseful romance, or a police procedural. All subgenres within the mystery field are included: fantasy, science fiction, espionage, political intrigue, crime dramas, courtroom thrillers, and more with a definition guide of the subgenres for a better understanding of the genre as a whole.

A ReQueered Tales Original Publication.

The Male Homosexual in Literature: A Bibliography *and* The Male Homosexual in Literature: Supplement (2020)
Ian Young

Ian Young's bibliography has served as a basic guide to English-language works of fiction, drama, poetry and autobiography concerned with male homosexuality or having male homosexual characters. Entries include titles published through 1980. Works of primary importance (thosein which homosexuality is a major aspect or which are otherwise of particular relevance) are marked with an asterisk for the convenience of researchers and collectors. Works are identified by author, title, place of publication, publisher, and date. For easy reference, entries are numbered and a title index is provided at the end of the main text. Five highly acclaimed essays on gay literature by Ian Young, Graham Jackson and Dr. Rictor Norton, including essay on gay publishing, round out the listings. A title index of gay anthologies completes the work.

The present *Supplement* includes titles overlooked in the *Bibliography* Second Edition, plus works written before the 1981 cut-off date but published later, including works published for the first time in book form.

$\mathcal{CB}$

**If you enjoyed this book, please
help spread the word by posting a short,
constructive review at your favorite
social media site or e-book retailer.**

We thank you, greatly, for your support.

And don't be shy! Contact us!

*For more information about current and future releases,
please contact us:*

E-mail: *requeeredtales@gmail.com*
Facebook (Like us!): www.facebook.com/ReQueeredTales/
Twitter: @ReQueered
Instagram: www.instagram.com/requeered
Web: www.ReQueeredTales.com
Blog: www.ReQueeredTales.com/blog
Mailing list (Subscribe for latest news): https://bit.ly/RQTJoin